Surprised by Shadows

Karen J. Hasley

Cover image – Sunlight on the Platte River, Nebraska

"'An old maid—that's what I'm to be. A literary spinster, with a pen for a spouse, a family of stories for children, and twenty years hence a morsel of fame, perhaps~'" Jo March

Thank you, Louisa May, for leading the way and giving us Jo to say all the right words.

This is a work of fiction. The characters described herein are imaginary and are not intended to refer to living persons.

ISBN: 1545207682

ISBN-13: 978-1545207682

New Hope, Nebraska, 1881

Railroad/Train Station	**N**	RR stock pens
Freight office		Livery/Blacksmith
alley		Fire Dept
Telegraph/Post Office		Variety & Groc
alley		Carpentry &
Feed & Grain	**Main**	Undertaker
Boot & Shoe Maker		Jail
Leather Goods	**Street**	Bliss House Hotel
City Meat Market		and
Dry Goods & Notions		Bliss Restaurant
Gooseneck Hotel & Billiards		Bliss Music Hall
Hardware, Agric Implements & Stoves		Meeting –
United Bank of Nebraska		Entertainment Hall
W ←School]	**←Alley/Church St→**	[Church→ **E**
↑Photography Studio↑		↑Tull's Beer↑
←Laundry] Dress Shop		Barber Shop
Nebraska Café		Law Office
Hart's Boarding House		MD/Drug Store
	S	
	River	

"There is strong shadow where there is much light."

Johann von Goethe
Writer, Philosopher, Statesman (1749-1832)

1

When I bought my train ticket, I put all the money I could spare on the counter in front of the agent and told him I wanted to go as far west as that money would take me. The man didn't blink. He counted the money, perused his train schedule, looked back up at me, and said, "New Hope, Nebraska." I didn't blink either.

"New Hope it is then," I said. I took my ticket, grabbed my bag with one hand and my artist's box with the other, and clambered aboard the train. That's how easy it was to start a new life.

At the beginning, the people of my new home mattered more than the place itself because I needed my neighbors to be tolerant, respectful, and accommodating. People who could live and let live. I never thought about, let alone cared about, making friends or fitting in or becoming a member of the business community, although I eventually did all three of those things. From the moment the ticket agent counted my money and gave me the ticket to New Hope, it was only and ever about finding a place where I could be the woman I was destined to be: Bathsheba Fenway. Painter.

New Hope today has not changed much from my first look at it six years earlier. One broad street of hard-packed earth that turns to a swirling river of mud with every thunderstorm and an unorganized assortment of stores and business establishments aligned along its east and west sides. It's true that the number and variety of establishments have increased and that some of the older buildings have acquired more polished façades since my first sight of them. It's also true that a side alley running east has since been officially named a street, but the general look of the place, that of a small, satisfied community doing its best to keep up with the times, hasn't changed one bit.

Once off the train in New Hope, the station agent offered advice about accommodations. "There's always the Gooseneck," he said. After giving me a second, careful look, he added, "But I wouldn't suggest the Gooseneck for you. Clear on the other end of town is Ruth Churchill's boarding house. You can't miss it; there's a sign out front with the name Hart's. That would be the place for you. No bedbugs there that I've ever heard." Unlike the Gooseneck, was his unspoken inference, which made up my mind for me.

I walked past the freight office, the telegraph office, and the feed and grain store, past the storefront that advertised leather goods, and on past the Gooseneck Hotel, which shared space with a billiards hall. At the bank, I stepped down from the boardwalk to cross a wide alley and back up again until I eventually stopped in front of Hart's, the very last building on the west side of the street. It was a large house, neatly painted, surrounded by a pristine white fence and a front gate that did not squeak when I pushed it open. All good signs. The sun setting behind the house lit up the whole place, creating a halo that turned the ordinary brown clapboard golden. I'll paint it someday, I thought, and call it *New Hope Heaven.* Later, settled into life there with Ruth Churchill as a good friend, I would think the name more accurate than I ever could have imagined at the time. Not heaven, of course, if there is such a place, but a peaceful, contented town, and isn't that what we expect out of whatever we imagine our own heaven to be?

When I entered the front door and stepped into the foyer of the boarding house that first time, the woman standing behind a tall desk looked up.

"Good afternoon," she said. She set down her pen and shut the ledger book she had been writing in before coming out from behind the desk. "I'm Ruth Churchill. Are you here for a room?"

Ruth Churchill had a pleasant face, startling green eyes, dark blonde hair knotted against the back of her neck, and a fair complexion just beginning to show its years. Older than I, I judged, but not by much. Her hands, which always tell more about a person than one might expect, were more worn than the rest of her, indicating a woman used to physical labor. She wore a plain gold wedding band on her left hand.

"Yes," I said. "I'm just off the train and the ticket agent recommended your boarding house. I passed the Gooseneck Hotel on my way here and understood why the fellow cautioned me not to stop there. Something about bedbugs."

"It's a small town. Word gets around, both good and bad," said Mrs. Churchill, "but the Gooseneck suits some and Bert Gruber, who owns the place, does his best with it." Over time, I would learn that Ruth Churchill was a woman of great kindness, who tried her best to find the good in people, events, and circumstances, but I think even she found it a stretch to speak of bedbugs in any kind of constructive way. She handed me the pen from the desk and turned the guest book so it faced me.

"It's fifty cents a night. There's a bath room at the back of the hallway where for an extra nickel you can relax in a hot bath as long as you like. The linens are clean, and the rooms comfortable and safe. How long do you plan to stay?"

I finished writing my name in the book before I said, "I hope to settle here permanently, Mrs. Churchill."

Her pretty eyes lit up. "Well, that would be grand, Mrs.—" she turned the book to read my name "—Fenway, just grand. I've lived in New Hope for the last seven years, and I truly believe you couldn't find a better place to put down roots."

"It's Miss Fenway," I corrected, "and I appreciate your

comments. I didn't see a dressmaking establishment on my walk down here or notice any place that offered tailoring services. Unless I didn't look carefully enough."

"We don't have anything like that, but I've long felt that if a person with those particular skills were to establish herself in New Hope, she wouldn't have a problem supporting herself. Is that something you'd consider?"

"Yes, I would." How confident my words sounded, despite the fact that I didn't know the first thing about setting up and owning a business, that I had never lived on my own or been responsible for my own livelihood in all my life!

"That would give us four female members of the Merchants' Organization, Miss Fenway, and I'm all in favor of expanding women's voices in New Hope."

"A suffragist, Mrs. Churchill?" I eyed her.

"My husband was an admirer of John Stuart Mill." At my blank look, she added, "He was a great philosopher in England, who advocated for universal suffrage. Duncan came from England and brought Mr. Mill's enlightened view to New Hope. He set quite a few people on their ears in the process and enjoyed every minute of it." She smiled at the memories. "I thought Cap Sherman would topple over from horror at the very idea of women voting. He survived the shock, but he's been a constant critic of women having a say in the Merchants' Organization ever since."

"Your Duncan needs to set that man straight," I said. At my words, Ruth Churchill's bright face and warm smile dimmed. It was as if someone had turned down a lamp for the night. I feared I had said the wrong thing but didn't know what.

"I'm a widow, Miss Fenway. My husband died last year," her tone suddenly bleak and sad.

Here is a woman who loved her husband dearly, I thought, loved him without restraint. I'm not a portraitist, but I'm still an artist and can often see below the surface and paint what I see. If I had painted Ruth Churchill at that moment, it would have been in subdued colors of gray and indigo, the colors of a cloudy day with silver streaks of rain dripping down a window like tears. A figure who watched the world from a safe distance, longing for but fearful, as well, of the warmth and color she had once known.

"I'm sorry," I said and felt how inadequate my words were in the face of her grief.

"So am I, Miss Fenway, but that doesn't change the facts." She straightened and left me standing alone as she stepped down the hall to push open the door.

"Danny," I heard her call, "will you come, please, and carry our guest's bags to her room?" She returned, followed by a boy who couldn't have been older than ten. I know very little about children, but he looked awfully young to me.

"This is Danny Lake," she told me. "He's my ward and the best help a woman could have. Danny, this is Miss Fenway, and she'll be staying with us a while. Carry her bag up to room four, please." To me, Ruth Churchill said, "Will you want a bath, Miss Fenway?"

"Is the sky blue, Mrs. Churchill?" I replied, which made my landlady smile.

"It certainly is today. Would after supper suit?"

"That would be heaven," I said.

"The Nebraska Café is right next door," Ruth Churchill told me, "and Ezzie Liggett, who owns the café, has been looking for someone to buy the small addition off the north side of her place. It's more space than Ezzie needs because when she decides to expand, it'll be out the back. It wouldn't take a lot of effort to wall off that extra room and turn it into a shop on its own, and we have a fine carpenter in town. In my opinion, the new space would fit a dressmaking establishment perfectly, but, of course, I'm no expert on that. I can't sew a straight seam for love or money." The boy had hefted my bag and was already climbing the stairs to the second floor of rooms as she talked

"Thank you, Mrs. Churchill."

"You might as well start calling me Ruth," she said. "I have a feeling we're going to be friends." I would come to learn that Ruth was right about most things, but the fact that she was a kind-hearted woman sometimes caused her to give the benefit of the doubt when the benefit of the doubt was not warranted, a fault from which I do not suffer. I have worse faults altogether, which compared to Ruth Churchill's make her as close to an angel as one is likely to meet on this earth. *New Hope Heaven* not so far off, after all.

"Then I'm Sheba."

Ruth said my name aloud in a considering way before she said, "I'm partial to names from the Good Book. Is that short for Bathsheba or is it just plain Sheba, like the queen who came to visit wise King Solomon?"

"Bathsheba, I'm afraid."

"Why *afraid*?"

"Her conduct wasn't always admirable," I said. "A married woman taking a bath on the roof and then – well, all the events that occurred subsequent to that bath."

Ruth Churchill laughed softly. "I always thought Bathsheba was a woman who did the best she could in a situation that must have been trying. Would a woman have been allowed to say no to the most powerful man in the country? I wonder. And then for the poor woman to be dragged from house to palace without a by-your-leave, shooed on home as soon as things got uncomfortable for the king, and then to lose her baby on top of everything else – well, I think she paid her dues and then some."

After a thoughtful moment, I said, "I'm not much of a church-goer so you might be right about that, I couldn't say, but I hope you're right when you said we might be friends. I like the way you think, Ruth. I like the way you give someone you don't even know the benefit of the doubt."

"I learned that from my husband. He was a charitable man." She paused, then nodded toward the stairs. "You're in the second door on the left upstairs. Danny's already gone to fetch you some hot water so you can freshen up a bit. We don't have facilities indoors, I'm afraid, but you'll find what you need in your room if you wake in the night and don't feel like traipsing outside. The regular facility is out back and it's as neat and clean as you'll find anywhere in New Hope. You're probably used to finer accommodations back East, Sheba, but you'd have to go all the way to Omaha to find any place better than Hart's. Danny and I live in The Addition, the rooms just off the first-floor hallway and if there's anything you need, just let us know by rapping on the door and we'll get it for you."

I thanked her, but in all the time I spent at Hart's, I never needed to ask for anything. Ruth Churchill knew how to run a first-rate establishment. In fact, as I would come to find out the next day, she knew how to run two first-rate establishments.

After a comfortable and sound night's sleep, I descended the stairs in the morning in desperate need of hot coffee and met Ruth Churchill at the front door of the boarding house on her way out.

"I mentioned my intention to Mrs. Liggett over supper last night," I told Ruth, "and she showed me the space she's willing to sell. I think you're right about it being a good size for the shop I have in mind, but I'll need to talk to your Mr. Sellers about the details of building it, and I'll need to stop by the bank, too. In fact, I should probably do that first." We both paused on the front porch at the top of the steps that led down to the walk and the front gate.

"Abner Talamine's a shrewd man, and he has a vision of what New Hope will be one day," Ruth told me. "I'd guess your proposal is in line with his plan for the town, but if not, let me know. I'd be willing to loan you what you need to get started." The words made me shoot her a quick glance. Most of the women I knew did not have ready access to money of their own or, worse yet, had lost all control over their own money once they married.

"Well, thank you," I said. "That's a generous offer."

"It's a practical offer," she replied. "I'll charge interest, you know."

"I'd expect you to."

"But it'll be a fair rate."

"I'd expect that, too." We stepped down to the walk side-by-side. "You're out early this morning."

Ruth smiled as she pushed open the front gate. "I need an early start today because I left the shop somewhat untidy when I closed yesterday."

"The shop? I don't understand."

"I'm sorry, I thought someone would have mentioned to you that I'm New Hope's resident barber."

"No, no one mentioned it. You run the boarding house and the barber shop?"

"I do." We stopped in front of the Nebraska Café, where I planned to fortify myself with a hearty breakfast before braving the banker. I gestured across the street.

"That barber shop? *Duncan's*?"

"The very same." For a moment, I saw fleeting sadness in her expression, the same emotion I had noticed the day before.

"Ah," I said, remembering yesterday's conversation, "your husband used to be the barber."

"Yes." With a movement so slight a person could have missed it, Ruth straightened her shoulders, much the way a soldier would do before heading into battle, and added, "Don't forget my offer about helping with the dress shop."

"I won't."

"I mean it, Sheba."

"I know you do." We each met the other's gaze, two women conducting business on Main Street. That was the moment I knew New Hope, Nebraska, would be home for me. As it was, almost from the start.

Mr. Abner Talamine, president of the United Bank of Nebraska, listened to me with uninterrupted attention, nothing on his face – neither blink nor twitch – giving a hint of his intention. When I finished explaining that I hardly had a cent to my name but that I understood fabrics, could take a Butterick pattern and easily adjust it for any size man, woman, or child, possessed an eye for color and style, a firm grasp on the concepts of profit and loss, and a good-faith commitment from Ezzie Liggett to sign over part of her space for my little dress shop, the banker gave a slight smile and quoted a dollar figure. I stared at him wordlessly until he explained, "That's the amount the bank is prepared to loan you, Miss Fenway. It's all I can offer. The country's economy isn't strong right now, but the railroad's arrival in New Hope has provided us with some financial protection, and I have it on good authority that our little community is in dire need of a dressmaker and milliner." At my continued silence, he smiled again – I would learn over time that Abner Talamine was an austere but likeable man – and added, "Mrs. Talamine has told me on more than one occasion that the female population of New Hope is languishing for lack of proper fashion."

I let out the breath I was holding and said, "Well, we can't have that. Languishing, I mean. The amount you quoted will be sufficient," and knew it would have to be because regardless of Mrs. Talamine and the fashion-starved population of New Hope, Nebraska, I wouldn't be able to wheedle one more cent out of the banker.

Through those first weeks, I came to know the inhabitants of New Hope, Nebraska, appreciate most of them, ignore one or two, and find in Ruth Churchill the kind of friend I had always needed but never realized I needed. Now, settled in New Hope for six years, established, accepted, and able to support myself, I sometimes wonder how I made it through the first years of adulthood without the support of such a friend. There is nothing more valuable than the aid and encouragement of a good woman friend.

With the appearance of the Union Pacific Railway in central Nebraska, little New Hope burgeoned into a larger and busier New Hope. Before my arrival, the town was delighted to be even a single stop on the busy U.P. line, but within three years of my arrival, the railroad added two more stops and the population grew accordingly. The Merchants' Organization, its name later changed to the Merchants'

Association, approved building a small church the year before my arrival, and a young minster arrived in New Hope soon after the construction project was finished. Ruth attributes that to the working of the Almighty, but she's a devout, trusting woman and I'm not. It's more likely that Gerald Shulte – a fine man of staunch moral character, I'm not suggesting otherwise – heard about a small town seeking a resident preacher and made his way over to New Hope with his new wife in tow, praying he would be just what the town wanted. That he was had more to do with personal initiative and good timing than divine intervention, but I don't suggest that to Ruth. She credits the man and his message for helping her overcome the deep grief she felt after her husband's death. My experience has been that time is equally as effective but again, I respect Ruth's deeply held beliefs too much to say such a thing to her. Besides, I like Gerald and Lydia Shulte, so why cast any doubt on the importance of the reverend's message and work? It's not that he's hurting anyone, and in Ruth's case, he certainly helped.

Following the quick success of their church venture, the town merchants turned their attention to a school. Once the schoolhouse was in place, they advertised for a teacher and were – again – quickly rewarded with the arrival of Arthur Stenton, not the most likeable of teachers, but an effective one and the best squelcher of childish high spirits I have ever met, a trait approved by every parent with students enrolled in the school. Arthur arrived in New Hope the same month I arrived and while one might think that two newcomers would find a mutual connection, that wasn't the case with Arthur and me. We were too alike, both private individuals content with our own company and feeling no need to mingle indiscriminately with other inhabitants of the community. I had my business and more importantly my art, and Arthur had his commitment to education and his books. Neither of us ever showed a desire to be more than head-nodding acquaintances. That's how I liked it, and I assumed it was the same for Arthur. We weren't hermits and we both interacted with a variety of people on a daily basis, but I always pictured Arthur Stenton returning to the privacy of the small house New Hope built for him with the same sigh of contentment I gave when I turned the sign on the dress shop door to closed and headed for my paints waiting in the back room.

Since my arrival, we've added new faces to the Merchants' Association: Joe Chandler from the hardware store, Con Tull, owner of the beer garden, a skilled cobbler named Mitch Lowe, and a photographer who spends more time traversing the county than he does taking pictures in his shop. And then there's John Bliss.

John arrived in New Hope later in the same year I settled there, but he did so with more confidence, experience, and cash than I ever displayed. With the ruthless purpose for which he's known, he bribed the Merchants' Organization to give him the space already claimed by Dr. Danford. From the start, Tom Danford wanted his drug store and doctor's office at the very end of Main Street, but unfortunately for Tom, the arrival of the railroad expanded Main Street south well past his office. When John Bliss offered to build the Danfords a new pharmacy shop, doctor's office, and living quarters on the far southern end of Main Street in exchange for giving him their original space, Tom and Margery boxed their belongings and shifted location without a word of complaint. The Danfords were satisfied and so was Bliss because he ended up with much of the east side of Main Street at his disposal. He wasted no time – or money, either – constructing the grand Bliss House Hotel with its equally grand Bliss Restaurant and the more common but just as appreciated Bliss Music Hall all in a row. He was a man who enjoyed seeing his name on a sign, I thought.

Once, after a merchants' meeting, I muttered that opinion to Ruth, and John, walking just behind us, overheard my words. They brought nothing but a smile.

"That's observant of you, Miss Fenway," he said. "Five easy letters, after all, and who doesn't like the idea of a little bliss?" I thought his smile, which lit an otherwise swarthy and saturnine face, was more mocking than friendly, and I would have made a rude retort except Ruth spoke first.

"I agree, Mr. Bliss," she said. "Imagine if your last name was – oh, I don't know – something like manure or poison. People would be less inclined to eat in your restaurant then." The words made him laugh out loud, which for a moment gave him the appearance of a much younger man.

"I couldn't have made the point better myself, Mrs. Churchill." We were outside on the boardwalk by then, and he dipped his head in cordial courtesy as he stepped past us.

"That man has an air of arrogance about him that I find unattractive," I said. In return, Ruth gave a laugh and shook her head. "What?" I demanded. But my friend would not be drawn out further.

"Nothing, Sheba. You may not find John Bliss all that attractive, but other members of the Merchants' Organization, myself included, hold a more charitable view."

"You find his money attractive." I heard the scorn in my voice and wished I had used a less superior tone, but Ruth didn't disagree.

"Of course, we do," she said, "and you can't argue with our reasoning. John Bliss and his money offer New Hope growth without us having to break the bank, and as a business owner yourself, you can understand why that appeals to us." At the time, the organization met in the back room of Bert Gruber's Billiards Hall and both Ruth and I walked south together, she toward the barber shop and I to my dress shop.

When she stepped down to cross the street, I said, "You're right, Ruth, but the money and the man are two different things. I can appreciate the one without taking the other to heart." Then, satisfied that I had dealt with John Bliss and gotten in the last word, too, I pushed open the door of my little establishment, still marveling that I was an independent and solitary business woman.

That exchange took place several years ago now and except for the Emmett Wolf unpleasantness in '78, New

Hope stayed peaceful and unremarkable, even as it grew. The people that stepped down from the train brought prosperity to our little community, ate in Ezzie's Nebraska Café and in the Bliss Restaurant, got haircuts at Duncan's, enjoyed the simple overnight luxuries of Hart's or the more expensive trappings of Bliss House, studied the hats and apparel I displayed in my front window and sometimes made a purchase.

Cattlemen brought their herds as far as the New Hope stock pens and loaded them onto cattle cars bound for eastern appetites, and in so doing infused Abner Talamine's United Bank of Nebraska with a steady flow of cash. After days spent looking at the backsides of cattle, the cowboys who tended the herds enjoyed the amenities of New Hope with enthusiasm, some of their enthusiasm morally questionable, but the members of the Merchants' Association decided early on that it took enough effort to monitor their own consciences and they were not going to set themselves up as the keepers of other folks' morality, as well. Reverend Shulte might wish his congregation's collective scruples were a little more sensitive, but as long as no violence was involved and everyone was a willing participant, New Hope maintained a practical tolerance for Saturday night activities. That good-natured detachment was what had attracted me to the town in the first place and what kept me a contented citizen for several years. I wasn't the least interested in changing anything that affected my life and my town. In New Hope, Nebraska, I was as happy as I had ever been, and I could have, would have, continued on with my satisfying routine of designing, sewing, painting, and creating. Except along came the summer of 1881 when my life was suddenly overturned and overtaken by the past and just as suddenly surprised by the present. Eventually, for better or worse, the unexpected jolts to my life that took place that year ended up turning my future into something I never anticipated and could never have imagined.

2

There is something about sunlight that draws me like a wasp to an open jam jar, something about how it turns the river to diamonds, slashes through clouds, sets the foliage of a red oak tree on fire, and transforms the rough-hewn roofs of little New Hope, Nebraska, into gold leaf. The sun's early morning light and its farewell streaks at the end of the day could almost be from two different celestial bodies. My infatuation with sunlight is why John Bliss and I became friends.

We didn't start out as friends. At the beginning, I found him arrogant, too fond of being right, and confident to a fault. When I enumerated those criticisms to Ruth one afternoon, she laughed herself silly. Laughed herself to tears and back, as my mother used to say. I knew that under the kind counsel of Reverend Shulte, my friend had begun to reclaim both the peace of mind and a touch of the happiness she must have enjoyed before her husband died, but I didn't think her reaction to my comments had anything to do with her healing heart.

"What did I say that was so funny?" I demanded.

Ruth took a quivering breath and lifted the corner of her barber's smock to wipe her eyes before she answered.

"I'm sorry, but oh, Sheba, do you really not see the humor in you of all people criticizing someone for being sure of his own opinion and always thinking he's right?" She glanced at my unsmiling face, took another deep breath, and answered her own question. "Apparently, not, so please forgive me. It was just that – well, never mind. Will you please forgive me?"

I ignored her plea and said, "Me of all people, you said. Are you suggesting that I—?"

"No, of course not. Of course not. You, my friend, are a meek and humble soul, nothing like John Bliss at all."

"I should hope not," I replied firmly but then had to concede, "Well, he and I might share one or two small traits, but nothing significant." Ruth smiled and said nothing, effectively ending the discussion, but on my walk home, I realized that despite the fact that she hadn't spoken, my friend had still somehow managed to get in the last word.

It was my fascination with sunlight that brought about the friendship John and I eventually enjoyed. Many times, loaded with easel and paints and heading out my front door to catch the first streaks of color along the eastern horizon, I would cross paths with the man, and at first, I found his early morning presence highly suspect. New Hope was usually still asleep when I pulled my door shut behind me, even if by the time I reached the corner of the alley leading east toward the church, I could see a few lights glowing behind an assortment of windows. New Hope's merchant families rising for another day, but the day still dark and the street still empty. Except for John Bliss.

The very first time we met was in the late fall of my first year there. His first year, too. That morning in '75 was autumn-dark with a hint of winter in the air, and I was bundled in a woolen coat with my heavy hair pinned up under a stocking cap. I could see a figure standing in the darkness on the other side of the alley where I was headed. I didn't have the sense to be afraid, still innocent enough to think that crime happened only in big, crowded cities, not in little New Hope, Nebraska, so I didn't pause in my march forward. When I got closer, the figure turned to face me, and I saw who it was. That was before John had filled that eastern section of the street with his several businesses, with his hotel and restaurant and music hall, and before he built and donated the town's meeting and entertainment building. None of those buildings was there then. It was just a barren stretch with Dr. Danford's office the first building to come into view with sunrise.

"Good morning, Miss Fenway."

I thought he touched the brim of his dark hat by way of greeting, but it was too dark to tell. *He* was too dark to tell, also, a black-haired man of swarthy complexion who made it his habit to wear dark coats.

"Good morning, Mr. Bliss." We stood facing each other on either side of the alley.

"You look like you're headed for an early stroll," he said after a moment's silence.

"I could say the same about you."

I heard his low laugh. "I'm not an early riser by choice or habit, but I felt the need to take a look at my property."

"*Your* property?"

"The east side of Main Street from the doctor's office south to the church alley, the deed says."

"So it's true then. You uprooted Dr. Danford and his wife so you could get the property you wanted. I heard some rumors about that." My lack of cordial tone didn't seem to bother him.

"It's true, but the doctor and his wife don't see it as being uprooted. They have what they want, and I have what I want."

"That sounds like congratulations are due then."

"I like to think so." Pause. "You don't approve."

"It's not for me to approve anything, Mr. Bliss. I'm as green as you are when it comes to living in New Hope, Nebraska. I just wouldn't have expected you to want to put down roots in a small town."

"I doubt New Hope will stay small very long."

"Because of the railroad, you mean."

"The railroad carries people, Miss Fenway, and people

bring business. Don't tell me you wouldn't welcome more customers for your dresses and hats."

I shifted my easel from one arm to the other before I said, "Of course, I would. I hope to stay in New Hope for a long time."

"We have one goal in common then."

I thought that one goal was all we would ever have in common, but I said only, "As much as I'm enjoying our little chat, I'll lose the sunrise if I stay any longer."

"I would never get in the way of an artist and her inspiration." I didn't catch any mockery in his tone. "I hope the sunrise offers what you're looking for." He glanced east down the alley. "Even to my amateur's eye, the colors look striking this morning."

I followed his gaze and frowned. "It's not the colors I crave, Mr. Bliss, it's the—" I paused, unable to find the words to explain the intangible qualities of light that I sought. Piercing. Soft. Diffused. Revealing. Everything I hoped to find in the morning sunrise contradictory at best. He waited for me to finish my sentence, and finally I said, "I can't say exactly what it is I'm looking for, but I'll know when I see it. I always do." Without more words, I turned and trudged down the alley toward the church and the curved horizon behind which I could see the first thrusts of light. Whether I would find what I sought for that particular morning remained to be seen, but the expectation and the surprise were part of what drew me to painting: that one moment when everything came together in my head and my heart and poured out onto the canvas. My own private and personal miracle. What I lived for. I watched the slow arrival of the sun with a critical eye as I walked, then picked up my pace, eager to be seated, my paints at the ready when morning finally spread itself across the sky.

Behind me, Bliss said something. "Good day," perhaps, or "Good bye." Maybe he said my name, too. I hardly heard him, couldn't tell and didn't care. I was interested in only one thing, and it wasn't John Bliss.

That first year, I don't recall seeing John in full daylight very often, but there were numerous occasions we met on my early morning excursions to capture the morning. From the start, I knew I was not the attraction for his early presence, and as I grew to know him better, I realized that what he enjoyed watching was not the arrival of morning light but rather the slow and steady rise of what would come to be "his" side of Main Street, the *Bliss Bonanza* as Ruth named it early on, intending no disrespect or unkindness because Ruth doesn't possess an ounce of either of those unbecoming qualities.

After he ensured that Dr. Danford and Margery were happily housed on the far southern end of town, John commissioned Harold Sellers, New Hope's resident carpenter, to start work on the grand buildings that would come to carry the Bliss name: the hotel with its antebellum pillars and ornate entry porch, the restaurant, its menu posted prominently in one of the large windows that flanked a welcoming double door, and the music hall identified by the words *Musical Entertainment* embellished with a great many curlicues on a sign swinging under the overhang. Ruth was right to name it a bonanza because from opening day, the Bliss enterprises were a huge success, always busy with a stream of both men and women taking advantage of some or all of the services Mr. Bliss advertised. As the presence of the railroad increased, so did the man's profits. Where he got the idea and the money to make the idea a reality I never knew and he never said, but from the start John knew what he was doing. And from my perspective, it seemed that he was as interested in getting exactly the right light fixtures and rugs and furnishings for his businesses as I was in applying exactly the right colors to my paintings, each of us creating works of art, although what we used to create our masterpieces was as different as night and day.

Through the years, I continued to meet John Bliss on my early morning painting excursions, but as his businesses flourished it was almost always after he had closed the Music

Hall and was on his way to his private rooms in the hotel. Bliss House, the restaurant, served a late supper but closed at midnight, and the Bliss Hotel remained staffed only until the last train had come and gone. The Music Hall, however, with its side area of gambling tables and the fine mahogany bar that traversed the entire front of the room didn't close until early morning. The Merchants' Association was at first concerned about the Music Hall in a town of respectable families, worried there would be a ruckus when the place closed its doors in the early morning hours, but there was never a moment of trouble. John stayed through the closing, escorted any lingering customers outside and made sure they found their way to a resting place, even if it was only a stall in Cap Sherman's livery stables. *No vagrants on the streets* was one of the Merchants' Association's rules and while I always considered John Bliss even less inclined than I to follow the rules, in that matter he never wavered, argued, or stepped over the line. It was a relief to know that John's calm but still ominous presence could send even the rowdiest patrons of the Music Hall home without any kind of fracas, regardless of the hour. We appreciated his ability to quell trouble with a low-voiced comment because in those early days, New Hope didn't have its own law enforcement constabulary.

John and I became friends over time, good friends, and even better friends in '78 when the town had to deal with the outlaw Emmett Wolf, but we stayed friends and nothing more. For a while, John kept close company with a woman he brought in to manage the restaurant, but that cooled after a time and she left for new horizons, there one day and boarding the western train the next. She was a beautiful woman, dark-haired and full-figured with skin the color of cream, the kind of woman more suited for Denver or San Francisco than little New Hope, even with the draw of John Bliss.

John didn't look woebegone when she left and never seemed to miss her. A pebble in a pond to him, I thought, and believed all women would have that same effect on the man. He was self-contained and independent, and it seemed to me that even at his most courteous he held the ordinary citizens of New Hope, Nebraska, at arm's length and in tolerant scorn. Never a popular man, he still knew how to stay on everyone's good side with well-placed and timely donations. The town's Meeting Hall was built largely from his generosity, and he donated a room full of very fine children's desks for the new schoolhouse. People could forgive a lot when the train dropped off something new and expensive for the town's enrichment. His double donation for the new fire engine clinched his acceptability. John Bliss was as welcome in New Hope as rain after a lengthy drought.

I never believed John would stay in our little community very long, a clever man always interested in the next opportunity waiting over the horizon, but in that regard, I was wrong. Stay he did, and put down roots the same as I. He chose his friends very carefully, was partial to Ruth – well, who wasn't partial to Ruth? Her face wears a transparent kindness that comes directly from her heart – and eventually became partial to me, much to my surprise. I never planned to like him and expected he felt the same about me, but that changed the first time he saw my paintings.

I had propped four of them against the shaded wall of the alley that ran alongside my dress shop – the spot where George Young built his small photographic studio – and was perusing them with a critical eye when John stepped around the corner of the alley and took a quiet stance next to me. I was deep in thought and unwilling to be interrupted, but after a moment, conscious of his stillness, I turned my head to look at him. He turned his gaze to me at the same time.

"You're very good," he said.

I couldn't help but feel pleasure at his remark. Painting is private and absorbing and one is never really sure if the work holds any merit at all. It's almost impossible to be dispassionate about it, any more than a mother can be detached from her baby, and it felt good to hear someone else say what I always hoped and sometimes believed to be true.

"Thank you."

We stood shoulder-to-shoulder looking at the four paintings for a longer while until he asked, "Are any of them for sale?"

I stared at him, having never given the idea a thought. I didn't paint for profit or for any kind of commercial recognition. Who among the merchants and ranchers and farmers of New Hope, Nebraska, and its vicinity had money to spend on wall paintings? No one I knew of. I painted because I had to paint. Because not painting was as impossible as not breathing, and either would kill me.

"I suppose so," I said.

He pointed to my favorite of the four. I would come to find out that John Bliss had an excellent eye for all the things that make good art good, for composition and color and perspective and balance and beauty. And light. Maybe especially for light because the painting which he wanted showed the schoolhouse and the few trees by its side as dabs of darkness against a sunset backdrop, the sun's last desperate streaks of brilliant light piercing through clouds of azure and deep rose. There was something both despairing and hopeful in the painting. Did the schoolhouse, did education and children and their contribution to the future, somehow reflect those same contradictory feelings? I don't know how it all fit together – though I knew on some level that it did – but I could recall the moment and relive the feelings of that early evening as I painted furiously. It was on my mother's birthday.

"I don't know what to charge," I admitted. "No one's ever bought one of my paintings before."

"I can't understand how that's possible," he said. "If you'll trust me with it now, I promise to send over something to you tomorrow. It will be a fair price."

Bliss was known to be a fair employer, generous even. The people who worked in his restaurant never complained, whether cook or clean-up, and he always had a string of happy-looking girls ready and willing to serve customers at the dining tables. Even without knowing John Bliss very well at that time, I knew he would be fair. More surprisingly, I did trust him, the result of those early morning chats, I suppose.

"All right," I said. I watched him heft the selected canvas and felt a pang as he carried it away. Did mother birds feel that same bittersweet jab when their babies left the nest?

The next day one of John's young helpers from the hotel brought me an envelope. The contents made me gasp. Too much, I thought, but I didn't offer to return a single dollar.

A week or so later, Mort Lewis, New Hope's attorney, stopped by my shop.

"Do you have other paintings for sale, Sheba?" he asked.

"Other paintings?" I repeated. I am usually a quick-witted woman, but the question took me by surprise.

"I saw the one you did for John Bliss."

"I didn't paint anything for John Bliss," I replied in a tone that sounded too tart, even to my ears.

Mort was quick to backtrack. "I meant that Bliss bought from you."

Mollified, I asked, "How do you know about that?"

"He's got it hanging in the lobby of the hotel in a fine burnished frame. Sure lifted the tone of the place. If you've got others, I'd like to take a look at them. My office could use something to give it a little distinction."

Adding distinction, I thought with a sigh, was not why I painted and was not the effect I hoped for, but I had paintings stacking up in the back and what else was I to do with them?

Over time, enough New Hope businesses displayed my paintings that people off the train searched me out, and I made the odd sale to railroad men, as well, who visited New Hope for one business reason or another.

I gave a painting as a gift to Ruth, one I did just for her because she had been so welcoming and supportive from my first day in town, had put me up at her boarding house and not charged me a cent until I got my business feet on the ground. A small thank you for lavender soap and clean sheets, for a friendly smile and the offer of a loan made straight from her heart. That painting, one of the few I titled, hangs in the lobby of her boarding house in a prominent place of honor over the hearth. It's one of the first things her boarders see when they walk through the front door. I called the painting "Ruth's River" because sunlight sparkles and dances across the Platte like a flurry of diamonds and Ruth's friendship is dearer to me than any jewels.

Six years into planting myself in New Hope, Nebraska, I was happy, or as happy as I knew how to be. I'm not by nature an especially happy person, but I'm not morose or unhappy, either. My temperament is simply not given to excess. The times I experience joy have to do with painting, with the moment when I know I've captured something just right and a warm wave of satisfaction washes through me. There, I tell myself, there is happiness. That brush stroke. That hue. That moment.

Of course, I was happy for Ruth when she remarried. She found a good man, a man who loves and appreciates her, but even then, I wondered to myself how and why she would give up her independent life – and eventually her barber shop – for a husband, no matter how good a man he was. She probably guessed my sentiments, we had been friends a few years by then, but I never voiced them outright. The glow on her face the day she married was a beautiful thing and held a light all its own. Later, I tried to paint her but could never quite capture Ruth's settled happiness.

I'm a good citizen and supporter of New Hope. I donate to causes that the Merchants' Association designates, attend the school's end of the year program and pretend to be entertained (I realize that children are necessary for the continuation of the human race, but other than that, I've never had much interest in them), attend church on the major holidays, and converse pleasantly with people on the street. I call several people friends besides Ruth, the Chandlers, for example, and the Talamines, but I prefer my solitary life to any social occasion. I even enjoy dressmaking. How satin feels under my fingertips and the way color gleams from a bolt of silk are satisfying. But all the things I mentioned would be worthless if I did not have the freedom to paint. New Hope gives me that. No one ever speaks a critical word when I forget to open my store because I'm in the back room painting or raises a disapproving eyebrow at the sight of me in a paint-stained smock and my hair held back by an inelegant bandanna. A religious person, someone like Ruth, would say that God brought me to New Hope, Nebraska, but I always thought God already had plenty to worry about the year I went searching for a new home. The Tong wars in San Francisco, the great economic national depression that drove people to desperate poverty almost overnight, shipwrecks and Indian wars and all matter of events worthier of divine intervention than one woman looking for a place to settle so she could paint in uninterrupted peace. It doesn't seem to me that the Almighty intervening in so small and private a life as mine would have shown good use of His time.

Whatever the truth of the matter – and I have little time to spend on such weighty issues – I lived in New Hope contentedly for six years, no complaint on my part and none, so far as I know, on anyone else's part, either. Until late in the summer of 1881 when Bert Gruber, owner of the Gooseneck Hotel and Billiards Hall, suggested to the Merchants' Association that we host an evening of entertainment for the town by inviting a traveling song and dance troupe to spend time with us.

"They can stay at the Gooseneck," Bert said. "That'll be my contribution."

That and bedbugs, I thought as I met Ruth's look across the meeting room. I knew when she glanced quickly away and stifled a giggle that she had the same thought.

Discussion followed. And followed. Bert said he had just returned from the neighboring community of Gothenburg and people there were still talking about the variety production they had recently enjoyed.

"I just bet they were," said Luther Winters. Luther is our expert on all things cosmopolitan because he has a brother who works for a newspaper in Kansas City. The words *Lou says* trip off Luther's tongue as easily and as often as giggles from a schoolgirl. "Lou says the city council there in K.C. bans more of that entertainment than they allow. Nothing I'd let Millie or Sally see, I can tell you that." Luther was also our expert on all things proper, although we knew he took his direction from his wife, New Hope's voice of respectability. I often wondered how I escaped Millie Winters's censure, but I never asked about it. I get seasick when the boat rocks.

I was surprised that Bert, not one to argue, spoke quickly in return. "Now that's not fair, Luther. Not American, either, to make a judgement based on hearsay."

"We're not talking about a court of law," Luther grumbled, but Bert wouldn't be silenced.

"I tell you, there were plenty of ladies in attendance in Gothenburg and not a one I talked to had anything critical to say about the show."

"We've got our own brass band," stated Cap Sherman. "Don't know why we need anything else."

"That's all well and good for the Fourth of July," Bert replied, "but I'm talking culture here. Fine music and dramatic presentations. Real honest-to-God entertainers. People who sing and dance and act for a living." Bert gave grave emphasis to his final three words. Not hotel owners and undertakers and butchers and dress makers, he might have said, but people who did something worthwhile for a living, something enjoyable, something world-expanding. We took his meaning without taking offense and the tide of opinion began to turn.

In the end, after the vote was taken, Cap Sherman stomped out of the meeting – but then he always stomped out when he didn't get his way so the rest of us remained unfazed – and Joe Chandler, head of the Association, commissioned Bert to find out more about the traveling company that would soon be departing its current host city of

Lexington, things like cost and timing and – mindful of Millie Winters's sensibilities – the content of the performance.

Bert Gruber beamed. I would have said he was an easy-going man who didn't feel strongly about most things, but he certainly had strong opinions about hosting an entertainment troupe. Well, I couldn't blame him. Bert was a single man with neither wife nor children to keep him occupied, and if I didn't paint, I might have felt somewhat bored myself. New Hope's brass band had its limitations.

"What harm can it possibly do," I asked Ruth later in the day, "to enjoy an evening of song, dance, and drama?"

At the time, I thought I knew the answer to my own question and only nodded when Ruth responded, "No harm that I can see. I enjoy Mr. Stenton's end of the school year programs, but it would be nice to see something with a little more polish. If I can last that long." Big with her first child, she laid a hand on her belly. "Tom says I have a few weeks to go yet, so if Bert gets a move on, I might be able to enjoy some light-hearted entertainment before the baby comes." Her tone told me she'd rather have a baby than a variety show any day of the week, but that as long as she could have one without giving up the other, she was perfectly amenable to Bert's suggestion.

If Ruth and I had had access to a crystal ball that day, we might have come to a different conclusion, but we didn't, of course. To my knowledge, there was not a single crystal ball in all of New Hope then – or today, for that matter. And I don't believe that a crystal ball, a gypsy soothsayer, and a magical deck of fortune-telling cards all thrown together could have predicted how that traveling troupe of entertainers would turn my world and my life upside down and backwards.

3

Bert Gruber made excellent time with his assignment, and by the end of that week posters announcing the arrival of The Alice Variety Theatre of the West began to appear around town. The citizens of New Hope and its surrounding area were promised "Vocal and Instrumental Entertainment," "Magic Transformations," and a dramatic presentation titled "Brittle Silver, or How a Mine and Maiden Were Lost and Won." The event became the main, if not sole, topic of conversation throughout New Hope. We were not New York or Philadelphia, with a theatre on every corner and a selection of entertainment available for every social level and price range. We were Nebraska and barring an unanticipated wedding or funeral, The Alice Variety Theatre of the West would very likely be the pinnacle social occasion of our year.

I experienced a rush for new ladies' hats and was pinning ribbon and flowers onto bonnets up to the very day of the performance. My big-city pretensions had vanished years ago, and I found myself humming under my breath, as happily anticipatory as any of my fellow townspeople. These were folks who valued hard work, saved their money, were appalled by waste and scornful of sloth, who took care of their families and always kept an eye on the future, no matter how tedious or demanding the duties of the present were. With little time for luxuries in New Hope, the arrival of The

Alice Variety Theatre of the West was as close to a luxury as they had seen in a long while. As *we* had seen, for that matter, because I looked forward to the evening with the same excitement as everyone else.

Bert Gruber brought back colorful handbills from the Lexington performance and word from Lexington's mayor that he had attended the show and could assure us that there was not a single word or action the entire evening that would not have been enjoyed by his maiden aunt – if he had a maiden aunt, which he didn't, but his point was well taken. It sounded like whatever happened on stage would pass the narrowed eye and superior taste of Millie Winters without a hitch.

Bert offered the theatre troupe free accommodations and meals and the Merchants' Association agreed to hand over 90% of ticket sales to the theatre group, an arrangement so generous that Peregrine Alice, owner and general manager of the traveling show, agreed to the offer immediately. With three other engagements already in place, one of which was in a neighboring county, New Hope had to wait two weeks for the troupe's arrival, which gave volunteers from the Merchants' Association time to scrawl the date, time, and cost of the performance onto the posters Mr. Alice provided and nail the announcements all over town. They would be up for two Saturdays, which would give people living in the country time to read about the show and get as excited as we city dwellers.

The six resident performers of the traveling Variety Theatre arrived in New Hope the night before the performance, stopped at the Gooseneck Hotel long enough to drop off their valises, and took up immediate residence in the town's Meeting Hall, which had transformed into the *Entertainment* Hall as soon as the posters showed up around town. When I went to bed the night of their arrival, lights still gleamed from the building that would be the site of the performance. Painting is a private and individual preoccupation, group public performance its exact opposite, so I had little knowledge of what went on behind the scenes of a dramatic presentation. Years ago, in what seems like the life of a different woman completely, I had attended both theatre and opera, but I am a visual artist and all I recall of those times are brightly-lit stages and an array of colorful costumes. I never spent a moment wondering about the preparation for such a performance. That night, however, standing in my shop doorway with the bright lights and snatches of laughter from the Entertainment Hall rivaling the nighttime activities of John Bliss's Music Hall, I realized I was smiling at the thought of the next evening's entertainment, which meant that after six years, I was as much a Nebraskan as anyone born and bred in New Hope. The idea pleased me.

Harold Sellers constructed a stage at the front of the Meeting Hall and stretched a rope across in such a way that blankets could hang on either side of the stage and be opened and closed by hand as needed. It couldn't hold a candle to the Eagle Variety Theatre Hall in Manhattan, which I had visited as a girl or Chicago's lavish Exposition Building that was described in detail in *The Grand Island Independent* a few years ago, but by New Hope standards, it was a very fine arrangement and when I arrived the night of the performance, the room buzzed with happy anticipation without a critic in sight.

I saw Ruth seated toward the front of the room and elbowed my way toward her. Fortunately, Lizbeth Ericson, the pretty sixteen-year-old who helped Ruth with the boarding house and Ruth's companion that evening, had an empty chair to her immediate right and after one glance at my approach, slid to the empty seat. I sat down between the two, greeted Lizbeth, and turned my attention to Ruth.

"How are you feeling and why are you here without your husband? Last time I saw him, it was clear he didn't want to let you out of his sight."

"I'm feeling fine, Sheba, but I'm big as a barn and I should probably have claimed two chairs for the evening." Ruth waved the single program page in front of her as a fan. "And since I am now married to the head of the *county* constabulary, we've both had to adjust to a less routine schedule."

"Trouble somewhere?"

"A bank robbery outside of Seeley this morning."

"Was anyone hurt?"

"No, thank the Lord."

"I can understand why the county sheriff needed to show up, but I'm still sorry you're by yourself."

"Lizbeth's here," Ruth reached across me to tap the girl lightly on her arm, "and you're here, too, so I'm not by myself. I'm in good hands. The town's in good hands, too, because Silas left Monty in charge of New Hope." Ruth and Lizbeth shared a smile. "Besides," Ruth continued, "being married to man who puts on a pleasant face but is always relieved when the school's end of the year program concludes, it wouldn't surprise me to discover that the robbery was nothing but an excuse to miss tonight's show."

"Ha!" I said. "You'd be very surprised and I would, too. The man is more protective about you than a mother bear with her cubs. Being as far away as Seeley must be awful for him."

Ruth smiled at that but said only, "We've both survived worse," and turned her attention to the stage, saying, "Harold did a nice job." At my murmured agreement, she added, "I imagine this must seem awfully crude to a sophisticated person like yourself."

I did not talk about my past and Ruth never asked, so I was surprised at a statement that might have been considered prying.

"No," I answered, "and truth be told, I bet I'm just as excited as Lizbeth here." At the sound of her name, the girl turned toward us with a bright, open smile.

"I admit I'm pretty excited, Miss Sheba," Lizbeth said, "getting to see the show and then spend the night at the boarding house – well, it's a big to-do for me."

She was a kind, fair-haired, pretty girl, besides being as smart as a whip. I had underestimated her at first but over time had learned to respect both her intelligence and her appetite for hard work. While Ruth had two sisters of her own, they lived a considerable distance from New Hope, and through the years, Lizbeth had gradually taken on the role of a beloved younger sister, one who returned Ruth's affection with fierce and loyal devotion. In some ways they were two of a kind, both tender-hearted and uncomplaining, but while Ruth was light dancing across the water, I would have painted Lizbeth with a darker current to her. Something strong and irreversible ran through her that would not be stopped once it took hold. There was iron in Lizbeth Ericson, a will set on the future and a mind of her own, a girl with hidden depths that she chose to keep to herself. She'll be a force to be reckoned with someday, I had thought on more than one occasion, and even now, Lizbeth still hovering somewhere between child and woman, I would not be brave enough to get in her way if she had set her mind or her heart on something.

We settled into our chairs as comfortably as their hard backs and harder seats would allow and waited without further conversation for the show to begin.

After a few more minutes, a handsome man with a dark goatee, chiseled sideburns of which Ruth would certainly approve, and long hair just beginning to show gray appeared on the makeshift stage. The black suitcoat, pin-striped pants, and silver-hued waistcoat he wore gave him a distinguished appearance. He had a voice to match, deep and clear and carrying without being bombastic

"Good evening, ladies and gentlemen," he began. "On behalf of the entire company, welcome to The Alice Variety Theatre of the West. We have an evening of entertainment planned for you, and I have been told by the most discriminating of critics that what you are about to see could not be rivalled were you seated in the finest performance hall of New York City. Speaking for all the members of our group, I extend our sincere hope that the performances which we offer for your pleasure tonight will make it an evening you will not soon forget."

I don't recall everything that occurred on stage that night. In fact, I've forgotten everything after the fourth performance. Mr. Peregrine Alice, the man who had welcomed us, recited several sections of Shakespeare, and as I recall he did justice to nearly every speech. Two men then appeared and lightened the mood by acting ridiculously moonstruck over a young songstress, who stood at a distance and studiously ignored their silliness throughout. I remember laughing at them. In fact, I remember that laughter rumbled through the entire hall so I wasn't alone in being entertained by the pair, but today I couldn't give back a single specific of their lovesick foolishness. One of the men then stayed behind to play a few familiar songs on what appeared to be a mandolin and managed to get most of the audience to sing along with him. When he finished, he pulled the improvised curtain to the center to close off the stage from view before he exited. I remember looking over at Lizbeth and being as entertained by the delight on her face as I had been by the performances I had just witnessed. The last thing I recall before the evening went out of control was Mr. Alice stepping to the center stage in front of the curtain and announcing that he was honored to present the stirring drama titled *Brittle Silver* with renowned actress Miss Fannie Newell in the lead role of Bronco Kate.

"I don't recognize her name," Ruth whispered to me. "Have you heard of Miss Fannie Newell?"

"No," I whispered back. "Maybe her renown is limited to places other than Nebraska."

My friend gave me a quick grin, then tried to resettle her bulk into her inadequate chair before turning her attention back to the stage.

A young man appeared and pulled back the curtain to reveal Miss Fannie Newell standing in the center of the platform with one hand pressed over her heart and her gaze fixed over our heads as if seeing a vision in the far corner of the entertainment hall. So convincing was her stance and her expression that more than one person in the audience took a quick peak over his shoulder to see if there really was something hovering in the back of the room.

Miss Newell was a slender woman with thick auburn hair, a fashionably pale complexion, and a generous mouth enhanced by face paint. At my first glimpse of her, even before I was conscious that I knew who she was, I felt my heart speed up and my stomach turn, the two reactions occurring simultaneously. My painter's eyes often see and interpret things before my mind and the rest of my body have a chance to catch up, and it must have been so that night. Ruth told me later that I inhaled sharply with a gasp audible to my companions. I don't remember doing so, but I do remember being suddenly as fixed on the actress as she was on that imaginary scene in the distance. It could not be, I thought, and yet I knew it was. Her first words – "Oh, Pa, where are you? I wish you were home!" – confirmed what I suspected. No flat Nebraska tones there; it was Pennsylvania I heard in the vowels and the syllables. It wasn't the West reflected in that clear, modulated voice speaking from the stage, it was the East, specifically Main Line Philadelphia. I knew that as well as I knew my own name, as well as I knew the real name of the actress billed as Miss Fannie Newell.

She was a credible actress, more talented than I would have expected, and I know she made the character of Bronco Kate come alive for the audience because I heard sniffles in the hall when the onstage drama forced Kate to be parted from the man to whom she had pledged her heart, and at the happy ending, the relieved audience broke into spontaneous applause at the sight of Miss Newell being embraced by her sweetheart, the man who an hour earlier had entertained us on the mandolin. If nothing else, they were a troupe of many and varied talents. At the performers' stage bows, I heard a loud and enthusiastic male voice call "Hoorah for Miss Newell!!" several times and thought it sounded a lot like Bert Gruber.

Somehow, I managed to sit through the entire variety

show, which was, so I've been told, both entertaining and edifying. It must have been Mr. Alice reciting from The Bard that earned the evaluation *edifying* because I don't recall anything else that happened on stage that night as being in the least instructive. But then, it took me a while to recover the full use of my senses and regain an awareness of my surroundings so for all I know, Plato's *Republic* might have been read in its entirety followed by a dramatic exposition of the Constitution of the United States. In fact, by the time I was myself again, breathing normally and able to consider what I should do about the shock I had experienced and whether I was prepared to bear its repercussions, all the members of The Alice Variety Theatre of the West, six performers joined by the skinny boy who had managed the curtain and the few props, stood onstage giving their final bows for the evening. I took a quick glance to my right at Lizbeth who sat completely oblivious to my presence, applauded for all she was worth, and stared at the stage with a glowing face. When I looked to my left, however, Ruth was not watching anything or anyone on the stage; she was watching me. When I met her gaze, she raised both brows in a question that did not need words.

I shook my head in response to her mute inquiry. Even if I had tried to offer some kind of explanation, my words couldn't have been heard over the applause and the sound of escalating voices. It's difficult if not impossible for the citizens of New Hope to remain quiet for an extended period of time even without a variety show to discuss, so after more than two hours of enforced silence, there was a lot that needed to be said. We are a community that enjoys life and holds an abundance of opinions about it.

Ruth stood, placed both hands at the sides of her waist, and stretched her shoulder blades back as far as she could manage without toppling over. Studiously ignoring me, she said to Lizbeth, who had also risen, "Did you enjoy the show, Lizbeth?" Lizbeth turned her head to look at Ruth, her wide smile as much an answer to the question as her words.

"Oh, yes, Miss Ruth! It was simply…it was simply –" The girl paused, seeking the right word, and then found it, "–splendid! It was simply splendid!" There was something about seeing Lizbeth Ericson so happy that briefly made me happy, too, despite what I feared was going to complicate my life indefinitely.

I remained seated with Ruth standing on my one side and Lizbeth on the other until I looked up at Ruth and said, "You two go on. I need to stay behind a while."

Lizbeth opened her mouth to speak, caught Ruth's slight headshake, and simply squeezed in front of me to slip her hand under Ruth's arm. Whether for Ruth's support or her own was hard to tell because the audience seated around us was moving toward the exit doors with the inevitable force of an ocean tide, and it wouldn't have taken much for either of my companions to be stepped on or over.

"All right," Ruth said to me in a mild tone and drew Lizbeth a little closer, "if you're sure."

"Oh, I'm sure." I didn't bother to hide the certain grim resolve that had crept into my tone. I know my duty but most of the time I don't like it. This was one of those times.

Lizbeth gave me another quick, puzzled look and then allowed herself to be pulled along by a determined Ruth, now as eager as everyone else to be out of the entertainment hall and headed for home. As close as she was to giving birth to her first child, she probably felt an equal need for both a cushioned chair and the water closet, not necessarily in that order. Nevertheless, for all her desire for the comforts of home, I saw her stop at the door when John Bliss briefly rested a hand on her shoulder and leaned down to say something to her.

She gave a brief reply accompanied by a slight shrug and then allowed John to clear the doorway of people who had stopped for friendly chatter and inadvertently caused a bottleneck in the flow of exiting patrons. Ruth was smiling but relentless in her desire to be outside, and John was just the man to help her get there.

He may have been in New Hope nearly six years, but there remained about the man an intangible but certain menace – the word *menace* seems strong and yet it is no exaggeration – that made his fellow citizens think twice about entering into any kind of disagreement with him. There were still disagreements, of course, because we all work and live and make community decisions in close proximity to each other, but when the topic had anything to do with John Bliss, it was broached carefully and respectfully. I had never seen John anything but even-tempered and mildly caustic but like everyone else, I sensed that something darker than self-mocking good humor rested behind his black eyes. No one wanted to be the one who let that particular genie out of the bottle.

I waited until the hall had emptied of people before I rose to my feet. From somewhere behind the drawn curtain I could hear the murmur of voices as the members of The Alice Variety Theatre of the West celebrated another successful performance. There was no exit door on that end of the Meeting Hall, and the cast began to appear from behind the curtain with valises in hand, trudging their way toward the door and eventually across the street to the Gooseneck Hotel. For whatever reason, Bert had told me that he was going to put out modest after-performance refreshments for the cast in his adjoining Billiards Hall – I would never have guessed that unassuming Bert Gruber was such an ardent supporter of the thespian arts! – and because that must have been an uncommon occurrence in the small towns in which the Alice Variety Show performed, there was a lively air among the performers as they pushed the curtain to the side and stepped down from the stage.

Two men and the young songstress appeared first, interrupting their chatter long enough to look over at me and smile.

"Fine entertainment," I said, because I felt I had to say something, and they responded with bright smiles and a chorus of "Our pleasure," before disappearing out into the street.

Another somewhat older man followed on their heels – a juggler and a master of the lariat, as I recalled, plus some other nimble-fingered act that had awed the audience but which I couldn't for the life of me remember.

Finally, Mr. Peregrine Alice appeared and stepped down from the stage, reaching up a free hand to Fannie Newell to steady her as she took a step to the floor. I moved forward unable to take my eyes from the woman's face. Even with the time I'd had to accept the fact, her presence in New Hope was still astounding enough to hinder rational thought. Of all the small towns in all the states of a country that stretched between oceans, why New Hope, Nebraska?

Observing my approach, Mr. Alice paused, removed his hat, set down the soft-sided valise he carried, and turned to give me an inquiring but shrewd look. Perhaps he thought I was an adoring female who wanted to express my admiration for the troupe's performance or even for him in particular. He was a very handsome man, and I supposed admiring females were common enough for him, but I watched his welcoming, slightly complacent expression fade as he noticed my gaze fixed firmly on his companion.

Closer, Fannie Newell seemed thinner, paler, and more fragile than she had appeared on stage. When Alice stopped, Miss Newell dropped her hand from his arm, sent him a quick, puzzled, and slightly annoyed glance, and then turned her attention to see what it was that had interrupted their exit. For just a moment, her face was blank, no doubt experiencing the same uncomprehending disbelief I had felt at my first sight of her, and then her face changed. Her eyes widened, her jaw literally dropped open, and she teetered slightly on her feet. Alice reached out to offer support, but his companion shook off his touch and stepped toward me. She seemed as speechless at my appearance as I had been throughout the entire second half of the theatrical show. No doubt it was a shock for both of us. Finally, because I had had time to adjust somewhat to her presence and she still shook her head in disbelief, I spoke first, an unplanned, rambling greeting.

"Hello, Dee. Yes, I'm astonished, too. Not that I'm not happy to see you, of course, but whoever could have imagined that we would meet after such a long separation in New Hope, Nebraska, of all places? Lord Byron was exactly right: Truth really is stranger than fiction."

I wouldn't have thought it possible that the woman's complexion could fade to a shade whiter than it already was, but she definitely turned even paler before she closed her eyes and with the poise one would expect from an accomplished stage actress, sank to the floor in a graceful swoon, first to her knees and then toppling over at the last moment so that her head came to rest obligingly on the large cloth bag that rested next to Mr. Alice's feet.

For a moment, Peregrine Alice and I stared at the recumbent figure as if we had never seen her before. Then he dropped to one knee and took one of her hands in his.

"Fannie? Fannie?" he asked. "My dear, can you hear me?"

Some things, I thought with an inward sigh, never change, then admonished myself for the thought because she truly hadn't looked either well or strong. And her face, even those beautiful and admired full lips which were always one of her finest features, had definitely lost all color. If one believed in ghosts – I don't – the pallor of the woman lying on the floor would have resembled one.

"She's fainted," I said. "I'll get the doctor," and stopped abruptly on my way toward the door when a childish voice asked, "Mama? Are you all right? What does *fainted* mean, Mr. Alice?"

I halted mid-step and turned back to view the scene. A small, dark-haired boy knelt beside Alice, and when the man did not answer, the boy lifted his head to look at me and repeated his question. Because of the dim light of the hall's lamps, I could not make out the details of the child's face with any clarity, but there was no mistaking the word *mama*. Good heavens! Intent on Fannie Newell and still coming to grips with my own shock, I had managed to miss the presence of the small boy entirely – and I considered myself a keen observer of details? Perhaps I needed to reevaluate all my self-proclaimed talents.

"It means she has temporarily lost conscious thought," I said to the child.

"Will she be all right?" Nothing panicked or fearful in his tone, just curious inquiry.

"She will be fine."

"Do you promise?" Curious - and insistent - inquiry.

"I seldom make promises, but you may trust that what I say is true."

"I don't know you."

"You don't know me yet," I corrected, "but that will change soon enough. Your mama will be just fine, and the doctor will agree with me when he arrives." Then I hurried outside and down the boardwalk in search of Tom Danford, somehow managing to continue to breathe as I did so.

4

Eventually, Fannie Newell, Peregrine Alice, and the child all ended up in the rooms attached to the rear of my shop, which had always seemed roomy enough when I resided there on my own but now seemed suddenly cramped and tiny. The doctor gave Miss Newell a quick but thorough examination: took her pulse, pulled back an eyelid, laid a gentle hand over her heart, then stood and pronounced her in no medical danger.

"But," Tom Danford said, "she does appear thinner and paler than what I consider to be healthy. Does she eat?"

He fixed his stare on Alice, who stumbled a bit in his reply. "I don't know, Doctor. I mean, I assume she eats, but I'm not responsible for her meals." He looked at the little boy. "Does your mother eat, Jem?" *Jem.* I felt my heart give a painful lurch.

"Yes, sir. Most of the time, anyway."

"Most of the time?" I asked. "What exactly does that mean?" Jem turned his dark-eyed attention to me.

"Mama usually eats when she's hungry," he explained.

"Except–" I said, reading his tone.

He nodded at my understanding and continued, "Except yesterday, and today she said she didn't feel hungry. She was just tired, she said." A curious silence settled on the rest of us because the dignity of the boy's tone was betrayed by the slightest quaver in his voice. A person might almost have missed it.

Dr. Danford didn't miss it, however. He rested one hand briefly on Jem's shoulder before saying to Peregrine Alice, "My professional opinion is that Miss Newell is exhausted and too weak to continue on a demanding performance schedule. I prescribe rest."

"Rest? We're playing in Curtis tomorrow night."

"*You* may be playing in Curtis, Mr. Alice, but Miss Newell is resting in New Hope," I said. "I'm sure the young woman who regaled us with her singing is more than competent and will be delighted to take on the role of Bronco Kate. Now, if you will, please lift Miss Newell and follow me. She'll be much more comfortable with me than at the Gooseneck Hotel. It's this way."

When I turned toward the door, I was halted by a small hand sliding into mine.

"I'm coming, too," young Jem said with calm assurance. I squeezed his hand.

"Indeed you are," I agreed.

After Tom Danford offered parting advice about warm food and plenty of rest, Peregrine Alice, Jem, and I stood around the bed watching Fannie Newell's chest rise and fall in light but regular breaths.

"I suppose Penny can take on the role of Bronco Kate," Alice mused aloud. "She may not have Fannie's flair for the dramatic, but she's six years younger and that makes up for a lot." I refused to dignify the remark with a comment. To me, he said, "I can't pay for her care, you know. She's due something for tonight and that's all. I'll send it over before we leave town."

The man seemed to have adjusted to the loss of his leading lady with remarkable ease. Perhaps success at his kind of traveling life depended on being flexible, quick-thinking, and hard-hearted when required. Perhaps success at any kind of life depended on varying degrees of those same qualities.

"By all means, send it over," and turned to Jem to tell him

to stay with his mother while I saw Mr. Alice out. "I'll be right back," I told the child.

"Yes, ma'am." He gave me a quick but serious look and perched on the edge of the bed next to his mother.

"You're not going to cry, are you?" I asked from the doorway when I looked back at the two figures.

"I don't cry."

"Ever?"

"Well, maybe when I was a baby, but not since I grew up."

He was a very small boy, and I hadn't the heart to point out the obvious just then.

"I'm glad to hear it," I said. "I'm not very handy with crying children." He didn't appear surprised by my confession.

Alice and I walked through my shop, and he paused in the front doorway before exiting.

"This is very kind of you, Miss—"

"Fenway. Sheba Fenway."

At my name, he fixed his gaze on me in an unwavering stare and something appeared in his eyes as he studied me, a speculative surprise or curiosity, before he finally resumed his air of debonair self-assurance.

"Fenway. Not all that an uncommon name, I suppose." Before I had a chance to comment on his remark, he said, "Fannie knows where we're headed the next couple of days. When she's ready to catch up, she can wire and let me know." He adjusted his coat and pulled down his shirt sleeves so each cuff peeked out neatly at the wrist, a clever man who regardless of the height of the fall would always land with both feet squarely pointed forward.

"I'll tell her," I said, but as I shut the door after him and turned back toward my small living quarters, I already knew that Fannie Newell and her son had seen the last of The Alice Variety Theatre of the West.

When I returned to the room where Fannie Newell slept, the boy looked over at me. He still sat on the edge of the bed but had taken his mother's hand in his. Something about the sight brought a brief lump to my throat, which disappeared when I said, "Your mama is very tired, and I imagine she'll sleep a while yet. What about you? Are you hungry?"

"Yes, ma'am."

"Come into the kitchen then, and I'll see what I can find. We'll put down some blankets on the floor and you can sleep right next to your mama's bed."

He nodded at the wisdom of my idea and stood. "Then when she wakes up, she won't be scared."

I had meant the sleeping arrangements to be a comfort to the child but didn't correct his words. "Yes, indeed," I said.

Jem sat at my little kitchen table and watched as I warmed leftover potatoes and ham from a previous night's meal, poured a glass of milk, and set the food in front of him.

"Aren't you having anything?"

I admired his restraint and the good job his mother had done teaching him proper manners. His eyes widened at the sight of the plate of food, and I suddenly realized that he was much hungrier than I had originally thought. Is that why he seemed so slight? The lump in my throat briefly reappeared.

"I had supper before the performance," I explained. "You go ahead and start while I go check on your mother. Then I'll come back and keep you company."

He didn't need a second invitation, and by the time I pulled out the chair across from him, he had managed to do serious damage to the plate of food.

"She's still sleeping," I said and refilled his milk glass before I sat down.

The boy nodded but continued to eat with the solemn self-discipline of a very small but dignified old man. I tried to picture him playing marbles or rolling an old wheel hoop down a hill or racing around with other children in a game of tag, but I couldn't see him doing any of those activities, all too rowdy and too childish for such a serious boy.

"My name is Sheba Fenway," I said, finally. His reaction was immediate and almost comical for its astonishment.

"That's my name, too!"

"Your name is Sheba Fenway?" I asked, coloring my tone with an innocent surprise I didn't feel.

"No." The syllable held a faint disgust at the ignorance of adults. "Not *Sheba* Fenway. I'm a boy. My name is James Cameron Fenway."

Hearing the name made me blink quickly. How long had it been since I had heard that name spoken aloud? Too long. Years. And yet, it still had the power to prick at my heart. Only a small poke by now, the same feeling a person might get when someone bumped accidentally against a healing bruise or a tender scar. Not quite healed enough to be wholly inured to pain but almost there.

"I thought Mr. Alice called you Jem?"

"Jem is what my mama calls me." He stopped to consider what he had just said and added, "Unless she's mad at me. Then she calls me James Cameron."

"What a considerate mama you have, to warn you in advance when she's mad!"

I watched him shake his head again at my lack of understanding and open his mouth to explain that I had it all wrong, then stop and contemplate me with a grave and mute expression. After a moment, when he understood that despite my serious tone I was teasing him, he gave me a quick smile, a burst of sunshine that lit up his face and his eyes. I could have wept at the sight.

"You're having me on," he said.

"Yes, I am." I returned his smile for a moment before I stood. "Now, I'm going to go fix you a place to sleep on the floor. I put a pan of water on the stove to keep warm while you go through the back room and out the back-door where you'll find the privy. Then come right back and give your hands a good scrubbing. All right?"

"Yes, ma'am."

The boy was as good as his word. While he was gone, I opened the traveling bag Alice had dropped beside the bed to look for something the boy could sleep in, but it was too dark and the search was useless. Instead, I found an old but clean painting smock of mine and pulled it over Jem's head after he slipped out of his shirt and pants. In his under drawers, he looked even younger, all skinny wrists and bony knees and arms thin as match sticks. Not under-nourished, I thought, because there was some meat on his bones, but the meat couldn't keep up with how fast he was growing. He'd still be thin when he was all grown up, I thought with certainty, lean and tall, possessed of a certain grace and the same thoughtful intelligence he possessed even now.

He lay down atop the multiple layers of quilts I had arranged on the floor, and I pulled a light blanket over him up to his chin.

"Are you warm enough?" I asked.

"Yes, ma'am." A pause. "Where are you going to sleep? In the back room with all the pictures?" So he'd noticed them, had he, even in the dim light? I had the impression that he was a boy who did not miss much.

"No, in the rocking chair by the fire in the kitchen," I said but doubted I would be able to sleep. Too much to take in. Too much to think about. "I fall asleep there sometimes when I'm reading at night, so it's nothing new for me."

"All right then," he said, as if giving his approval to the idea. His lashes feathered down onto his cheeks and he slept. Did all children fall asleep that way? One moment talking and then just like that soundly asleep?

I pulled the covers up to Fannie Newell's shoulders and for no reason laid a hand against her forehead. She wasn't sick and I knew there was no fever to detect, but I couldn't help myself. She slept on, her chest rising and falling in a quiet rhythm, a young woman as thin as her son, though in her it wasn't growing pains but something else. Exhaustion? Worry? What was her story?

I left the door to the room open and went into the kitchen, cleared the table, used the last of the warm water to wash up Jem's dishes, and got ready for bed myself. I suppose I should say, got ready for *chair*. I had told Jem the truth: I did fall asleep in the old chair often enough, but the difference was that when I eventually awoke, I crawled into my own comfortable bed for what remained of the night. Not so this time. I took off my dress and pulled a nightdress over my chemise and then stretched out in the rocking chair with my legs draped across a packing box topped by an old pillow to cushion against the crate's rough edges. This will never work, I told myself as I pulled a coverlet over me and then, Jem-like, fell instantly asleep.

New Hope begins to stir about the same time the sun begins to show. With my shop situated right next door to Ezzie Liggett's Nebraska Café, I can tell when people start moving around and if I'm not already out and about painting the morning light, I generally rise when I hear activity. Ezzie offers fine coffee, and when I hear the café's door open and shut with customers intent on their first cups of the day, I'm usually right there with them. In exchange for breakfast and all the coffee I can drink during the day, I take care of Ezzie's mending, both professional and personal. It's the kind of arrangement that adds to my enjoyment of living in New Hope. We are a convivial and practical group of merchants and know enough to play to the others' strengths. Mending a few tablecloth seams is a fair trade for piping hot coffee with the added touch of fresh cream.

The morning after my houseguests arrived, I washed my face, pulled on yesterday's dress, and peeked into the bedroom, noting that sometime during the night young Jem had crawled into bed next to his mother. The two slept on in oblivious innocence. Their faces, relaxed in sleep, bore a subtle resemblance to each other, both pale and perfect ovals embellished with dark, dramatic brows. Jem's hair was dark, his mother's dark auburn, but their curls were the same. In fact, both slept with a tendril of hair flopped across their foreheads in the exact same pattern and place. I quietly pulled the bedroom door shut before I headed next door to the café.

With my own breakfast finished, I asked Ezzie for a plate of hotcakes and sausage to take with me. She obliged and juggling the plate of hot breakfast in one hand and my usual pot of hot coffee in the other, I managed with the help of one of the café patrons to make my way outside, then used one foot to open the unlatched door of my shop wide enough for me to enter.

All remained quiet. With the hotcakes and sausages deposited on the stove awaiting future consumption and my two houseguests still soundly sleeping, I returned to the front of the store, turned the sign to open, and began the day. Two shirts to cut out for Bert Gruber, whose bachelor status offered modest but consistent business, the finishing touches to a traveling dress for Mrs. Talamine, and a lengthy fitting with Ellie Chandler. I liked Ellie a lot and admired her patience with twin four-year-old sons who were adorable scamps but scamps nonetheless. Her husband, Joe, thought the sun rose and set in his wife and after the recent birth of their third child, a robust girl named Mary Marie, had requested something "new and pretty" for Ellie.

"Not that she'd ask for anything," Joe hastened to tell me, "because Ell would never think of anything for herself. Me and the boys and the baby, that's what Ellie puts first, but I'd like her to have something new, something made just for her, maybe something in a pretty pink?" Then, because he wanted to assure me of his serious intentions, he added, "I can afford it, Sheba. Whatever Ellie wants." Which was not something pink but yellow instead, pale like early-morning sunshine and scattered with delicate violet nosegays, a lovely shade for Ellie's rosy skin and blonde hair.

That morning, the pinned dress carefully removed from Ellie's slim form, she picked up baby Mary Marie from the makeshift egg-crate cradle where she slept and turned back to me at the door.

"I hear you have company, Sheba." I didn't speak, and Ellie said quickly, "I'm not meaning to stick my nose in your business, only I wanted to tell you that we ordered a new mattress from the Montgomery Ward catalog and we'd be happy to loan you the use of the old one as soon as we get the new one. You could put it on the floor if you need sleeping space. It was just an idea I had in passing."

Ellie looked suddenly worried that she had somehow offended me, and I said with a smile, "I do have company, Ellie, and that old mattress might come in handy. Thank you. Let me know when your new one's in. Maybe I could buy the old one from you." I knew I had a reputation as being somewhat prickly but never toward Ellie and Joe Chandler. They had experienced hardship in their past and in the early years of their marriage, and I had nothing but admiration for the way they stuck together, the way they cared for each other and faced their difficulties head on together.

Baby Mary had awakened and begun to fuss, arching her little back and turning her head restlessly against Ellie's shoulder. Hungry, I thought. I recognized the symptoms.

"We'll see about that. Just so you know it'll be there if you need it." She rearranged the baby against her other shoulder and stepped outside while I shut the door behind her and turned the store sign to closed. I should have realized that New Hope would know all about my business by breakfast; the town allowed few secrets among its inhabitants. Everything was a trade-off, I told myself. Always something – privacy, for example – to be given up in exchange for getting something. In this case independence and the freedom to paint while living among decent, tolerant people. When I thought about the situation that way, I thought I still had the better of the bargain.

When I stepped into the back room, two faces lifted in my direction. I hadn't heard any sounds from behind the bead curtain, but Ellie had been chattering as I worked and we had both enjoyed a few laughs about this and that, so it wasn't a surprise that I had missed the rustle of two hungry people sitting down to a lukewarm breakfast.

"Did you think to heat it up?" I asked.

The actress, dressed in a skirt with the old shawl I had left behind thrown over a plain white shirtwaist, rolled her eyes at me. At her expression, I repeated the unconscious thought I'd had the night before: *some things never change*, and said, "You were never interested in anything domestic before, sister. Don't tell me you've learned to cook in the past—how many years would it be? Nine?"

She still looked pale and thin, but her smile made her recognizable and suddenly younger. I felt the quick warmth of affection.

"Yes. Nine. I remember waving at you as the ship pulled away. That was the last time I saw you. You had on that ridiculous hat." I remembered the hat, too, feathers and an abundance of satin roses.

Across from her at the table, Jem set down his fork, gave a contented sigh, took a last large gulp of milk, and asked, "May I be excused, Mama?" Then he turned to look at me. "Good morning, Miss Fenway." The boy had the manners of a society matron.

"Good morning, Jem," I answered and walked over to the coffee pot that sat on a low flame on the stove.

"To answer your question, Sheba, I did somehow manage to warm breakfast and I figured out how to keep the coffee hot for you, besides. However, I still have no love for cooking or any domestic skill, for that matter, but –" here she gave a shrug and a small grimace "– alas, life has forced me to ignore most of my personal inclinations." Something there in her tone, not bitterness but weariness, perhaps, and a kind of sadness. She looked across at Jem and I saw the tenderness on her face. That was where her personal inclination lay now, I realized. In that little boy.

"You're excused," she told him. "Set your dishes on the counter by the sink and then make your bed. I want to talk to Miss Fenway in private."

"I have an old catalog you might like looking at," I told the boy. "After you've done what your mother said, you can go through to the front of the store. The book is on the little table by the mirror. You can take it and go sit on the bench outside and watch the folks go by in the street. I always find that entertaining. If your mother says it's all right, that is."

Jem caught his mother's quick nod and skipped into the

bedroom, reappeared after what must have been the fastest anyone has ever made a bed, and disappeared into the store. We heard the little bell on the front-door jangle once, then again as the door clicked shut behind the boy. I sat down in the chair Jem had vacated – if there would be three of us for a while, I thought, I'd need another kitchen chair – and looked at the woman over my coffee cup, both of us apparently at a loss for words.

"You didn't come home for Jem's funeral," I said, trying to keep any telltale emotion out of my voice.

Unsuccessfully, because she met my gaze and said with terse antagonism, "I didn't know, Sheba. Not until a long time afterwards. Do you think you were the only one in the family that loved him?"

I fixed on the first part of her reply. "Didn't know? Father wired Great Aunt Hortensia and while it took some time to track the two of you down, he said he finally did. You were in Florence, I think. She sent condolences for the two of you – Father showed me the telegram – and said she'd do her best to arrange return voyages home as quickly as possible."

"I didn't know," she repeated, "and Great Aunt Hortensia didn't know a thing about it, either," adding at my skeptical expression, "For god's sake, Sheba, Father was determined to exile me for two years and nothing, not even his only son's death, was a valid reason to change his plans. You understand as well as I that Father was not a man to change his mind or admit a wrong or believe anyone knew better than he." She pushed herself to her feet. "Think what you want. You will, anyway. I know you too well. Now I'm tired and I believe I need to rest again. Isn't that what the doctor said last night?"

"Yes." In truth, she did look exhausted.

"As soon as I get a little stronger, we'll get out from under your feet."

The stubborn set of her mouth reminded me of all the times we had argued as girls. She had had a certain look that I came to recognize as a warning not to bother her with further talk because she was done with listening. Our father wasn't the only member of the family to believe he knew better and more than other people. I read her expression with a mix of affection and exasperation. Doubt, too. My sister had a gift for playing fast and loose with the truth. Always had. It was a family trait even I had resorted to on occasion. Still, her few words had tilted my world a little, had turned a long-held resentment on its ear.

I shook my head and said, despite my belief that she would ignore me, "I wish you'd stay a while, Dee. It's not very fancy, but you and Jem are welcome here as long as you want to stay." She stared at me as I continued, "It appears there's a lot I don't know, and I'd like to. I'd like to catch up."

Because what if she told the truth? What if all I had been told about her behavior eight years earlier had been a lie? They were so alike, Father and Dee, that either or both could have lied then, as likely as she was lying now. I thought I had left all the conflicts and confusion of my old existence behind, but it had caught up with me, despite my efforts to get as far away as possible. The difference now was that I had a new life here in Nebraska, had freedom and friends, had grown used to the clarity and candor of typical New Hope conversations. However annoying or painful clarity and candor might be, they made everything easier in the long run. Those had been lacking in my life a decade ago. I was stronger now, surer of myself, had discovered the pleasure of community and the straightforward joy of independence. It was time for truth. Past time, really. There was Jem, besides. Named after his uncle and resembling him in all sorts of indefinable ways. I didn't want to lose him so soon.

At my invitation, something softened in her face. "There's a lot we *both* don't know, I imagine. We'll see, Sheba. You'll watch Jem?"

"Yes. He'll be fine. He's a good boy."

"You don't know the half of it." Without another word, she went into the bedroom and closed the door softly behind her.

I cut myself a piece of bread and a slice of cheese and stood next to the counter as I nibbled on lunch, considering what I had just been told, remembering the way grief for my brother had engulfed me and made me vulnerable to memory and imagination and incoherent thought. I hated to admit it, but here in the clear air of New Hope, Nebraska, I saw that I might have gotten some things wrong during that difficult time so many years ago, might have been told only what was intended to keep me close to home. Well, truths or untruths, that plan hadn't worked out so well for Father, had it? While he stayed behind in his fine Philadelphia mansion, I found a home along the Platte River in the rolling Nebraska foothills, happier than I had ever been in those earlier Philadelphia years. With a short-sightedness I would recognize later, I didn't see how the sudden reappearance of my sister could possibly change the life I had made for myself in New Hope.

5

My nephew sat contentedly on the outside bench until Ruth crossed the street to my shop. She took the steps up from the street to the boardwalk carefully because her bulk and the force of gravity conspired to keep her on the hard-packed earth of the street. When I stepped outside to see if Jem remained occupied with the pages of the Montgomery Ward catalog, I saw Ruth approaching and waited for her with an outstretched arm. She took hold of my hand with a grateful, maybe even desperate, grasp and with me as leverage pulled herself up the steps.

"Thank you," her voice somewhat winded from the effort.

"You're welcome," I responded and followed her gaze to the child who sat watching our efforts. "Jem, would you come here, please?" I asked. "I'd like you to meet my friend." With his usual serious courtesy, he hopped off the bench and came over to stand beside me. "Mrs. Carpenter," I said, "this is Jem. Jem Fenway. Jem, this is my very good friend, Mrs. Carpenter."

Ruth sent me a quick, sharp look when I spoke the boy's last name and then turned her attention and a warm smile back toward him. "How do you do, Jem?"

"Fine, thank you. My real name is James Cameron Fenway, but you may call me Jem." With that homage bestowed, he looked past her and asked, "Is he yours?"

Sitting on his haunches at the top of the steps Ruth had just barely managed to ascend was a large, black dog. Mouth open in what resembled a big canine grin, panting a little, tongue lolling to the side, eyes and ears waiting for any of the magic words: *walk, treat, play, stick, bacon* sat Othello, the boarding-house dog.

"Is that your dog?" Jem asked, staring at Othello as if it was the first dog he had ever seen, a strange new creature descended from another planet.

Ruth thought a moment and then said, "Well, yes, I guess he is, but I'm not his first choice." Jem shifted a puzzled look to Ruth. "He belongs to a young man named Danny, but Danny's gone off to the army on an adventure and I'm afraid poor Othello is stuck with me. He's not very happy about it, either."

"'O, now, forever, farewell the tranquil mind,'" Jem said. "'Farewell content.'" Our turn to stare at the boy.

"From the play *Othello*, I believe," I said by way of explanation to Ruth, and to Jem, "Isn't that right?"

He nodded, his attention once more on the big, old dog. "Third act. Will he play with me, do you think?" Not Othello, of course. The dog.

"He would love it," Ruth said firmly, "and he'll be your friend forever. He's particularly fond of fetching sticks."

"Come over here, Jem," I said, and we stepped down into the side alley. I pointed west in the general direction of the schoolhouse. "Down the alley behind my shop is the outdoor facility we use, and I'm pretty sure I saw some large twigs blown up against it from the last norther that came through. Go gather some up and I guarantee Othello will not be able to resist the lure. It was his favorite game to play with Danny, wasn't it, Ruth?"

For a moment I was afraid my words would make her cry – she missed Danny terribly and she was only days away from childbirth, besides; just about anything could make her cry – but she rallied and nodded.

"Yes, it was, and now there's no one to throw the stick.

Poor Othello. You'd be doing him a kindness, Jem."

While Jem was off in search of good-sized throwing sticks, Ruth said, "We need to talk, Sheba. It's been less than twenty-four hours since I last saw you, but I feel like I'm behind on everything."

"Let's talk later. I've got to get the bodice of Mrs. Talamine's dress finished so we can have her final fitting in the morning, and I need to make room in the store somewhere for an order of lace and buttons."

"I imagine your place seems a little crowded all of a sudden with a house guest."

"Two house guests."

Jem returned with his hands full of sticks before Ruth could say anything more to me except, "We definitely need to talk later." She turned to the waiting boy. "Come up here on the boardwalk, Jem, and say Othello's name a couple of times in a loud voice. Then wave the biggest stick you've got in the air and say something using the word *stick*." At Ruth's use of the word, Othello's ears perked up and he roused himself to all fours from his previous bored, slouched position.

"Say something like what?" Jem asked.

"It doesn't matter. Recite a poem. Talk about the weather. As long as you say s-t-i-c-k a few times." Ruth spelled the word letter by letter so as not to spoil the treat for Othello, the illiterate boarding-house dog.

Jem, mystified, did as he was told. "It's sure a fine day to throw a *stick*," he proclaimed in a loud voice, his serious, intent expression so reflecting his namesake that I felt like weeping for a moment, and I didn't have any of Ruth's excuses for the emotion. "I found this *stick*, Othello, and I'd be happy to throw it." Putting all his energy into the experience, Jem turned sideways toward the alley and brandished a large stick in the air. "Something tells me you're the perfect dog for fetching *sticks*." To Othello, the third time hearing the magic word shouted in the loud voice of a child was the charm, and the hound seated himself on Jem's foot staring upward with fixed interest at the child's waving hand.

"Well, go ahead," I said. "Send it sailing down the alley with all your might and then be ready to tussle him to get it back. You've teased that poor old dog long enough." After Jem followed through, both he and Othello were racing down the alley. I couldn't have said which was the more delighted of the two.

"A nice boy," Ruth observed.

"Yes. Was there a reason for your visit or were you just out to stretch your legs?"

She nodded toward the side alley where we could hear Jem laughing and shouting, "No, give me the stick, Othello! How can I throw it if you don't give it to me?"

"Danny always said that, too. The silly old dog never figured it out with him, either." She shook her head as if to clear the memory and answered my question. "I heard some talk is all, Sheba."

"Naturally. About my having company?"

"Yes. About someone being carried to your house after the show because she was ill. I wanted you to know we had an open room at Hart's, but all things considered, I doubt that you want to take me up on the offer."

"No." There was so much of the past I'd have to share, and I had neither the time nor the heart for it just then.

Ruth patted my arm. "Never mind. You don't have to tell me anything, and if you ever want to, do it on your terms, not mine. I just wanted you to know I was here if you needed me."

A good woman friend is worth her weight in gold, I thought, and even with, especially with, her current bulk that remained true of Ruth Carpenter.

"I know. It's all been a shock and I have to get some things straight with my sister first."

"Of course. Well, if you need anything, dishes or linens or such, let me know. I have a ready supply at the boarding house." She turned to head down the boardwalk toward Hart's and stopped long enough to ask, "Did I mention I sold the barber shop?"

"What?! No, you never mentioned that."

"I forgot, I guess," her tone not quite apologetic since she remembered that I was keeping secrets. "It was just getting too much. I told Silas I had to get rid of something and it was either the barber shop or him."

"Whew!" I said. "I imagine he breathed a sigh of relief once he heard your decision."

Ruth laughed. "It wasn't even close, but don't tell Silas that. I like to keep him on his toes."

"Who's the new barber?" I asked.

"A young fella named Hezekiah Corker. Goes by the name Corky. I liked him right off, and he's agreed to keep the name on the sign."

"Still *Duncan's* then. That seems fair."

"Fair." Ruth said the word quietly, stretching out the syllable with thoughtful consideration. "I don't know what that means any more, Sheba. I'm more inclined to say that seems right, and let it go at that." She turned and began her slow way down the boardwalk, past the café toward the boarding house.

"We'll talk soon, Ruth. I promise," and meant the words when I said them, but Ruth went into labor and for quite a while after that, a new baby in the house and all, she naturally had her hands full. As did I, but for entirely different reasons.

Once prompted – the boy having been taught the same manners as previous Fenway generations: that children do not volunteer information unless and until such information is requested – Jem regaled both Dee and me with the wonders of Othello. So smart, so friendly, so tireless, so endless a list of saintly qualities that finally his mother said, "I'm glad you made such a good friend, Jem. Perhaps he's waiting for you outside even now for more play time. You may be excused from supper to go check."

"If not," I added, "look for him in the back yard of the boarding house. You remember where that is? On the other side of the café. Ruth won't mind. I know for a fact that she doesn't allow the dog in the house when the weather's good, so I'll bet he's there."

"Be home by dark," Dee called after him as he disappeared into my back room and outside through the door there. To me she asked, "It's safe, isn't it?"

"Yes, quite safe. New Hope quiets down after supper and Ruth Carpenter is the kindest woman I've ever met."

"A friend of yours?"

"Yes." After a pause, I asked, "How do you feel?"

"Tired. I'm just tired is all."

"Jem said you hadn't been eating."

Dee gave an expressive palms-up gesture with her hands. "I had to feed two on one person's wages, and the money didn't go very far as it was." She must have caught a skeptical look on my face because she said with faint dignity, "I'm not the woman I was, Sheba. Well, –" she amended, "– not entirely, anyway. I have a son now." At my continued silence, she went on, "I'm never going to be saintly and meek and unselfish. It's not in me, and we both know that. I doubt it's in you, either. But I'll do whatever it takes to give Jem the life and future he deserves." I didn't doubt her sincerity.

"He reminds me of his uncle at that age."

"He does, doesn't he?"

"Does he know anything about his family?"

"The Philadelphia Fenways, you mean? No. I was afraid the old man might try to take him away from me, try to turn him into a proper Fenway."

"A proper Fenway," I repeated softly. "Sometimes I almost felt sorry for Father, longing so desperately for a proper heir of the family name and being disappointed at every turn. His only son dying young and you and I – well, look at us."

Dee laughed, not kindly. "I never wasted any pity on the old devil. He certainly never wasted any pity on me, or you either, I'd wager. I'm not sorry he's gone. He left all his money to charity. Did you know?" At my nod and shrug, she eyed me across the table and said, "You haven't asked me about Jem's father."

"If it was Mr. Alice, I doubt he'd have sent over your last wages in a plain envelope without bothering to say good bye."

"Perry's not a bad sort, but you're right. He's not Jem's father." The question hovered between us until she said, "Jem's father is dead. I told Jem his father was a soldier and that he died bravely in battle. He wasn't and he didn't, but Jem doesn't need to know more right now. Sometimes the truth can bite you, and I don't want that for Jem."

There was so much unsaid between us, so many unknowns and mysteries, I doubted we could ever regain all the ground we had lost.

"You're still painting, I see."

"Yes."

"I took a look in the back room while you were busy in the store. You've done some good work."

"Thank you." I didn't want to speak about that part of my life to her, the part that brought me my greatest joy, that gave my days and my life value.

She heard the distance creep into my voice and said with a touch of her former, younger haughtiness, "We won't be in your way very long, Sheba. If I can rest here for a day or two, we can catch up with the show. Perry'll be glad to have me back once he figures out that young Penny isn't quite the stage presence he anticipates. A pretty girl, of course, but there's nothing in her to bring a tear to the audience, unless it's that high G she can never quite hit. That's made me cry often enough."

Despite myself I laughed at her words. That was the sister I remembered from our younger years, keenly observant, using the truth to cut, and always unencumbered with any sympathy for another's feelings. I had many of those same traits myself but living in New Hope had filed down my rough edges.

"I was hoping you'd stay longer. One of my friends volunteered a mattress and I'll put it in the back room where I can sleep. I spend a lot of time back there, anyway. Ruth offered all sorts of extras from the boarding house. I've no doubt you're used to better accommodations, Dee, but for Jem's sake, you should be sure you're healthy and strong before you think about taking to the road again. What about Jem if something happened to you? He'd be lost among strangers."

She knew I was right but simply said, "We'll see," and rose. "I'm going to go find Jem. Down the street, you said?"

I nodded, "Yes, south, just past the café. A big handsome house with the name Hart's on the sign. You can't miss it for all the barking and shouting." I grinned at my sister and she returned it, the first time I had felt any sort of true bond with her since she appeared in costume on the stage of the town's Meeting and Entertainment Hall. Maybe there was hope for us yet.

It was August, but that evening began what I think of now as my own personal Nebraska spring, a slow thaw of emotions that had long been frozen. Without any further direct discussion about the matter, Dee and Jem took me up on my offer to stay on. After that, it didn't take long for color to return to my sister's cheeks, sparkle to her eyes, and a refined lightness to her voice.

As for Jem, the little boy blossomed in New Hope. Why wouldn't he? He had Othello and the Chandler twins to play with and all the loud, chugging trains coming and going, besides. Paradise for a child who had been on the road and in back rooms for most of his life. He surprised me by calling me Aunt Sheba out of the blue one day, using the name with a nonchalance that suggested he had expected all along that he had an aunt by that name. No surprise, no shyness in his tone, just Aunt Sheba-something-something and then he was off down the street to play. His mother must have discussed the family relationship with him, but neither of them mentioned it to me. For a moment, hearing the name aloud made me catch my breath. Would so close a connection cause me to forfeit something from the independent life I had come to treasure? Would I gain any warmth or joy in exchange? But there was no going back, and "Aunt Sheba" had a secret appeal I admitted only to myself.

Thinking about my past over the following days, I couldn't recall exactly how or why my sister and I had lost touch in the first place. Well, that's not exactly true. I was outraged when Dee didn't rush home at the news of our brother's unexpected death from a sudden fever, and because of my own deep grief at his loss, I believed every word Father told me. Chose with a kind of purposeful ignorance to believe every accusation he threw out about Dee, even when I knew he remained furious at what he perceived as my sister's shameful and immodest conduct, when I well understood how implacably vindictive he could be and what a long memory he possessed. Our father was a man who demanded obedience, who ruled his household without an ounce of flexibility or empathy, and Dee was a young woman with a fearless, foolhardy, and disastrous need to challenge every one of his rules and constraints. Perhaps if our mother had lived, all our lives, even Father's, might have ended differently, but she died young and left three children with a man more comfortable with his past military training than with his present motherless family.

When I recollect my childhood – something I do as infrequently as possible – I remember most, remember only really, what it felt like to be caught between an autocratic parent and an admired but rebellious older sister, the constant anger, the sneer of voices at the dinner table, the many, many times I feared some violent action would take place, whether on my father's or my sister's part I was never quite sure. He was a man who set great store by propriety and to strike a woman, even one as infuriating as Dee, would not have been acceptable, regardless of provocation. But our fine mansion in the very best Philadelphia neighborhood reeked of anger and unhappiness, even if no one ever came to physical blows. Words have it in them to be cruel and painful, too.

I did my best to be peacemaker, but in the end, dear Jem buried in the family mausoleum and Dee apparently continuing to enjoy her travels uncaring of our great loss at home, when Father turned to me, his last opportunity, and demanded I forego the great passion of my life – painting – to be that biddable child for which he longed, a decorous, genteel, unremarkable, and fitting reflection of the Fenway name, I could not do it. Would not do it.

Not long after my eighteenth birthday, finally in legal possession of a small inheritance from my mother's side of the family, I left a brief note addressed to the fierce man I called Father on the parlor mantlepiece, walked one last time down the front steps of the fine brick mansion where I had lived all my life, and entered the Pennsylvania Academy of the Fine Arts, which had accepted the application I made under the name of B. L. Fenway – I feared losing the opportunity if they knew I was a woman. I never let Dee know where I was, never spoke to my father again, never returned to mourn at his grave or the graves of my brother and mother. My mind was made up and the past well and truly gone. In its place, I found all I needed in light and color, in the swirl of oils and the quick soft strokes of pastels and the frenetic sketches of charcoal, in the smell of turpentine and the play of light and shadows through a window. At last, when I had soaked in all I could absorb from the very best teachers in the country, I used the last dollars of my inheritance and bought a one-way railway ticket to New Hope, Nebraska, where I was happy as a meadowlark living in the present without a smidgen of the past to interfere. Until one summer evening I attended a performance of The Alice Variety Theatre of the West and that past returned with a vengeance.

I waited three days after my unexpected guests arrived before I loaded up my easel, paints, and brushes and headed out to capture the early morning sunrise. By then, Ruth had given birth to a healthy son, one Alexander Paul Carpenter, Joe Chandler had delivered the mattress his wife had offered, and despite my misgivings, Dee, Jem, and I had settled into a kind of routine. It would be untrue to say I never missed my solitude because there were times, especially in those early days, that I longed for it with sharp intensity. But I could escape to the shop or to the back room to put finishing touches on paintings, Dee rested a great deal of the time, and Jem was busy discovering the adventure of life in a small town. Neither Dee nor I was inclined to be a perfect companion in the best of times and we recognized our limitations. From the start, however, Jem was a pleasure to be around.

I'm not a woman to coo over babies and have never experienced a moment of longing for one of my own. Truly, whenever I spent any time observing children's behavior, I almost always felt either annoyed or baffled. Children can be very loud and get very dirty. I don't wish any of them harm, of course, and I realized that it was perfectly normal for parents to see in their children endearing qualities that were invisible to me, but with Jem I began to understand why people found their own offspring so lovable. My nephew bore more than the name of his dead uncle, he wore the imprint of my brother on his face, in grave, dark eyes, in a quick, mischievous smile, in sudden bright laughter, and even in the few but very pronounced rebellions he displayed. He wasn't a perfect child, only a delightful one. Jem wasn't all Fenway and must have had something of his father in him, but in those early days I was so charmed by the child's resemblance to the dear brother I had lost ten years earlier that I never gave the boy's father a thought. For a long time, Dee never spoke of him, and her silence kept Jem's father invisible and irrelevant. I wish now that I had asked more questions, had made my sister tell me about him, had at least found out if Jem was the product of a legal union. If I had known the whole story, events might have played out differently.

The first predawn morning after Dee and Jem's arrival that I stepped outside was clear and pleasantly cool for late August, the dark sky to the east just streaking with the special morning light I could never quite capture. I thought that it would always be elusive and no matter how old I got, I'd still be hobbling outside, cane in hand and an ear trumpet dangling from a cord around my neck, for just one more attempt to catch that creamy morning light on canvas. The broad main street was empty and quiet, but I heard the tinkle of a store's door bell from farther down and took a quick look to locate Isaac Lincoln's compact figure in the dim light as he stepped outside. The adults in his family – his mother, his wife, and himself – had been born into slavery, slowly moved west after the war, and eventually found their way to New Hope. Like me, the Lincolns were accepted by the town without comment and like me, they decided to stay on. When Isaac opened his meat market, it was a quick success and kept him busy buying and selling. He liked to escape to the river to fish now and then, however, and every once in a while, when our morning timing was right, we would each lift a hand toward the other, I trudging east down the alley and he heading south toward the river. I never saw the man catch anything but a little private time in those morning forays. Perhaps that's exactly what he was fishing for.

John Bliss fell into step beside me that morning. I hadn't talked to him for several days, since before the Alice Variety Theatre of the West had swept into New Hope and changed my life, but neither of us felt any need to leap into a conversation. John and Ruth were the two people I was most comfortable with. Both of them had the knack of quiet, knew how to listen, knew that sometimes saying nothing was the best response.

After a stretch of silence, John said, "Morning, Sheba," as he walked and without glancing over at me. A pause, then, "You picked the best morning of the week. Look at that." We stopped simultaneously. Ahead of us, the fledgling sun rising behind a bank of stubborn clouds had outlined the clouds with a thin border close to the color of spring lilacs, something between pink and purple, only much, much brighter. A dazzling color that made me inhale deeply at the beauty of it.

"Is it the best morning?" I responded. "You'd know, I suppose, but I wouldn't."

"You've been kept busy."

His words made me give a subdued snort. "As if you haven't heard about my visitors from every citizen of New Hope that stopped into Bliss House for the lunchtime special."

"It was meat loaf yesterday," John said, "and it always draws a crowd, but no one mentioned your name that I heard." I gave him a steady look, waiting for the clincher. "The boy on the other hand was a very popular subject. Seems he's joined up with the Chandler boys to catch bank robbers. I expect Si Carpenter will be deputizing all three of them before long." The picture of Ruth's husband doing so made me laugh, as John intended.

I unfolded my easel, dug into my large cloth bag, and lifted out a smooth, thin cut of primed pine board because I was in the mood to practice and play a bit that morning. A canvas wouldn't appear until some kind of picture had taken shape in my mind, and just then my brain felt as blank as that piece of wood.

"The boy conspiring with the Chandler twins is my nephew." I looked at John. "Did you hear that, too?"

"I did."

I crouched down to squeeze some oil colors onto the palette before I stood, brush and palette in hand, and faced John to explain, "My sister and I lost touch years ago. Our family wasn't close, and it just happened. I didn't know I had a nephew until the night of the variety show." Because John Bliss knew how to keep his distance, I didn't mind him knowing.

"Their staying with you isn't disagreeable." A question more than a statement.

"No. Not yet, anyway. If it were just Dee, we'd probably be snipping at each other within the week, but Jem makes it all right. Better than all right, to tell the truth. I had a much-loved brother, also called Jem, who died years and years ago.

It was a painful time. There's a lot of my brother in the child."

"Ah, I see," and I thought that for all John's reticence, he did see.

If Ruth hadn't recently given birth, she would have been the person I shared that information with, but she didn't need my family's history infringing on her and Silas as they began making a family history of their own. I dipped my brush in the splash of white oil paint, and John took the hint.

"Well," he said, "if you need anything, just ask. There's extra of everything at the hotel." I stopped long enough to smile at him.

"Thank you. No doubt there are any number of items that would be helpful, but where would I put them? On the roof?"

His turn to smile. "Now that would be something noteworthy enough to overtake the meat loaf special in people's conversations." He glanced up. "Those clouds didn't last long."

I followed his gaze. The silhouette of clouds had disappeared and the bright rosy lilac color with it.

"No, but I've still got them in my head."

He took the hint. "I'll let you get to it."

He turned away and I did the same, poised my brush, squinted at the wood remembering, made a quick, short stroke and then another and another. Hopeful I'd get it right this time, but I was conscious that the sharp edge of color in my mind had already faded. Not that its dimming surprised me or even mattered because it was more the physical act of painting than the final result that stirred me with joy and hope. I couldn't explain it properly but thought that in some strange way, each attempted color held a promise for tomorrow and each brush stroke was an investment in my future.

6

The addition of two people into my life certainly changed my routine, but as usually happens, another routine developed in its place. They didn't rise until I opened the store for business, and Dee used my morning absence to hold lessons for Jem at the kitchen table. I told my sister that school would resume in earnest as soon as the early crops were harvested, that in Mr. Arthur Stenton New Hope had found an excellent teacher, and it would do Jem good to attend school with other children. Dee agreed that sounded like a good idea, but her heart wasn't in her words. It would be hard for her to pass that private time with her son on to someone else. Neither Dee nor Jem was stellar when it came to arithmetic, but everything else from geography to history to grammar could be found in Shakespeare's plays, and they both had a flair for the theatrical. Once the words "Howl, howl, howl, howl! O, you are men of stones!" shouted in Jem's young voice blew into the store with such gusto that I was startled enough to poke my finger with a needle and draw blood.

"Lear?" I asked Dee that afternoon after Jem had disappeared outside, for all I knew to get his deputy's badge from Si Carpenter. "Do you think that's a good idea for a child his age?"

Dee raised both brows and spoke as if I were the child.

"It's art, Sheba. My goodness, you of all people should understand that." She had regained a rosy color to her complexion and put on just enough weight to fill out her face and figure. Rest and the kind of security she found with me seemed to have put her on the way to good health. Perhaps knowing Jem was happy in New Hope added to her happiness, too.

After supper, Jem usually went in search of Othello for their usual flurry of stick-throwing at the end of the day, and more often than not, Bert Gruber appeared at the door of the dress shop around the same time.

The first time I opened to his knock, I said with a mix of surprise and anxiety, "Bert, is everything all right? Do you need something?" The man standing in my doorway outside of business hours was not a common sight.

Behind me, Dee said, "Mr. Gruber has kindly offered to give me a tour of New Hope, Sheba."

My sister has always had a way with men, has always enjoyed their company and sincerely found their conversation stimulating in a way I've never understood. Under her frank, direct, admiring, and interested gaze, I could well understand why a man would become enticed by Dee's attention and entice her to all sorts of unacceptable behavior in return. That kind of reciprocal fascination is what got her into several compromising situations as a younger woman, infuriated our father, and eventually caused her to be banished to the European continent. The look on Bert Gruber's face as he looked past me to where my sister stood was proof that she had lost none of her natural allure.

Many days later, into September by then with a hint of fall creeping into the early evening breeze, I sat with Ruth on the porch of the boarding house. She looked herself again, if slightly worn from sleep lost to the needs of the new baby, who lay in a cradle at Ruth's feet. Without conscious intent, Ruth brought her foot gently down on the cradle's rocker every time young Alexander stirred, and the cradle's gentle motion sent the baby right back to sleep. My friend was a woman of quick intelligence and humor, but this mastery of exact timing was a new skill. I had noticed that motherhood equipped women with all sorts of new and heightened talents. Funny how such a small thing as a baby could make such big changes in a person's life.

I was wondering about Dee, about how she had managed those first days after Jem was born and if she had been on her own at that time when Ruth said, "Bert Gruber certainly finds a lot of reasons to visit the dress shop." She was purposefully not looking at Bert and Dee as they strolled on the boardwalk across the street from Hart's, apparently returning from a walk along the river. I wasn't nearly as discreet in my attention and squinted openly at the couple before turning to look at Ruth.

"Just one reason," I said.

"Well, yes, but one reason is all a man needs. Bert seems smitten with your sister, I must say."

"Dee draws men like bees to clover. She always has."

"I haven't seen anyone else buzzing around your doorway."

"New Hope has a limited number of unattached men."

"There's John Bliss. I would have thought he'd find a woman like your sister to be exactly his cup of tea."

"I know for a fact that John doesn't drink tea," I retorted, my voice sharper than the remark warranted. I didn't know anything of the sort, but the mental picture of my sister walking next to John in the same manner she clung to Bert, speaking in a low voice and smiling, pressed closed to his side and her hand tucked firmly under John's arm, made me unexpectedly cranky.

"Fancy you knowing that." Ruth's tone was mild, but we had been friends a long time, and I recognized her teasing tone.

"I know a great many things about several of the inhabitants of New Hope, but I choose to keep my own counsel."

"I was just saying to Silas this morning that your prudence

was an example for all of us, Sheba." Mild again but this time I met her glance and we both laughed.

"I have never in my life been credited with that particular virtue," I said, then turning my attention back to the couple across the street I added, "I hope she doesn't break his heart. Bert's not a bad man."

"No. In fact, he's one of the kindest people I know," Ruth paused briefly. "I think *he's* wise enough to judge the situation and take care of his own heart."

I caught the stress she gave the word *he's* and might have continued the discussion with some emphasis of my own, but despite the gentle rocking of the cradle, the baby woke up and began to cry with such volume I could hardly believe the sound came out of that little body. Ruth picked him out of the cradle and stood.

"Suppertime for this little boy," she said. With her hand on the front door of the boarding house, she turned to say over her shoulder, "You'd tell me if there was anything you needed, wouldn't you?" At my nod, she said, "Good night, Sheba," and went inside.

I remembered John Bliss's similar offer and felt a quick spurt of gratitude for good friends, for New Hope, really, and for all the parts and pieces of my life in it. From the outside, nothing here would match the grandeur of the imposing mansion in the exclusive Philadelphia neighborhood where I had spent my younger years, but while I'd be the first to admit that New Hope, Nebraska, didn't possess a single speck of grandeur, for me it seemed grand, all the same.

I clearly recall that night with Ruth on the front porch of Hart's boarding house because it was the last I knew of peace for a long time, for many weeks. That night I was happy, and surprised that it was so. I found I almost liked my sister – had she changed? had I? was it simply growing older? – and I was already really fond of my nephew. I never thought I missed not having family connections, but my contentment with Dee and Jem's presence in my home and in my life made me better understand the draw of family, why Si Carpenter's gaze always sought out Ruth before anyone else regardless of the crowd or occasion, why Ellie Chandler's voice softened when she related Mary Marie's latest accomplishment and old Mrs. Lincoln made *my son Isaac says* the final word on any subject.

When Jem came racing around the corner of the boarding house, I pushed myself up from the porch steps calling, "Time for bed, young man," and heard Ellie Chandler in my voice. Jem came to an abrupt stop, considered if he should argue the fact, decided against it, gave Othello a scratch behind the ears by way of good-night, and waited for me at the front gate. We walked side-by-side back to the dress shop.

Later, lying in bed, Jem informed me, "Mama says I'm to go to school when it starts up." That was news to me, but I was happy my sister had listened to my advice.

"I'm glad to hear it. Mr. Stenton is a fine teacher. Strict, though. No foolishness allowed. No dogs, either." I remembered how years ago, when Ruth's ward, Danny, had been Othello's hero, the dog would wander glumly around town until in the way dogs had of knowing things, he would suddenly rise from wherever he lay and race with ears flapping toward the boarding house, Danny home at last!

I know," Jem said. "Mama explained it all, how I'd need to sit and pay attention and do what I was told and make her proud. She didn't tell me about the no dogs part, though. Are you sure?"

I smiled. "Absolutely, but if you think I might have that wrong, we can ask your mother in the morning." I pulled the covers up under his chin. "She's still out with Mr. Gruber or we could ask her tonight, and you'll be asleep before you can say Jack-be-nimble."

Jem being Jem, he had to repeat the phrase right after me, give me a grave look, and say, "I'm not sleeping yet, Aunt Sheba," but five minutes later when I peeked into his room, he was, mouth slightly open and his hair tousled against the pillow.

Dee came in not long after and we talked briefly, I don't remember about what, only that Bert Gruber didn't come into our conversation. I was tired and left her sitting at the kitchen table when I went off to my mattress among the pictures in the back room.

When I awoke in the morning, the first thing I recalled was how skeptical Jem had been about the no dogs rule at school. It would be a good idea, I thought, to let Dee know so she could repeat the rule for emphasis. I went into the kitchen to put water on the stove for a quick morning wash, smiling at the picture of Jem and Othello sitting side-by-side in one of those fancy desks John Bliss had donated to the school, and with my thoughts so occupied, I didn't at first notice the envelope propped on the kitchen table. Finally seeing it, I stared as if I'd never seen paper before. *Dee*, I thought, knowing it had to be from her, and then with a sinking heart thought, *Jem*. There was something about the black scrawl of my name on the envelope that bespoke bad news. I just knew it. She's taken Jem and they've both disappeared from my life, I thought. This will teach me to base happiness on other people. As quickly as they come they go. I knew it as surely as I knew my own name. But I was only half right.

Sheba,

I have some business to handle and I'll be gone a while. I don't know when I'll be back. I told Jem last night that he was to stay with you, that you were his family now and you'd take care of him until I got back. I wouldn't trust him with anyone else, and he's happy here. You don't need to know where I've gone or bother trying to find me, either. I've learned how to hide in plain sight. I'm an actress, remember, and I can turn into another woman any time I want.

Don't trust any strangers that show up at

your door and don't believe everything you hear about me. I wish I'd have told you that a long time ago, before I ever left, but I never thought you'd doubt that I loved our little brother.

I'm glad we found each other after all these years. It's almost as if it was meant to be.

Take care of my son, Sheba.

Your sister,

Delilah

I stood abruptly and went to push open the door to the bedroom. Jem lay sprawled in sleep, looking much the same as I had last seen him the night before. She hadn't lied about that, at least, but I didn't know what else to believe. I glanced around the room. Everything that belonged to Dee, clothes, hairbrush, shawl, that big traveling bag of hers, was gone, and without the vitality of her presence, the bedroom seemed even smaller than I remembered.

My sister didn't need to remind me that she had taken on the life of an actress – though I gave a quick thought to our father, a man who valued the ordinary and proper above all things yet ended up with one daughter a painter and the other on the stage; well, it served him right – because all her life Dee had created her own kind of drama wherever she went, playing out the Bard's words in literal translation. "All the world's a stage, / And all the men and women merely players; / They have their exits and their entrances, / And one man in his time plays many parts." One woman did, anyway.

I went over to the stove and poured a cup of coffee, took it to the table and reread Dee's note. I had some ideas about finding her, but even as I was still dealing with my surprise and disappointment and anger, I realized she was probably right, that I wouldn't be able to track her down. And close on the tail of that realization was the thought that maybe I shouldn't even try. It was what Dee wanted and what she expected from me. But it was that little boy sleeping in the next room that confounded me and kept me from knowing the right thing to do. I had lost my mother as a child, and on the right day, the memory could still stir a twinge of melancholy. I didn't want that for Jem. But, I argued with myself, Dee isn't dead, only absent for an unknown amount of time. She wouldn't willingly abandon the child. Surely, she would return for him. My jumble of thoughts was prompting a headache, and I had just decided to grab a sketching pad and some charcoal and head toward the river to occupy my mind and my hands when Jem sat down at the kitchen table. I had been so immersed in my thoughts, my unseeing gaze fixated on the table top as I deliberated my immediate actions and alternatives, that I missed the boy's entrance and was startled by the scrape of a chair on the floor.

"Good morning," trying to make the words cheerful as I examined Jem's face for tears or other signs of worry. No sign of tears past or present, that was certain, but then at our very first meeting, he had told me with firm authority, "I don't cry," and perhaps the words were truer than I realized. Six going on sixty.

"Good morning," he responded, a child trained in the courtesies. Then, "Last night Mama told me she was going away for a while."

I gave the note in my hand a half-hearted wave. "She told me the same thing in this letter she left."

"Then I guess she's really gone."

"Yes. Your mother was always a person to follow through on what she said." I hesitated, then asked, "Did she tell you where she was going?"

"No, ma'am." The little twitch of his lips, not quite a tremble but the closest thing to distress I could detect, said he told the truth but didn't much like it.

"She didn't tell me, either."

The two of us sat without talking, Jem staring at my face and me watching the flicker of hope in his eyes fade as he realized his mother had really and truly left without him, hadn't told either of us where she was going or when she planned to come back. I pushed my chair away from the table a bit.

"Would you mind sitting on my lap for a while?" I asked. "This has come as something of a shock, and I believe it would be a comfort to me," but I was not the one in the kitchen who looked bereft and a tiny bit lost. I held out my arms, palms extended toward Jem, and he crawled up onto my lap. He sat too stiff for a moment – I wasn't his mother and we both knew it – and then all at once and with a barely audible sigh, he relaxed against me.

"I don't think she plans to be gone very long," he said, his tone less convincing than the words.

"No doubt you're right. It's probably just some business she needs to attend to, something she can take care of in a twinkle."

"Mama says that sometimes, too. 'I'll be ready in a twinkle,' she says." A touch of mama-sickness there, I thought, and my heart went out to him.

"Well, I can remember our mama – your grandmother, that would be –saying the same thing so I guess that's where we learned it."

He thought about my words a while, then said, "Aunt Sheba, there's something I'd like to know."

"All right. Go ahead. I promise I'll tell you whatever I can, but it may not be much."

I couldn't see his face but imagined all sorts of troublesome questions must be jostling around in his young mind: how could my mother leave me like this, or why did she have to make it such a big secret, or (I especially worried about this one) do you think she's really coming back? All questions for which I had no answers. My few moments of worry and trepidation were wasted and unnecessary, however, because what Jem asked had a simple answer.

"When school starts up, can I go? I'd sure like to."

I let out my breath and slid the boy from my lap. "Yes, you may. I would be delighted if you went to school."

He gave a big grin. "Well, that's all right then," he said and moved to sit in his regular chair.

"I take it you'd like some breakfast."

"Yes, ma'am. Is there any bacon?"

At last a question with an answer I was certain of. "There certainly is," I said, "and by the time you've washed your face and hands and dressed for the day, I'll have it ready. We don't eat breakfast in our night clothes. I've got fresh bread, too. Does a bacon sandwich suit you?"

"Yes, ma'am," said with a great deal of enthusiasm as he skipped back to his bedroom. "That will suit me just fine, and Othello, too." I was thankful that the earlier pensive and slightly sad tone in the boy's voice was gone and threw two extra pieces of bacon into the pan without complaint. Othello was as partial to bacon as Jem, and my relief at not having a weepy child on my hands put me in charity with both the child and the dog.

It would take time to try to track Dee down, and in her absence, I would have to give Jem's welfare more attention than I was used to. The shop wouldn't run itself and I still needed to paint. Now more than ever I needed to paint. My calling. My passion. My freedom. What gave me hope for tomorrow. What made me happy today. I could never, would never give it up, no matter how many dresses had to be pinned or nephews had to be looked after. Yet somehow, despite the sudden and unexpected responsibilities that I had awakened to that morning and that would now almost certainly crowd my days, I was surprised that my anger toward Dee was gone and that I didn't feel overwhelmed or aggrieved or resentful, emotions I had expected to battle. After a moment's quick contemplation, I realized that was all due to Jem's broad smile as he anticipated a bacon sandwich. If I can keep the boy happy and safe, I thought, then everything will be just fine, and if it takes tossing a few extra slices of bacon to a big black boarding-house mutt every morning for that to happen, so be it. My nephew's well-being was worth every single sizzle.

Mr. Copco, the ticket agent at the railway station, was certain he had not sold a ticket to my sister or to anyone that looked remotely like my sister.

"Sheba, I can assure you I would recognize your sister if she showed up at my counter asking to buy a ticket, and if she had done that, I wouldn't be averse to telling you where that ticket took her seeing as how she's your sister, but she didn't so I can't." Mr. Copco was not intimidated by my scowl. "And now if you don't mind, there's a line of people behind you who unlike you want to buy tickets, so—" He allowed his voice to trail off and looked over my shoulder at the man standing behind me. "Yes, sir?"

I took the hint and departed, stopping at the next-door freight office to see if by some wild stretch of the imagination, Dee had caught a ride with an outgoing freight delivery. No luck there, either. Knowing that my sister wouldn't have hiked to wherever she was going, I made a final stop at Cap Sherman's livery.

"Sure, I seen your sister around town," the old man told me, "but I ain't never spoke a word to her and she sure didn't ask to hire any of my property, either, not wagon or beast. Wouldn't have allowed it, anyway."

Cap Sherman, old, grizzled, and foul-tempered, wore an expression that dared me to ask the inevitable, which I did because I needed information, not because I was in the mood for any of his foolishness.

"Woman didn't have any meat on her bones that I could see. Arms like sticks. I'm not fool enough to trust my property to a woman who can't hold on to it."

I might have argued with his tone, but his words had enough truth to them that all I said was, "Thank you," and turned back toward my shop.

Millie Winters stepped outside the grocery store just as I passed and asked, "Is everything all right, Sheba?"

Millie and her husband had settled in New Hope right after the war ended and opened their Grocery and Variety Store the same year Cap put up his livery, all of them waiting for the railroad to come to town and ensure their success. The railroad was a little slower than everyone expected but its arrival, when it finally came, put New Hope on the map, almost literally. The livery and the general store, the bank and the carpentry, the café and Ruth's boarding house all thrived. More businesses followed and more railroad stops got added and more passengers got on and off the train and New Hope had been thriving ever since. Millie Winters had stuck it out through the hard times and while I didn't particularly like the woman, who had a nose in everyone's business, I didn't begrudge her a comfortable life.

Her unprovoked question made me pause and send her a sharp look. "Why wouldn't it be, Millie?"

Millie is not a woman to be cowed by a cool tone or a raised brow. "No reason especially except—" For a moment each of us waited for the other to speak, and then Millie continued, "I saw young Lonnie running a telegram down to your shop yesterday. I hope it wasn't bad news."

Of course, she knew that was the first I had heard of a telegram and of course, I wasn't about to admit to that ignorance. Millie and I are well-matched in some areas.

"Not bad news, at all, but I appreciate your inquiring. Do you know if Mr. Stenton is back from his trip yet?" She didn't blink or hesitate at my abrupt change of topic.

"Yes, I seem to recall seeing him step off the train a day or two ago."

I thanked her again, started to walk away, and stopped long enough to say, "That yellow muslin came in for Sally if you want to send her down for a fitting."

"I'll do that, Sheba. She's going to visit my sister in Sidney and wants to take the dress with her."

"A long stay?"

"Six weeks." Sally was the Winters' only child and the woebegone tone in Millie's voice made me feel a little more charitable toward her.

"She'll enjoy the time away," I said. "Doesn't she have a cousin the same age?"

"Yes, my sister and I had our girls a month apart."

"No doubt they'll have a fine time then. Girls of that age have a way of entertaining themselves."

"Seventeen," said Millie. "It's hard to credit. Seems like just yesterday she was seven and going off to school."

I thought of Jem. Would it seem the same with him, six today and sixteen tomorrow?

"Well, send her down when she has some time so I can get the dress done before the start of her adventure. With all her dark hair, Sally will look as pretty as a picture in that shade of yellow."

"Thank you, Sheba."

I nodded and headed home, Sally Winters and yellow dresses forgotten as soon as I took a step. A telegram I didn't know anything about delivered to my shop, I thought, must certainly be connected to my sister's sudden departure.

I knew I was right when I broached the subject to Lonnie Markman, the young man who oversaw the responsibilities of both the telegraph office and the post office, which shared the same location in a building close to the train station.

"Yes, I did, Miss Fenway," Lonnie replied in answer to my question. "I had a wire for the doctor, too, and I delivered them both yesterday morning."

"I was at the Talamines yesterday morning."

Lonnie's look said he didn't know what that fact had to do with the present discussion, but he was sensible enough to say only, "Yes, ma'am," adding after a moment, "but the telegram was for Miss Newell, so I didn't think to look for you." When Lonnie Markman started at the telegraph office as a fresh-faced youth just off the farm two years ago, I could browbeat him with ease, but two years of experience had toughened him up.

When I asked, "What was in the telegram, Lonnie?" he pulled himself up ramrod straight and answered with dignity and only a slight quaver in his voice, "I'm not allowed to tell you that, Miss Fenway."

"Not allowed? Whose rule is that?"

"The Western Union Company's rule. When I finished my training, Mr. Jones made me take an oath that I wouldn't share the private information that came in a telegram with anyone but the person it was addressed to."

"Miss Newell is my sister, Lonnie."

"Yes, ma'am, so I've been told."

"Well, surely you're allowed to give private information to a person's sister."

Lonnie swallowed hard enough to make his Adam's apple bob. "No, ma'am, I'm not."

We stared at each other a long moment until I conceded, "All right. I certainly don't want you breaking any rules on my account." Both of us knew that wasn't true, but I soldiered on, regardless, "Can you at least tell me where the telegram was sent from?"

Lonnie pondered my question, my request setting him atop the pointed and uncomfortable horns of a mental dilemma. He's a letter-of-the-law type of young man, which was why he was particularly well-suited for the job he held, everything spelled out in a rule book and the dots and dashes of communication unambiguous.

"I guess I could do that."

"Good," I said and waited while he pulled out a wooden box of receipts printed on flimsy paper.

"It was sent from Dawes City."

I repeated the name. "Is that in Nebraska?" When Lonnie nodded, I asked, "Where in the world is it? I've never heard of it."

"It's up in the far northwest corner of the state, ma'am, at the Dakota border. There's not much else up that way, just Bowen, I think, and then it's a good hundred miles south before you get to Antelopeville or Potter. They're both on the railroad line so I know about them."

"And who sent the telegram?" I asked the question in a casual tone, hoping Lonnie was so caught up in his Nebraska geography that he'd answer it without thinking, but the boy was made of stronger mettle than I realized.

At my question he stopped talking, drew himself up ramrod straight again, and said, "I can't tell you that."

"Lonnie, I'm not asking you what the telegram said, only—"

"No, I mean I really *can't* tell you that because I don't know. The sender's name isn't on my receipt here." He waved the paper in front of me.

"You'd know if you looked at the copy of the message you keep in your file. No doubt the person who sent it put his name at the end."

"No doubt." Lonnie Markman stood in front of me, and from the part apologetic, part defiant, part fearful look on his face, it was clear it would take a lot more effort on my part to get any more information from him. Yes, Lonnie's expression said, there definitely was a name at the end of the message but no, he definitely wasn't going to tell me whose name it was.

I'm not proud of the moments I spent weighing my chances of success if I stepped up my bullying efforts, but after one final squinty-eyed glare at the young man, I gave up the attempt. Like many in New Hope, I had a soft spot for the telegraph clerk because of what happened to the previous young clerk from three years earlier, so I surrendered. For the moment.

"All right, Lonnie. I hope The Western Union Company appreciates you, although I might just send the sheriff down to get the information I want. No matter what the company's rule book says, you'd have to give Sheriff Carpenter any information he asked for, wouldn't you?"

I could see from the young man's suddenly stricken expression that such a circumstance had never before crossed his mind and that it wasn't covered in the rule book, but as ridiculous an idea as it was – the only woman in New Hope who had the right and especially the courage to give Si Carpenter an order was his wife – I didn't bother to set Lonnie's mind at ease. My behavior when I'm annoyed can often border on the petty.

Nevertheless, that evening, once more seated with Ruth on the front porch of the boarding house, baby Alexander in his cradle and Ruth's rocking foot at the ready, I brought up the idea in a casual tone.

"Silas thinks the world of you, Sheba," Ruth answered, "but I don't see how he could possibly justify sneaking information from Lonnie just to satisfy your curiosity. No crime's been committed, has it?"

"I wouldn't say sneaking," I retorted, ignoring Ruth's question and her continued silence until I finally had to admit, "No, no crime that I know of."

"I would never tell you not to do something you've made up your mind to do. What would be the point? And I know you're not a woman to take the easy way out, so go ahead and ask Silas, but I doubt even you can bully my husband into getting you what you want."

"Sneaking and bullying," I grumbled. "What a fine opinion you have of me!"

Ruth laughed. "You're a good friend, Sheba. I couldn't ask for a better, and there's no woman I admire more than you. Well, maybe Mrs. Garfield, poor woman."

The words made us both quiet for a moment as we thought of our president, who had been seriously wounded by an assassin earlier in the summer. The newspapers did not hold out much hope for his survival, and of course, Ruth would admire a woman on the verge of widowhood. Hadn't she herself grieved the loss of a dearly-loved first husband years ago?

She took a breath that sounded more like a sigh and continued, "What I meant was—"

"I know what you meant, Ruth, and I hope I'm honest enough with myself that I can admit that if sneaking and bullying would get me what I wanted, I wouldn't hesitate to do either or both. The problem is that I couldn't make young Lonnie do what I wanted, so why would I imagine I'd have any more success with Si? Your husband isn't a man to be swayed by anybody, present company excluded, of course."

Ruth didn't bother to dispute the point. "Imagine Lonnie Markman holding his own against you!" she said instead. I caught her teasing smile and had to smile in response.

"Oh, hush," I said, but added, "I still wish I knew where Dee went or who in Dawes City, Nebraska, would be sending her a telegram. I don't know what to tell Jem."

"Yes, poor Jem, though I have to say he doesn't seem all that upset about his mother's departure." As we sat on the porch, an assortment of barks and shouts drifted around the corner of the boarding house.

"That's because he expects she'll be back soon."

"And you don't?"

I shook my head, troubled by my secret thoughts. "No. My sister has a habit of running. She ran away with a young man when she was barely sixteen. Father tracked them down and dragged her home, but that was the start of a long history of abrupt departures."

"Poor Dee then."

"Why *poor* Dee?"

"Maybe all that running isn't towards something. Maybe she's running away from something."

I thought about that, remembered the constrictions of Philadelphia society and the weight of our father's expectations. As usual, Ruth saw more than I would have imagined.

"Yes," I agreed, "maybe she is. That's what I did, isn't it?" I didn't talk much of my past, but over time, I had shared some of my history with Ruth.

"Anyway," Ruth said, ignoring my question as adeptly as I had ignored hers earlier, "there might be someone else who has the answers you're looking for."

I didn't know who she meant and said so.

"For goodness' sake, Sheba, think. We haven't sat here an evening without commenting on your sister's ability to find regular company for a walk and yet tonight, I didn't see anyone come knocking at your shop door."

"Oh, of course," disgusted with myself. Had I left my

brain next to my coffee cup this morning? "You're right. Maybe Bert knows something about Dee leaving."

"Maybe? He didn't show up for a walk tonight, did he, or come around anytime today to find out what happened to Dee? That seems unnatural behavior for a man as beguiled by your sister as Bert is."

I stared at my friend and said at last, "I consider myself a capable and intelligent woman, but I swear, Ruth Carpenter, you put me to shame."

When I stood, Ruth added as warning, "But don't think Bert's any more likely to give you the information you seek than Lonnie Markman. Or Silas either. Most men have a line they won't cross, no matter what."

"And you think Bert's line has something to do with Dee?"

"Oh, Sheba, I'd bet money on it," Ruth said.

I was glad I didn't take my friend up on her wager because as usual, Ruth read Bert Gruber exactly right. I don't know how she learned to do that, whether it always came natural to her because of her innate kindness or because it was a benevolent byproduct of the years she spent grieving her beloved Duncan. Regardless of the reason, she guessed right about Bert. There was indeed a line he wouldn't cross, and the line wound itself around, over, and through my sister.

When I stopped at the Gooseneck Hotel the next day, Bert didn't bother to deny anything. Or admit anything, either. All he said was, "All I can tell you about Miss Newell, Sheba—"

"It's Miss Fenway," I interrupted. "We're sisters and I should know what her last name is."

"She prefers Miss Newell." Since the man clearly believed he was an expert on the life and times of Delilah Fenway, I resisted rolling my eyes and let him finish. "All I can tell you about Miss Newell is that she's perfectly safe and healthy. She has some business to attend to, and I was happy to be of some help to her in the matter."

By the end of our discussion, the only information I had

that I didn't have before I stopped by the Gooseneck was that Bert had driven Dee out of New Hope in a wagon. Where he left her, whether a final destination or only a stop along the way, and what her pressing business was were details he would not divulge. Or perhaps could not divulge, I thought, because I had the distinct impression that Bert didn't know much more than I did. But the man was blinded by admiration and infatuation, which made him feel so honored that my sister would turn to him for any help whatsoever that he was content with his ignorance. I, on the other, neither admiring nor infatuated, was simply irritated.

Grumbling under my breath at Bert's stubborn reticence, I stomped down the boardwalk toward the dress shop, preoccupied enough to forget to watch where I was going. I would have tripped off the boardwalk, no doubt landing off balance in the alley's dirt, if John Bliss hadn't caught me by the arm and pulled me back.

"Sorry," I said, "and thank you. I was lost in thought."

"Is that what it was? Looked more like a temper than a thought to me."

We stepped in tandem down into the alley, John still keeping a firm hold on my upper arm, and I looked west toward the schoolhouse.

"I understand Mr. Stenton got back a while ago," I said out of nowhere, "and I heard the early wheat's in. Do you think that means school will be starting up soon?"

"And you think I'd know something about that?" Spoken with slight amazement.

"You bought the desks," I retorted, bringing my gaze back to John's face, "and you're not a man to lose sight of an investment." He took his hand from my arm.

"I considered it a gift," he said, something in his tone that surprised me. Was it disappointment that colored his words?

"Of course, it was a gift. I know that, but—"

"I don't know when Stenton plans to open school for the fall, Sheba. He's the person you should ask about that," John's tone back to normal.

We stepped up onto the boardwalk on the other side of the alley and stopped in front of the dress shop. I knew I had work waiting but for some reason was loath to get to it.

"I know you've been preoccupied lately, but you've missed some fine sunrises," John said.

"Preoccupied is an understatement. I had some personal errands to take care of the last day or two, but I wish I'd gone painting instead for all I accomplished."

"This has to do with your sister, I imagine."

Without thinking about it, I sat down on the bench that sat by the front door of the shop and John sat down beside me. I turned sideways to face him.

"Since the night New Hope opened its doors to the Alice Variety Theatre of the West, everything in my life has had to do with my sister and only my sister."

"And the boy, too."

My tone softened. "Yes. Jem, too," adding, "I'm glad she didn't take him with her when she left. He's happy enough with me now."

"But you don't think that will last?"

"Jem believes his mother will be home in a few short days at the most, but I have my doubts about that. If only she'd said something to me before she left, told me why she had to go or where she was going, I wouldn't have such a bad feeling about all this. It's that blasted telegram." At John's question, I answered, "Dee got a wire from someone and whatever was in it sent her on the run. Lonnie Markman's suffering from a case of Western Union conscience and won't tell me what it said. Bert Gruber helped Dee leave town, but I don't think he knows much more than I do. I have a bad feeling about it." I repeated myself and then was silent. John, too, for a few moments until he stood.

"If I hear anything, I'll let you know," he said, looking down at me where I sat.

I tried to smile. "I'd appreciate it. Not that anyone could ever make Delilah Fenway do something she didn't want to do, but for Jem's sake I'd like to know she's all right, at least."

I rose, too and added with a sigh, "And now I've got work to do that I can't put off no matter how much I'd like to."

"It's not putting off work that makes you testy. You need to grab your paints and easel and take in a sunrise. You know that's all it takes to make you feel better."

I wanted to say I wasn't testy, but there was no denying any of what he said. How had John Bliss come to know me so well from only casual, early-morning conversations held in an alley, him always going one way and I another?

"You're right," I agreed. "Maybe tomorrow."

"Maybe, but old Eb Fry said his big toe was forecasting rain."

"Eb's big toe has been known to be wrong," I said, laughing a little. Simply talking about painting had lightened my mood. "And anyway, a rainy morning has its own kind of light."

"Maybe I'll see you in the morning then."

"I wouldn't be surprised," I said as I opened the door to the dress shop, stopping long enough to add, "Thank you for the chat, John. I didn't mean to load you down with my troubles."

"Isn't that what friends are for?" A terse reply but said with a smile. Then he walked past me headed for either the café or the boarding house – although why, with a hotel and a restaurant of his own, he'd be going to either of those places beat me – and I stepped inside my shop. The afternoon would be full of cutting and pinning and basting and sewing, but John's observations had convinced me to make other plans for early the next morning.

7

Mr. Arthur Stenton has the look of an Old Testament prophet about him, which is not necessarily a bad thing if one is enclosed in a room with more than thirty rambunctious children over an extended period of time. It isn't that our schoolmaster wears a long, white beard or parades around New Hope in the flowing robes artists tend to ascribe to Moses or Elijah. It's something intangible in his demeanor that fits the comparison, something stern but not unkind or unfair or judgmental. Personally, I would not have a moment of doubt about following the man across the Platte River or experience the slightest surprise if the waters parted in front of us. Mr. Stenton has expectations for his students, not just academic expectations but deportment and moral expectations, too. There is something about him that makes a person – not just children, either – fear disappointing him, and the fear would not be attributed to feeling the thwack of the rod. Rather, so I have been told by people who know, it is the look on his face, how he draws back when he's dissatisfied and frowns and shakes his head in a kind of stunned disbelief. Until Jem came into my life, I had enjoyed – I use the word purposefully – little interaction with the teacher, but with the start of a new school year, I recognized that needed to change.

One afternoon, I saw his trim figure through my shop

window striding along across the street toward the drug store. I caught up with him as he exited the store.

"Arthur, could I have a moment of your time?" It took all my will not to call him Mr. Stenton, but we were both adults and had known each other from a distance for over five years, and I refused to bow to his innate authority. We had settled in New Hope the same year and we were equals in any way that mattered.

"Yes, Miss Fenway?" His tone pleasant, his expression not smiling but pleasant as well. What was there about the man that made me feel momentarily six years old again? Ever cordial and fearfully patient, he removed his hat and waited.

"You've been away for the summer and may not be aware that my nephew now resides with me."

"I believe I heard something to that effect."

"His name is James Cameron Fenway, but he goes by the name of Jem. He's a good reader but has never to my knowledge attended school anywhere."

"How old is your nephew, Miss Fenway?"

How odd that I had never asked that exact question to either Dee or Jem! "Perhaps…six?" Impossible to miss that my words were more question than answer.

To his credit, not a trace of incredulity at my ignorance showed in the man's expression or sounded in his tone. "Old enough to attend school then."

"Yes."

"And is he willing to attend school?" The question was his, this time, and I was happy to be able to give at least one solid and certain response.

"Not just willing but eager. He asks about it daily."

Arthur Stenton replaced his hat. "Very good then. I'll be sure there's a desk ready for him. Next Monday. Eight o-clock sharp. Good day, Miss Fenway."

"Good day, Arthur."

And that was that, no rules, no advice, and only the two questions. Was brevity his secret to managing a room full of high-spirited children? Did he say only the very minimum necessary to communicate his wishes and then move along to the next subject? I'm ashamed to admit that for the first time in my life, I realized that teaching might demand as much technique and discipline as painting.

Jem went off to school the next week with a big grin on his face and came home grinning, too. He loved his first day, loved every day afterwards, too, and thought the sun rose and set in Arthur Stenton. Whatever the teacher's technique, it worked on Jem, and because the boy was happy, I was happy, too. Happy until Archie Sloan pushed open the door of my little dress shop and stepped inside and my life changed. Again.

In autumn the light alters. To this day, I don't have the words to describe what happens, how the sky shrinks and the morning dims and early sunlight fades to the color of fresh cream, everything occurring so gradually and so inexorably that one might almost miss the shift from summer to fall. Unless you painted, of course. Then it was impossible not to notice how summer slowly disappeared into fall.

There was nothing special about the fall day I met Archie Sloan, although his acquaintance would make it special and not in a good way, either. Like all the preceding autumn days, I started with an hour or so of trying to capture the milky color of diminishing morning sunshine, eventually hurried home to get Jem up and off to school, and then spent the remainder of the morning and all of the afternoon working on this dress and that shirt, the ordinary tasks of my ordinary day that put food on the table. Two mouths to feed made me view my customers and my business more seriously and, unfortunately, added an air of drudgery to my work, too. I didn't understand why that should be because nothing to do with the dress shop had changed. Only before Jem, the shop had been a means to an end, and if I decided to hang the closed sign early so I could spend the afternoon painting down by the river, what did it matter? If I lost business or missed an order, I didn't care because I knew other customers would come along, and if they didn't, as long as I could pay for paints and canvases, I could always figure out a way to make ends meet. But now there was Jem, who read every book he could get his hands on, ate enough for three boys, and outgrew his clothes almost before I had the last stitch in them. I didn't want him to live on less. Remarkable how one little boy affected the way I looked at the world! I never thought it could happen to me.

So that September day, when the bell on the shop's front door gave its little jingle, I took a moment to pin down the velvet band on the hat I was refurbishing for Margery Danford before I looked up.

"May I help you?" I asked the man who entered and straightened from my task at the work table to meet his gaze straight on. Eyes dark green as summer grass returned my stare before he smiled. He had a young, clean-shaven, unlined face and dark hair that brushed the top of his shirt collar.

"Yes, ma'am, I hope so. The way you were studying that hat, you must be the local dress and hat lady."

"I'm Sheba Fenway."

"That's good then, because you're just the person I was looking for."

He closed the door carefully behind him and came closer to where I waited. Not so young, after all, I thought with the distance between us lessened. Lines along his mouth showed pale against his sun-browned skin. An attractive man still, but I added a few years to my first estimate of his age. A pleasant smile, too, but it caused me to shift my stance, nevertheless, something visible only to my artist's eye making me suddenly cautious.

"How fortunate for you, Mr.—" I stopped and waited.

As if remembering his manners, he removed his hat with a flourish – a flat-crowned affair of heavy, dark wool felt and a woven leather cord encircling it above the brim. Hats are part of my livelihood and I peruse enough catalogs to recognize when a hat is more South America than Nebraska.

"Excuse my manners, Miss Fenway. My name is Sloan. Archie Sloan."

"Now that we've had proper introductions, Mr. Sloan, I'll ask again. May I help you?"

"I hope so. I was told you were Fannie Newell's sister."

He might as well have poked me with a sharp stick. Dee's stage name was the last thing I expected to hear come out of his mouth.

"Whoever would have told you that?" I asked, uneasy now and unsure about why this smiling man should be asking about my sister.

"The old man at the livery. Did he get it wrong?" Archie Sloan's eyes were as sharp as cut glass, much too sharp to have missed my initial hesitation.

"No. Cap Sherman doesn't get much wrong when it comes to New Hope, Nebraska. Fannie and I are sisters." Then taking the bull by the horns I followed up with a blunt question. "Why do you want to know?"

"Fannie and I are longtime friends, and it's been quite a while since I've known the pleasure of her company. I was hoping to renew an old acquaintance." He looked over my shoulder toward the bead-hung doorway that led into the back kitchen. "Is she here now?" Not as transparent a question as the words made it seem, his tone too eager and faintly foreboding. Mental alarm bells that would have rivalled the town's Fire Department tolled in my head.

"No."

He turned his attention back to me. "Well, that's a disappointment, Miss Fenway. It surely is. Do you expect her back soon?"

"No."

He repeated the single syllable and added, "Not here now and not expected back soon."

"That about summarizes it, Mr. Sloan," I said.

"I hope you can understand how disappointed I'd be if I missed seeing an old friend after such a long time. Good friends are hard to come by."

"They are," I agreed.

"Then would you mind telling me where I can find

Fannie? I'd hate to leave without seeing her."

"No doubt that's true, Mr. Sloan, but I'm afraid I can't help you strengthen your bonds of friendship with Fannie. I don't know where she is."

"Her own sister doesn't know where she is?" A casual playfulness in his tone that clearly showed he didn't believe me.

"That's the truest thing either of us has said so far." I spoke with a smile and tried to match his light tone. "My dear sister, ever a woman of mystery and surprise, departed New Hope for parts unknown some weeks ago, and I have not heard from her since. But rest assured that if I do, I'll be certain to let her know you came asking after her."

Archie Sloan never stopped smiling, but there was an edge to his words that did not match the smile. "You be sure to do that, ma'am. You be sure to tell her that Archie Sloan came looking for her and was sorry to miss her."

He replaced his hat and turned to leave. I could tell he doubted my story but recognized there was little more he could do at the time. He's a man to watch out for, I thought, but if someone had overheard our conversation, they wouldn't have understood my disquiet, every word innocent enough on the outside.

Just as Sloan turned to exit, the front door burst open and Jem came barreling in followed by Othello lumbering a little behind, unable to keep up with the boy's liveliness.

"Aunt Sheba, Mr. Stenton said that in another country a girl the same age as me found a cave full of old paintings. He said the paintings were done thousands and thousands of years ago and that I should ask you if you knew anything about them because you're a painter. But what I really want to ask you is if there are any caves around New Hope that Othello and I could explore." The dog's tail began wagging at the sound of his name coupled with Jem's enthusiasm. To his canine brain, adventure awaited.

The boy, talking a mile a minute, suddenly realized there was another adult present and pulled himself up short, took an inhale that sounded as audible as a gulp, gave a sideways glance toward Sloan, and said, "Excuse me for interrupting."

"You're excused," I said, unreasonably eager to get Jem out from under the keen gaze of Archie Sloan. "I'll tell you what I've read about those cave paintings when I'm done here. Go back and have a cookie – there's one for Othello, too – and I'll catch up in a minute."

"That's interesting about those old paintings, boy," Archie Sloan said, but I didn't think it was paintings in a cave that interested him. "Maybe they were made by Indians."

Jem gave the idea a moment of consideration before he responded. "No one knows who made them, sir." Jem is always polite. "That's what Mr. Stenton said. And I don't know if there are any Indians where those caves are. It's a place called Brazil. Mr. Stenton showed me where it was on the globe at school."

"You go to school, do you?"

"Yes, sir."

"Every day?"

"Not on Sunday. We go to church on Sundays."

I put both hands on Jem's shoulders, turned him around, and gave the boy a gentle nudge.

"We have some grown-up business to finish up here," I said, trying to make my voice sound more stern than nervous. What was there about Archie Sloan's interest in Jem that quickened my heartbeat? He hadn't said a single thing that could be called suspicious or dangerous. But still…still…

"Yes, ma'am," and the boy disappeared with his canine fellow-explorer close on his heels. From the kitchen, I heard the clink of the cookie jar's lid.

"Boy looks a lot like his mother." I didn't respond. "A lot like his father, too."

Of course, I wanted to ask about that comment, ask what Archie Sloan knew about Jem's father, but the knowledge that doing so was exactly what Sloan wanted me to do kept me from saying a word.

"Well, thanks for your time, Miss Fenway. You won't

forget to tell Fannie I was here, will you?"

"As I told you, Mr. Sloan, I don't know where my sister is and I haven't heard a word from her since she left town, but if that should change, you can be certain she'll hear about your visit."

"That's all I can ask." In the doorway, he turned for a final word. "That's a nice boy you got there, Miss Fenway. Apple of his mother's eye, I imagine. Of yours, too, looked like. Hard to replace a boy like that."

After he pulled the door closed behind him, I stood motionless for a few moments, turning over his last remark in my mind and wondering why I heard a threat in it. Was that what loving someone did to a person, made her feel unnaturally protective, made her fearful where no danger existed? But even as I berated myself for being alarmed at nothing, some part of me knew better. For all his easy smiles and harmless comments, Archie Sloan was not harmless. He was a man to be watched. A man to be feared.

Sloan showed up two days later, out of the blue and where I least expected him, a pattern of behavior I would learn to associate with the man. Morning and I was bundled against a cool breeze, carrying only a sketch pad and charcoals with me with an old woolen blanket thrown over my shoulder. I was trying my hand at a series of charcoal sketches of New Hope against different horizons and had turned west at the corner alley so when I faced the town, I would catch the angles of all the roofs against the rising sun. New Hope was a town thrown together with haphazard enthusiasm at word of the U.P. Railway's approach, but when the sun played against the variety of establishments, it turned the uneven roof line into soft silhouette and sent shadows where you least expected them. I liked the idea of shading the charcoals to match that morning effect. I hoped to do the same at dusk, too, but feeling the nip at my fingertips, I thought that effort might have to wait until spring.

I walked past George Young's Photography Studio and Ruby Strunk's small house and laundry shed, then stopped at the crest of the ridge that was just high enough to hide the schoolhouse from plain view of town. I threw the blanket onto the ground, laid the charcoals and pad down on top of it and still standing, turned east to study the view. That morning I was interested in John Bliss's businesses: the hotel, which was the tallest and the fanciest building in New Hope, and the adjacent music hall, somewhat shorter than the hotel, squat and more substantial. John wasn't a showy man by any means, but he had ornamented the corners of both buildings with unusual wooden curlicues that gave the establishments a vague European air. The only structure in town even slightly similar was Hart's, Ruth's boarding house, which had originally been built by a wealthy railroad man as an imposing home with curlicues of its own and an impressively towering chimney. Hart's, however, was for another day. Satisfied with the way the lines of John's grand rooftops peaked above the shorter roofs on my side of the street, I turned to reach for my sketch pad and was shocked to find Archie Sloan standing on the other side of the old blanket, not doing a thing but watching me. I must have been more intent on the landscape than I knew or surely I would have noticed his approach, felt his gaze.

My audible gasp of surprise that bordered on alarm caused him to say quickly, "I didn't mean to scare you, Miss Fenway. You were caught up in the view." He looked down at the blanket. "It doesn't look like you're here to paint this morning. I was told that was a common practice of yours, but maybe I got that wrong."

I didn't bother to respond to his comments but asked, "What are you doing out so early?" If the man didn't make me so blasted uneasy, I might have found his smile attractive.

"Admiring the view, just like you. Admiring the schoolhouse, too. Your little town has a fine building there." I made no comment. "I can see why Fannie's boy would like it, him being dragged along behind his mama all his early years. Now me, I never had much time for school. What I wanted to learn wasn't going to be found in books, no ma'am."

"What do you want, Mr. Sloan?"

"I want to talk to Fannie."

"So you told me a couple of days ago."

"I thought maybe you remembered something is all, something about where Fannie might be, something she told you that you forgot about when we first talked."

"No," I said. "I haven't remembered anything new."

"Maybe the boy then. Maybe he knows something."

"No," I said again. "Jem knows less than I do."

"Maybe if I asked him myself—"

"If you come near the child, I'll report you to Sheriff Carpenter."

Sloan tried to look surprised. "Report me to the sheriff?! What will you tell him I did? Is it a crime in this little town of yours to inquire after an old friend?" He was right, of course, because he had not raised hand or voice to me, had not threatened Jem with anything but a conversation.

"I don't know what you're playing at, Mr. Sloan. Something to do with my sister obviously, but I'm not my sister and I don't know where she is. Even if I did, though, I doubt I'd tell you. I don't think I like you very much." He watched me, unsmiling, as I reached down, picked up the charcoals, pad, and blanket, and turned back to give New Hope a lingering look. "And you've managed to ruin a perfectly good sunrise, which makes me like you even less."

"You'll have to try again tomorrow. You walk out on your own nearly every morning about the same time, I hear, same as the boy heads off for school every morning. Not many secrets in a small town like this."

"Are you threatening me, Mr. Sloan? Is that what this is about?"

"Threatening you? I don't know where you get your ideas! It was just an early morning walk, Miss Fenway, and I was just making conversation." He paused before asking, "Did I mention your sister has something that belongs to me?"

"No." He wanted me to ask what that something was, and

I was equally determined not to display a bit of curiosity. Sloan's game had palled. I was eager to be done with the conversation and didn't bother with more words, just turned my back to him and began to walk back down the broad alley that connected to Main Street. John Bliss lounged at the corner of the photography studio, waiting for me. Watching for me, I thought, and was so relieved to see him that I was finally able to take a deep breath. There was none of Sloan's threat in John Bliss's attention.

"You had company today," John observed, straightening from where he leaned against the building's corner.

"Yes."

He heard something in my voice that made him say, "Not invited then?" His own tone had flattened out and lost its usual sardonic edge.

"No." I started walking and he did the same. "His name's Archie Sloan. He says he was a friend of Dee's. Wants to know where she is, and I get the definite feeling he doesn't believe me when I tell him I don't know."

"He worries you."

"I don't like him," I replied carefully, "but he's always polite and keeps his distance. I couldn't tell you why I don't like him, just that I don't. He frightens me."

John stopped at the words. "I've never known anything to frighten you, Sheba, not man, beast, or nature." I stopped, too, and turned to face my companion.

"I don't like the way he talks about Jem, but on the surface, his words are as innocent as a Bible reading." I shrugged. "I must be getting soft in the head."

"In the heart, maybe. You care a lot about the boy."

"I do," I admitted. "I've never had much to do with children and I never understood why people fussed over babies, but Jem is – special. He's special to me, anyway. When you care about someone, it makes you let down your guard. That's why I've always kept to myself. Caring for someone changes things, makes you worry more and spend time thinking about them when you could be doing other things." I sighed and started walking again. "Anyway, I'd say my feelings about Archie Sloan were just my imagination, but I know that's not true."

"I'll see what I can find out about the man." We reached the alley's intersection with Main Street.

"Would you, John? I don't want to be a bother, but I'd appreciate it."

"That's all right. I can tolerate a little bother now and then." When I stepped up onto the boardwalk in front of my shop, John said my name, and I turned back to look at him where he stood on the hard-packed dirt of the alley.

"If the man troubles you again, you come and tell me before anyone else, before you say a word to Ruth or Carpenter or anyone. Will you do that?"

I eyed him. "So you can do what, exactly? Ride like one of King Arthur's noble knights to my rescue?"

The idea made him laugh. "You should know by now that there's nothing noble about me. And I don't know any woman less in need of rescue than you. What you told Ruth the first time you and I knocked heads was right on the money. I am arrogant, and I like to be right, but I also like that painting you did that's hanging in the hotel lobby. People notice it. You'd be surprised how often people comment on it. I expect the time may come when the name Sheba Fenway turns out to be a draw for our little town, and that would mean more business for my hotel and my restaurant. You see my point?"

My turn to laugh then. "I do, John. One business owner to another, I do, though I can't imagine anything like that happening in the foreseeable future."

"Maybe you're right, Sheba, but business is business, and I don't let anyone interfere with what's mine. You have any problems with Sloan, if he bothers you in any way, you come to me first. Agreed?" I met his gaze and gave a slow nod of assent. He nodded in return, the agreement between us sealed at that moment. He crossed the street toward the music hall, and I pushed open the door of the dress shop, my thoughts shifting away from everything that had occurred that morning to getting Jem's breakfast on the table. Later, however, seated and busy hemming my way through a stack of trousers, I went over both of the morning's conversations in my mind, surprised that it was John's words that gave me the most pause. He never had told me what he'd do if I complained to him about Archie Sloane's behavior, and maybe that was all for the best.

I finally made a decision, more a mental leap than a decision, really, for which there was no sensible explanation. Only that I was tired of worrying about Archie Sloane's presence in New Hope and why he was so insistent about finding my sister. I didn't like feeling jumpy about Jem, either and was annoyed with myself that I had allowed a stranger to make me uneasy and uncomfortable for no reason I could put my finger on. So when Millie Winters stopped in the dress shop and I asked how Sally was enjoying her stay with her cousin in Sidney, I was already primed to take some kind of action. I never expected Millie to be the person to light the fuse, but that just shows you how life never goes the way you think it will.

Millie pulled out a folded paper from her dress pocket. "She's having a fine time, Sheba. Put her and her cousin together and they always enjoy themselves. It's been like that since they were little girls. No doubt my sister has her hands full with the two of them, but it's only high spirits and Pris and I were exactly the same when we were their age." Millie smiled at the memory and handed the crumpled paper to me for a look. "Sally sent this along with the letter I got today. Looks like that traveling variety show we had here, the one your sister was in, has been touring Nebraska like a house afire, not that there's many settled towns along the Wyoming border. Sally enjoyed it so much the first time, she said they were going to see it again in Sidney. They'd have seen it by now, but I thought you might be interested, your sister being a part of it and all." I paid only partial attention to Millie's rambling words as I smoothed out the rough flyer she handed me.

The words *THE ALICE VARIETY THEATRE OF THE WEST* stretched across the upper half of the paper in big, bold, black capital letters and underneath that fancy heading was the line *Fresh from a String of Successful Shows.* Toward the bottom of the page were the double-underscored words *Enthralled Audiences from Dawes City to Rush Creek to Antelopeville* and underneath that line, with the two city names and dates hand-written into the appropriate blank spaces, was *See us in* Sidney Sept 14 *and in* Potter Sept 20. The concluding line at the very bottom of the flyer next to a crude drawing of a stage and a closed curtain was the guarantee *THE BEST TWO BITS YOU'LL SPEND ALL YEAR!*

I stared at the paper a long while. According to the flyer, the traveling entertainment troupe had been in Dawes City a while ago. Dee received a telegram from Dawes City also a while ago. I didn't know if the *whiles* added up, but I thought they might. Was it Perry Alice who wired Dee? Did he lure her back to that vagabond life? But if that was all it was, why the suddenness and the secrecy on Dee's part? Why not just tell me? And would she have left Jem behind without giving him those details? I shook my head slightly as if doing so would clear my puzzling thoughts and looked at Millie.

"May I keep this paper a while, Millie?" The woman smiled.

"You can have it, Sheba. I thought of you right away when I saw it. I believe it would be hard to find family you haven't seen in a long while and then lose touch so soon when you didn't expect to. I know I wouldn't like it." There was sympathy and understanding in Millie's tone and in her expression. I've misjudged her, I thought, at least on occasion. A tendency toward gossip doesn't mean a person couldn't also be kind or feel true sympathy. In a rare burst of self-reflective humility, I considered that my tendency to put people into boxes and close the lid on them might need to be altered.

"Thank you," I said and laid the paper down on the table.

"Now let me go get that shirtwaist you came for. I think you'll like it, Millie. The color's right for you," the two of us back to the business at hand. The flyer was never out of my thoughts, however, and after Millie left the shop with her purchase, I gave the flyer one more long look, turned the sign on the door to closed, took money from the can I kept in the kitchen, and walked down to the train station. I wasn't sure how much a ticket to Potter, Nebraska, would cost, or how long it would take to get there, but Lonnie Markman had told me Potter was on the railway line and that was enough for me. The Alice Variety Theatre of the West would be in Potter in a few days, and so would I.

8

Like New Hope, it was the Union Pacific Railway that put Potter, Nebraska, on the map, and like New Hope, Potter was a small town with big ambitions.

"Have you ever been there?" I asked Ruth when I stopped to see if she'd watch Jem while I was gone.

"No. Potter's three counties and 140 miles to the west. Why would I take the time to visit a place that I'd guess looks exactly like New Hope? The railway was midwife to both towns, after all, and right about the same time, too. I'm not sure why you feel the need to make the trip, but I'm happy to keep an eye on Jem for you. He can have Danny's old room. He's a good boy, Sheba, and no trouble."

I hadn't told Ruth the whole story about why I planned to be away from New Hope for two days, but at her words, I felt guilty enough to volunteer, "I heard that the Alice Variety Theatre was scheduled for Potter so I thought maybe—" I stopped, realizing how ridiculous it could sound: I thought maybe the show was still in Potter. Maybe my sister had gone back to performing with them. Maybe I'd get an answer as to why she left so abruptly and so secretly. Maybe I'd have something to tell Jem about his mother. A lot of *maybes*, I thought, and not a single guarantee of anything except an uncomfortable trip on a dirty train several hours and three stops coming and several hours and three stops going.

Fortunately, my friend understood without my having to finish the sentence.

"Then, of course, you need to go, and don't worry about Jem. The fact is, with Silas out of town, I'll be happy to have any kind of human conversation over supper, and Jem is full of all sorts of information I didn't know."

"He is, isn't he?" I smiled. "You know Mr. Stenton isn't one for praise, but he told me in passing that in all his years of education, he's never taught a child with the level of curiosity Jem possesses. I didn't pursue the comment, just took it as a compliment and said thank you." Changing the subject, I said, "I didn't realize Si was gone again. Is there new trouble?"

"A train robbery this time, over by Brady Island." Ruth appeared somewhat on edge.

"How many does that make now?"

"I can't say for sure, but too many. The first one was the night the variety show came to town, and since then I'd guess three or four more all around Lincoln County. Silas says it's the same wild bunch every time, men looking for easy money and careless about people's lives. By the time Silas gets there, the robbers are long gone and they don't leave much of a trail."

"I haven't heard of anyone being hurt," my small attempt at comfort.

"Yet. No one's been hurt yet." Her words told me my attempt wasn't as successful as I had hoped. Ruth had lost one husband and while she never said the words out loud, I knew she feared losing a second. But she was a woman possessed of an admirable mix of good sense and hope, and concluded, "And that's how Silas wants it to stay, so he and Lucas rode east late last night to try to pick up a trail or get some kind of description. So far, the robbers have worn kerchiefs over their faces and kept their hats pulled low, and that hasn't given Silas much to go on. This time he wants to stay on their trail longer." I understood the shadow of worry in her eyes.

"Si and Luke will be gone a while then."

"Yes, but Silas left Monty in charge so New Hope's in good hands." Monty, Si's junior deputy, looked awfully young to be a threat to anyone, but if my friends had confidence in him, who was I to question their judgment? Ruth cocked her head to the side, hearing something I didn't, something I couldn't, I suppose, and said, "There's the baby. I have to go. When do you leave?"

"It's the first train out in the morning. Can I send Jem over for breakfast?"

"That'll be fine. I'll be up with Alexander. Othello and I will take care of Jem until you're back, whenever that is." As I pushed open the door to leave, Ruth added, "Sheba, you wire me first thing if you run into any trouble. I mean it, if you have any trouble at all, you let me know."

"I will, but with Silas gone, I don't know what you could do if I did run into trouble."

"Silas isn't the only man you can count on, Sheba."

I looked at her, puzzled, and might have questioned further except by then even my non-maternal ears could hear the lusty baby cries coming from the back of the boarding house.

"I don't expect any trouble, Ruth, but I promise to let you know if anything goes wrong. Now you'd better go take care of that baby. He's got a powerful voice on him."

"Don't I know it?" Ruth said, pride in her voice, and tolerance, and love. Mostly love.

Monday morning, I sent Jem over to Ruth's after an early breakfast to wait for Mr. Stenton to open the schoolhouse, and I boarded the 6:35 train to points west, one of which was Potter. I hadn't been on a train since my arrival in New Hope six years earlier, and while the *Grand Island Independent* was always prosing on about progress in Nebraska, apparently that progress didn't apply to the seats in a railroad car. Or maybe Sidney Dillon, the railroad's president, didn't read the *Independent*. Whatever the reason, the wooden bench on which I sat felt exactly as hard and uncomfortable as the seat I recalled from my trip west years before. Either I or the wooden bench or both of us needed more padding. Fortunately, I remembered to bring along a small drawing pad and charcoal pencils and was able to pass the time sketching portraits of my fellow-travelers. I wasn't then and am not now very good at the human form, although I was tutored by the finest portrait artist of our time, George Peter Alexander Healy. Mr. Healy was a genius with faces and figures; I was not.

"Landscapes suit your eye for light, Miss Fenway," he had said at the end of our time together, "and you might try your hand at still-life, but I don't anticipate you will make a name for yourself in portraiture. However, there's a group of painters in Paris that's become known as the Impressionists. They experiment with light the same as you. You might consider learning more from them." Nothing unkind, but to hear yourself critiqued by a master artist was humbling, nevertheless. The hours I spent on the train that day gave me the opportunity to practice my portrait skills, but by the time I reached Potter, there was nothing in my sketch pad that proved Mr. Healy wrong.

Ruth's words about Potter came to mind when I stepped onto the train platform. The place carried the general air of a town established solely because the train made a stop there. New Hope had started out the same way, but where New Hope had taken advantage of cattle that came north from far southeast Texas and Oklahoma Territory, Potter's location was too far west to do the same. Abner Talamine's bank certainly helped, too, because in my first stroll down Potter's main street, I didn't spot anything resembling a bank. Potter, I decided, was what New Hope might have looked like ten years ago: smaller, less inviting, less vigorous, and less promising. New Hope had flourished and Potter hadn't.

With only the small lunch I had brought with me on the train, I was hungry and stopped for a meal at one of Potter's two cafés. No elegant Bliss Restaurant. No solid, respectable Hart's Boarding House, either, and I decided to spend the night in the train station. Not an inviting prospect but it was clean and safe and on a few occasions in my past, I had survived worse. I could survive the wooden benches in the waiting area of the Union Pacific Railway's station in Potter, Nebraska, if I had to.

"I heard The Alice Variety Theatre of the West has a show in Potter tonight," I said to the woman who brought my chicken and dumplings, "but I didn't see any signs posted about it."

"No, ma'am. Of course, the show had to be cancelled."

I stared at her as if she spoke Russian and repeated, "Cancelled? But why?"

"Well, it would hardly be proper to go on with it in the light of what's happened."

"I've been on the train since early morning, and I don't know what you mean. What exactly is it that happened?"

"President Garfield died last night," the woman told me. She might as well have inserted the word *finally* into her explanation because we both thought it. The President had been shot over two months earlier and had been lingering all this time since. I remembered Ruth's sympathy for Mrs. Garfield, the feeling truly warranted now. Poor woman. Poor President Garfield, too. He was a man who held a lot of promise for the nation. Many of us had held high hopes for his presidency, but he had been in office for fewer than four months before a madman shot him. Whatever hope and promise James Garfield once possessed were now as useless to the United States as dust. I felt a momentary pity, not just for the dead man and his wife and family, but for all of us. Chester Arthur was president now, and what little I had read about the former vice president wasn't flattering.

"I didn't know," I said, remained quiet for a moment out of respect, and then asked, "Is the variety troupe still in town? I've come quite a distance to see one of the members traveling with it."

"Last I knew they were staying over at Lulu's. There was talk of postponing the show until tomorrow night, so I'd guess they're still there."

After I finished the chicken and dumplings – acceptable but not nearly as good as the dumplings I was used to at the Nebraska Café – I crossed Potter's main street to where I recalled seeing Lulu's. With its plain store front, block-letter sign, single door, and one unadorned window, it was anybody's guess what the place had on offer, but when I entered the establishment I recognized it as Potter's version of New Hope's Gooseneck Hotel. Beds available for a night's sleep but nothing fancy and probably with the same bedbugs the Gooseneck offered. The thought of sleeping on the bench on the train platform suddenly took on the attraction of a featherbed in a big-city hotel.

The woman behind the front counter introduced herself as Martha and nodded when I asked if the members of the performing troupe were still in town but added that while some were in their rooms, Mr. Alice, the man I inquired about, was down the street at city hall.

"It's a shame about the President and I understand about being respectful, but it's not like cancelling the show altogether is going to make anybody feel better, so Mr. Alice said he was willing to stay over a night if we wanted him to put on his show tomorrow instead."

"That makes sense," I said because a response seemed warranted and then asked, "Is there an actress from the show staying here by the name of Fannie Newell?"

The woman ran her finger down the book on the counter and shook her head. "No, no Fannie Newell. There's a Penny—" she squinted "—something, I can't make it out, but no Fannie and no Newell, either."

I thanked her, got directions to Potter's city hall, and left, wondering as I walked if the absence of Fannie Newell's name meant that my sister wasn't there or that she was travelling under a different name. If she was running from someone, from Archie Sloan probably, it made sense that she would create a new name and a new identity to keep from being found.

I recognized Potter's city hall only because it had a small sign hanging in the front window with those two words stenciled on it. Otherwise, it looked exactly like what the much larger sign said it was: a store that offered "Merchandise and Sundries." Well, New Hope's buildings would have had to do double duty, too, if it weren't for the generosity of John Bliss and his contribution of the Meeting and Entertainment Hall. That and the fine desks at the schoolhouse and the new pews on order for the church all helped give New Hope an air of settled prosperity that Potter lacked. Somehow, I hadn't thought about John being as invested as the rest of us in our town's success, but his discreet generosity indicated otherwise. He was a quiet man, a man who watched and listened and paid attention to things without drawing attention to himself. Sometimes I thought I enjoyed his company as much as I did because I was reserved like that, too. It was a relief to know that because he understood me, I had no need for pretense when we were together.

I was thinking about John Bliss so intently that I bumped into a man exiting the store. He backed up quickly and murmured an apology, even though it was my lack of attention that caused the collision. We recognized each other at the same time.

"Miss Fenway."

"Mr. Alice," equal levels of surprise in both our voices. I hadn't expected to track Peregrine Alice down so easily and of all the people he had expected to see in Potter, Nebraska, I was probably at the very bottom of the list.

"This is a surprise," he said. He had looked startled to the point of shocked at first sight of my face, but he was an actor and now his expression was pleasantly quizzical and nothing else.

"Not for me," I replied. "You're the reason I'm here." I put a hand on his sleeve and pulled him through the doorway and out onto the boardwalk. "Can we talk a few minutes?"

He must have known what the topic of conversation

would be, but he adjusted his hat with thumb and forefinger and held out his arm to me as if we were promenading down Fifth Avenue in New York City.

"Of course." I laid my fingertips lightly on his forearm and we began to walk slowly back toward Lulu's.

"Did you get your stay extended?" I asked.

"I'm relieved to say I did. It's our last engagement this side of Denver, and we need the cash to get to Colorado."

"You've picked a hard life," I observed.

I heard the smile in his voice. "It might appear that way to some, I guess."

"But not to you."

"No. I wouldn't do it if I didn't like it. I took to the stage early and I've never regretted it."

After a long moment, I said, "I'm looking for my sister."

"From the resemblance, I suspected you were sisters, but I left her with you in New Hope. Why would you be looking for her here?"

"I believe it was you that sent her a telegram a few weeks ago and right after she got it, she disappeared without a word. That's why I'm here. I'd like to talk to her. I'd like to understand what made her leave like that."

"You didn't see her for years and you never tried to find her, did you?"

I felt shame at the question because he was right. I had periodically wondered where my sister was and what she was doing, but I never tried to find her or gave a moment's thought to doing so. The death of our brother, Jem, had set a distance between us that I believed could never be bridged. How curious that another Jem was now drawing us back together!

"No. We were never close, and she left without a word years ago. I didn't think she wanted to be found. She never made any gesture toward me that would make me think otherwise."

"But now—"

"Now," I said, "we're all grown up and life is different.

And there's Jem."

"Ah, it's the boy." Peregrine gestured to the two straight-backed chairs that sat on the boardwalk under the overhang shading Lulu's front window, and we sat.

"Yes," I agreed, "it's the boy. What can you tell me, Perry? Do you know where I can find my sister? Do you know what she's running from?" When I turned in my chair to look at him, I could practically hear the thoughts debating in his mind.

Finally, he said, "I don't know what your life's been like, and I don't know all that much about Fannie's, either, come to think about it, but I do know that she's a woman who likes to take chances. She took a chance with me and my traveling show, and it worked out all right for both of us. But there were other times—"

He paused so long that I prompted, "Other men, you mean."

"Yes. Other men. Fannie wasn't a – I mean, she was a woman finicky about companionship. Always knew what she wanted. She never had to sell herself, but that wild air about her sometimes caught the attention of the wrong kind of man."

"Archie Sloan." My saying the name surprised Alice.

"Definitely the wrong kind of man there. Did Sloan make it to New Hope?"

"Yes. He's been hanging around town for a while," I said, "hanging around Jem and me especially and asking where my sister – my sister *Dee* – is." I stressed her given name. "I don't like it. I don't like him, and I want to understand what he's really looking for. I thought at first it was Jem, that he was Jem's father, but now I think even if that's true, the boy is just a means to an end for Sloan. There's something else going on." I thought about Alice's question and what it suggested. "Was it you that told Sloan about Dee staying behind in New Hope?"

Alice's turn to feel shame now. I heard it in his voice. "I've never made a claim to courage, Miss Fenway, and Archie

Sloan is a dangerous man. When he wants something, there's nothing he won't do to get it. Nothing. He tracked the show to Dawes City – I don't know how – and he wanted to know where Fannie Newell was. He could have gotten the information he wanted from anybody in the company, so why should I die over it or let him hurt somebody else? I put him off as long as I could, but eventually I had to tell him. I wired Fannie, told her Sloan was closing in on her and he wasn't a man to take lightly. She knew that probably better than me. I take it she acted on my telegram."

"She left right away. No word where or why." I thought about my sister running from a dangerous man, living the best she knew how, hiding, then running again. No matter the reason, she deserved better. I felt a quick, sharp pang of compassion and outrage.

"Why is Sloan looking for her?" I asked, but in answer, Alice simply shrugged.

"I don't know any more than you do, and it's probably better for both of us that way. I always knew she was running from someone, but I never asked and she never volunteered."

"And that was enough for you?"

"Whatever Fannie chose to give was always enough for me. She's—" memory softened his tone "—special, your sister. I've never met anyone like her. I don't think I ever will again. She was so good on the stage! She sparkled. She drew them in. Drew me in, too. I miss her."

"Do you know where Dee is, Perry?" That was the question I had come to ask and the one answer I wouldn't go home without.

"If Fannie wanted you to know, she'd have told you." My patience slipped a notch.

"I'm her sister and I have her son and there's a dangerous man who won't leave us alone," my words clipped and stern, "so right now I don't really care what my sister wants. I need to know what I'm up against so I can keep Jem safe. That's what matters to me. So I'll ask you again, do you know where Dee is?" I heard his sigh before he answered.

"Not exactly."

"Don't try —" I began angrily, but he held up a hand.

"I think she might be in Ogallala. In my telegram, I gave her the name of a man I know that owns a high-class place in Ogallala and told her she could look him up if she wanted. It was a place to start, anyway. Marty puts on a show every night, singing and dancing and the like. Respectable entertainment, nothing bad, nothing you couldn't take your old mother to, though I'm sure Marty offers other comforts on the side. He never was a man to miss an opportunity, and I hear Ogallala is full of opportunities in the summer, so maybe that's where she headed. I never heard back from her, yea or nay."

"What's the man's name?"

"Marty Chip."

I repeated the name and asked, "What's the name of his place?"

Perry Alice stood up before he answered, stretched a little, and then looked down at me. "I don't know, Sheba. I knew Marty a long time ago, and it was just by chance that I heard he had settled into Ogallala and was doing all right by himself. Somebody told me in passing that his show could give mine a run for its money, and that's not something I was likely to forget." I would have asked more, but he raised his hand again. "I don't have anything else to tell you, Sheba, not about Fannie or Marty Chip or Archie Sloan or anybody else. I hope you get your questions answered, but I'm not the man to answer them for you. Now I need to let my folks know that we have a show to get ready for tomorrow night."

I looked up at the man, his goatee and sideburns as trim as I recalled, handsome in the way theatre people are handsome, with something not quite genuine about him. But I couldn't fault him for it. That was his life, and it wasn't just show people who lived behind a mask.

"Thank you, Perry," I said. "I appreciate your help."

With the same courtly gesture as before, he touched the brim of his hat lightly with thumb and forefinger.

"You're welcome, Miss Fenway," the familiarity of *Sheba* replaced with stage manners. I knew I had to be grateful for the small truths he had shared with me. Peregrine Alice was a man who played at make-believe for a living, after all. Like my sister, I doubted that truth was essential to his nature.

After he entered Lulu's, I sat for a while longer, thinking through my next step. Ogallala was on the rail line, too, due east, between Potter and New Hope. We had made a brief stop there on my way to Potter and would no doubt stop there on the way home, too. I didn't know much about the place, only that, like New Hope, a lot of Texas trail herds converged there in the summer to take advantage of the rail line. Because of that and the fact that neither Ogallala nor Keith County had its own Silas Carpenter keeping order, the town's reputation did not invite visits from ordinary, law-abiding, peaceful people. But it was September now, most of the herds and their wild wranglers long departed, the community slowing down and its disreputable elements soon to move on to other, more lucrative parts. What if Marty Chip closed down his establishment for the winter and left for greener pastures, too? I couldn't take the chance. There was no way I could merely watch the notorious cow-town through the train window as we passed it, no way I could afford to lose this opportunity. If my sister was working in Ogallala at a place owned by a man named Marty Chip, I wouldn't leave before I found her.

I had several hours to pass before the next, and last, train east was scheduled to arrive, so I settled myself as comfortably as possible on the train platform and leaned back against the wall. Late afternoon light in autumn has a mysterious quality about it, a brooding, subdued feeling with the invisible ability to send one looking for a lamp to light against the coming darkness and the coming winter. Looking north across the empty tracks at the broad expanse of empty prairie, it was all I could do to keep myself from being downhearted.

I'm a level-headed woman, someone who contemplates a

matter, giving all sides equal attention, and then concocts a plan based on the results of that exercise. I left home for art school after just such a deliberation and never had a moment's regret about the decision, but for some reason that day, I felt as close to melancholy as I had been in many years.

Did I truly need to find Dee? And if I did, why? Was it really about Jem, as I so boldly asserted? In a moment of truth, I realized the quest I'd assigned myself was likely more about me than Jem, about my guilt over believing the worst of my sister, even when I knew how deeply my father scorned her and disapproved of her behavior. Why had I never questioned what he told me? Why had I thought that her love for our brother was less than mine? Did I owe Dee something now because I had been so easily swayed then? But she was the elder. Shouldn't she have watched out for me? Is that what family came down to – obligation and responsibility and duty? What of shared memories? What of a common childhood? What of love? For all my complaining about space and privacy, I had liked sharing my home with Dee and Jem for that short time, had enjoyed the feeling of being part of a family, however small. Yet if my sister didn't want to be found, was it selfish of me to try to find her anyway because I wanted to keep those feelings in my life, because I discovered regrets and longings I hadn't realized were there? With my own life and my art built on a deeply-held belief in independence and single-mindedness, what right had I to impose something different on Dee? Shouldn't she be allowed to come and go as she pleased? But there was Jem now; there was always Jem to consider.

The thoughts swirled in my head and would not be silenced, and I stood and began to pace up and down the platform, swinging my arms vigorously. I trusted action and brisk outdoor air to put me back on track, even if I wasn't sure where the track led. With my back to the station doorway, nearly three hours before the next train's arrival and my mind deep in thought, I missed seeing a man step out of the train station onto the platform. It was only when I pivoted and turned back toward the station that I saw him. In the dim light of early evening, I could tell only that the figure was someone I knew and for a moment I thought with dismay, Archie Sloan. But then I breathed a sigh of relief. Not Archie Sloan but John Bliss walked toward me, the difference between night and day, between darkness and light, between fear and safety. All the difference in the world.

Just seeing the man lightened both my mind and my heart in a way I hadn't expected. I had known John for several years and certainly considered him my friend, but this feeling of deep, uncomplicated happiness at the sight of him was a new sensation that surprised, even shocked me. My feelings might have showed on my face, I couldn't know that, but I was fairly certain they couldn't be detected in my voice.

"What in the world are you doing here, John?" I asked, making no attempt to hide the incredulous disbelief with its slight edge of suspicion. I couldn't help it. Had he been following me all this time? For all the pleasure I felt at seeing him, the idea that he had been on my heels without saying a word was oddly unsettling and as unexpected as my earlier happiness. It's because I thrive on light, I thought, and in people, honesty is the same as light. I need honesty in my friends the way I need light in my art. It's all that counts.

"Hello to you, too, Sheba." His tone was relaxed enough, but now that I could see his face clearly, his eyes looked as dark and hard as flint. He could almost have been angry, but I couldn't think of any reason he should be mad at me.

"All right. Hello, John." I paused for effect. "Now that I've satisfied the courtesies, what in the world are you doing here?"

Without answering, he walked toward the bench where I had waited earlier, with me following a step or two behind just as silent. Once he sat, he motioned toward the empty spot next to him.

"Would you mind sitting, Sheba? I'm happy to tell you what I'm doing here, but it's easier to talk if we're on the same level."

I sat, dropped my bag off my shoulder, and turned sideways on the bench so I could see his face. Our knees almost touched.

Without additional amenities, John said, "I'm here looking for you. As I recall, that's what you wanted to know."

I studied his face a long moment, then asked, "If you had bad news for me, you'd tell me straightaway, wouldn't you?"

"I would."

I took a breath. "Then you're not looking for me to tell me something's happened to Jem. Or Ruth. Or the dress shop. No fires. No late-season tornadoes. The Platte hasn't floated New Hope and all its inhabitants away."

"No."

"That's something, anyway." I gave him a stern look. "Did you come on the train with me without letting me know you were there? Did you follow me, John?"

"No and no. I rode over straight from New Hope, no train ticket required," a slight upturn at the corners of his mouth as if my questions amused him.

"Then why are you looking for me?" was all I could think to say. The man's words were simple enough, but for some reason they didn't make any sense. Maybe I was more tired than I thought.

"I was—" he considered several words before settling on, "—concerned when I couldn't find you. Ruth told me you thought your sister might be in Potter and with Sloan nowhere to be found, I wanted to make sure he wasn't watching you from a distance, waiting for you to lead him straight to the person he wants to find."

I didn't know how to react to his explanation, whether to be annoyed or touched that he had come all this way because he worried I couldn't take care of myself. On the whole, I was inclined to be grateful.

"That was kind of you, John." At that, he turned fully to face me, dark brows drawn together, his turn now to decide if my response annoyed or gratified him.

"Kind," he said. "Is that what you think this is, Sheba? Me

being kind?" Something in the intensity of his words struck me mute. "I know you see the world different from other people, that for you morning sunshine holds more color than a rainbow and water's another kind of light, but sometimes you're blind about what's going on around you. An intelligent woman like yourself. How is that possible?" He lifted my chin with one thumb, steadied my face with his fingers on my cheek, and leaned to kiss me, a hard kiss, a kiss like the man himself, confident and demanding. I was taken aback by both his words and his kiss, but not for long. It hardly took a second for me to react, to lean into him and return the kiss as I brought up one hand to rest over his.

"Kind and something more then," I said finally, dropping my hand and drawing back from him. "I'm not in the mood to argue right now." He kept his fingertips against my face for a moment longer, then he, too, straightened, smiling in the way he had that made a person wonder what mischief he'd been up to. As it was, I had a pretty good idea about that.

"That doesn't happen very often," he said in an easy, unruffled voice.

"No, I guess not." I hadn't been kissed in a long time, not since art school, and had forgotten how enjoyable it was, but kissing John Bliss – good lord, I thought with passing astonishment, I just kissed John Bliss like I meant it! – had to take second place to finding Dee. She was the reason for my trip, after all. "Dee's not here in Potter, John. According to Perry Alice, she never was." I proceeded to tell him everything I was told and everything I guessed.

'Was Ogallala your next stop?"

"Yes."

"And all you've got to go on is the name of a man called Marty Chip?"

"Yes." He shook his head.

"You were just going to – what? Go up and down the street and in and out of saloons and cathouses and ask for him?"

"I suppose so. I don't know. But I'd have figured something out before I got off at Ogallala."

His eyes weren't on me any more. Instead, he sat looking straight ahead at the train tracks in front of us, elbows on his knees and his chin resting on his clasped hands. It was dark by then, but a pair of gas lanterns hung on the wall on each side of the bench where we sat. When he turned his head toward me, the light from the lamps brought the planes of his face into sharp relief. There's as much darkness as light in this man, I realized, but I didn't find the idea alarming.

"I know you would have, Sheba. I have no doubt about it, but I can help you with this, if you'll let me. Will you?"

I appreciated that he asked, that he didn't think he had a right to be involved in my life because he was a man and knew better than a woman, or because I had kissed him long and hard and without restraint just a few minutes before. John Bliss was not a man to force his way into a woman's life; he was a man who would wait to be invited. I liked that about him, liked it a lot.

"Yes. Do you know Marty Chip?"

"No, but I know Ogallala and I know a few people there. I can ask around for you. Why don't you stay here and get on the train like you planned? Get off at Ogallala. I'll be waiting for you at the station. You've got at least an hour and a half before the eastbound train gets here. I don't have to follow the rails and as I recall, you have a lengthy stop in Sidney so if I leave now, I can get to Ogallala before the train does, maybe do a little digging before we meet up."

"You've been on the road all day, John. I can't ask you to get right back on the road again."

He smiled and stood. "I don't recall you asking. I'll be all right."

I stood, too, suddenly awkward and having a hard time getting out the words, "Thank you." There was more I should say, that I wanted to say, but I didn't know what or how. Accepting help or being in another's debt was new territory that I'd have to get used to. He brushed the back of his hand against my cheek, a light, casual, friendly gesture as if he were aware of my discomfort.

"You're welcome. I'll meet you in Ogallala."

"It's a deal," I said. He put on his hat, which he'd set on the bench between us, turned away and disappeared into the train station without another word or a backward glance.

Well, I thought, as I settled myself back onto the bench to wait for the train, I wasn't expecting that. Dee. Jem. Now John Bliss. I was pretty sure those were all the changes in my life that I could handle for a while.

9

It was fully dark when the train reached Ogallala, but the station was lit and busy, Ogallala being a lit and busy town that catered to a clientele partial to nighttime activities. When I picked out John's figure from the crowd on the platform, the strongest feeling I had was relief. I might pride myself on being self-sufficient, but I also enjoyed a wide streak of good sense and having John along on this quest was a stroke of luck for me.

As soon as the train screeched to a halt, I watched John straighten from the wall where he'd propped himself, toss his cigarette onto the ground and grind it briefly under his heel, then step forward a little, watching the cars to see where I'd emerge. He couldn't see me observing him from the window where I sat, so I took a moment to study him. A tall man thickly built, not handsome but imposing in an intangible way that was reflected in his stride and in the way he ignored his surroundings, indifferent to anything except his own interests. Which now somehow included me. When exactly in the past six years had that occurred and how had I missed it? I rose, slung my bag over my shoulder, and made my way down the aisle. One question at a time, I told myself. First, where is Dee, and then, why is she running? Any questions about John Bliss had to be pushed far down on the list, not forgotten or ignored but saved for a later time.

When we finally stood face-to-face, I once more skipped a greeting and said simply, "You look tired." I thought so, anyway, but he was a dark-complexioned man and another person might not have seen the weariness on his face.

"I'm all right, Sheba. You look about the same. It's been a long day for you. Are you up to a walk?"

"Did you already find Mr. Chip?" I sent him a surprised look.

"Not exactly, but someone I know told me where to find him. She said he puts on something called a vaudeville show six nights a week."

"What kind of a show is a vaudeville show?" If I had heard the word before, I didn't recall it.

"I asked the same thing, but when she described the particulars to me, it sounded exactly like a variety show, just with a fancier name."

She. He had said it twice so I hadn't heard wrong. I couldn't help but wonder how and why John Bliss knew a woman in Ogallala, but of course that wasn't any of my business.

"But is it playing tonight? Potter canceled Perry's variety show out of respect for the President's death."

"Potter's a respectable community. Ogallala's not. The show's scheduled tonight. I saw a poster for it and got us a couple tickets."

We walked down the platform and stepped into the single broad street that ran south of the tracks. Ogallala, Nebraska, in all its rough and ready splendor, spread out before us. On both sides of the street were store-fronts with light and noise spilling out their windows and a stream of men coming and going out their doors.

At the sight, I stopped and said, "I heard Ogallala slowed down in the fall."

"Another two weeks and it will. The mild weather we've had made a difference, and word is there's a late herd of Longhorns coming in from Texas this week. No one'll risk missing out on that business."

Once we started walking again, John shifted casually to my other side so he was between me and the store fronts. A gentleman in his own way. Rules of proper conduct shared common elements, whether in Ogallala or Philadelphia, it seemed. We passed The Cowboy's Rest, the piano music jangling outside from its smoky interior not all that restful in my opinion, and stopped in front of a windowless place with lanterns hanging on each side of a front double-door and the name *The Poker Chip* painted on a sign that hung crookedly over the door. Tacked on a front wall was a poster with the words *Vaudeville Show Tonight* written so large and so dark that I could make them out from where I stood. Two men brushed past me and pulled open the door, allowing both light and noise to splash outside. One of the men turned around, saw me, stared a little too long, and backed up.

"Well, ma'am," he said, "if you'd like to see the show, I'd be happy to have you as my guest. I don't believe we've met." He was a skinny, balding, bow-legged fellow with an engaging grin. There was nothing threatening about him, and I smiled.

"That's kind of you, but we already have our tickets, thank you." Looking over my shoulder, I asked, "Don't we, John?"

The fellow caught sight of John behind me, gave him a look, swallowed, and said, "That's all right then. No disrespect meant."

"None taken," I replied, still smiling. "Have you seen the show before?"

"Oh, yes, ma'am. Yes, ma'am. I seen it many times, but I can't get enough of it. I'll be sorry as hell – beg your pardon – when Marty takes it on to Lincoln like he's talking. We ain't never seen the likes of Miss Delarose here in Ogallala. I swear, when she's Little Nell, the whole place gets to bawling like a baby."

"You live in Ogallala year-round, do you?"

"Yes, ma'am." His waiting companion said something in an impatient tone that I couldn't make out, and the man said, "We want to get a front row seat, but since you've got your tickets, why don't you just come in and find a chair, too? No use you having to wait for Marty's okay. He knows me well enough. Lord knows I'm here two or three times a week."

"That's very kind of you," I said. "We'll do that." He held the door open until John came around in front of me and placed one hand on the edge of the opened door.

"Obliged," John said. "I've got it now." He didn't raise his voice and there was nothing except cordiality in his tone, but the man swallowed noticeably once more before he nodded.

"Yes, sir. I hope you enjoy the show." He disappeared inside with his friend and John looked at me.

"Working your magic, Miss Fenway?"

"Terrorizing the natives, Mr. Bliss?" We grinned at each other before continuing inside.

The Poker Chip was nowhere near the size of New Hope's Entertainment Hall, and the rows of chairs were squeezed uncomfortably close together. John separated one chair from its row and motioned me to be seated.

"You're not having a seat?" I asked.

"I'll be right behind you. The wall looks more comfortable." I eyed the way the audience, now entering the place in significant numbers, sat crowded shoulder to shoulder and had to agree with him. Apparently, Marty Chip was not a man to sacrifice profit for comfort.

By then, I was more tired than I realized and was content to sit, wait, watch, and think. Mostly think. Is this the life my sister wants, I wondered. Did she know it would come to this, to rooms filled with the smells of smoke and unwashed bodies and cattle dung in towns no one had ever heard of? Did she care? I had picked the life I had in New Hope deliberately, knowing what I was getting into and willing to make whatever trade-off was involved for the freedom to do what I loved, but I didn't think it was the same for Dee. I ran willingly toward a dream and a passion, but thinking about the past, it seemed to me that Ruth might have been right about Dee when in my friend's usual wise and quiet way she had observed, *maybe all that running isn't towards something. Maybe she's running away from something.* Even if it wasn't that way at first, it surely was now with the threatening figure of Archie Sloan on her heels.

Marty Chip, owner of the establishment, stepped onto the makeshift stage, offered an extravagant welcome, and outlined what was in the evening's show. He mentioned some poems by name, included a sonnet or two by William Shakespeare, and ended with the announcement that Miss Florence Delarose would once more dramatize several scenes from the popular play *Uncle Tom's Cabin.* He tried to add that that particular performance was one of Miss Delarose's most requested presentations, but at the actress's name, the men began to whistle and stamp their feet so loudly that Chip's words were drowned out. Eventually, the room grew quiet with anticipation and Chip drew apart the crude curtain and there was Dee, dressed in something white, high-necked, and virginal, the very picture of sweet maidenhood as she stood and recited Charlotte Bronte's poem titled *Life.*

"'The day of trial bear,'" she ended, her hand over her heart, "'For gloriously, victoriously / Can courage quell despair!'" The audience loved it, loved her even more, and applauded wildly, but I turned to where John stood against the side wall. His gaze met mine and I nodded. She had dyed her hair black and wore it loose around her shoulders in girlish fashion, and the change in her appearance, that regression to sweet youthfulness, might have fooled someone who saw her from a distance and didn't know her as I did. But the actress Florence Delarose was definitely the actress Fannie Newell and how many other actresses, besides, I didn't know. Didn't care, either. All I knew and all I cared about was that the raven-haired woman now reciting the words of Elizabeth Barrett Browning from the crude stage of a rough place called The Poker Chip in a west-Nebraska cattle town was Delilah Fenway, my sister and Jem's mother, the firstborn child of a Philadelphia judge, a woman I had lost and found and lost and found again. If she was still running away from something, maybe I could help her stop, if that was what she wanted. All I wanted was the chance to try.

At the break, before the planned and highly anticipated concluding showcase from *Uncle Tom's Cabin*, I rose and made my way to John.

"I don't need to see the rest of the show," I told him. "Is there someplace we can talk?" He nodded, cupped my elbow in one palm, and guided me to the door.

"I wouldn't have recognized her," John said once we were outside.

"I know. I had to take a second and third look myself." We walked without further conversation until we reached the last building on the street. A small, graceful sign nailed to the wall next to the ornate front door read *Ogallala House.*

"They have a good dining room here that stays open late," John said, holding open the door and waiting for me to step inside. "You'll think better with something in your stomach."

His words made me realize how ravenous I was, the satisfaction of the chicken and dumplings I had enjoyed in Potter hours ago long gone. After we sat down, I surveyed the room, which was outfitted with linen covered tables, bright gas sconces, and several paintings on the walls.

John followed my look and said, "The quality of the food here doesn't need any improvement, but I can't say the same about the art work."

"You've become an expert on art now?" I asked, smiling.

"No. More an expert on the artist." I gave him a long look and he shrugged, smiling a little himself.

"Well, maybe not an expert exactly, not yet, anyway." We might have sparred a little more, both of us sensing that the friendship between us – if friendship was the right word – had begun to shift delicately and covertly into something else, something new, but a woman appeared at our table and interrupted the conversation. I looked up at her, expecting to see a woman ready to take our order, but with a closer look at her face, I knew this woman was no mere server.

At her presence, John stood and said, "Caroline," giving warmth to her name. *Caroline*, I thought. Well. She hadn't traveled so very far from New Hope, after all, the *she* of

John's Ogallala acquaintance identified.

"Hello, John," warmth in her tone, too, but I didn't think I heard anything more than warmth in either voice, not passion, not love. Of course, I'm no expert in either of those categories, and my hasty conclusion could have been far wide of the mark.

"You remember Sheba Fenway," John said to her and then to me, "Sheba, this is Caroline Moore. Caroline lived in New Hope for a time."

"Yes," I said, smiling at her and holding out a hand, "I remember, though I don't recall we were ever formally introduced. I was trying to get my shop established during those years, and I'm afraid I wasn't very sociable."

She took my hand, gave it a surprisingly firm shake, and said, "It's kind of you to remember me, Miss Fenway. I didn't stay in New Hope very long – a year maybe?" She looked at John for affirmation but he didn't respond. "And then I got an offer from Mr. Gast to run Ogallala House for him and I took it."

"Greener pastures," I said.

"You might say that," an ambiguous response. "It suits me and I can't complain. Sit down, John," she motioned him back into his chair. "Will you have the usual?" *The usual*, I thought. Well. How often did it take for something to become *the usual*? Not that it was any of my business, of course.

"That'll be fine." John looked at me. "They serve the best steaks east of Denver, Sheba."

I doubted it was the steaks that drew him to Ogallala but replied, "You've convinced me," and turning to Caroline Moore added, "I'll have whatever he has, thank you." She had watched the small exchange between John and me with interest.

"You won't regret it, Miss Fenway."

"Sheba, please." Caroline nodded at that and drifted away to another table to make conversation with the two well-dressed men eating there. She was a graceful woman, younger than I remembered; I'd guess not yet thirty. Warm brown eyes with black lashes, skin the color of cream, a coil of gleaming, dark brown hair at the back of her neck. Her high-collared dress gave her figure an appealing fullness. Graceful and attractive. Any man would find her appealing.

I followed Caroline's figure as she moved away, and when I turned back saw that John was watching me watch her. Did he expect me to comment about the woman, about her presence in Ogallala, ask how well they knew each other and how often they saw each other? If that's what the "expert" anticipated, I would have to disappoint him. I thought it likely I would bring up the topic sometime, but some *other* time, not tonight, when I had more serious matters on my mind.

Our meal came quickly, the sizzling fragrance of the steaks everything promised and then some. Eventually, having stuffed as much as I could possibly stuff into both mouth and stomach, I set down my fork and leaned back in my chair.

"Remind me to take your advice more often," I said and John smiled.

"Now that I've got your permission, believe me, I will. Are you ready to talk about your sister now?"

Brought back to reality, I nodded. "Yes. I need to talk to her, John. Do you know where she stays?"

"Chip's given her rooms on the second floor. Word has it that she doesn't socialize much, despite being the most popular person in Ogallala."

"No doubt she's trying to keep herself as hidden away as possible. Can I get up to the second floor of The Poker Chip without causing a fuss, do you think?"

"I have a better idea, thanks to Caroline. The Ogallala House sends a late supper over to your sister after every show, and Caro says they've become friends, of a sort."

Caro, I thought. Nicknames now.

"She said she could let her know you were here and that you wanted to talk to her."

"Maybe Dee won't see me if she's warned in advance that I'm here."

"She will if she doesn't know why you're here, if she thinks there's trouble about the boy."

I thought about it and finally nodded. "All right," I said. 'To tell you the truth, John, I doubt I'll be able to find the right words. I feel all out of ideas right at the moment."

"No wonder. You're tired and you've had a long day." The look he gave me had a touch of tenderness to it, something I wasn't used to. I felt my heart tighten in my chest at the sight. "But you've been worrying over this conversation ever since your sister left, and now's your chance to get the answers you want. If I know you, you'll figure out what to say. I've never known an obstacle you couldn't get the better of. You'll be all right."

The man's more of an expert than I gave him credit for, I thought, and said aloud, "I hope you're right. Miss Moore had a good idea. Should I—?"

"I'll take care of it. Just sit there a minute and catch your breath." I followed orders as he rose and disappeared through the doorway that led to the kitchen. John was right on two counts, at least: I was tired, and I was worrying over how to talk to Dee. I hoped he had the rest of it right, too.

Caroline Moore followed John back to the table where I sat and poured two cups of steaming coffee before she looked at me. "I'll take over something for Florence and when I see her, I'll tell her you're here and want to talk to her. Is that all right?"

"Tell her I need to talk to her," I said, stressing the word *need*. "Wherever she wants to meet but it has to be now. Tonight. Don't let her put you off." I heard how demanding my words sounded and added, "I appreciate that you're willing to get involved in my problem, Miss Moore. Thank you. I didn't mean to sound bossy." I gave a rueful smile. "It's one of my many bad habits, I'm afraid, and I hope you'll pardon me if I came off sounding less than grateful."

She didn't bother to argue my bossiness, which raised her in my estimation, only replied, "We can all get a little bossy when we're tired and worried. You and John wait here until I get back. I asked Susie to bring you a plate of our special pecan cookies to go with the coffee. On the house."

After she left, I said, "She's a nice lady."

"She is." He looked like he was going to say more but took a sip of coffee instead, and then a girl, Susie I assumed, delivered a plate heaped with large, soft cookies and neither John nor I said anything else for several minutes.

Finally, I sat back and said, "Slap my hand with that fork if I reach for one more cookie. My goodness, you'd think I had never seen one before."

"Maybe you ought to try painting one. It would be just the thing to hang on the wall at the Nebraska Café. Increase everybody's appetite."

That made me laugh and for the next few minutes, until Caroline Moore returned and sat down at the table with us, John and I enjoyed the easy banter that had been common to us for the past few years. He was a man who knew what it took to make me laugh, and never at another's expense. He had a knack for making me see and laugh at my own foolishness, instead. The kind of thing one good friend does for another to help her keep her feet on the ground. A rare and valuable attribute. At Caroline's approach, I stopped mid-word and turned toward her, waiting until she sat down, waiting to hear what message – if any – she brought.

"Meet her in ten minutes in the alley next to The Poker Chip. There's a side door. She said she'll wait for you there."

"All right," relief obvious in my voice. "I didn't know what to expect. Thank you."

Caroline nodded and rose. "You're welcome." She examined my face a long moment. "Now that I know you're sisters, I can see the resemblance."

"Even with the black hair?"

"Oh, it's nothing to do with the hair. It's something else I can't quite put my finger on, but there's a likeness for sure. Maybe more in attitude than looks." She shrugged and said to John, "It was good to see you again, John. Don't be a stranger."

He stood at her words. "Good to see you, too, Caro. Thanks for your help here. You'll let me know if you need anything."

"I will." They exchanged smiles. "But the Gasts are very good to me, and I like it here well enough."

"That's good to know, but my offer stands."

"I know it does," and with a final smile and nod in my direction, she walked away. I wondered what there was about Ogallala House and Mr. Gast that made her prefer them to John Bliss and his establishments. Lovers' tiff? And yet neither of them acted like there was a falling out between them.

I banished my curiosity – not permanently, I knew, but for the time being – and stood up, slinging my bag over my shoulder the way a soldier off to the wars would do, which wasn't that far from the situation when I thought about it.

"You can enjoy another cup of coffee while I'm gone, if you want, John. I doubt Dee is going to give me much of her time, but there's no use you—"

John shook his head. "It's probably better if you don't wander around Ogallala by yourself this late. We aren't in Lincoln County, and there's no Si Carpenter to keep the peace."

The two well-dressed men at the neighboring table opened the door of the restaurant and stepped outside, letting in the sound of loud and furious voices raised in argument somewhere out in the street.

"I guess not," I said. "I'll appreciate the company."

John grabbed his hat from one of the hooks on the wall and we stepped outside into a pleasantly cool night. Another month and we'd have wool blankets piled on our beds, but tonight was more late summer than early fall. A sliver of moon showed in the cloudless heavens, and there were stars everywhere, scattered in the dark ocean of sky the way a child might fling a handful of pebbles into a pond. The furious argument I had heard was fading as the men involved staggered east, their voices hardly intelligible. Politics? A woman? Money? Whatever the cause of the argument, either one or both of the men seemed to be losing interest.

A part of me was apprehensive about the coming conversation, but another part of me found walking with John Bliss by my side both comforting and reassuring. A new sensation for a woman who made her own decisions and treasured her privacy, who went where she wanted on her own and without a by-your-leave to anyone. Independence, I thought, shared a kinship with loneliness. That was a new idea for me, too. I remembered how at first, I had resented sharing my home with my sister, had disliked the cramped space and sleeping in a chair. Now here I was, after a long day of playing hide-and-seek, getting ready to invite her to come back to New Hope and move back into my little home. Surely the Fenway sisters could handle the likes of Archie Sloan. And there was Jem. We both loved him, the same way we had both loved his namesake. John and I stopped where the alley joined the street.

"I'll wait here," John said. "Will you be all right?"

"Yes." I stepped into the alley, looking for the side door Caroline Moore had mentioned, and went only a few steps before a slim, shadowy figure stepped from the doorway into view. Delilah. My eyes had adjusted to the night, but it was still hard to make out the distinct details of her face.

Without a greeting, my sister hurried forward and asked, "What is it? Is it Jem? Has something happened?" in a strained voice. Too dim to tell if she looked her age, but for that moment she certainly sounded it.

"Jem's safe enough for the time being. I left him at Ruth's." I sensed more than saw her shoulders slump from relief.

"You scared the hell out of me, Sheba. What are you doing here?" Then, considering my words, she added, "What do you mean *for the time being*?"

"I know the telegram you got in New Hope was from Perry Alice telling you there was a man looking for you, and that's why you left in such a hurry. Well, that man turned up in New Hope. He calls himself Archie Sloan, and he asks about you. A lot. Now he's started saying things about Jem, about where he plays and where he goes to school and wouldn't it be a shame if something happened to him. I don't like him, Dee. He's dangerous. He told me you had something that belonged to him. Is that why he's looking for you?"

My sister stood still as a statue as I talked, taking it all in, and I didn't expect her to answer my question. Dee had grown into a woman of shadows and secrets, but she surprised me with a ready answer.

"Yes."

"What did you do to set that man on your trail? Is he Jem's father? Jem favors him, I think."

"Archie Sloan?" The disgusted outrage in her tone answered the question. "No, never. How could you even ask such a thing? A man like that! But he had a brother, Cole," Dee's voice softened on the name, "and while Archie and Cole spent a lot of time together, they were different as night and day, as different as you and I, Sheba. Cole's the one I picked. We were married in Kansas City."

"Married."

"I'm sorry to spoil the picture you've built up of my prodigal past, but yes, married. Happy, too, for the little time we had. When I ran, I was still Fannie Newell to Archie and I needed to leave the Sloan name behind, so it made sense to make Jem a Fenway. He was just a baby. What difference would it make to him?" She shifted on her feet.

Another Jem Fenway, I wondered, to make up for losing the first Jem, for not saying a proper good bye?

"Cole Sloan wasn't perfect, Sheba. He liked to take risks and like Archie, he wasn't above breaking the law, but he had a heart and he cared for me. It was Archie who was the bad one. He was so jealous of his brother, and Cole could never see it. After Cole died, when I told Archie I planned to leave, he wouldn't let me go. He said it was because I knew too much about what he and Cole had been up to, but there was more to it. I think that even after Cole was dead, Archie needed to prove something. He told me I wasn't going anywhere and then used his fists to make sure I understood. So one day when Archie was gone, up to his usual dirty business, I grabbed Jem, a tin box full of cash, and left. No warning. No questions. No good-byes. I just left. Did he think I'd let him treat me like that? If he ever laid a hand on Jem, I knew I'd have to kill him, so it was better all around if I disappeared."

"Sloan didn't see it that way, though, did he?"

"No. He's like a dog – a mad dog – with a bone. Not a man to be bettered, especially by a woman."

"Have you been running ever since, Dee?"

"Not exactly. It wasn't long after I left that Archie ended up in a Kansas prison for hurting a man over cards in Wichita, and life was all right for a while, but a few months ago I heard he got out, and I knew he'd come looking for me. He'll never forget that money."

I digested everything my sister said, everything she didn't say, too. "Do you still have that money? Where is it?"

"Why does it matter?"

"Because you could give it to Sloan and then we'd be done with him. He'd go away and leave you, leave Jem, alone."

"It's my money now, Sheba. I've got plans for it."

"It's not your money. You stole it."

"Well, so did Archie Sloan, and the way I look at it, it's finders keepers."

"You'd let a man like that threaten your son because you want to keep money that doesn't belong to you? How much money are we talking about?"

"Ten thousand dollars." The words hung in the air between us. A fortune. My mouth must have dropped. "Two railroad payrolls and a north Kansas bank. Ten thousand dollars, Sheba. Enough for Jem to have the best education in the finest universities in the world. In the *world.* No backwater education, no scrounging for a living. He'll never want for anything, not ever. I swear my son will have that money, every cent of it, when he's old enough to appreciate it. I won't have it otherwise."

I stared, unable to make out all the details of her face but hearing in her voice all I needed to know. There was no compromise in Delilah Fenway. There never had been, as far back as I could remember.

"So you'll risk Jem's life now for his future later."

"Archie Sloan isn't a fool. He won't hurt Jem as long as Si Carpenter is keeping the peace in New Hope. It's me he wants. I don't know how you managed to find me, Sheba, but it can't be helped now, I guess. You just keep telling Archie that you don't know where I am, and in a couple of weeks I'll be gone and you'll be telling the truth."

"Gone?" Not returning with me, I thought with a sinking heart, not moving back into my little home, not crowding around the old kitchen table, no dramatic lines from *King Lear* disturbing my work day. How could I feel such sharp disappointment for something that I had never desired?

"Gone." She reached for the handle of the side door. "I'm tired, Sheba. Go back to New Hope. Keep telling Sloan you don't know anything. Tell Carpenter – no, tell John Bliss – that you've got suspicions about Sloan. There's no way Bliss will let anything hurt you." Dee gave a little laugh when I started to protest. "Good lord, Sheba. What's the matter with you? Too much time spent behind your easel and not enough with the people around you I'd say. That man loves you. It was clear the first time I saw the two of you together. And from what Caroline says, he knows how to take care of his own. I may circle around to New Hope once in a while, but with you and John Bliss and Si Carpenter and everybody in that nice little town of yours watching out for Jem, he'll be safe enough." She was gone then, the door closing behind her and no more of a farewell than there had been a greeting.

I stood motionless a long moment, long enough for John to get worried, I guess, because I heard his steps behind me in the alley.

"Sheba."

I turned toward him. “I’m all right.” He didn’t ask more and I didn’t volunteer anything just then. “I think I’d like to go home now,” I said and repeated, “I’d like to go home.”

“The train won’t be here ‘til the morning, and I’m not in charge of the schedules.”

I smiled at that. “I know. I thought we could find something at the livery, not wait for the train, and leave for New Hope right now.”

“It’s almost midnight, and it’ll be a cold, long trip. Going cross-country, we might beat the train, but not by much.”

“I know it’s a lot to ask, but I don’t recall that I’ve ever asked anything from you before, anything personal, that is, so maybe you can live with one request every five years.”

“Can you live with it, is more the question.” I heard a smile in his voice.

“I’ll have to,” I said, “because I’m asking you if you’ll take me home now, home to New Hope, not wait for the train but leave now. I can’t do it by myself.”

He must have heard something in my voice, something new for both of us – humility? need? – because I think he was startled. Then he pulled me into his arms and held me tight against his chest. I could feel his heartbeat. With a soft voice against my hair, he said, “I’ll do whatever you ask, Sheba, whatever you want.” He kissed me, hard, then pushed me away enough to lay a hand on my shoulder and turn me toward the alley’s entry. “The sooner we start, the sooner we’re home.”

I couldn’t argue with that, so I tucked my hand under his arm and let him lead me back into the street and down toward the train station where the livery was situated. He had to roust out a boy sleeping in the loft to hitch up a wagon for us, all the boy had available at the time, but before I knew it, we were on the road headed east, me perched on the hard wagon seat next to John Bliss and John’s horse tied up behind clip-clopping right along with us.

Sheba, I thought to myself, you’ve got this man next to you and what are you going to do with him? I truly had no idea. At that moment, I didn't know much of anything except that I wanted to see Jem's little face and have a long talk with Ruth and watch the sun come up over New Hope, dip my brush in paint, and try to catch the way morning light sparked gold off the changing leaves of the cottonwood trees. I was comfortable, the sliver of moon enough to show the road and the night very, very quiet. I took hold of John's arm, pulled myself closer to him, and laid my head against his shoulder. I felt him rearrange himself to give me a little more support. I'd figure out what to do with John Bliss later. Between the two of us, we were sure to come to a conclusion of some kind, but for the time being, he was the closest thing I had to a pillow. Despite the rough road and the hard wagon seat, the cool night air that had suddenly taken a turn toward winter and my ungainly posture holding on to John's arm with both hands, I felt something almost like contentment. Safe with John Bliss and happy to be going home, I fell fitfully asleep.

10

We stopped once, a quick, moonlit pause to murmur a few inconsequential words and take care of necessities before continuing toward New Hope. I stayed alert for a while afterwards lost in thought and then dozed again, never losing hold of the man next to me. When I awoke in earnest, I straightened and stretched the cramps out of my back and shoulders. John turned to look at me when he felt my grasp on him slacken.

"I was going to wake you," he said. "I didn't think you'd want to miss that." With both hands firm on the reins, he had to lift his chin at the sunrise that lay before us, a lovely scene with streaks of red and rose that made me think of a campfire's flames.

I watched it for a while before saying, "I believe a storm might be in our future."

For some reason my words made him laugh out loud, but his only response to my suspicious look was an easy, "I wouldn't be at all surprised."

I would have pursued the matter except I saw the lines of weariness on his face and hadn't the heart to say anything but, "You've had a long night, John Bliss, and I owe you for everything you did. I don't have more words than thank you, so – thank you." I said the two words with sober firmness, rested one palm briefly against his cheek, and said thank you again, only softer, adding, "I'll never be able to repay you."

He swallowed before he spoke, a man of cool pride who for one quick moment looked neither cool nor proud, and then tried to regain his composure with the words, "Isn't that what friends are for?"

I shook my head. "Oh, *friends*! Is that what you think, John? An intelligent man like yourself? How is that possible?" With deliberate care, I mimicked his tone and his words to me from yesterday afternoon and knew he recalled the moment because his cheeks gained color. His complexion made it hard to tell, but I knew what I saw and was satisfied with the results of my gratitude and my teasing. Something to add to the list of conversational items we would get to someday, right under the name *Caroline Moore*. I hadn't volunteered any information about Delilah, either, and he deserved to know her story, too, but all of that would have to come later.

We came into New Hope following the train tracks, passed the train station, and pulled up in front of Cap Sherman's livery and smithy. The double doors were open and John hopped down from the wagon, took a long, leisurely stretch – for the first time in the years I'd known him I noticed, really noticed, what a strongly built man he was, how his shoulders filled out his coat, how little effort it took for him to swing himself down from the seat – and walked inside the stable, returning with old Cap. I can take or leave Cap Sherman, but most people who know him would rather do the latter because he's a cantankerous, judgmental know-it-all. There's no way around that fact, but because the good people of New Hope accepted me as I was, I always felt it was my duty to do the same with others, even someone as difficult to be around as Cap Sherman.

Cap shot a look at me where I sat on the wagon seat, and I dared him to say something, anything, but with John standing within arm's reach, the old man just gave a shrug and a twist to his mouth. I could almost hear the words he was thinking - *shameless woman* - but while he might have the worst temper in

New Hope, he doesn't lack for brains.

"Make sure you brush all three of them down well. Keep 'em warm for a while, too. It was a cold trip. Then give them an extra measure of oats. There'll be somebody on the evening train to take the team off your hands." John ran a hand down the withers of his own mount, a handsome gray animal with a white blaze on his forehead that John called Caesar, and then counted out money into Cap's outstretched hands. "That should cover everything."

"I don't need you to tell me my business, Bliss," was Cap's gracious reply. Because all the regular citizens of New Hope had learned to ignore the old man's foul temperament, John came around to my side of the wagon, reached up for me, and lifted me down without further comment to Sherman, it being the wise choice to ignore the little irritations of life that will never change no matter what.

We walked south down Main Street toward our respective homes and stopped in front of Bliss House.

"Well," I said to him, "yesterday was an adventure I hope not to repeat in the near future. You don't have to walk me any farther. I'll stop home for a moment and then go over to Ruth's to get Jem. You look like a man who's been on the road all night."

"I had good company so it wasn't that bad."

"Good company," I repeated with an unbecoming snort, "who slept the whole way. Don't make me laugh. I know I owe you an explanation of my conversation with my sister, but that will have to wait."

"You don't owe me anything, Sheba, but if you're feeling particularly obliged, I could use something for the wall behind the check-in desk, something that shows New Hope in the best light."

He made the little play-on-words without cracking a smile until I said, "Sometimes you're too clever for your own good, John Bliss, but be that as it may, I imagine I can find something to suit your fancy."

"I imagine you can," he responded, and I didn't think he

was talking only about paintings for his hotel. "I'll watch until you get to the dress shop."

"This isn't Ogallala. We're back in New Hope now. I can walk to my own establishment without a threat of danger."

"Maybe. Maybe not. I don't think this story is over."

This story, I thought. Did he mean the story about an unrepentant woman on the run with a fortune she stole from a thief? Or the story of him and me and a future I couldn't picture, no matter how many Nebraska mornings I painted? Not that it mattered because whichever story he meant, he was probably right.

"I don't either, John. I'll talk to you later."

When I opened the door of the dress shop, I turned back to look down the street toward Bliss House and give a brief wave, which I didn't think John could see for the distance between us. Maybe the man had better eyesight than I gave him credit for, however, because only after my casual wave did his still, dark-suited figure disappear into the hotel.

I took enough time to grind beans and bring water to a quick boil for a cup of coffee before I walked to Hart's. By then, I had heard the whistle from the first train of the morning and New Hope had begun its day. A trickle of people made their way to the neighboring Nebraska Café, Tom Danford waved a hand in greeting from across the street as he opened his drug store, and the shade on the bank door was up indicating that as usual Abner Talamine was already seated behind his desk doing whatever it was bank presidents do. Everything was comfortingly familiar. Unlike Ogallala, New Hope quieted at night and burst into energy in the morning, acting the way a town should act. Then I had to laugh at myself, at how respectable, how mundane I had become. Me, Sheba Fenway, rebellious artist and independent woman. A stick-in-the-mud before I was thirty.

Still smiling at my thoughts, I entered the foyer of Hart's, took a sidelong look at the wall where Ruth had hung the painting of the Platte River I gave her years ago, walked as far as the large butler's desk on which the boarding house's customer book rested, and stopped. From the Addition, the rooms off the back hallway where the Carpenters lived, I heard a baby crying halfheartedly, complaining about something but not with any real outrage, just trying out his lungs to make sure they still worked. It didn't sound like the best time to interrupt my friend, so I turned back to sit down in one of the comfortable foyer chairs. I had thought the jingle of the bell on the front door had been drowned out by the baby's crying, but I was wrong.

"Good morning, Sheba." Without my hearing him, Si Carpenter had come down the hallway and now stood beside my chair. "Is everything all right?"

I stood to face him. "Yes. I just came to collect Jem. Thank you for keeping him for the night."

Silas Carpenter, the sheriff in charge of law enforcement for Lincoln County, is a lean man of average size, gray eyes, and dark hair with a touch of silver beginning to show at his temples. At first sight, there is not one thing that sets my friend's husband apart from any other man of similar build and color, and yet just his name is enough to quiet a disturbance or calm a man yearning for a fight. Si carries an authority about him that is recognizable without words and without the badge he has been known to leave at home on purpose. Of all the mistakes a person might make with Si, the greatest one – and perhaps the last one – would be to underestimate him. I know of at least one occasion when that happened, and the man who made the error is no longer with us.

"I'm not due any thanks. I just got home late last night myself."

"That's right, Ruth said there was another robbery around Brady Island. Any luck?"

He gave a slow, thoughtful shake of his head. "No. I'm beginning to think there's something other than bank and train thievery going on. It doesn't feel right." I must have looked puzzled because he shrugged. "Just me thinking, Sheba." He allowed himself a small smile. "Sometimes that's as dangerous as chasing bank robbers. Ruth mentioned you didn't like this Archie Sloan hanging around. Does he bother you?" Does it snow in winter, I asked myself.

"Not bother, exactly," I replied, "but he thinks I know where my sister is and pesters me about it once in a while."

"You want me to talk to him?"

"No," a quick answer because now that Dee was in possession of stolen money, having the law involved didn't seem quite as desirable as it once had. "He's never been disrespectful, just insistent." The baby's cries from the back of the house got louder. "I guess I could say the same thing about your son: not disrespectful but insistent."

"He's a boy with pronounced opinions."

Si Carpenter never seemed more human, more a man like other men, than when he talked of his wife. Saying her name changed the tone of his voice. Seeing Ruth across a room or across a street, for that matter, softened the lines that time and weather and hard-living had etched into his face. Now I saw it was the same for the new baby. The effect that love has on a person, I thought, isn't always handsprings and sonnets and love songs at the moon. Sometimes it's just a momentary look on a man's face.

Si walked to the coat tree behind the door and grabbed his hat. "Go on back, Sheba. Ruth's in the kitchen, and I heard Jem stirring a while ago so I imagine he's up by now. You let me know if there's anything I can do for you."

"I will." He nodded and stepped outside, closing the door behind him.

Ruth looked over at me when I entered the kitchen. It was quite the tableau. Jem was seated at the table with Othello next to his chair and both stared fixedly at Ruth, who stood by the stove using a large fork to move something that sizzled and smelled delectable around in a frying pan. Baby Alex lay in a cradle on the other side of Jem's chair, flailing his little fists and fussing. It seemed the lure of bacon started at a young age.

"Good morning," I said.

Jem turned his head toward me long enough to say, "Hello, Aunt Sheba," before returning his gaze to where Ruth stood at the stove. The moment lasted all of two seconds. I wouldn't have been surprised if the boy had followed up his greeting with the question, were you gone somewhere?

Ruth grinned, looking a little tired but still cheeky, despite a new baby that hadn't managed more than four consecutive hours of sleep since the day he came into the world.

"Yes, hello, Sheba. The bacon variety show is about to start. Why don't you sit down and join us? There's plenty for everyone, which you can tell from the blissful look on Othello's face." She stopped long enough to set an empty plate on the table in front of me.

"Not just Othello's face," I replied, pulling out a chair, "and I don't mind if I do."

"Did you just get off the early train?"

"Not exactly."

"Oh?"

"John Bliss caught up with me in Potter – which he says he found out about from you – and we came home from Ogallala last night in a borrowed wagon."

To her credit, the only reaction my friend made to my explanation was to repeat, "John Bliss. Ogallala. Wagon," and then add, "I see." She brought the skillet to the table and pushed eggs and bacon onto Jem's and my plates, then dropped two pieces of bacon onto a plate by the door for the dog. Alexander's racket had subsided because he was gnawing away at his little fist that had found its way into his mouth. Ruth peered down at him and said, "You, young man, will have your breakfast in just a few minutes."

Because she is a woman of excellent timing, Ruth didn't ask any questions of me, just set a pot of fresh coffee in the middle of the table and sat down at the table, too. Jem and I, alike in our appreciation for a hot breakfast highlighted with crisp bacon, ate without speaking until I looked up at Ruth.

"You're not having anything?" I asked.

"Oh, I'll get there, but it was too entertaining watching

you and Jem attack those eggs."

I wiped my mouth on a napkin and tried for some dignity but guessed it was too late for that.

"A woman can be forgiven for indulging in a hearty breakfast if she just spent yesterday and all of last night on the road."

"Where'd you go, Aunt Sheba?" Jem had stood, ready to gather and carry his used dishes over to the sink but stopped at my words.

I didn't hesitate. "You remember. I told you I was going to visit a friend in Potter."

"Then why were you in Ogallala?"

"To visit another friend."

"Oh." Jem's forehead furrowed as if the idea of me having more than one friend was a knotty puzzle he had to work out, but eventually he shrugged and finished clearing his side of the table.

I stood and followed his example before saying, "I put your lunch on the kitchen table at home. Go home and wash your face and hands, and then you and your lunch should get to school."

Jem's face lit up. "Aunt Sheba, do you know that Mr. Thomas Edison has invented something called an incandescent bulb that gives off light from electricity?" His excitement at the idea gave off its own kind of luminescence.

"I may have read something about it," I replied.

"Mr. Stenton says we're coming to a time when everyone in the country will use electricity and bulbs, and no one will need lanterns or gas lamps any more. He says Mr. Edison's bulb is going to change everything."

"If Mr. Stenton says it, then it must be so," I said. "Now off with you. Wash your face and hands, get your lunch pail, go to school. In that order. What do you say to Mrs. Carpenter?"

Jem turned toward Ruth. "That was very fine bacon," he said soberly.

Both Ruth and I let out little explosions of laughter at the words; I recovered first.

"Bacon aside, what else do you have to say to Mrs. Carpenter?"

"Thank you, Mrs. Carpenter, for letting me stay at your house and for letting Othello sleep on my bed." At the sound of his name, Othello's tail thumped once against the floor and he pushed himself to his feet. At the sight of his gray muzzle, I felt a little pang. Jem set such store by the dog, and Othello was getting old. When he passes, it would be an awful grief for a little boy. This is love, too, I thought, this desire to spare another person heartache.

Jem set the last of the dishes by the sink pump and with Othello following close behind, the two went into the hallway. Ruth and I heard the back-door slam shut.

"You never let Othello sleep in the house when Danny was here," I pointed out.

Ruth smiled, but there was sadness on her face, too. "Well, that was then and this is now. Danny's all grown up and in the army, and Othello and I both miss him. Poor dog needed a boy to sleep with. Blankets can be washed easy enough, but loneliness—well, it takes more than soap and water to get rid of that." Ruth knew about loneliness, of course, knew what it was like to love and lose and grieve. She loved Si Carpenter deeply, but that didn't always soften the memory of the heartache she'd felt when her first husband died young of consumption. Light and darkness, love and grief can live side by side in a person's heart, Ruth had once told me. The words made more sense to me now than they had at the time.

"I have a work day to get to," I said, "and you have a hungry baby. I'll tell you about my trip later."

"Can you at least tell me if you found Delilah?"

"I did find her."

"But she didn't come back with you."

"No."

"She must have her reasons."

"Delilah always has her reasons." I couldn't hide the little twist of bitterness in my voice and was tempted to sit right back down at the table and tell Ruth the whole story start to finish. But the baby began to fuss again, this time in earnest – I could hear the difference in his cry – and I said, "Thank you, Ruth, for watching Jem. I appreciated it more than you know. I'll talk to you later."

I greeted Lizbeth as we passed each other at the front door of the boarding house and on the walk home gave weighty thought to the conversation I had just had with my dear friend. It made me uncomfortable and a little sad to realize that no matter how much I might want to, I was not going to tell Ruth everything about yesterday's quest. She was married to the county sheriff, the man in charge of law and order throughout all of Lincoln County and who took his responsibilities seriously. My sister holding onto stolen money wasn't anything to bring to Si Carpenter's attention, and if I told Ruth about it, there was no way she could keep it from him even if she tried, not with that open face of hers. The knowledge that I had my own secrets and shadows I intended to keep from my best friend made me sigh. Life had been much less complicated when all I needed was morning light to make me happy.

The day started off busy and stayed that way until I closed the shop in the late afternoon. Miss just one day, I thought with a grumble, and you ended up doubling your work for the whole week. Then I had to laugh at my complaining because for the first year or two I had been so desperate for customers that I had contemplated parading up and down Main Street with an enormous placard on my back, and here I was unhappy about having more business than I knew what to do with. Isn't that just the way human beings go through life, I thought, always wanting what they don't have and then complaining when they get it, whatever "it" happens to be.

Jem came home from school enthused about yet another invention Mr. Stenton had shared. "Moving pictures," Jem announced, shaking his head with wonder. "Imagine that, Aunt Sheba. You look at a picture and it moves while you sit still." Like looking at you, I thought, feeling such a rush of affection for the child that I had to force myself not to give him a hug. I had learned over time that while Jem tolerated hugs, he did not especially enjoy them.

"Boys are like that," Ruth told me when I mentioned my discovery. "Don't take it to heart."

I replied that, of course, I didn't take it to heart. We both knew that wasn't completely true, but I didn't want to be the kind of aunt that pinched little boys' cheeks and supposed that from a child's viewpoint hugging fell into the same category.

The storm I had seen on the horizon as John and I approached New Hope hit with a vengeance during the night, bringing thunder and lightning and torrents of rain. I woke at the racket and when I looked down at the mattress next to my bed, saw Jem in the dim light, sitting with his arms hugging his knees.

"It's just a thunderstorm," I told him. I could tell that he turned his face toward me and imagined the serious look in his dark eyes. Did being comforted fall into the same category as cheek pinching and hugs? He was still a little boy.

"I know," he said, then, "If Othello was here, I'd feel a lot better." Something else not to take personally.

"How about some hot chocolate?"

"It's the middle of the night."

"The middle of a stormy night," I corrected, "and that calls for something out of the ordinary, don't you think?"

In the kitchen, I added sugar and chocolate shavings to milk I heated on the stove and poured both of us a small cupful. We were quiet as the crashes and snaps outside slowly diminished.

"It will be cold tomorrow," I said. "You can hear the wind blowing summer away."

Jem tilted his head to listen and then nodded. Out of nowhere, he said, "I hope Mama's dry and warm tonight." His voice, trying hard to be grown up, was wistful enough to twist my heart.

"I'm sure she is." I gave a brief thought to telling him that

I had seen his mother and she had been perfectly well, but Archie Sloan came to mind and then the knowledge that Dee was complicit in several major and unresolved robberies so I was quiet. I rose and picked up the empty cups.

"Back to bed now," I told him. At the doorway to his bedroom, I rested a hand briefly on the top of his head. "Your mama really is safe and warm, Jem. I guarantee it."

"Yes, I suspect she is," he replied. "She knows how to take care of herself." An odd turn of phrase from a little boy, but not one with which I could disagree.

With forethought, I had sewn a respectable winter coat for Jem, suede with a wool collar and wool cuffs that could be pulled down over his hands for warmth. He examined it with care and then pronounced it fine. Manly enough to wear without fear of being mocked, he meant, and I was relieved it passed inspection. I had once proposed he use a lunch bag I made for him of bright blue felt but at his look of horror, I immediately transferred his sandwich and apple back to the empty lard pail he and all the other boys favored. Children seemed destined to remain a mystery.

Othello met Jem at the back-door and together the two of them sloshed their way – happily sloshed their way, it looked to me – through the fresh mud toward the schoolhouse. I gave the canvases stacked against the walls in my back room a longing look, but I had to catch up with the work my trip to Potter had delayed. The back room of my little house was as close to a working art studio as I would ever have. Harold Sellers had installed two small glass windows that met at the southwest corner of the room. Hardly ideal when it was eastern light I favored, but it couldn't be helped, and in the end, any natural light was better than none at all. I had four finished pictures, one of the church steeple against a sunrise that I especially favored and two more pictures I had started but wouldn't be able to finish as they were. Rework was called for, and a lot of it. Why those two were wrong, it would have been hard for me to explain; they just didn't work, and I would have burned them before allowing them out of my sight. But the church painting – I paused in front of it – was very good, the rising sun creating an aureole of light behind the cross and the splashes of orange and rose spreading across the sky a subtle promise of something bright and hopeful. This is the one I'll give to John, I thought. He'll appreciate the feeling behind it, and the idea of the church hanging on his wall made me smile, besides. It's not like it would hang in a beer garden, after all. A hotel is perfectly respectable, even if it shared a wall with a music hall of more doubtful repute.

I stopped for a little lunch that day, Wednesday, and carried my jam and bread from the kitchen with me into the shop when I heard the bell announce a customer. So much for the word *closed* hanging on the door.

"Hello, Sheba." Bert Gruber stood just inside, holding his signature bowler hat in both hands.

"Hello, Bert." I popped the last bit of bread into my mouth. When he made no move to speak, I asked, "I hope everything's going well with you, Bert. I haven't talked to you in a while." He nodded the way a person nods when he isn't really listening.

"I seen you get on the train Monday morning, Sheba, and I don't know why I thought it, but I said to myself, Sheba's off to find Fannie. Was I right?"

"Her name's Delilah, Bert, and she is my sister. I was worried about her." A cautious response that didn't answer his question.

He examined me with a gravity that made the short, rotund, sometimes foolish man seem suddenly dignified and wise.

"There were a lot of years you didn't worry about her, though, weren't there? A lot of years nobody worried about her or cared about her at all."

The words were true enough that I bit back a sharp retort about it being none of his business, something I would have done by instinct and without apology only a few months ago.

"Yes, I think that's true," I said at last. "We went our own ways, and we both got lost in the process. But now it seems my sister wants to stay lost, and that's something I can't do a thing about."

"You found her in Ogallala, didn't you?"

"Did you know she was there all along?" answering his question with a question of my own. Let him hear how outraged I felt. That Dee should share her whereabouts with this man, someone almost a stranger to her, a man who didn't even call her by her given name, yet not let her own sister and son know where she was stirred up familiar feelings of disappointment and annoyance.

"I make it a point to keep track of her. I love her." I felt the prick of meaning behind his words. People keep track of the people they love. What did it mean that I had walked away without a backward glance or passing thought to my only sister?

I don't think Bert meant the words as chastisement, however, because he spoke them without a trace of self-consciousness, the way he might say, it rained last night or, we're holding a Merchants' Association meeting tomorrow. I didn't know what to say in response.

"That sounds laughable, I guess, a man like me and a woman like Fannie Newell—" He caught my look and shrugged. "I know she's Delilah Fenway to you, but she'll always be Fannie Newell to me. That's the way it is, Sheba."

"I can see the way it is, Bert," I said, but gently. Who was I to say who was allowed to love another person?

"Then you can see I'll never betray her, never put her in danger."

I knew from his words that while I had to go in search of my sister and practically pry her past out of her, she had told Bert Gruber everything. Was that what they talked about on their evening promenades, her hand tucked under his arm and her head lowered so that only he could hear her words?

If I have to bite my tongue one more time, I thought, I'll draw blood but said meekly, "I appreciate knowing that, Bert, and I know Dee must appreciate it, too. Are you asking if I feel the same?"

"You can't trust Archie Sloan, Sheba. You can't tell him anything."

"I agree. I don't trust Archie Sloan, and I won't tell him anything. I promise."

My promise seemed to offer Bert small comfort. "That's good, because he's a bad man, a very bad man. He hurt her before, and he'll do it again. She had to run, don't you see?"

"No," I said. "I don't see. If she'd give that bad man what he wants, she wouldn't have to run, wouldn't have to leave Jem behind without reason or explanation." The memory of the child's voice when he said, "I hope Mama's dry and warm tonight" sharpened my tone.

Bert put on his hat, his face thoughtful. "I admit she has a blind spot about that little boy. She loves him so much she can't reason about him, but she sure loves him, Sheba. You know that."

I did know that, and knew Bert was right about Dee not being able to think sensibly about her son, as well – for a lot of reasons, love being one of them, but also because one Jem she had loved was cheated out of a bright and promising future and the first Jem's sister was not going to allow history to repeat itself with the second Jem.

"Her secret's safe with me, Bert, and you can tell her so. Will you know when she leaves Ogallala?"

"She promised she wouldn't go anywhere without letting me know. Fannie knows love when she sees it; she knows I love her."

The dignity of his last words touched me. I will never see Bert Gruber with the same eyes again, I realized, no longer a plump, sometimes ridiculous little man who owned a barely reputable hotel and billiards hall. That Bert Gruber was gone, and in his place stood a stalwart champion. I hoped my sister appreciated what it was Bert offered her. More than love, although that certainly had its worth, but devotion, faithfulness, kindness, and acceptance. If Dee had any sense at all, she would not risk losing such rare and generous gifts.

11

Rain returned by the end of that day and continued on and off through the next day, as well, the weather keeping me inside but too reflective about my recent trip to Potter to be cranky about it. I woke early on Thursday and worked on a half-finished painting I thought held some promise, then spent the rest of the day sewing until my eyes squinted without any effort on my part and my shoulders ached from strain.

Leaving Jem at the kitchen table working on a science report for Mr. Stenton about how a thorough downpour could have both helpful and damaging effects – not just science, I determined, but an exercise in logic and rational thought as well; Mr. Stenton was a shrewd teacher – I threw a shawl over my head to protect against the remaining cold drizzle and hurried down the boardwalk to Hart's. A talk with Ruth was long overdue.

"So you couldn't convince Delilah to come back with you to New Hope."

I hadn't told Ruth many of the details of Ogallala, only that Dee had found temporary work there that seemed to suit her. Ruth took everything I said at face value, but we've been friends several years so I'm sure she realized there was more to the story than what I shared. Instead of trying to pry out more details, however, she only stated the obvious and poured us both a second cup of tea. Silas was out on his evening rounds through New Hope and baby Alex was sleeping with fits and starts in his cradle.

"No," I answered.

"That's odd, in a way, don't you think? With her son here, and you, and a place she can rest for a while."

"My sister isn't a particularly restful woman."

"It must run in the family." I shot her a look that made her smile. "I'm glad to see you aren't mad at me for letting John Bliss know where you were headed. I couldn't not tell him. You and Mr. Sloan being gone at the same time worried John. Worried him a lot."

"That's what he said when he caught up with me in Potter."

She waited for me to say more and when I didn't, volunteered, "It wasn't easy for John to come hat in hand asking for information about you so be kind to him."

"When am I not kind to John Bliss?"

"I can recall a few instances."

"That was years ago," I pointed out, "when we were both newcomers to New Hope. We've managed to get along just fine for quite a while now."

"John has some shadows in his past, I think," Ruth said, her tone thoughtful, "but then everybody's got something they don't talk about, don't they? Everybody's got a secret memory or two they prefer to keep to themselves." I thought about her husband's past and all the years he spent intent on vengeance, chasing a deadly phantom. I thought about Delilah, too, on the run from a past she couldn't let go – or that wouldn't let go of her.

"Of one kind or another, I suppose," I agreed and stood. "I passed Othello on my way here. I imagine he scratched at the back-door until Jem let him in, and now he's stretched out on the floor next to Jem's chair. I hate to shoo him out into the damp. Do you mind if he spends the night in my kitchen?"

"Having Jem around has taken years off that old mutt's

life. If you don't mind, why would I? Another year or two and I bet Alex gives Jem some competition for that dog's attention, but right now I'm glad Jem and Othello have each other. Othello was a comfort for Danny, too, after his family died."

"Have you heard from Danny lately?"

"It's been over a month, but in his last letter he said the army was moving him to Wyoming Territory, and he sounded so excited about it I knew I wouldn't hear any more until he got settled in there."

"Army life suits him."

"It does, doesn't it? He spent enough time at Fort Cottonwood before it closed to know army life was what he wanted. Danny always loved an adventure, even as a boy." She smiled at a memory. "All those long, long thoughts of his." We walked into the hallway and through the lobby of the boarding house, stopping at the front door. "Sheba, if there's ever anything you want to talk about or—" Ruth stopped mid-sentence. "Listen to me, talking like I'm an old grandmother with all the answers to life. Never mind."

The front door opened before I could reach the handle, Silas home for the night as long as New Hope stayed quiet.

"Sheba," Si said, but his glance slipped quickly to Ruth even as he greeted me. It was always like that when she was present – Si's way of reassuring himself that his wife was safe and well, visible and touchable. Si Carpenter had come close to losing her once, and the experience left its mark, its own kind of shadow.

"I'm just leaving, Si," I said. "Good night."

When I entered the shop, I was puzzled by the sound of voices from the kitchen. Jem reading his report aloud to Othello, maybe? But no, nothing so innocent. Archie Sloan sat at the kitchen table next to Jem, the two of them conversing like old friends. Othello, smarter than his boy, sat in a corner with his attention fixed firmly on the pair, never shifting stance or glance even when I spoke. He isn't a growly kind of hound, but I would have sworn I heard something low and grumbly coming from his throat. Clever dog.

'Well, here she is." Sloan stood at my appearance. "You said she'd be along."

My heart beat so full and fierce in my chest that it took me a moment to find room for breath and speech.

"What are you doing here?" Jem lost his smile at my tone.

"Waiting for you. Visiting with the boy."

"How did you get in?" Sloan raised his brows as if my question shocked him.

"I knocked on the back door, Miss Sheba. I know my manners. And Jem here let me in."

Jem said, "Mr. Sloan reminded me about landslides, that too much rain can cause landslides bad enough to cover a whole town. That's right isn't it?"

"Yes," I said, "that's right."

In a jovial tone, Archie Sloan added, "There's danger everywhere, Miss Sheba, and it can show up when you least expect it. Never does to let down your guard, does it?"

Not bothering with a reply – we both understood the message he was sending, so why bother? – I said, "It's time for bed, Jem, and Mrs. Carpenter said Othello can spend the night."

"Can he sleep on the mattress with me?"

"Yes."

"Well, all right then!" Jem was more enthusiastic than I at the prospect of sharing a small, unwindowed room with a damp dog long overdue for a bath. "Good night, Mr. Sloan. Good night, Aunt Sheba. Come on, Othello!" The dog didn't need a second invitation. He made a wide berth around Sloan, sent the man a last warning glance, and followed Jem into the bedroom.

Once the door closed, I turned to Sloan, whose gaze had remained on me, Jem being only a means to an end for him.

"Don't ever do that again," I said. Fury made my voice slightly unsteady.

"All I was doing—"

"I know exactly what you were doing, but whether you

believe it or not, I don't know where my sister is any more than Jem does. No matter what you do or how you try to scare me, it won't work because I can't tell you something I don't know."

He eyed me. "I heard you took the train out of town while I was gone. Where'd you go?"

I have never found it very difficult to lie. I had to make up stories to get out of Philadelphia and into art school and doing so didn't trouble me at the time. My inclination is to tell the truth, but that's not always possible.

"I went to Sidney," I said, "if it's any business of yours."

"I wonder if the ticket man would agree with you."

"You'll have to ask him, I guess, but I understand the railroad has rules about those things."

"Rules don't mean nothin' to me." A pause. "I hear you and Bliss come back together, real cozy like. Was Bliss in Sidney, too?"

"You'll have to ask him."

"I might do that. He's a man needs to be taken down a peg. Had the nerve to knock a friend of mine into the street."

"Your friend must have deserved it."

"I don't know about that. Bliss seemed to think he was watching you a little too close for comfort, but with all that red hair, you're a woman to draw a man's attention, make him wonder if the rest of you heats up red hot, too. Now if you and Bliss are spending time together, I can understand why the idea of another man taking his place might rile him up, but still —" A speculative glance at me. "Maybe I should take a ride over to Sidney."

"If that means I won't have to see you or listen to you, I think it's a fine idea. The sooner the better." I shifted my stance and looked past him toward the back room so he couldn't misunderstand my words. "I want you to get out." I might as well not have spoken.

"I doubt I'll find her in Sidney," Archie Sloan mused, "or you wouldn't have made such a show about telling me where you went. You're too smart for that."

"I want you to get out," I repeated. "Now. Stay just one more minute and I'll get Sheriff Carpenter." Sloan reached for his hat on the table.

"I'm going, I'm going. I guess you got a temper, after all. I always heard that about red-haired women." He grinned at me, but no humor reached his eyes. "Your sister's got something of mine, and I ain't one to forget or forgive somebody that steals from me."

That's rich, I thought, coming from a thief, and said, "You've got ten seconds left." Without further speech, he turned and walked into the room I used for a studio. The back-door clicked behind him.

Tomorrow I would ask Joe Chandler to install locks on both that door and the front door. Joe would wonder about that, of course, because nobody in New Hope locked their doors except Mr. Talamine at the bank, although that Emmett Wolf fracas three years ago had changed the way we felt about being safe in our own homes, had made us suspicious and fearful for a while. New Hope is well-named, however – a hopeful, ambitious community from one end of Main Street to the other – so most people managed to put what happened behind them. Still, that sad and sorry business taught us all a lesson in life we'd rather not have learned.

In the end, it didn't matter to me what Joe thought. I'd have locks put on both doors tomorrow, and I'd have a serious talk with Jem about Archie Sloan, too. Sloan's words, no matter how coarse, couldn't hurt me, but there was one way he could do me damage from which I would never recover. We both understood what – who – was at play here. If Sloan ever truly believed I knew where Dee was, he would not hesitate to use Jem, to hurt Jem, to get the information he wanted. I knew that to be as true as winter following fall. What I didn't know and what I hoped I'd never find out was whether I would hand over my sister in exchange for my nephew. A barter straight from the devil. *With you and John Bliss and Si Carpenter and everybody in that nice little town of yours watching out for Jem, he'll be safe enough.* My sister's voice had held the ring of confidence, but even at the time, I knew what she said wasn't always true. New Hope was my home and its people were my friends, but a good home and good people aren't always enough to keep wickedness away and everyone safe. Sometimes evil arrives when you don't expect it and stays when it isn't invited. That was the main lesson in life we learned from Emmett Wolf, and none of us would ever forget it.

To Joe Chandler's credit, he never said one curious word about the door locks, just showed up at the shop at the end of the next day with the locks and his tools in hand. Joe's reticence probably says less about his self-control than it does about how the people in a small town know everybody's business. Whatever the reason, Joe put two of the latest Yale locks on the outside and was finishing up with the sliding bolt locks for the inside when John Bliss made an appearance.

I hadn't seen John since our return three days before, but that doesn't mean I hadn't thought about him. He pushed open the front door where Joe knelt putting on the bolt, apologized for bouncing the door off Joe's nose – "No harm done," Joe announced, but his eyes watered a bit from the impact – and stepped over to where I stood.

"Sheba," John greeted. He may have intended to smile, but with a closer look at Joe's activity, any smile he intended disappeared, replaced by a frown and the words, "You feel a need for locks now?" spoken in a tone suddenly so devoid of human feeling that Joe looked up at John, catching something ominous behind the words.

I heard it, too, saw Joe's quick, understanding glance, and said, "Hello, John. Come back for something hot to drink so we don't distract Joe and I'll explain." John followed me through the bead curtain into the kitchen. "Tea or old coffee?" I asked.

He set his hat on the table but didn't sit down. "That's a hard decision, but tea will do."

I put the kettle on to boil, filled two tea balls with leaves, and said, "Sit down, will you? When you hover, I get nervous." John sat and I did the same.

"I don't think anything makes you nervous, Sheba, at least nothing I've seen in the years I've known you."

"Things change."

"I can see that. Is it Sloan that's made you feel the need to put locks on your doors?"

I told him the story of last night, the shock of coming home and finding Archie Sloan big as life and arrogant as sin sitting in my kitchen next to Jem, the memory still so shocking that my feelings must have showed on my face.

"Why didn't you get someone to throw him out?"

"He left on his own, John, and he didn't do anything that would have seemed wrong. He knocked like any person would do and Jem let him in, and when I told Sloan to go, he went."

"And the next day you're putting locks on your doors."

"Yes."

"I don't like that, Sheba." The teakettle began to whistle, and I jumped up to grab it.

"I don't like it either," I said over my shoulder, busying myself with the water and the tea. When I returned to the table with two cups of steaming tea in my hands, Joe appeared in the doorway.

"I'm done, Sheba. I left the keys to the Yale locks on the counter. They're small enough to keep in your pocket."

"Thanks, Joe. If it's all right with you, I'll stop by tomorrow and settle up."

"That's fine. It's Saturday. You know where I'll be."

After Joe left, I set the sugar bowl on the table and sat down again. Neither John nor I spoke.

Finally, he said, "Sheba," his tone no longer grim, just quiet, just kind. When I lifted my eyes from my cup, I found his gaze on my face. Warmth there and the same tenderness I had seen that night in Ogallala. My heart shifted a little, also the same way it did that night in Ogallala. "Why don't you tell me?"

"Is that why you came, to get all your questions answered

about what happened in Ogallala?"

"I came because I wanted to see you, because you're the handsomest woman I've ever seen, because I'm partial to blue eyes, because I have a strong desire to kiss you again, because I like being around you – most of the time, anyway. Will those reasons do or should I keep going?"

"That's enough for a start," I answered and spooned more sugar into my tea, smiling to myself as I did so.

"Where's Jem?"

"I sent him down to the telegraph office to ask Lonnie Markman how the telegraph works," I answered. "I doubt Lonnie will be able to answer all of Jem's questions, but I'm sure he knows more about the telegraph than I do. I've never figured out how sounds can run through a wire."

"But you can paint water so it glitters like diamonds."

I smiled again, this time right into his eyes. "Yes, sometimes I can do that, John." I paused to take a breath and without further prompting began to tell him about my sister. Not about Fannie Newell or Florence Delarose but about Delilah Fenway, my beautiful, rebellious, puzzling, curious, secretive, fearless sister. I talked and John listened. There was some of me in the telling but more of Dee and our younger brother and our inflexible father and our stifling life among the Philadelphia elite. I told him how Dee's wild behavior caused her fall from grace, how she was banished to Europe with our stern spinster aunt as chaperone, how she abandoned Great Aunt Hortensia and disappeared as soon as their ship docked in New York City, how she and I lost touch, and I concluded with the very little I knew of her life since. I told John more than I shared with Ruth. I told him everything and did not soften my own conduct in the telling. I had a sister. I let her walk out of my life and I never once tried to find her.

"All these years I blamed her for ignoring our brother's illness and death and making me shoulder the burden of his dying, but now I realize our father never told her. I should have trusted her. I should have done more," I said quietly.

"How could I let my sister walk out of my life and never make an effort to find her? What does that make me?"

John reached across the table and put a hand over mine. "Human," he said. "It makes you human like the rest of us."

"But we don't throw away the people we care about. I should have—" His hand tightened.

"The world's full of *should'ves* and if you let them, they'll suffocate you. You took care of yourself, Sheba, and no one would fault you for that. Was anybody looking out for your interests? Was your sister?"

I shook my head, my throat suddenly too tight to speak. In all my life, no one had ever put my interests first. No one had even cared enough to ask what my interests were. But at that, I had to give my head another shake, this one quick and hard. I was too close to sliding into self-pity, and I despise that kind of self-indulgence, in others but especially in myself.

"Not that you needed anyone to act for you," John said, removing his hand. "You seem to do fine on your own."

"I do," I said, "but it's still nice to know—" I didn't finish the sentence because I thought it would have backed John into a corner, forced him to say something that should never be forced. "Anyway, now you have the whole story, and it's not me at the center of it."

"With all he's got at stake, Sloan's never going to give up. You and the boy are his only link to the money. That explains why, even when the man himself isn't around, he has someone watching you."

I recalled Sloan's comment. "Was that the man Archie Sloan said you knocked into the street?"

"The same. I didn't like the way he watched you. It wasn't for the normal reasons a man might let his gaze dwell on you." He smiled slightly. "That I understand well enough."

"So that's how Sloan knew I'd been away." I paused, thinking about the past weeks. "That means Sloan isn't travelling alone, which is no surprise, I guess. How many men do you think he has with him?"

"More than just one. Four or five, maybe, but he's careful

about having them around at the same time. I've seen him talking with four different men over the past few weeks, each time thick as thieves." We both smiled at his choice of words.

"Interesting," I said. "I wonder what Mr. Sloan and his friends get up to when they're not in New Hope."

"I think Si's asking the same question."

"It's hard for an old dog to learn new tricks," I observed. "Not that Mr. Sloan is all that old, but it's only human nature to fall back on what you know." I stood. "Is it too much to hope that the man gets caught in an act of thievery and has to spend the next twenty years in prison?"

John rose, too. "Five years or twenty, Sheba, Sloan's not a man to forget an injury. As long as he doesn't get what he wants, he'll be a danger to you."

"More of a danger to Dee and Jem than to me, surely."

"It's not worrying about Dee and Jem that keeps me awake at night." We stood facing each other, close enough that he could touch my lips with his fingertips, which is what he did. In an instant, I was in John's arms, his mouth insistent and warm on mine, his hands at my waist pulling me closer, everything where it should be and neither of us in a hurry to pull away…until Jem let the back-door slam and burst into the kitchen.

"You'll never guess, Aunt Sheba! It's just like Mr. Edison's bulb!"

I heard John murmur an impolite word with a touch of laughter behind it. I jerked away, embarrassed but determined to act as if it was the most common circumstance in the world for Jem to find me kissing a man in the middle of the kitchen.

"The telegraph, you mean?" I asked, trying unsuccessfully for a normal tone. Even to my ears, I sounded breathless.

The way Jem's head tilted as he examined first my face and then John's reminded me of Othello when I talked to him, that little tilt of the dog's head that said I don't understand a word you're saying, but I'm paying attention and trying to figure it out.

"Hello, Jem," John's tone even and pleasant.

"Hello, Mr. Bliss. You were kissing Aunt Sheba."

"That I was."

"Mr. Bliss was just leaving, Jem." I turned to John with a stern expression but with enough regret in my eyes to spark a return look from him that made me want to shoo Jem right back outside. Here was another way having children around made you do things you didn't want to do. It was a wonder people with a first child ever managed a second. "Good night, John."

He reached for his hat. "Good night, Sheba." A nod toward the child. "Jem."

"Good night, Mr. Bliss." The amenities complete, John departed the kitchen, and I went over to the stove.

"You can tell me what you learned about the telegraph while I heat supper," I said. "It's got something to do with electricity, doesn't it?"

My question, intended to move Jem's thoughts away from kissing in general and from my kissing John Bliss in particular, worked.

"That's what Lonnie told me," Jem agreed and proceeded to regale me with more information about the telegraph than I wanted or needed or could have possibly understood, even if my thoughts hadn't been entirely focused on John Bliss and the pleasure found in his arms. Jem was not a boy to skimp on information about things that interested him, however, so after he stopped talking about the telegraph, he started in on the intricacies of Morse Code. Later, Jem in bed for the night, teeth brushed and face washed, I went in to listen to his prayers and had to admit I wasn't nearly as clever at the art of distraction as I thought. In the middle of a string of requested blessings that always started with his mother and moved along to me, to Othello, then to Mrs. Carpenter and baby Alex and Mr. Stenton and the new president of the United States, Jem stopped abruptly and squeezed open one eye.

"Aunt Sheba."

"I'm listening," I said, in case he thought I was

daydreaming about other, more worldly activities instead of paying attention to his prayers.

"Should I ask God to bless Mr. Bliss, too? I mean, with you and him kissing and all, maybe I should add him to the list."

I narrowed my eyes at the child, looking for mischief, but there was none. James Cameron Fenway was a little boy who gave everything serious thought, even – especially – praying. The grave expression on his face made me smile.

"Yes," I said, "that's a good idea. No doubt Mr. Bliss can use all the praying he can get."

Then, thinking about Archie Sloan and the pull of ten thousand dollars and the look in his eyes when he told me, "I ain't one to forget or forgive somebody that steals from me," I thought it wasn't just John Bliss who might benefit from a few extra prayers.

12

The next day was a busy Saturday, as every Saturday is, but with the chilling breath of winter blowing down our necks, I had a rush of customers requesting all things warm – on the outside heavy skirts, snug vests, and fitted shirtwaists and on the inside flannel camisoles, long drawers, and wool knickers. I took the orders without complaint knowing my painting would suffer, but I had the care of a growing boy whose bony wrists stuck out of his shirt's sleeves by the third washing. I never realized children lengthened so quickly.

The Reverend Gerald Shulte is not only a good man but one possessing good sense, as well. Not with so much as the twitch of an eyelid did he ever express any level of amazement when I began to attend church regularly. It was all due to having Jem in my household, of course, which Pastor Shulte no doubt understood, but because he encourages his flock not to question Providence, I have no doubt he lives by the same creed. He's that kind of man, both honorable and kind, so each time he greeted me as he stood in the church doorway at the end of the service, he assumed God had arranged my visit and said only, "Hello, Sheba. It's good to see you," when his worldlier inclination might have been, "Hello, Sheba. I'm as astonished to see you this morning as I've been astonished to see you every Sunday you've shown up. Apparently even in this modern age, miracles do happen." Our numerous discussions about religion in general and God in particular could well have prompted such a comment, but neither the man's good nature nor his good sense would have allowed it. A simple good morning was what he said and what I returned, Jem's presence in my life changing more than I could have anticipated. Sometimes, with Jem sitting next to me and the little church filled with a rousing rendition of *From All That Dwell Below the Skies* – breaking into spontaneous four-part harmony on the alleluias – I found myself thinking that maybe Reverend Shulte and Ruth and Ellie Chandler and Jem now, too, and all the other people I knew who held to the same simple belief might, in fact, be right, and I was the one who didn't see or understand any of the truths all around me. Fortunately, Sunday is the only day that encourages that kind of profound introspection, and if I walk home briskly enough, the thoughts have usually vanished before I reach the front door of the dress shop.

That Sunday, the Sunday after the new locks, Bert Gruber caught up with me as I reached the end of Church Street. Jem had already run on ahead when I heard my name and turned.

"Something here for you, Sheba." Bert handed me an envelope.

"But it's your name on the envelope, not mine," I said after a quick look.

"Be that as it may, it's for you," then in a lowered voice, although there wasn't a soul nearby to overhear our conversation, Bert added, "She knows you're being watched. Knows he's not averse to robbing trains, either. It seemed safer this way."

It wasn't the cool September breeze that made me shiver, it was Bert's words. The old days, the days when New Hope, Nebraska, meant home and safety and freedom to me were long gone.

"You spent time with her, too, Bert." Unconsciously, I lowered my voice the same as Bert. "Are you sure Sloan's not having you watched, too?"

"Oh, he came calling early on." Bert rubbed his hand against the side of his face as if recalling a bruise, "but one look at me and he figured I wouldn't know anything. A man who looks like me won't win any beauty prizes, Sheba, so the idea of a woman like Fannie with someone like me gave Sloan a good belly laugh."

A man like you, I thought, adding the words and the humble tone in which they were spoken to the reasons I already had to despise Archie Sloan.

"Not that that's a bad thing," Bert went on, "because none of 'em bothers with me now, and I can come and go as I please. Better all around that way, Sheba." I folded the heavy envelope into my coat pocket.

"Thank you, Bert." I might have asked more questions but knew there would be no point to it. Bert's loyalties weren't divided.

Jem asked permission to go down to the Lincolns' to play with Frederick, the Lincolns' only child, and after assuring me he would come home the moment Mrs. Lincoln pointed a finger toward the door, the boy was off. He and Frederick – never Fred – had met each other at school and become friends over time, both of them interested in inventing things and exploring places, not necessarily in that order.

I planned to drag my easel and a blank canvas west to paint the setting sun behind the stand of dark trees that grew next to the schoolhouse but not with Dee's letter burning a hole in my coat pocket. The envelope was addressed to Bert Gruber, Gooseneck Hotel, New Hope, Nebraska in block letters that could have been printed by man or woman, and the inside message was equally unrevealing.

Sheba,

Jem turns 6 October 2. Get him something nice, and don't tell him it's from me. That way he can't let something slip in front of the wrong people. I'm all right. Sounds like you and Jem are doing all right, too.

That was the extent of it, a brief note, no signature, and a ten-dollar greenback folded lengthwise and lengthwise again and tucked into the writing paper. Ten dollars. For someone in my circumstances, the amount was a windfall, even though I had no doubt it was stolen money, money that didn't rightfully belong to me any more than it rightfully belonged to my sister. But there was no way to return the money just then, and a boy didn't turn six every day, so the first thing Monday morning, without experiencing one moment of doubt or regret at the idea, I deposited the bank note into my account at the United Bank of Nebraska. Whoever owned that one particular greenback would have to wait a little longer before he got it back.

When Ruth suggested I bake a birthday cake in honor of the occasion, I looked at her as if she had told me to compose a symphony or build a castle.

"I have never baked a cake in my life," I said.

"Never?"

"Never."

"Not one?"

"Not one. Not ever. That's what *never* means." I could tell my friend thought I was exaggerating so I added for emphasis, "I have never in all my life baked a cake for any occasion whatsoever, and I don't intend to start now, not even for my favorite nephew's birthday."

Ruth digested the information. "Sometimes I forget how different we are, Sheba, I really do, but then something like this comes up, and I think we must have been born on different planets."

"We had a live-in cook when I was growing up," I admitted. Why should I be embarrassed that I was raised in and by a houseful of servants? But I was. "I never had to learn anything practical as a girl. French lessons and how to walk with a book on my head are about all I remember."

Ruth sent me a quick smile. "Well, I can't paint a picture to save my soul so it all evens out in the end. Ask Ezzie. I know for a fact that she serves cake at the café often enough."

"That's a good idea, Ruth. I should have thought of it myself with Ezzie right next door. Do you think it's all right if I invite a couple of Jem's friends to share the cake with him? Maybe I could have lemonade and—I don't know. Does lemonade go with birthday cake, do you think?"

Ruth laughed out loud at that. "I have never heard you sound so helpless, Sheba. It's a child's birthday, not the inner workings of Mr. Bissell's carpet sweeper." As usual, Ruth's laughter made me laugh, too. She had a way of making that happen.

"You don't turn six every day," I said at last.

Ruth's look was warm with understanding. "That's true, Sheba."

"And turning six without your mother," I continued, "well, I know what that's like. I just want Jem to have a happy day." In a rare expression of affection, Ruth gave me a light kiss on the cheek.

"I know you do and I'm sorry I teased you. Ask Ezzie to bake a cake and don't bother with lemonade. Luther's got a new soda pop called root beer – it's not real beer, Sheba; don't look at me like I've lost my mind – down at the Variety Store, and I haven't heard a single person complain about it. Just the opposite. I guarantee you can't go wrong with cake and root beer and little boys."

Ruth was right, of course. In the end, Jem, Frederick Lincoln, Jerry Shulte the Younger, the Chandler twins, and Othello sat in my kitchen on a sunny but blustery Sunday afternoon, ate too much cake, drank too much root beer, discussed horses, bugs and electricity, made a few rude noises, and eventually put on their coats (clever Othello never took his off,) and raced outside to do whatever it is boys do when they're together in a group. Always a mystery to me and even more so after that afternoon.

That evening, I handed Jem two small packages, one a leather pouch of brand new marbles – "As fine a bag of aggies as you're like to find anywhere, Sheba," Hans

Fenstermeier told me in his accented English – and the other Mr. Verne's novel *A Journey to the Centre of the Earth*, the superior edition with illustrations. I had Hans to thank for both presents because while the marbles were on the shelf at his Dry Goods and Novelties store, the book wasn't, and he had to put in a rush order for me so I would have it in time. The cost of the book and the rush order made me gulp, but the look on Jem's face when he removed the brown wrapping and saw the exciting cover with its intrepid band of explorers crossing a dangerous bridge made everything – the cake, the root beer, the rush order, my fretting and uncertainty, everything – worthwhile.

"I expect Mama would have been here today if she could have come. She's partial to cake."

I sat on the edge of my bed and looked down at the floor where Jem sat on his mattress, covers tossed to the side, the marbles and his new book within arm's reach in case he woke in the night and felt the urge to play or read. I tried to gauge the feelings behind his words, which sounded remarkably practical for a six-year-old boy.

"Is she? I don't remember that being the case when she was a little girl." He looked back at me with wide eyes, always interested in stories of his mother's childhood. "But my goodness, did she ever favor oatmeal cookies! No oatmeal cookie was ever safe in our house, no matter where the cook hid them. When it came to those cookies, your mother was like Othello with a bone." I paused a moment and tried to match his practical tone. "I know your mother would have been here if she could have, Jem, and I'm sure she thought about you all day and wished she was here." He nodded, satisfied that our thoughts were in perfect unity, and began his prayers. Children can accept things better than adults, I thought, and didn't know if that was their blessing or their curse.

The next week was Indian Summer, a mocking tease of a week. See, it says, winter's not right around the corner. No, siree. Look at all this sunshine. Shed that coat; you won't need it. Believe me, I've got it all under control. This is the year the seasons will move in reverse. Guaranteed.

I fell for the week's sassy weather wink every year and did again that October. It was unthinkable to waste a bright and paintable morning, so I woke very early, threw on an old dress, tied my hair back with a kerchief, and left Jem still asleep as I headed east to try to capture the light of an Indian Summer morning as it peaked above the horizon. In a way I can articulate only with brush and paints, it is light unique to only one week a year, and I didn't want to miss it.

I suppose I didn't see his figure until it was too late because I felt happy that morning, happier than I had been in a long while, thinking about Jem's birthday the day before and the next two unfettered hours of painting, thinking about John Bliss, too, and how we had moved from friends to—what, exactly? Something more than friends, certainly, but what? What did John expect from me and more importantly, what was I prepared to give? Serious contemplations, perhaps, but serious in a happy way. Lugging easel and canvas and with my paints and brushes tied up in a cloth bag over my shoulder, I walked east down Church Street, reached the alley that separated Tull's Beer Garden from its vacant neighbor – rumor had either a dentist or a newspaper going in, either of which would be a welcome addition to New Hope – when Archie Sloan stepped from the side alley and planted himself directly in front of me. I gave a gasp, more of shock than surprise, and backed up a step.

"Pretty morning, ain't it?" he said. "I thought you'd be out early to take advantage of the good weather. That's your painting on the wall over at the big hotel, isn't it? You know what you're doing when it comes to pictures, I'll say that."

"Thank you." I moved to step around him, but he moved in the same direction at the same time and so nothing changed. Both of us still stood face-to-face near the corner of the vacant building.

"Doesn't seem smart you being out on your own, though, does it? Not smart or safe, either."

"Mr. Sloan, I'm losing good light while you stand there prattling on about God only knows what."

"But you know what."

"Yes, you're right, I probably do know. You're probably on about my sister, about where she is and what she did and how she's got something that belongs to you. To tell the truth, I'm sick of hearing about it."

"Are you now?" As fast as a snake, he lifted his arm to my throat hard enough to back me up against a wall in the side alley. "Well, I'm getting sick of it, too, Sheba. Sick of both the Fenway women, in fact." His forearm pressed against my throat under my chin, not so tight that I couldn't breathe but tight enough. I could feel the rough wood of the wall pricking into my back through the cloth of my dress.

"Here's what I know, Sheba. You never went to Sidney, never set foot there. You got off the train at Potter, but you spent most of your time in Ogallala. That's what I know. You're a woman people notice, a woman men notice more like, and a lot of men noticed you in Ogallala. Was she there? I know she wasn't in Potter, but was your thieving bitch of a sister in Ogallala? Is it the boy keeping her close? I know you have to know where she is. I'm no fool."

I felt panic at the words because he was right, he wasn't a fool, he was a man who watched and waited and followed and knew more than he should. Why had I ever thought I could best him? He was a man of relentless greed and limitless arrogance, a man to fear. I saw it. Why couldn't Dee? Suddenly I felt nearly sick with the need to push him away from me, to get his face out of mine and distance myself from the sight and sound and smell of him. I needed time and space to think. What did Archie Sloan know for sure? *What did he know*?

"Get away from me," I said. "Who do you think you are?"

"I'm a man that always gets what's coming to him. I learned that at my daddy's knee. Hold on to what's yours, boy, he told me, and don't let nobody get the best of you. Man or woman don't make no difference because nobody ever gets the best of Archie Sloan." I tried to loosen his hold but every time I moved, his arm pressed just a little harder. "Your sister has something that belongs to me, little thieving whore that she is, and after I get it back, she'll pay. Or you'll pay or the boy'll pay. Nobody steals from Archie Sloan."

Between his arm against my throat and my heart beating faster than the wheels of a runaway train engine, I could hardly get a word out, but besides being frightened I was furious, and I can always find breath to speak when I'm angry.

"You go near Jem, and I'll have the sheriff on your back so fast it'll make your head spin."

"I can handle the sheriff."

"But can you handle me?" John Bliss, thank God, stood directly behind Sloan and asked his question in a casual, low, and mocking voice that belied the look in his eyes, which were black with rage. He put both hands to Sloan's shoulder and whirled him around so it was the two men who now stood face-to-face. I put a palm to my throat, swallowed, and then took a startled breath because from nowhere it seemed John had drawn a small, silver-handled, very sharp blade that he pressed into the soft spot at the base of Sloan's throat. Sloan's eyes had chilled, had faded from a dark green that sparked with anger and scorn to the pale color of a still summer pond. John might be holding the knife, but in its own way, Archie Sloan's expression made him equally as fearful.

"Not now I can't," Sloan said. His tone was relaxed, but I noticed he didn't move a muscle and barely breathed. "You're the man with the knife, Bliss. Now me, I don't have a weapon on me, not knife or gun. You kill me, you'll be killing an unarmed man, and it won't be me that gets the sheriff on his back."

"No," John agreed almost cheerfully, "because you'll be dead, and like you, I'm willing to take my chances with Si Carpenter." Sloan tried to shrug but the knife pressed more firmly into that soft spot and John's deliberate words: "Don't.

Move." changed the man's mind about shrugging. "I'm only going to tell you this once, Sloan. Just once. This woman is off-limits, her and the boy both. If you ever lay a hand on her again, it will be the last thing you do. Do you understand that?" A tiny drop of blood showed at Sloan's throat.

I had to give Sloan credit for nerve because even at the threat of being slit stem to stern, he managed a slight laugh.

"Lord, yes. Like I told your lady, I'm no fool, and it's not her I'm interested in." As John slowly lowered the knife, I thought Sloan would either bolt for the safety of the street or try some underhanded way to move the confrontation to his advantage, but he did neither. Instead, he thumbed that fine felt hat of his farther back on his head, pulled at his vest to straighten it, turned to me, and said, "I'm sorry if I alarmed you, Miss Fenway." *Alarmed?* I thought. Try terrified or enraged or sickened. Any of those would be a truer description.

But I didn't respond aloud, just stared at him long enough for John to say, his voice now back to normal without that cold and dangerous edge, "You're not wanted here, Sloan. Time for you to move along." John held the knife loosely in one hand, poised very slightly on the balls of his feet in case sudden action would still be needed. He reminded me of a big cat I'd once seen in a traveling circus. The lithe and beautiful creature paced its cage, something anticipatory in its eyes as it slowly swung its head back and forth to examine the people crowding forward. Swing open the door just a crack, it seemed to say, and let me show you what I can do. I had admired the gorgeous thing more than feared it, and knew an even greater sympathy, remembering what it was like to feel restless and trapped, unable to use the abilities I had been given.

"I'll do that. Nothing would suit me better." Archie Sloan made a point of giving me a cordial nod before he sauntered away, a man without a care in the world but one: his aggrieved and deadly lust for ten thousand dollars. Less the ten that rested securely in Abner Talamine's United Bank of

Nebraska, of course.

"Sheba? Are you all right?" I shifted my gaze back to John, and instead of answering his question asked one of my own.

"Do you carry a knife in your boot, John?" Just curious and nothing else.

From his face, I knew he hadn't expected those words, but he isn't a man easily thrown off balance, an attribute I find particularly appealing.

Answering my question with a gesture, he bent, lifted his pant leg, and slid the blade into what might have been a small sheath on the inside of his boot.

"Have you had that with you every time we've been together?" I asked, still curious.

He nodded. "Yes, ma'am. Every time." A small smile, no doubt thinking what I was thinking.

"I can't imagine any of those proper young boys that came calling back in Philadelphia had a weapon of any kind with him," I mused.

"No? Well, you must have noticed by now that I'm not proper and I'm not young and we're not in Philadelphia."

I planted myself right in front of him and put both arms around his neck. "Well, thank God for that," I said and pulled his head down to kiss him. The kiss surprised him for just a moment, but only a moment, because before I knew it, I was where I'd been just a few minutes ago, backed to the wall of a vacant building with a man's body pressed against me, but the sensation was as different from the feel of Archie Sloan as night is from day. *Definitely not proper* was my last rational thought for several minutes. Some sound out on Main Street brought me to my senses, and I pushed John away.

"Now look what I've done," I said with annoyance, aware of morning sunshine creeping into the alley. For a minute, the man who had been kissing me with expert and relentless abandon looked suddenly like an inexperienced boy, flushed, somewhat disheveled, and confused. What was going through that dangerous mind of his? Did he think I expected something in the nature of an apology? He must have been able to tell from my response that I had no need for or interest in a request for forgiveness.

He said my name, but his voice was hoarse, so he cleared his throat and tried again. "Sheba, I—"

I gave him a quick, light kiss on the mouth and slipped away from where I stood between him and the wall.

"Hush," I said. "It's not your fault I've lost the best light of the morning." I bent to get my easel, canvas, kerchief, and bag from where they had scattered during the sudden altercation with Archie Sloan and when I stood upright, juggling all the items in my arms, John looked himself again. A lean, saturnine man with a knife in his boot.

"No, but it still feels like my fault. Do you need some help there?" He indicated the jumble of items I held.

"No, I'm fine now, but before, when I truly did need help, with Sloan I mean, you were there and I appreciate that. Did I say thank you?"

"In a manner of speaking." We smiled at each other, but the predicament I found myself in was never far from my mind.

"Sloan knows I was in Ogallala, John, and why I was there. Why he didn't find Delilah is a mystery, but maybe she was already on to the next place. He'll never believe I don't know where she is. Never." This time it was my turn to catch a breath and swallow. "What should I do? Would it be better to have the law track her down to get the money back? Would they send her to prison? What if Sloan finds her first? What if he uses Jem against her, against me? I don't know what to do. I don't know what the best thing to do is."

John reached out one hand to tuck a loose curl behind my ear. "I know."

"I feel like it's all up to me, and I don't want it to be. I just want to live my life and paint and sew and mind my own business. I want it to be like it used to be."

"Except for the boy. You don't want that part of your life the way it used to be."

He was right, of course. I wanted the blessing without the trial, as Gerald Shulte had preached just the previous Sunday. I wanted everything on my terms. I had to smile because it was the first and would probably be the last time John Bliss would remind me of Gerald Shulte.

"No, you're right."

"We'll figure something out, Sheba."

I might have called his voice loving, it was so soft and kind, so tender, but maybe the heated time we just spent against the wall of a vacant building in an empty alley had given me thoughts that wouldn't hold up to daylight or to ordinary life. Better to think no further than *kind* for the time being.

"In the meanwhile," John continued, "keep a sharp eye on Jem and on your own coming and going, besides. Expecting to find you painting the morning sun and finding Sloan with his hands on you instead was something I wasn't prepared for." He paused, serious. "If he'd had a weapon on him, I'd have killed him. You know that."

"I know there was a moment you wanted to, but what you would have done had things been different, I can't say, and I hope I never find out." I shifted my stance to let him know the conversation was over. "I have the lesser part of an hour left of the morning, John. I don't want to lose that, too."

With no further conversation, we walked to the end of the alley where I turned east toward the rising sun and he went west. My work day was just beginning and his, at last, was drawing to a close.

13

The fine weather held all week, and I was able to finish the painting I began the day Archie Sloan surprised me in the alley. Eventually it would hang on whatever wall John Bliss chose because I knew that was the picture he should have by way of thanks, not the sunrise over the church steeple but this one, to keep him from forgetting how easily I'd come into his arms that morning and how willing I had been to give him whatever he wanted to take. Something powerful lay between us but what? I wondered if he thought about that morning and wished we had taken more time to sort things out. One way or the other. I scrawled *Indian Summer* at the bottom of the painting and the initials B. F. and set it to the side for the right moment to give to John.

I thought seriously about asking Bert Gruber to convince my sister either to come back to New Hope, turn the money over to Si Carpenter and take whatever consequence would come to her for possessing stolen property, or leave Nebraska entirely and go as far west as she could go. California sounded big enough to hide her. But I didn't talk to Bert at all. Was I being watched and would a visit to the Gooseneck Hotel and Billiards Hall look suspicious? I never went there otherwise, and I didn't want to draw anyone's attention to Bert, who was my only link to Dee. Besides, I doubted Bert could convince my sister to do anything she didn't want to do. She would hold onto that money for Jem's future, even if doing so killed her – and remembering the brutal push of Archie Sloan's arm across my throat, remembering the vicious tone that punctuated his threatening words: *she'll pay or you'll pay or the boy'll pay,* I thought with a shiver that it could well come to that.

In a strange but quite definite way, I understood Dee's intention and purpose, even while I thought she was short-sighted and the results could end up deadly. We were sisters, after all, each of us determined to go her own way and get her own way, and while Jem was my nephew and loved because of that, he was Dee's son. Her son. She had carried him all those months, had felt his kicks before he was born, had pushed him out of her own body, had nursed him and cared for him, and with his father dead, had been the child's only protector all this while. Sometime in those years, she had also decided possessing the best of everything money could buy was the key to Jem having a happy life. In that way, however, we had each learned different lessons from our childhood. Sisters, yes, but what made all the difference between us was the way we viewed money. And the way we loved Jem.

Friday of that week, Harriet Lincoln came to the shop to order a new dress. To my thinking, Harriet was the most beautiful, the most paintable woman in New Hope, her dark skin smooth and glowing and her dark eyes the same. She had a wonderful smile, too, and the regal carriage of a queen, yet was as friendly and down to earth as anyone could be. I wondered if I had come out of bondage or had lived my childhood under the threat of beatings and being sold whether I would carry myself with the same gracious poise that Harriet did. I doubted it. I've never been known for possessing either patience or dignity.

"Something in a light wool, I think, Sheba." Harriet looked at the bolts of fabric on the side table and then back at me. "It's Isaac that's insisting. I'm happy enough with what I've got, but he has his mind set on getting me something new." She spoke in a shy voice, but I could tell the idea pleased her. Not so much a new dress but having a husband that loved her and wanted to buy her a new dress.

"Then we shouldn't disappoint him," I replied. We went over to the fabric table and after some study, I pulled out a fine wool in a light cream color with a soft and hazy plaid of blue and rose as background and edged with tiny flowers in the same blue and rose colors.

"What about this?" I asked. "The cream color will make your skin glow even more than it already does, and the flowers? Well, who doesn't like the idea of flowers in the middle of a Nebraska winter?"

Harriet fingered the fabric, smiled at something only she could see, and nodded.

"You have the artist's eye, Sheba," she said. "This'll do fine." She stayed long enough for me to take the necessary measurements and said on her way out the door, "Frederick sure enjoyed the party for Jem. All he talks about is root beer now."

"I'm sorry," I said with a grin.

She made a small wave with her hand. "Oh, Isaac's in full agreement with his son. Between the two of them, I figure they're the reason Luther can't keep any of that soda pop on his shelves." She hesitated. "Frederick said Mr. Stenton gave him and Jem a project to work on. Has Jem told you about it?"

"The map of the world you mean?"

"Yes. Mr. Stenton said they can use the globe from school to make the map and Frederick's all excited about it. He carried that globe home today like it was made of glass."

"Your son's bright, isn't he, Harriet?"

"I think so," she said. The pride in her dark eyes wasn't nearly as mild as her words. "So's Jem, and I wondered if you'd allow Jem to spend the night with Frederick tomorrow night so they can work on the map together. We bought some coloring pencils from Hans and a big piece of paper. We'll take good care of him, Sheba, and it would be a treat for Frederick to have Jem over. He's never had a good friend before. If you'd allow it, Jem could come over tomorrow after school lets out and you can collect him after church. If you think Jem would want to come, of course."

Jem, I told her without bothering to ask my nephew, would think it the best thing ever, which he did.

Saturday afternoon I gave the boy last minute instructions in good manners, reminded him to eat whatever was put on his plate, and told him the invitation did not include Othello. He nodded as if he was listening, which he wasn't, and was out the door before I was quite finished with my instructions. I followed him outside and watched Jem running down the boardwalk, darting around the people who weren't walking fast enough (which as far as I could tell included everybody) until he disappeared into the meat market.

He's safe enough with the Lincolns, I told myself, but knew a quick, sharp pang of worry that Jem would be out of my sight and care, even if it would be for fewer than twenty-four hours. Since his arrival in New Hope, we had been apart only for the one night I went in search of Delilah, and I was surprised at how much I missed the boy's presence from the moment he dashed out the door. I sat down on the bench outside my shop and leaned my head back. I knew it was silly to worry, but I did, anyway. How had I come to this? Love isn't always reasonable, I thought, and there was the threat of Archie Sloan, besides.

I opened my eyes and sat upright as the weight of someone sitting made the bench shift. Having the thought of Sloan in my head made me pull away sharply, but I realized even before I turned that my bench companion was John Bliss. Somehow over the past weeks I had come to recognize the feel of his presence without needing to see him in the flesh. Although seeing him in the flesh had its own compensations. A strong mouth and big hands and powerful shoulders could give a woman ideas.

For a moment, I must have looked alarmed in some way because John said quickly, "Sorry. I didn't mean to startle you. I should have said something first."

When I turned to face him fully, I was reminded of something Ruth once told me: *John has some shadows in his past.* I thought Ruth's words were more than true, that this was a man who held as much darkness in him as light, but I also knew that no longer mattered to me when it came to John Bliss.

"That's all right," I said. "I was thinking." I pulled my skirts closer to make more room for him.

"About?"

"This and that," adding, "I haven't seen Archie Sloan around since Monday. Is it just me, or is he really gone?"

"Gone for the time being, him and the men I suspect ride with him."

"Is that good or bad?"

"Whether that man's absent or present, it's always bad if he's not gone for good, Sheba." John sat back and stretched out his legs. "Was that streak of lightning I saw racing down the boardwalk Jem?"

His light words made me laugh a little. "None other than," I answered and told John about Jem being invited to stay overnight at the Lincolns'. "I know Harriet will keep as good an eye on him as she does on Frederick, and I know Isaac Lincoln is as solid and safe as the United Bank of Nebraska, but still—" I let the sentence dangle and John reached over to put his hand over mine where it lay in my lap.

"You've got to stop fretting, Sheba. It's not like you."

"I know. Only," I picked my words with care, the way a person might sneak in late and tiptoe carefully up the stairs, trying to miss all the squeaky boards along the way so he didn't give himself away, "once a person lets down her guard, it changes the way she feels. About other people and about herself." It wasn't just Jem I meant, but Dee, too, and the man seated next to me. Especially the man seated next to me. "Once the walls are down, I don't think you can ever get them back up the way they were. Like it or not, you're changed forever, and I worry about what that might mean for me. Will it make me a different person? Will it change the way I see the world? Will it change the way I paint? If I lose that part of me, John, I lose everything. For a woman used to controlling her own life, it's unsettling and scary."

"For a man, too." Something in his tone made me turn my head to look at him. "Scary as hell. I know, Sheba." He gave a shrug that told me we were both making our way up the same squeaky steps and stood. "With Jem taken care of, let me treat you to supper."

My hand went to my hair in a reaction as typically female as a corset. "Not the way I look!"

He reached out a hand and waited. "Exactly the way you look. Don't fuss, Sheba. You could be wearing a burlap sack and you'd still put every other woman in the place to shame. Turn the sign on the door and come on. I know a place that serves the best food in town."

Hearing John Bliss so light-hearted was a rarity, like someone had picked up a fiddle and begun to play a bright and happy tune. I stood, marched over to the door, and did exactly what John said.

"There," I said. "Closed. Happy?"

Something flared in his eyes, an emotion that made me slightly breathless. I was glad I wasn't the one expected to answer, although John didn't seem to have any problem with a reply.

"Yes," he said, "happy. What man wouldn't be?" Then, without a moment of hesitation or self-consciousness, he reached for my hand and didn't let it go until he needed both hands to pull out my chair at the finest table Bliss Restaurant had to offer.

Later, walking home with no handholding this time, I pulled my shawl tighter around my shoulders against the night air and thought how pleasant it had been to sit across from a man that found me attractive, to laugh at little things and talk about nothing in particular. Normal, like my life used to be, but a little improved because of the look in John's eyes when he smiled at me. I'm only human, after all.

The Meat Market sits across the street from the Bliss

Restaurant, and I couldn't help but sneak a look in that direction as we stepped outside after supper. Of course, the place was dark. The Lincolns had built their living space out behind their market the same way my rooms were in the rear of the dress shop. Isaac and Harriet and Isaac's mother, Pleasant, were good people and had immediately fit right into the buzz of the New Hope hive. Isaac joined the Merchants' Association, Frederick started school, and the whole family came to worship every Sunday. Good people, solid and dependable. But even knowing all that was true, I simply couldn't help that quick glance across the street.

"He's fine, Sheba."

I had to chuckle. "Am I that obvious? You don't miss much, do you?"

"Not when it comes to you I don't." He didn't even look at me when he said the words, but they surprised and touched me, nevertheless.

When we reached the dress shop, I pushed the front door open.

"No key?" John asked.

"I'm still getting used to the idea," I replied, "but I knew you'd be with me when I came home tonight so I didn't bother with the lock."

He followed me back to the kitchen, no surprise visitor sitting there tonight, and waited until I turned up the lamp I had left dimly burning on the table.

"Well," he said. "I believe you're in safe and sound for the night," and turned to go.

"Stay for tea, won't you?" I knew I didn't want him to go, and it was all I could think of at the time.

When he turned back to face me, he said, "No old coffee on hand tonight?"

"No, just tea. Please stay, John. It'll only take me a few minutes."

He sat down without another word and watched me as I put the kettle on to boil and took down the jar of tea leaves. As I bustled and he watched, I was conscious of his presence in a way I had never been before. The back of my neck felt tingly and I feared that when I turned back with the filled teacups, he would see that I was blushing.

If I was, John didn't remark on it when I put his cup in front of him and joined him at the table. I picked up my cup with both hands to blow the tea cool, but he didn't touch his. Not generally a tea-drinking kind of man, I thought, and reminded myself to buy coffee beans.

"Do you have a knife in your boot right now?" I asked. The question coming out of the blue didn't faze him.

"I do. I'm never without it."

"Never? Do you wear it to church?"

"I'm not a regular church-goer, Sheba, but on the few occasions I've joined the congregation, yes, I had a knife in my boot even there."

"Huh." I had to think about that. "I guess I don't really know you, John, or understand you, even after six years."

"There's not all that much to know or understand."

"I doubt that's true."

"Maybe I should say there's not all that much I'd want you to know."

"You know just about everything about me," I reminded him. "I told you where I grew up, and why I left home, and what I've been doing since then. I didn't hold anything back, even though a lot of what I said wasn't anything I was proud of. I don't have a lover in my past, either."

"I'm glad to hear that, but it doesn't matter all that much to me in the end. It's not your past I'm interested in." He looked at me and smiled a little. "Is that your way of asking about Caro?"

Smart man to listen between the lines, I thought, and said, "Yes."

"I doubt it's what you think, though I can't tell you I don't have lovers in my past."

"Not with a straight face," I agreed, then added, "I'd still like you to tell me about Caroline Moore."

He began his story without further introduction, just

started speaking and kept talking until the story was over.

"My mother worked the honky-tonks in St. Louis. You could buy a dance from her and more than a dance if you had the cash. She was occupied a lot and mostly I just got in the way. She wasn't unkind, but she didn't know what to do with me so she never spent much time on me."

I thought of Dee and how she doted on Jem and how knowing you were loved could make bad situations seem not so bad. Poor little boy to be only a bother to his mother.

"She died when I was nine. Some sickness from her trade, I imagine. I never knew. She was there and then she wasn't. I don't know what would have happened if some people named Moore hadn't taken me under their wing."

The name got my attention, but I was smart enough to stay quiet. I doubted this was a story John Bliss told many people, and I felt honored by the telling.

"Harlan and Daisy Moore were on their way out west with a train of folks from Ohio, and there I was running wild in the streets of St. Louis, hungry and thieving for food. They were salt of the earth, those two. Hard-working, generous, reliable, just plain good people. Like the Shultes and the Lincolns. Like a lot of New Hope. They took a bastard boy in and never expected any thanks in return. People who did the right thing without being asked. There were three older daughters I never knew, all of them out of the house with families of their own by the time I came along. Harlan used to laugh about it, how he and Daisy thought their family was done and maybe they could catch a breath now and enjoy a little quiet when along came a son. David. My age exactly. They raised him and me like brothers, no difference in anything. Same schooling, same scoldings, same care, same everything. We made it as far west as Fort Kearney when Daisy told Harlan she was too old for a wagon and she wanted a house, so we stopped and settled up where Broken Bow is now. Harlan set up a smithy there. That was his trade."

I stood and brought over the kettle to reheat his tea and

mine, then sat down again, added another spoonful of sugar to my drink, and watched John's face, willing him to continue. I thought the last part of the story would be sadder than the start and wanted it over, more for his sake than mine.

"Davey was the best friend I ever had. More brothers than friends, I guess. He was like his folks: never saw bad in anyone. After Harlan and Daisy died—" John paused with the words, as if saying them out loud still hurt a little "—Davey and I took off for Virginia City. We heard there was silver there and we were young. Just nineteen, green as grass, and looking for adventure."

I tried to picture the man sitting across from me with his dark, cool eyes and inscrutable expression so young and fresh-faced and excited about the future, but the vision wouldn't come. When did that knife find its way into his boot? And why?

"We got there in the middle of the silver boom. What a place! People said Virginia City was the richest place in the country and to two would-be prospectors from Nebraska, it was like—" John shook his head at the memory. "I can't describe what it was like then, Sheba. Like San Francisco or Chicago, maybe, only nothing about Virginia City was civilized. It was just silver, silver, and more silver. Davey and I worked like dogs that first year, and it was hot as blazes, too. I would have given up, I think, but Davey was sure our strike was right around the corner. And then one day it turned out he was right. We hit silver. Not anything like the Comstock but big. Big for us, anyway. We hooted and hollered like fools and then used the first money we got to buy up all the land around us."

He was quiet a long time. I could see the memories on his face and didn't interrupt. At last he finished the story.

"Then Davey met Caroline and everything went to hell, and there's no one to blame for it but me. She was a hostess at a dance and gambling hall, and I thought the worst of her because of it. I knew the kind of woman she had to be even before I met her. With Davey into sudden money, he was easy pickings for a woman like that, I told him, and she sold her services to the highest bidder. The things I said about her before I even met her still shame me today, but at the time, I couldn't see it. All I could think was that I promised Davey's parents I'd keep watch over him and that's what I was doing, protecting him from being hurt because I knew the kind of woman she had to be, knew better than he did. That was me, always smarter than everybody else. When I finally searched her out, I offered her money to let Davey be. I should have known from how she acted then that I was wrong about her, with her proud look and her scornful words putting me in my place. Another man, a smarter man, would have backed off and thought things through, but at the time I was so damned sure of myself, sure I knew best and had her figured right when all along I was wrong. Wrong all which ways to Sunday. Wrong to say the things I said. Wrong to judge her like I did. In the end, Davey and I fought about it. Well, he punched and kept on punching and I took it because I owed his family too much to hit him back. Then he walked away and never looked back, not once. Sold his share of the mine to the Irish Big Four and left Virginia City without speaking another word to me. Caroline went with him. That was in '73, just when the Big Bonanza got discovered and I tried to stay on. There were fortunes being made every day, but without Davey, it wasn't the same. So I sold out, too. Maybe I could find Davey and make amends, I thought. Make things right, turn back the clock, get back what I lost. All those things. I figured he might go back to Nebraska – I was wrong there, too – so I headed in that direction myself. I got to New Hope and liked what I saw and stayed on."

I digested the story, one I was certain John had never shared with anyone else, and finally spoke. "I know you found Caroline, but what about Davey?"

"Caroline found me, Sheba. It was pure chance she heard about a place called Bliss House in New Hope, Nebraska. She asked the right questions – Caro's a woman who always asks the right questions – and then she wrote me because she thought I should know Davey was dead." I gave a little gasp in spite of expecting the sad news.

"I'm sorry." He acknowledged my words with a bleak smile.

"They bought a spread in Wyoming Territory, but something happened. Caroline doesn't speak about the details, only that there was a fire that killed Davey and their baby and almost killed her. She has scars." Scars inside and out, I thought. What woman wouldn't? "She was hurt and laid up a long time. When she got better, she went to Denver and found a job running a restaurant on the railway line, which is how she heard about the Bliss establishment in New Hope and wrote me about Davey. I went to Denver as soon as I heard and convinced her to come back with me to New Hope. She stayed a year until Gast made her a better offer in Ogallala. She's been there over three years now, so I guess it suits her. We both understand she doesn't owe me anything. She can go where she pleases."

I felt such a wave of tenderness for the man when he finally grew still that I didn't know what to say. I had regrets, too, about Dee and even about Father, and over the past months had begun to wake in the night wishing I'd done things differently in my own life. *Make things right, turn back the clock, get back what I lost.* Such useless thoughts, but they prey on a person when it's dark and quiet.

At last I asked, "Have you made peace, John?"

"With Caroline? Yes."

"I saw the two of you together so I know there's peace between you. Affection, too. I meant peace with yourself."

"That's a task easier said than done, Sheba."

"But not impossible."

"No, not impossible."

We both knew he hadn't answered my question and wasn't going to. Wasn't able to? Maybe that was the truth, but I hoped for a different truth: wasn't able to *yet.* I rose quickly, remembering the picture and glad to change the subject.

"I have a gift for you, and I think it's dry enough to handle," I said and hurried into the studio. John followed behind me and went over to check the lock on the door before coming to stand beside me.

"It's too dim to see in here," I said, and we both went back to the kitchen. It was too dim there, too, I knew. The Indian Summer morning light of the painting needed good lighting of its own to be appreciated, but I hoped even if it didn't show to advantage just then, he would be able to appreciate the effort and understand the emotion I had put into it. "I want to give you more than this, John, for your help in Ogallala and your protection in the alley the other day and because you're the first man I've ever really trusted, but this painting is all I'm able to give you right now."

The words made him look at me closely for a moment. I have more to give you, I wanted him to know, but I can't give it tonight. When Jem is safe and I don't share my bed with the twin specters of worry and fear, I'll share my bed with you. No one else before. No one else after. Ever and only you. But not tonight. Not now. Not yet.

Whatever he saw in my face made him reach a hand to my cheek for a moment before he turned his attention to the painting, hefted it higher, moved closer to the lamp on the table, and gave it a long leisurely examination. It was smaller than most of my other works and the colors more vivid. The high emotions I had felt as a reaction to the events of that morning in the alley all showed in the painting. John would understand.

"I don't know how you do this, Sheba. It's like you caught the morning in a bottle and then spilled all the colors out on the canvas. It's fine work."

A compliment from the most demanding art critic in Paris couldn't have pleased or warmed me more than those three words from John Bliss.

"Thank you."

"I'll have Harold make a frame to do it justice."

I eyed the painting. "I think it's too small for the hotel

foyer," I said with a critical tone, picturing the walls of the hotel's entry, "which is where I thought you'd want to hang it. I have another painting that I was going to give you before I finished this one and changed my mind. That one's bigger and would look better—"

"Sheba." I was glad to see a true smile, one without bitterness or grief or self-blame, on his face.

"What?"

"This isn't going in the foyer, it's going over my bed. As a reminder and a promise."

I didn't ask as a reminder of what because I knew he had heard all my unspoken promises. I felt suddenly – and uncharacteristically – shy, which apparently tickled John because he laughed before he set down the painting, reached for me, pulled me into his arms, and kissed me long and hard.

Sometime later, he asked, "Remember how I told you that when I got to New Hope I liked what I saw and stayed on?"

His voice was barely a murmur against my hair and frankly, at that particular time, I wasn't especially interested in talking, but it seemed rude to ignore his question so I said, 'Yes," and hoped he heard me, pressed as I was against his chest.

"What I saw and what I liked was you." The words surprised me enough to make me push away from the safety of his arms and look at him.

"Me?"

"You. I saw you walking down the other side of the street on my first day in town. You were a sight, hair the color of oak leaves in autumn and striding more than walking. You looked like a woman taking a dare, chin out, arms swinging. Just a sight."

"I don't think that's a compliment," I said, unimpressed and slightly indignant.

"It is a compliment, my love." *My love.* The casual words made my breath catch in my throat. "Nothing but," John continued, "and I decided right then and there that I wanted to be the man to take you up on that dare, whatever it was, so

I stayed."

"Hmph. For a man of your – let's say forceful – temperament, it certainly took you long enough."

"You didn't make it easy, but be that as it may, it was worth the wait." He pulled me back against him and hovered over my lips long enough to add softly, "And then some," before doing his best to make me forget that he had just described me as a big-chinned woman with a manly gait. A successful effort from a man accustomed to success, whether business or pleasure because when John finally stepped outside with a final reminder for me to set the lock behind him, he had managed to find his way back into my good graces.

And then some.

14

Harriet Lincoln and I spent a long while thanking each other after church the next day. I had to believe that private time with John enjoying his company and some of the other skills he possessed outweighed Harriet's appreciation for giving Frederick a playmate, but I didn't plan to share the details of my evening with her and our mutual thank-yous eventually shifted into talk about the weather and what we planned for Sunday dinner, safe small-town topics that never failed.

In the afternoon, Jem and Othello came with me to the far side of the schoolhouse. I was going to try my hand at a water color of the setting sun against the hills done on canvas stretched across quite small frames. Neither water colors nor small were customary practices for me, but something about the last few days in my life had made me eager to experiment and try for new effects. What effects exactly I didn't know, but I was excited by the possibility to fly – if not higher, than at least in a new direction.

Jem had brought along his new Jules Verne book and was sitting propped against the western wall of the school for warmth, since it was evident we had squeezed the last drop of heat out of this year's Indian Summer. Othello lay with his chin on Jem's leg.

Later still, we meandered home, Jem full of the book's

adventures and asking what it would be like – *really* – inside a volcano while I worried that little New Hope, Nebraska, would erupt into a volcano of its own making if someone didn't do something about Archie Sloan. As it turned out, I was right to worry.

I worked at getting all my winter orders cut and pinned and fitted, then basted and sewed and delivered. The work was both grueling and satisfying as one by one dresses, shirtwaists, camisoles, and knickers began to take shape. Bent over the sewing table concentrating on hems and seams, a mindless pastime, gave me the chance to think about what, if anything, I should be doing about the two knotty problems in my life: my sister's stubborn refusal to part with money that didn't belong to her and Archie Sloan's menacing presence and threats. I'm not a person who normally believes she is at the mercy of others, but in those two cases, I couldn't see it any other way.

Sloan was on his second week of being absent from New Hope, and I swung between happiness and uneasiness depending on my thoughts at the time. It was delightful not to have the man anywhere in sight, but my delight was always tempered with wondering where exactly he was and what exactly he was doing. Had he found new information that pointed him toward Dee? Had he, in fact, found her? Was he even now taking an unspeakable vengeance on her because of her betrayal? My imagination had the ability to keep me up at night if I allowed it to do so.

Thoughts of John Bliss had the ability to keep me up at night, too, but for very different reasons. We saw each other in passing long enough for a smile or a quick greeting, and it might have seemed to the general population of New Hope that nothing had changed between John and me, that we were the same casual friends we had been for the past few years, relaxed with each other and with a teasing edge to our conversation, but, of course, for me everything had changed. Nothing I felt for the man now could ever be described as casual or relaxed. Those days were gone. That wall was down.

Simply the sight of him at a distance down the street stirred memories of his hands on me and kindled a low-burning heat in my belly. I knew all about what went on between men and women and with my girlhood behind me, had felt relieved I escaped the worst of all that complicated craving. I had my art, after all.

Yet here I was, like a girl with her first schoolyard crush, and even that wasn't really accurate because being in John's arms didn't make me feel anything like a schoolgirl. If innocence were on one side of the scale and experience on the other, I knew the direction I wanted the balance to tip. How did this happen and who could I blame? So I sewed and thought and worried and lusted all week.

Luckily, Jem was busy with school work and Jules Verne, Othello and a growing friendship with Frederick Lincoln. As long as his meals were on the table and I listened to his prayers, the child didn't allow my mental distractions to cause any distractions of his own.

Until very early Friday morning when my distractions became public property and New Hope, Nebraska, as it had done three years before, again became a community invaded by shocking violence and sudden death.

By October, Nebraska is cold enough to put frost on the pumpkin overnight, so I put on my painting gloves – old wool gloves from which I had cut the fingers – a heavy barn jacket and a close-fitting cloth hat before I left the shop that Friday morning with all my usual gear in tow. As had become typical, I had enjoyed only fitful sleep so it made sense to be up earlier than usual, enjoy a quick cup of coffee, and then leave for an hour or two of painting, the only peaceful time that remained for me, the only time I could escape from myself – another artist will understand what I mean – with my eyes, my mind, and my hands aware of nothing but the physical world around me. A glorious reprieve from all things troublesome.

No true morning light yet, only a hint of it along the eastern horizon, but by the time I picked my spot and set up my easel, the hint would be a promise and I would be ready for the moment that came only once every twenty-four hours. Unfortunately, that morning ended up being a morning lost, in more ways than one.

I shut the door of the shop behind me with an ungainly one-handed movement, adjusted my bag on my shoulder, and stepped into the street, so preoccupied with deciding where I would set up my gear that at first the horses stomping and snorting restlessly in front of the bank didn't register with me. New Hope's main thoroughfare was always quiet around this time, John's Music Hall closed and its patrons long gone to sleep off the effects of drink or bemoan the money lost at cards, yet in front of me were four restless horses and one man in the saddle with all the reins looped in his hand. I felt a sudden alarm and for just a moment was unsure what to do. Rush back inside the dress shop? Hurry farther down to Hart's and rouse Si Carpenter? Whichever deputy had drawn night duty would by this time be back at the jail on the other end of town getting ready to turn the keys over to Si for the morning. Daybreak in New Hope was the quietest time of its day, no train arriving, no stores open for at least another hour.

In the end, the decision was made for me. Even as I stood there, literally open-mouthed, an explosion sounded from inside the bank, nothing that could have been heard on the opposite end of town but enough of a blast and a quick quake of the ground that the bank's immediate neighboring establishment, the Chandlers' hardware store, would have experienced quite a jolt. Even from where I stood, with a broad alley separating me from the bank, I made a reflexive retreat from the sound of the explosion. Not a minute after the sound, three men burst out of the front doors of the bank, making no attempt at quiet. Contrary to what I thought would be a robber's desire to escape without notice, these men shouted as they ran toward their horses and once mounted, reined back with one hand and brandished pistols, shooting into the air with enthusiasm like something from the cover of a Ned Buntline dime novel. Nothing I saw made any sense, so if not Ned Buntline, then perhaps I had dropped into one of Mr. Verne's fantastical stories.

The four men turned south toward the Platte, passing right in front of me and still firing so wildly that I felt the rush of a bullet as it barely missed me and instead cracked into the front door of the dress shop splintering the wood. If the man had been aiming, I would have been dead, but even then, without any details other than the scene before my eyes, still shocked and flustered and frightened, I knew that this was the work of Archie Sloan. He wasn't one of the four men on horseback, but he was present, nevertheless.

At the sound of wood splintering behind me, I whirled, terrified that somehow the bullet had continued through the door and into the shop. What if the noise roused Jem? What if he had padded barefoot toward the front door, curious about the racket? What if—? I couldn't finish the thought but instead dropped everything from my arms and used both hands to wrench at the door, now crooked and unwilling to open. From a side glance, I saw a shirtless Si Carpenter standing before the open gate that led to the boarding house's walk. He held a rifle in one hand and was taking aim at the figures in the distance, but I knew that even Silas Carpenter, as cool and steady a man as you'd find in New Hope, would not hit any of those targets. All of them too fast and too far by then.

Sobbing a little for breath, I looked first at the dress shop floor – nothing, no one, lying there, thank God, thank God – and then hurried into the back to shove open the bedroom door, where Jem sat on his mattress. The room was too dim to make out the details of his expression, but Jem's voice was sleepy.

"I heard a bang," he said.

I started to speak, but because of relief and fear and shock and even more because of love I began to cry instead, both hands over my mouth to stifle the sobs so I wouldn't alarm the boy. Let them rob the bank every day, I thought, let them break open the vault and turn all the citizens of New Hope into paupers, I didn't care as long as Jem was safe.

"Are you crying?"

I took an unsteady breath that turned into a hiccup and was finally able to say, "Yes. I'm sorry. Something blew up in the bank, and I was worried about you."

"But I'm not in the bank. I'm right here." Puzzlement there, poor child. More baffling behavior from adults for him to consider.

"I know." I was saved from having to explain my illogical words by a man's voice calling my name from the front of the shop, a man's voice thundering my name, really. I half-turned to see John Bliss burst into the kitchen.

"I'm all right," I said quickly. "We're both all right. Some men robbed the bank."

"Robbed? Really?" Jem sounded excited, curious, and slightly regretful. He had missed the whole ruckus, after all.

John halted abruptly at the sight of me in the bedroom doorway and drew in a deep breath. Normal color came back into his face. His eyes thawed.

"I know," he said. "I was closing up for the night when I heard the noise. I thought I saw you standing outside your shop, but it was still dark and then when I got closer, I saw the door—"

"Missed me by a mile," I said, and we both accepted the lie because anything else was unthinkable. There was too much unsaid and undone between us. I turned to Jem. "You stay right where you are."

"But—"

"Right where you are, young man," I repeated with greater emphasis, "until I get back."

A mulish expression showed on Jem's face, which I ignored long enough to repeat my words a third time and pull the door halfway closed.

"Was anyone hurt?" I asked after I pulled John out into the shop and away from little ears.

"I don't know. I don't think so." I heard in his voice the

same unrealized fear and breathless relief I had heard in my own voice when I talked to Jem as he sat whole and well in front of me. When we most need our walls, I thought, they are nowhere to be found.

John said my name. I took a moment to pull off my hat and shake out my hair before I went purposefully into his arms, holding him against me as tightly as I could, as much for his comfort as mine.

"I'm all right," I told him, "but we should be sure everyone else is, too," which caused him to say the most extraordinary thing.

"I don't love everyone else, Sheba."

The words had nearly the same effect on me as Jem's "I heard a bang," but instead of once more bursting into tears, I said quietly, "I know, but we should still check on the others," adding, "We both know Sloan is involved in this somehow, and I can't rest until the matter is taken care of one way or another. This is no way to live."

He stepped outside, shoving the damaged front door completely out of the way as he passed it, and reached back for my hand. "Without you is no way to live," he said. "That's all I know for sure, but come on, let's check on our neighbors and see what Si's planning. The man will never allow something like this in his own town and near his own home." Together we walked hurriedly toward the bank where a crowd had already gathered, buzzing like someone had overturned a hive of honeybees.

I saw Ruth standing apart from the others, wrapped in a huge shawl and holding the baby tightly against her chest. Of course, it wasn't the same at all, and yet somehow in her tight, close hold on Alexander, I saw John and me just a few minutes before in our momentary intense embrace. Touching brings its own kind of comfort, I thought, a truth I had disregarded since the early deaths of my mother and brother. The somber look on Ruth's face told me she knew her husband would go after the bank robbers and while she would never say a word in worry or complaint, she was still a loving wife and mother and wouldn't rest properly until her Silas was once more home, his duties done and his responsibilities met. I let go of John's hand and drifted over to my friend.

Ruth turned toward me. "Oh, Sheba, I saw the door of your shop! That was too close for comfort!"

"It didn't seem to me that they were aiming for anything in particular. They just wanted to wake everybody up." I looked around at the crowd. "And it looks like they were successful. What about the bank?"

"Abner just went inside with John. Everyone's waiting to hear the bad news. Were you up when it happened?"

"Up and outside, ready to paint a little sunrise."

"Oh, Sheba!" Ruth said again and closed her eyes for a moment. "Thank God you're safe. What a shock this is for little New Hope!"

It is and it isn't, I wanted to tell her, because I was certain Archie Sloan was involved, even when I didn't know how or why, but at that moment Abner Talamine stepped outside onto the boardwalk in front of his bank and the crowd grew instantly quiet. The bank owner seemed to have aged twenty years since the last time I had seen him. His bearing remained upright, but he carried an invisible weight on his shoulders that none of us missed. We all recognized bad news when we saw it, and each of us standing there was thinking the same questions: Is every single dollar I worked for and saved lining the pockets of men who never worked a day in their lives? Is it my future they'll spend? From the lines on Abner's face, we knew the answers before he spoke.

"Friends," a pause, a deep breath, and, "you entrusted me with your money and I failed you. It's gone. The vault was blown open and the money taken. I don't know what else to say except I'm sorry and I'll make it right, whatever it takes." With a hand to each lapel, he adjusted his suitcoat and stepped down into the street where his wife met him and tucked her hand under his arm. Abner Talamine had been good to me and given me the benefit of the doubt at my arrival in New Hope, and I was sorry to see and hear him so beaten. I wasn't the only one who felt that way because several people clapped him on the shoulder or murmured something encouraging to the banker and his wife as they passed through the crowd, actions that showed what set New Hope and its people apart.

When I turned my attention back to the bank, I saw Si Carpenter in serious conversation with John before the sheriff gave a nod and stepped up to the place where Abner Talamine had stood a few minutes earlier. The seriousness of the situation and the general regard in which people held Si once again quieted the crowd.

"Luke and I are leaving now to track the thieves, and I want to deputize four men to come with us. Monty will stay behind in New Hope and I'll deputize Bliss to support Monty here at home. I had Monty wire all the local lawmen along the Platte south and north, anyone who might run across four men on the run, and he'll get word to the neighboring counties, too. I expect we'll accomplish what we set out to do, which is recover your money and send four men to the state prison for a long time." From the small collective exhale of relief around me, I knew all of us found comfort in the calm confidence of Si's voice. Our sheriff is a man who does what he says he'll do, a man to be trusted. If anyone could restore the lost fortunes of New Hope, it was Silas Carpenter.

"I'll take volunteers," Si concluded, "but not just anyone. You may want to do your part, but to do any good you have to know your way around a weapon and you have to be willing to take orders." The requirements narrowed down the possibilities – not Dr. Danford and not Mort Lewis, attorney-at-law, for example. In the end, tough, broad-shouldered Con Tull, who as a younger man used to fight for a living and now ran the beer garden, the two Lowe brothers, and Joe Chandler were the four new deputies.

I stood close enough to Ellie and Joe Chandler to hear their discussion as Ellie tried to dissuade her husband from leaving. Most of the time, Ellie's temperament is as cheerful and friendly as her face is pretty, but she should not be underestimated, nevertheless. I wasn't there to witness the time Ellie turned on crotchety old Cap Sherman and called him an old fool in front of half the town in a voice not to be argued with, but Ruth had seen it all and relished the retelling. I was sorry to have missed the exchange and would have enjoyed seeing young Ellie put old, grizzled Cap Sherman in his place. Any man who makes no secret about his disdain for women *is* an old fool and needs to be reminded of the fact on a regular basis.

Ellie's concern that Friday morning, however, had nothing to do with Cap Sherman and everything to do with her husband and the father of her three children heading off after outlaws. Ellie and Joe stood close with baby Mary Marie between them, and I tried to move away to keep from overhearing their conversation. Ellie's words stayed soft and private and while I could guess at what she said, I never understood an actual word of hers. Joe, on the other hand, started off quiet enough but by his last words, his tone was firm, decisive, and loud.

"When they blew out the vault, they put you and the kids in danger, Ellie. The store's right next to the bank. What if they'd miscalculated? What if something had gone wrong? You could have been blown up in your beds. I won't have my family put in danger that way. These are men who need to be cut down to size and reminded how decent people live. Si said he'll have me and I'm going."

For a long moment Ellie stared at her husband, then she shifted the baby to one hip and pulled Joe down to kiss him on the mouth and say something soft that only he heard. Just a whisper of something between them that made his face soften.

"I will," Joe told her, staring down into his wife's upturned face as if trying to memorize every feature. "Nothing could ever keep me away." He dropped a quick kiss on little Mary's cheek and strode off after Si.

Eventually, the crowd dispersed. Stores had to be opened;

breakfasts had to be fixed and eaten; work continued; life in New Hope went on, bank robberies or not.

"I have to get Jem off to school," I told John, "and then see if Harold has time to repair my front door."

"Make sure the lock still works, too," John said in a grim voice, "because Si says Sloan wasn't one of the four robbers." We didn't have time for anything else except a nod and a smile, but I thought about John's observation as I awakened Jem, who had fallen back asleep, and set out his breakfast.

"You remember what I said about not talking to Mr. Sloan, don't you, Jem?" I asked.

He looked up from his oatmeal, one of the few breakfasts I could make without doing too much damage. "Yes, ma'am. I'm not to get close enough to him to talk to him is what you said. You said he was a bad man and if he tried to talk to me, I was to run away and find you."

"That still holds. You won't forget, will you?"

"No, but—" his brow wrinkled with serious thought "Aren't we supposed to be kind to our enemies? That's what Mrs. Shulte told us in Sunday School. She said it's like putting hot coals on their heads when we are."

Emptying a bucket of red-hot coals onto Archie Sloan's head held a lot of appeal for me just then, but I said, "If you ask Mrs. Shulte, she'll also tell you you're supposed to obey your elders, which is what I am. You can be kind to Mr. Sloan from a distance."

Jem gave me a look far older than his years and finally said, 'Yes, ma'am," before turning his attention back to picking out each raisin one-by-one from his oatmeal. Jem is partial to raisins.

"You're going to be late," I told him finally, although that was unlikely to be a problem. Everyone in New Hope was unsettled by the morning's robbery, and there had been talk about canceling school for the day. I didn't protest the idea because I liked the thought of having Jem under my watchful eye, but Mr. Stenton announced that except for starting one hour later than normal – his sole concession to the upheaval a bank robbery inflicts on a peaceful community – school would be held with all its usual academic activities. Civilization and education will always trump lawlessness and chaos.

I didn't have a single customer that day, something that hadn't occurred since my first year when both the shop and I had been new to New Hope. The day of the robbery, however, I thought people might be reconsidering their orders, reworking the family budget, and reevaluating the debit and credit columns of their respective businesses. For many of us, especially those with families, poverty was just one bad month away and even a little money in the bank acted as a safeguard against hardship. I wouldn't be surprised to have orders canceled, with regret and apology but canceled just the same, and what would I do with goods I couldn't sell? I didn't dwell on it, which in my opinion would have been a waste of time and decided instead to trust that Si and Luke, Si's right-hand assistant, and the four men riding with them would return home with all the missing money and the men that stole it. New Hope had learned a few years ago that Silas Carpenter was a man who accomplished what he set out to do and why, I asked myself, would it be any different now?

Thinking about Si made me think of Ruth, so with the store empty of customers and my head full of *what ifs*, I closed the newly-repaired front door – Harold didn't even charge me for the work – and walked down to the boarding house.

Lizbeth looked up from the front desk when I entered. "Oh, Miss Sheba, Ruth said you saw the whole bank robbery. Were you scared?"

"I'm embarrassed to say that I was too preoccupied with other matters to be scared. By the time I figured out what was going on right in front of me, the robbers and all our hard-earned cash were only dust in the distance. It's the reason I make dresses and don't keep the peace."

"It was wicked to steal what people worked so hard for," Lizbeth said, that touch of steel I had noticed before sounding in her voice. "They will no doubt be sorry when Sheriff Carpenter catches up with them." I recognized a kindred spirit with her words; Lizbeth was another person who trusted Silas without reservation.

"No doubt," I agreed. "Is Ruth in the kitchen?"

"Nursing the baby in the bedroom."

"I'll just go back," I said. "I don't think she'll mind."

Lizbeth smiled her agreement and went back to polishing the large butler's desk and the wall shelves behind it.

"I hoped you'd come over," Ruth said when she saw me in the bedroom doorway. "I needed some company and while Lizbeth usually keeps my mind occupied, I didn't want to load her down with my thoughts today."

Ruth sat in a rocking chair next to her and Si's bed, not nursing anymore because the baby looked asleep but still rocking, more to keep herself occupied than anything else, I thought.

"I know you worry," I said quietly, "but you of all people know that Si Carpenter is a careful, thorough hunter. He's an expert at that kind of work, Ruth."

"I know that, Sheba, of course, I do, and I don't speak my worries out loud, but loving someone doesn't just increase your joys. It increases your worries, too." She gave me a sly look, not a typical expression for Ruth. "Haven't you figured that out by now?"

"Having Jem around has changed my view of things," I admitted.

"I wasn't talking about Jem."

If I was having the conversation with anyone but Ruth, I probably would have snapped out a quick and feisty reply and flounced off, but the only thing I had ever kept from Ruth was the fact that my sister possessed a stolen fortune and while I had a good reason for doing so, even that omission made me uncomfortable. In general, I can spin a falsehood if pushed to do so, but not to Ruth, not to a woman so filled with light.

"I won't say I don't know what or who you're talking

about, but it's too soon for me to make an intelligent comment. When I look back, it seems to me that one day John and I were just good friends and the next day—well, the next day we were more than friends and I have yet to figure out when and how that happened."

Ruth smiled. "It's a funny thing, isn't it? I fell for Duncan the very first time I saw him. We hadn't said a single word to each other, and yet I knew when he stepped off the train that he was the man for me. With Silas, though, it was like you said. We were friends for a while and then over time, being friends wasn't enough for all the feelings we had." I didn't want to talk about the feelings I had, not with Ruth or with anyone, and she must have seen that on my face because she shifted the subject.

"I've never seen my husband struggle with a decision the way he did this morning." At my questioning look, Ruth said, "Si knew he needed to go after those robbers, but he didn't want to leave New Hope. He said he had a bad feeling about whatever he decided to do because Archie Sloan was nowhere to be seen. That's a loose end for Silas, and my husband hates loose ends."

"Si can't be in two places at once," I responded, "but I think he's right to worry. I don't like it either." We sat in silence for a moment until I rose.

"I'm going to go home and finish Klara Fenstermeier's dress. Maybe she hid enough money under the mattress that she'll be able to pay for it," adding as an afterthought, "Poor Abner. He looked terrible, didn't he?"

"Yes. He's a man that takes his responsibilities seriously and we're all his friends, besides. He was carrying a heavy burden this morning."

"Well, if anyone can catch up with those thieves and bring our money home, it's your husband. He can take care of himself and he knows his business."

His *dangerous* business, Ruth might have amended, his *deadly* business, and I would have understood and agreed. But she wasn't a woman to give words to those kinds of thoughts so she only smiled, laid a quick kiss on the baby's head, and said simply, "I agree on both counts, Sheba. Thank you."

Later, working in the solitude of my shop, I considered what Ruth had said about how increased joys increased your worries, too. It was the same effect with art, I realized with surprise. Just as great happiness could by contrast make a person's fears appear darker, so the brighter the sunlight, the blacker the shadows the sunlight cast. How was it that I had gone so many years without recognizing the connection?

15

At supper that same night, Jem told me without the slightest attempt at modesty that Mr. Stenton had shown the world map he and Frederick had created using the school's globe as a model to all the students and said it was the best effort the teacher had ever seen in all his years of teaching.

"Congratulations," I said, feeling almost the same level of gratified pride as my nephew but also feeling it was my duty as the adult in charge to use the moment for some kind of lesson about life, so I added, "It's a fine feeling to work hard and be recognized for your effort, isn't it?"

"And Mr. Stenton asked Frederick and me to stay after school tomorrow," Jem ignored my efforts to build his character and continued, "to help him put the map up on the side wall. He said he wants to keep it up there for the rest of the month."

"He must like it very much then."

"Very much," Jem agreed happily. He took a last bite of potato and looked back at me to say in a tone older than his years, "I know, Aunt Sheba. 'Reputation is an idle and most false imposition; oft got without merit, and lost without deserving.'"

I stared at the boy and finally found the words to ask, "And that would be from—?"

"The second act of *Othello*." Jem did his best not to let any pity for my unfortunate ignorance about the plays of William Shakespeare show in his voice.

Six years old, I thought, and familiar with both *King Lear* and *Othello*, two of Shakespeare's most morbid tragedies. I felt warmed by a small burst of love for the boy. What an unusual mixture of adult and child he was!

"Mrs. Carpenter sent over molasses cookies," I said, because I couldn't think of an appropriate response to the words of William Shakespeare.

"Mrs. Carpenter is a very nice lady, isn't she?"

"Yes," I answered, "she is." I pushed the plate of cookies toward Jem. "You may have two." Which fortunately put an end to any continuing discussion about pride, hard work, reputation, and William Shakespeare. My day had been challenging enough as it was.

While busier with talk than purchases, I still stayed occupied well into Saturday afternoon. Farmers and ranchers from the outlying areas came in to make their weekly purchases, and I could recognize the ones who buried their money in a can in the backyard by the relieved expressions on their faces when they heard about the bank robbery. I hoped that one of those can-burying wives would need a new dress for winter because I didn't expect much business from any of the others.

By mid-afternoon, when a wall of cloud turned the sky gray and the wind rose, most people decided to start home. It wasn't until then, Main Street slowly emptying of traffic and the bell on the shop door motionless for more than an hour, that I began to wonder where Jem was. Even now, years later, I can't understand my lack of concern. Of course, I knew he and Frederick Lincoln were staying behind with Mr. Stenton to put up their map, but Saturday classes were only until noon and how long could it take to pin a paper to the wall? I should have been concerned much sooner, but I wasn't.

Monty, the younger of Si's two deputies, stopped by for a chat before continuing his rounds through New Hope, and that took up a little time. A diligent and steadfast young man, not yet twenty I would have said, Monty fairly worshipped Si Carpenter and took his job as an assistant peace officer very seriously. Si thought highly of Monty, too, and Ruth often set an extra plate for the deputy at their table. The young man's surname was Montgomery and his nickname Monty, but for all I knew, he didn't have a first name. After Monty left, I began to straighten the shop because it was obvious I shouldn't expect any more customers that day and then, as if someone had prodded me with a stick, I stopped what I was doing and straightened, suddenly upright and completely still. Jem should have been home by now, I thought. Something is wrong.

The moment seemed almost a stage cue, something right out of one of Shakespeare's tragedies because as a feeling of dread settled over me, the door of the shop opened, and young Frederick Lincoln entered. Alone.

One look at the boy's face and I said without a word of greeting, "What is it? What's happened?"

Frederick came closer and held out his hand, which clasped a piece of paper.

"He said I was to give you this." I didn't take the paper at first.

"Who said?" He flinched a little at my harsh tone, and I made myself speak more gently. "Tell me what's happened, Frederick." I took the paper from the child's hand and thought he relaxed slightly to be rid of the burden, the paper a weight he could hardly carry. It would be a heavy burden for me, too, I knew, and didn't look at it.

"A man told me to give you this. I don't know who he is. He came to the schoolhouse and he shot Mr. Stenton dead, I think, and he wouldn't let Jem leave with me. He told me to give you this note or he'd hurt Jem." The words came out in a rush. No wonder the paper had felt like an anvil in his hand.

Oddly, I felt everything in me slow down, my heartbeat, my breath, my motions, everything. Shouldn't everything be racing instead?

"Is that where Jem and the man are now, at the

schoolhouse?"

Frederick nodded. "Yes, ma'am." He watched wordlessly as I opened the note.

> I have the boy. You know what I want. Come to the schoolhouse. Keep it to yourself. You and me can work this out.

I refolded the paper. "You did a good job bringing this straight to me, Frederick. Now I'm going to give you three more jobs to do so pay attention. First, I want you to find Mr. Bliss. You know who John Bliss is, don't you?"

"Yes, ma'am."

"Good. When you find Mr. Bliss, tell him what happened at the schoolhouse and that you gave me a note like you were told to. Then I want you to find Mr. Gruber at the Gooseneck Hotel and tell him the same things, only I want you to give Mr. Gruber this note. Hand it to him just like you handed it to me." I took the boy's hand, placed the note on his open palm, and folded his fingers over the paper. Was it my imagination or did Frederick's shoulders sink once more under the weight of that small piece of paper? "Do you know who Mr. Gruber is?"

"Yes, ma'am."

"Good boy. Be sure you give him the note. The last thing I want you to do is go straight home. Don't talk to anybody along the way. When you get home, you tell your father and your mother everything that happened. They'll know what to do. You stay close to them." I placed both my hands on his shoulders and bent to look directly into his dark eyes. "Mr. Bliss. Mr. Gruber. Straight home. Can you remember all that?"

One more, "yes, ma'am," as answer.

"Thank you, Frederick. Jem and I are counting on you." We walked outside together and shared one more serious look. Then he jumped down into the street and raced straight across while I made my way toward the schoolhouse.

The wind had picked up enough to make it feel colder

than it really was, so while the street wasn't empty of people, the weather was urging those still out to get their errands done quickly and head for the warmth of home. No one paid any attention to me. When I stepped into the broad alley that led west to the schoolhouse, I picked up my skirts and began to run, past the photography studio and Ruby's house and laundry shed, up the small crest and down the other side until at last with the schoolhouse in view I had to stop for lack of breath. I was bent over, hands on my knees, and gasping. All my parts that had seemed to slow down when Frederick Lincoln first entered the dress shop now raced at top speed. The schoolhouse sat directly in front of me, and as I watched, still panting, the door opened to show a man's figure in the doorway. Even from that distance, I recognized him and the distinctive, flat-crowned hat he wore. The two of us stood looking at each other across the school yard where children usually played. No one played there now, but the breeze made it look as if invisible children rode the two small plank swings blowing back and forth from ropes attached to tree branches at the side of the schoolhouse. Neither Archie Sloan nor I spoke. Finally, my breathing back to normal, I walked purposefully toward the schoolhouse.

Still without a word, I got an arm's length from Sloan before I stopped. One arm across the doorway barred me from entrance and in the other he held a rifle.

"That's far enough," he said.

"I want to see him."

"You will when I get what belongs to me."

"You let me in, you son of a bitch. Do you think I'm stupid enough to bargain for something I don't even know for sure you have?"

"Boy," Sloan called back over his shoulder, "tell your Aunt Sheba you're in there."

A moment, then, "I'm here, Aunt Sheba." No quaver in his voice.

"I want to see him." I stared at Sloan.

"You and your sister. Two of a kind. Always think you

should get what you want." He stared back at me, defiant and for some reason angry, as if I held the gun. "I got no reason to do what you say."

"You won't hurt me," I said, "because I'm the only link you've got to all that money." I drawled out the last three words with an insolent slowness. "If you make the wrong moves here and miss out on your money, you won't have time to try to find my sister because you'll be too busy running from the law. Either we work together on this or we both lose, so get out of my way and let me see my nephew. Otherwise, I'll stand here until hell freezes over and don't think I won't."

Begrudging the effort, the man stepped aside and I entered the schoolhouse. Jem sat on the floor with his back against the big teacher's desk at the front of the room. One of Jem's legs was tied to the leg of the desk by a length of rope. The desk was heavy and the knots looked firm; the boy wasn't going anywhere. Sloan grabbed my upper arm as I passed and kept me from getting closer.

"Are you all right?" I asked Jem.

"Yes, ma'am, but," I could see his little Adam's apple bob with the gulp he took, "Mr. Stenton is hurt bad. I think he might be dead."

I followed Jem's gaze to the side wall where the teacher lay on his side. I had to dredge up my artist's eye in order to look at Arthur Stenton without reacting with horror to the sight. The colors were stark: a spill of dark red blood under his legs, a splinter of white bone protruding from a black pant leg.

"What have you done?" I hissed at Sloan.

"He wouldn't leave when I told him to. Said he wasn't about to leave the boy. I didn't have a choice." No apology in his voice but a slight regret because, I thought, he realized that murder made everything different. I realized it, too. One murder, six murders, a dozen murders and you can still only hang a man once. When Jem was no more use to Sloan, what would keep Sloan from killing the child, for spite if for no other reason?

I didn't have a chance to respond because Sloan suddenly whirled in the doorway, pulling me around with him so that I stood in front of him and we both faced outside.

"Not another step," Sloan shouted. "You come into range, and I'll blow this woman's brains out."

John came to an abrupt halt at the bottom of the ridge, panting. Close on his heels was another man, slim, young, and hatless. Monty.

"Turn her loose, Sloan. You might live longer if you do."

"I'll let her loose, Bliss, but all in good time. You stay right there, you and the other fella, and I'll send her out to you." To me, he spoke in a low voice. "You get your sister here with my money."

"I don't know where she is."

He gave my arm a hard jerk. "Then you better get busy and damn well find her because you got twenty-four hours."

"I can gather the money," I said, but I knew after the bank robbery that there wasn't that much money left anywhere in New Hope, even if I went begging from door to door. He knew it, too.

"You get her here and tell her she better have every last cent with her, otherwise I'll send that boy back to her piece by piece, finger by finger, one ear and then the other. Nobody wants that, do they?"

"He's your own flesh and blood, your brother's son," I said with disgust, "and you'd hurt him that way? What kind of man are you?"

"She told you that, did she? Like I should care about what belongs to Cole. Like I ever mattered to him. Cole." I heard envy when he said the name, and a kind of loathing and something else I couldn't place. Something softer and almost sad. Was it regret? Loss? "All the years we were growing up, people said he was the one with the brains and the looks. He was the one everybody took to. Oh, Archie, he'll never amount to nothing, but Cole now, he can't do no wrong. It was always that way. He never done nothing for me. I'm the one that saw Fannie. I'm the one that wanted her and should've had her, but he's the one that got her. They couldn't keep their hands off each other. It made me sick. Her and the boy are nothing to me."

"Sheba." The breeze threatened to blow John's voice away. "Let it be for now and come here."

"Yeah, you do that, Sheba," Sloan's voice was harsh against my face, "and don't come back empty-handed."

I hesitated, more torn with that decision than any other choice I had ever made in my life. Walking out the front door of the only home I'd ever known and leaving everything familiar behind was child's play compared to that moment. I knew I had to go, but how could I walk away and leave Jem tied to a desk, his only companion a man who threatened to cut off the boy's fingers one at a time? How could I go? How could I stay?

From inside the schoolhouse, Arthur Stenton groaned. The sound made both Sloan and me turn toward the wounded man's figure.

"He's not dead," me stating what was now obvious.

"Guess not." Sloan sounded surprised but indifferent.

For me, however, Arthur's groan provided the impetus I needed to make a move. "I'll leave, but I'm taking Arthur with me."

"No."

"Yes. You don't need him here. He doesn't have anything you want and maybe if he doesn't die, maybe if all you're guilty of is taking back what was owed you," – plus kidnapping, I thought, and attempted murder, and bank robbery, but I didn't mention any of that – "the law won't be on your tail quite so close. Maybe you'll have time to disappear. Mexico's not that far. But murdering a respected school teacher in Si Carpenter's town— well, you know Si will never let that go. Never. You must have heard his story, how he tracked a man to this very town and how he didn't stop until he got him. Why take that chance if you don't have to?"

"I told you I can take care of Carpenter. Got him out of

town, didn't I?" but I could see Sloan worrying his lower lip in thought. Then, "All right, you can have him."

I sent Jem a quick look that I hoped was reassuring but more likely appeared simply desperate and went to crouch over Mr. Stenton. He groaned again but didn't open his eyes.

"Arthur," I said quietly, "can you hear me, can you help me?" No response. "All I know for sure is if I leave you here, you'll die, so I'm going to try to get you to Tom. He'll know what to do. I'm sorry if I hurt you." Mr. Stenton was not a big man but without him able to help me, he might as well have had the bulk of Con Tull.

As I cleared desks for a direct path to the door, Sloan yelled out, almost certainly to John, "Stop! I told you don't move. She ain't come to no harm yet, but if you take another step, I swear to God I'll put a bullet in her back."

I crouched again by Mr. Stenton and with my back bent and both my hands under his arms, I began to pull – yank – haul his body toward the door. For what seemed an eternity, he was no more help than a burlap bag of seed corn would have been, and then I felt the burden lighten ever so slightly as Arthur tried to use his good leg to help, tried to push himself along as I pulled. I couldn't bear to look at the bad leg and the jagged edge of bone as it poked through and then disappeared again into his pants leg. If the man could feel anything, and now that he was giving me weak assistance I hoped, I feared, he could, the pain must be excruciating. At the threshold of the door, Sloan stepped to the side but didn't look down at me. His gaze was fixed on the men in the distance; not just two now, but three.

"Twenty-four hours," he said to me as I dragged Arthur past him. "You got twenty-four hours and they start now. You watch the shadows on those trees and get me what I want before sundown tomorrow or you'll get that boy back in pieces. She took something of mine; I'll take something of hers. Sounds fair to me."

I couldn't respond, not with the burden, the burdens, I bore. Instead, I made it over the threshold and then was outside, me with my back to the waiting men and still bent nearly in half, pulling Arthur Stenton along over ground that suddenly seemed as rough as railroad tracks. We bumped along. I yanked and pulled the best I could, and Arthur's good foot did its best to help by pushing himself forward. My pulling and his pushing, my labored grunting and his labored moaning, we just kept going, with my eyes on Arthur and his eyes closed. I couldn't tell if he was conscious enough to be aware of what he was doing. The two of us just kept going in what seemed an endless effort.

Until someone pushed me to the side and took over for me, did even more than that. The big arms of Isaac Lincoln lifted Mr. Stenton with ease.

"I got him now, Sheba," Isaac said, brusque and firm. He turned without any more words back in the direction of New Hope.

"Don't let him die, Isaac," I called to the man's back. "You tell Tom the same. Don't you let him die." No answer from Isaac but his pace picked up.

I straightened and pressed both hands to the small of my back, my mind busy with plans as I stretched.

"Sheba." John's voice brought my hands to my side and my eyes to his face. He looked different than I was used to seeing him, the skin around his dark eyes drawn taut into small creases. He spoke one word as a cautious question. "Jem?"

"He's in there, tied up, maybe scared, I couldn't tell, but he's fine for now." John exhaled and a little color returned to his face.

"Good. Are you—?"

"I'm all right, John, but I need to find Bert Gruber." For a moment I could see John wanted to pull me against him, to hold on and not let go, but while I understood the urge, I had work to do and only twenty-four hours to do it.

"Truly," I said, "I'm all right," and tried to smile. "But listen, John, Sloan will hurt Jem, I'm convinced of it, unless I get Dee to New Hope along with the money. I don't have much time, and I need to find her first. I don't know how to do that exactly, but I've got some ideas. You have to stay here and make sure no one makes a move toward the schoolhouse. No heroics. Will you do that?"

"Yes." Monty stood behind John, listening to our conversation and at my question, nodded in agreement as if I had been speaking directly to him.

"Thank you." I used both my palms to draw his face close to mine. "Thank you, my dear," I said and kissed him. Monty turned his attention elsewhere, still young enough to be embarrassed, but when John would have turned it into more than a simple thank you, I backed away quickly from the temptation of his arms. "I have things to do. I can't stay. Will you wait for me here?"

"Don't you know by now that I'll wait for you anywhere you tell me for as long as it takes?"

I wanted to say more but felt an overwhelming need to leave, to get wheels turning, to find Dee, to tell her what was at stake here, to make her understand that she risked something precious and irreplaceable for dreams only she possessed. John must have seen all those thoughts spread across my face because he used both hands to push me gently in the direction of the town.

"Go on, Sheba. I'll be here when you get back. I'm not going anywhere, not without you." I didn't need any more urging.

I didn't know where my sister was at that particular time, but I believed there was someone who did and who could find Dee for me. Bert Gruber. The problem became that I couldn't find Bert. Not at the Gooseneck and not at the billiards tables. Not anywhere.

At the Lincolns' meat market, Harriet looked up from behind the counter where she was getting ready to close for the day, wrapping the few remaining cuts of meat and placing them in the fancy icebox they had ordered from Chicago. She set everything down and came around to the front.

"Oh, Sheba, what terrible thing has happened?" Harriet

rested a hand on her chest as if trying to slow down her heartbeat. I knew the feeling.

"A bad man named Archie Sloan has been holding a grudge against my sister for a long time," I said. It would be the explanation I gave again and again, not completely true but true, nevertheless. "He's decided it's time to get even with her, and he intends to use Jem to do that."

Harriet nodded and asked, "And is Jem—?"

"Not hurt." I couldn't continue with that topic and instead asked, "Harriet, could I talk to Frederick a moment? He's here isn't he?"

"In the back with Pleasant. I'll get him." In a moment both the child and his grandmother appeared. I hadn't exchanged much conversation with Pleasant Lincoln and knew her more by sight than anything else. An elderly woman born into slavery, she was gray-haired with a permanent stoop to her back. Her name seemed to reflect her nature. I thought that age had bent her more than slavery ever could because despite the forward thrust of her shoulders, she remained dignified and proud. I greeted Pleasant and went to crouch in front of Frederick.

"Thank you for being such a help today," I told the boy. "I don't know what I'd have done without you. I don't mean to doubt you, but I need to be sure – did you give Mr. Gruber the note like I asked?"

"Yes, ma'am. I put it right in his hand."

"What did he do then? Did he say anything?"

Frederick's forehead wrinkled with his effort to get everything right. "He said thank you and then he read the note and put it in his pocket and he gave me a nickel and told me to go home."

"Did you notice if Mr. Gruber went anywhere after that?"

"I don't know. Not that I saw." He paused a moment. "Is Jem home safe?" Reflected in his eyes was the same worry I felt.

"Not yet, but soon, and Mr. Stenton's at the doctor's by now."

Behind me Harriet said softly, "Not dead then?"

I stood and turned toward her and Pleasant. "Seriously injured, but the last I saw him, Isaac was carrying him to Dr. Danford."

"I don't know what to make of all this," Harriet said.

The older woman made a small, scornful sound. "There's been wicked men since Cain killed his brother, Harriet. Did you think we'd be spared our part once we settled here?" She turned to me and gave a small smile that showed a mouth full of teeth so perfect that at her advanced years they were unlikely to be the original set. "Don't you worry, Miz Fenway. We been praying for Jem since Frederick brought the news home. The good Lord says, 'a wicked man is loathsome, and cometh to shame.'"

I didn't have the old woman's faith, but I appreciated the kind thought. "Thank you, Mrs. Lincoln. I hope that's right because it can't happen soon enough for me."

At the livery, Cap Sherman told me Bert hadn't borrowed either horse or wagon from him, but I had better luck at the train station window.

After explaining that Union Pacific Railway policy did not encourage him to give out information about passengers, Mr. Copco leaned over the counter and said in a low voice, "Bought a one-way ticket to Willow Island, Sheba. That's all I know."

"Willow Island's east isn't it?"

"Yes, ma'am. Five stations east."

Bert Gruber was on his way to find Dee, I guessed, and the only important question was whether he could find her and bring her back to New Hope before Sunday supper. But in case I was wrong, or Bert was wrong, there were other actions I needed to take.

First was to send a wire to Caroline Moore in Ogallala to ask if Dee was still performing there under the name of Florence Delarose or any name, for that matter, and if not, to find out if Marty Chip remained in town. If they were both gone, did Caroline have an idea where either or both of them were now?

I sent a second telegram to Potter, to the attention of Martha at Lulu's asking if she knew where the Alice Variety Theatre of the West was currently performing.

Finally, I asked Lonnie if he knew which towns on the telegraph line had law offices, and when he said he knew some but not all, I said that would have to do and dictated a telegram that said:

> Must get message to actress Fannie Newell (stop) also known as Florence Delarose (stop) needed at home immediately (stop) son gravely ill (stop) need help finding her (stop)

I used my name as signature, and when Lonnie had the list ready, I put a hand on his arm before he could click a word and told him I knew these were a lot of telegrams to send and sending them would cost a significant sum, which I wouldn't have until Sheriff Carpenter returned the stolen money to the bank. Knowing the resolve of Silas Carpenter, I concluded, that was sure to happen, but until it did, would Lonnie be accommodating enough to send the telegrams and send me a bill for the service at a later date? It was a fine speech.

Lonnie, unimpressed with my thoughtful rhetoric, shrugged and said, "I can do that, but I doubt I'll have to, not with you and Mr. Bliss being as close as you are. Everybody knows he's got money in more banks than Mr. Talamine's so he's good for it."

In a small town, a woman doesn't possess an ounce of privacy, I thought with a fleeting rush of indignation, and I certainly did not need John Bliss to pay my bills. But the part about John having money in other banks was news to me and I had more important matters on my mind than people knowing who I spent time with, so if the man's name and business reputation could get me what I wanted, I needed to swallow my pride, smile, and say thank you. I managed the first two, asked Lonnie with the sweetest smile I could muster if he'd bring any responding telegrams out to the schoolhouse where I would be spending the night, and then added the thank you like a period at the end of a long and rambling sentence. The sweetness of his reply – "I promise to do that, Miss Sheba, regardless of the time, though I won't be getting anything back until morning" – made me briefly sorry for all the times I had bullied him to get my own way.

My errands took time and when I left the telegraph office, it was well past supper time with only a slit of twilight still on the horizon. One more errand and I would head back to the schoolhouse, where I had no doubt a patient John still watched and waited.

Margery Danford, the doctor's wife, met me when I entered the drug store. I didn't need to say a word.

"He's still alive, Sheba," Margery said. "Tom says the leg is shattered but he may be able to keep it. If he lives, that is, and Tom's not willing to make a guess either way. Arthur lost a lot of blood and he's not a big man to start with." After that report, she asked about Jem. I gave a quick reply and left, sending a longing glance toward the boarding house directly across the street as I picked up my pace and made my way back to the alley and then to the schoolhouse.

Sometime in my absence, someone had brought a bench – it looked like the fancy one from outside the barber shop – and set it up at a distance from the schoolhouse, not close enough to be in rifle range but close enough to see if or when the door opened. There was no smoke from the tin chimney that poked up on the roof and no windows to tell if there were lights on inside. I thought of Jem sitting on the floor of a cold, dark room, tied up to a desk, a helpless victim of the actions of adults over which he had no control, one of the adults being a man that threatened to cut off the boy's fingers. I couldn't dwell on any of it too much.

Monty was nowhere to be seen. John, seated on the bench, turned as I approached and without a word I sat down next to him and pulled myself as close to his side as I could get, not for warmth, although the night's temperature was sure to drop, but for the feel of his body against mine. In need of something more substantial than warmth and for the time being able to find it only in John Bliss.

"Anything new?" I asked.

"No."

I told John everything I had done and concluded, "I don't know what else to do, John, but there must be more I could be doing. Can you think of anything?" Something in my voice caused him to place an arm around my shoulders and pull me even closer.

"No," a pause, then, "I might be able to gather up enough money to make Sloan happy, Sheba, but I can't get it here by Sunday night. Maybe if we told him—"

John Bliss had sold a silver mine, after all, so it was his willing generosity more than the offer itself that touched me.

"Thank you. I told Sloan something of that nature, but he said he wants to see Dee along with the money. I know he has his own plan in mind, some awful revenge. That's why I worry so about Jem, no matter what happens. There's got to be more I can do, but I'm at a loss." I shook my head. "I've never said that very often in my life."

"It's not always up to you, Sheba," John said in quiet response.

"Meaning?"

"Meaning it's up to other people now, to Bert and your sister and maybe Caroline or one of those lawmen who got your wire. Other people have a part to play as much as you do now. None of this was of your making, and you've tried to fix it the best you know how." Of course, he was right, but the knowledge didn't make my heart less sore, my worry less sharp, my anger less intense.

"What if she doesn't come?" I asked. "What will I do?"

"Monty and I have talked through a couple of ideas."

"But if Sloan thinks we aren't following his orders he'll—"

John said my name in as stern a tone as he had ever used with me and turned to kiss me squarely on the mouth before saying, "That's enough. I won't let anything happen to the boy. He's in there and not hurt, you said, and he'll come home the same way." There was enough moonlight that I could make out his serious expression.

"All right," I said at last. "I'm sorry. I'm not used to loving someone, and I can't always control myself."

"I know what you mean."

When I caught his look, I had to smile. After a moment I added, "Margery said Mr. Stenton might live."

"That's good news."

I straightened and looked around. "Speaking of Monty and your ideas, where is that young man?"

"I sent him back to town to get something to eat and make his rounds. There's nothing to be done here right now. He'll be back. He's young, but he doesn't want for nerve."

"I don't know much about him."

"He's been on his own all his life, with no Harlan and Daisy Moore coming to his rescue."

"I'm sorry for that."

"He'll do. Si thinks highly of him and Si isn't one to praise if praise isn't deserved."

As if talking of Si made her appear, Ruth's voice came quietly from behind us. "It's just me. I don't want to startle you." John and I both stood and faced her. "I have a pot of hot coffee and a wool blanket for you, if it's your plan to spend all night out here. Is it?" The question was directed to me.

"Where else could I be, Ruth? How could I stay home and sleep warm in my bed when Jem's here? I wouldn't want him to think I abandoned him." She set the coffee pot and two tin cups on the seat of the bench and reached a hand to pat me on the shoulder.

"I know. If it was Alexander or Silas, I'd do the same. I had a wire from Silas this afternoon, by the way." She turned slightly to include John in the conversation. "They caught up with Sloan's men outside of Norton, Kansas. The Norton County sheriff had heard about some men moving through his county fast and thought they might be the ones Silas was looking for."

"Was anyone hurt?" I asked.

Ruth's calm tone told me that her Silas and the others from New Hope were safe, but I wondered about Sloan's men. Her answer to my question was indirect.

"Silas said they had to wait in Norton for representatives from the Union Pacific to take charge of two robbers and get them to Lincoln. The governor's taken a special interest because it looks like these are the men responsible for the recent train and bank robberies in the state."

"Two robbers," I repeated, "when there were four to start with."

"Yes."

"I can't be sorry," my tone dismissive. They were men gone and better forgotten, as far as I was concerned. "Will we get our money back?"

"We will. Every cent."

I knew that was good news, good for the citizens of New Hope, Nebraska, and good for me, too, but I would have traded every last cent to have Jem home, feeding Othello from the supper table when I'd told him a hundred times not to and quoting from Shakespeare and adding names I didn't recognize to his ever-growing list of people he prayed for.

"That's good," I said. "Did you let Si know we're having a little trouble here?" To say the least.

"I did. He wired right back that he was leaving Lucas, Joe, and Con in Norton with the two prisoners and riding straight home with Mitch and Russ, but even if they rode straight through without a single stop, there's still no way he'd get here before tomorrow night. I'm sorry, Sheba."

"It's not his fault or yours. Sloan's plan was always to get Si out of town. That was the purpose of robbing our bank, not the money, at least not for Sloan. The only money he cares about is some money Dee took from him a long time ago, and for him it's more than that now. Sloan needs to prove that no one, especially a woman, can get the best of him, needs it so much that he can't think straight about it anymore. That's why I'm so afraid for Jem."

Ruth could have asked questions about the money, the first she had heard of it, but all she did was squeeze my shoulder for comfort. "I have to get back. I left Alex at Ruby Strunk's, and she's got enough on her hands with her own children, eight I think I counted. John, you take care of my friend."

"I'll do that, Ruth." In the moonlight I could see how she tilted her head a little to meet his look and then smiled.

"Yes," she said, satisfied with what she saw in his face, "I see that you will."

After she left, John and I stayed standing while I filled two cups from the pot and handed him one of them. We sipped our coffee in companionable silence. Finally, I moved the coffee pot to the far end of the seat and sat, pulling John down beside me. He took care to wrap the blanket around my shoulders and I thought I heard him make some kind of sound, not a real laugh with the seriousness of the situation but a more quiet and rueful sound, as if he were laughing at some action of his own that with hindsight now seemed ridiculous.

"What?" I asked.

John pulled a portion of the blanket more tightly around my shoulders. "We've spent two nights together, and neither one's what I was hoping for," he said at last.

I smiled to myself and without responding laid my head on his shoulder. The still, dark schoolhouse sat in the distance with just enough moonlight to silhouette the trees against the heavens. I sat with my head on John's shoulder and the rest of me curved ever-so-slightly against his chest. My left hand lay in his right. Our fingers intertwined. His warmth made me warm, and I thought that was how it should be between a man and a woman, willing to share whatever heat the other needed, willing to offer comfort and loan shelter.

"All right?" John asked, his breath warm against my cheek.

"Yes," I said.

We sat very close and not speaking well into the night.

16

Sometime later, past midnight I guessed, but nowhere near dawn, a voice behind us called a soft greeting that made me sit upright. I was somewhere between waking and sleeping, but John's figure next to me, while relaxed, never seemed anything but alert.

"Everything quiet in town?" John asked.

Monty came around to stand in front of us. It felt cold enough that I expected to see his breath in the moonlight when he spoke, but there was nothing. Sitting motionless had made me feel colder than the temperature warranted.

"Quiet enough. People would like to do more, but I told them no, told them it's better without a crowd around. You and me will handle this."

Monty's face was sun-browned from working outside much of his life, but otherwise he was fair, with shaggy blonde hair Ruth often felt compelled to take a scissors to and eyes somewhere between green and brown. Not much of a smiler but a pleasant enough young man, with the kind of face that would show its age only half as fast as the rest of us. Perhaps it was that quality that made him seem so very young. That night, standing between us and the schoolhouse, light from the moon behind him turned his hair pure white. I longed for my paints and a brush to try to capture the illumined halo that made the deputy look angelic.

"I can sit a while," Monty offered John. "Why don't you make sure the Music Hall shuts down like it should? They'll listen to you more than me."

When John would have protested, I said, quickly, "Why don't you, John? You've been here for hours and it'll stay quiet until you get back. I promise to take care of Monty so he doesn't get into any trouble." Both men smiled at my feeble humor.

"I wish you luck with that, Sheba," John said and stood. "I think I will make sure my place is shut down and quiet, though I know Benny can turn out the lights as well as I can." John leaned down to brush a light kiss across my lips. "I'll be back in a while." He exchanged a look with Monty, some kind of man-talk going on there to which I was not privy, and walked back toward town, striding up the small crest easily before his figure was out of view.

I patted the empty bench beside me. "You can sit, Monty. I appreciate the company." He had acquired a hat since I'd last seen him, which he took off and set on the bench between us.

"I'm sorry about the boy," Monty said.

"Thank you. Me, too."

"I don't know the whole story," and when I would have spoken, he continued quickly, "and I don't need to. It's never right to threaten hurt to a child. Never. I feel the same as Bliss about what's going on here." He stopped and added, "'Course you and me ain't – I mean, it's clear he'd cut off an arm if that would make you happy—"

"That would definitely not make me happy," I said firmly, "but I know what you're trying to say, and thank you for that, Monty." I wanted to fill the hours to make the night pass and at the same time wished the night would last twice as long as usual if that's what it took to find Dee. Talking seemed all I had at my disposal. "I don't think I've ever talked to you except a hello or a good night as we passed each other. I'm sorry about that. I guess I haven't been very neighborly."

"You keep busy with your painting," he replied, not

bothering to argue with my confessed unneighborliness. "That picture hanging at the boarding house is just about the prettiest thing I ever seen."

"You like the river?"

"I like the way you made the river look, all sparkly and clean. It's how things ought to be in life."

"Sparkly and clean, you mean?" He turned to see if I was making light of his comment, and when he saw that I was as serious as he, he nodded.

"Yes, ma'am. The world we got ain't always very pretty. People ain't always very pretty, either, but when I look at that picture I can almost see what it would be like if we took better care of each other. Peaceful like and bright. That's what brought me to the law. Maybe I can help make New Hope be more like that picture." He paused, suddenly self-conscious. "Well, that's the way it seems to me, anyway."

For a moment I thought I would embarrass both of us by weeping. I paint the world as I see it and then long for the finished work to mean something to someone, always in the back of my mind thinking that *someone* had to be a fancy gallery owner in New York City or a famous art connoisseur in Paris or a Chicago art dealer. And here was this unschooled boy with the face of an angel and a ridiculous cowlick that refused to be tamed talking to me about my paintings in a way that told me they really meant something to him other than filling a space on the wall. Young Monty – who deserved a proper first name, I thought, no matter how outlandish it was – had just paid me a high honor. He understood what art was supposed to do. Open windows. Tease the imagination. Take you places you had never been before. Force you to think thoughts you had never imagined before.

I was quiet so long I believe he thought he had offended me because his voice had a sheepish quality when he said, "Well, I don't know nothing about painting and such, so you can just forget I said that."

"I will never forget you said that," I replied, speaking forcefully so he'd understand I meant what I said. "It was kind of you and you know what? You got it exactly right. Paintings and books and music mean different things to different people, but all of it is food for our souls. A lot of people don't understand that, but I believe you do."

"All I know about the soul is what I hear in church. Pastor Shulte's been trying to explain it to me, but when I think about a man like Archie Sloan threatening to hurt a little boy, I wonder if some folks missed out on getting a soul altogether." His comment brought me back to where I sat and why I sat there.

"I don't disagree," I said.

We talked a little more, about what brought him to New Hope, how he admired Si Carpenter and adored – no exaggeration on my part – Ruth, how he liked living somewhere where he felt he belonged, and how he'd made friends in New Hope that meant a lot to him. He dipped his head when he spoke that last part, looking suddenly shy, and I thought one of those friends was someone special. I understood everything Monty said because it was the same way I felt about living in New Hope. Such an accommodating little town.

By the time John returned, I realized to my shame that I had learned more about Monty in the hour or two we talked that night than in all the months he had been Si Carpenter's junior deputy. You keep busy with your painting, Monty had said, and he was right. I couldn't argue. For me, painting was life. But people were life, too, in a different way, and didn't each somehow balance and affect the other? If there was a lesson to be learned from my vigil, it was that sitting on a bench through a dark and quiet Saturday night gave a person entirely too much time for reflection.

After Monty left, I said to John, "He's a nice young man."

"He is that," John said, then paused. "Should I be jealous?"

"No. Monty's nice enough, for sure, but I'm partial to men who carry knives in their boots."

"That's a relief." He gave me a light kiss and I settled back against him, accustomed now to the way we fit together. I'm going to hold on to this man, I decided. Having someone around who knows how to keep a person warm will come in handy in the middle of a Nebraska winter.

I rearranged the blanket and drew it more tightly around my shoulders. Closer to dawn than dusk now, and I couldn't help but shiver when I thought about what Sunday might bring.

How John knew my thoughts I don't know, but as if he had read my mind he said, "He'll be home safe and sound, Sheba. You'll see. In twenty-four hours this will all be behind us."

The words made my breath catch in my throat. Oh, but what if—? I wanted to cry, what if—? and refused to finish the question. Instead, I remembered what Monty had said: *I can almost see what it would be like if we took better care of each other. Peaceful like and bright.* This is just my time for darkness and shadows, I told myself, looking for straws to grasp, but hope and light will win out, must win out, in the end.

I dozed on and off until John said my name, and I came awake with a start.

"What? Is—?"

"Look," he said, and I followed his outstretched hand to a glorious sunrise, the early light streaked and gleaming, as sharp and brilliant as lightning and turning the few morning clouds into polished river stones.

"Your eye is as good as mine," I told him.

"No, it's just that I'm learning to see the world through your eyes."

I thought about those words as I trudged back to New Hope. Monty had shown up early, and he and John had moved away from where I sat to hold a serious dialogue. I could see by the way that John listened to the younger man that he respected his view, regardless of the deputy's youth.

I stopped briefly at the doctor's office to hear the good news that Arthur Stenton hadn't died during the night, which would be the only hopeful message I would hear all morning.

From there, I crossed the street to the dress shop so I could wash my face, replait my hair, and don a different shirtwaist before I took the coffee pot and cups back to the boarding house.

Ruth heard me enter and came out of The Addition to stand in the hallway. "It was a long night for you," she stated. She was still in her nightdress and wrapper.

"Yes, but I had good company."

Ruth gave a quick flash of smile before she said, "I don't know all the details, Sheba, but we'll have a prayer during service this morning for everyone involved."

I regret my next words. I was weary and sick with worry, but those are neither acceptable reasons nor valid excuses. "If you waste a prayer on Archie Sloan, I'll never forgive you," just like that, my voice as cold as the morning air.

"It's Jem we'll pray for."

"You do that, Ruth, if it makes you feel better, but how much good did it do at Duncan's bedside? All those nights you sat there praying and he's still dead, isn't he? It's not prayer that's needed here, it's my sister showing up with a bag of money."

To her credit, Ruth did not respond in kind, but I knew my words and harsh tone had startled her. She blinked once and said, "I understand."

I was instantly contrite. Of all people, Ruth Churchill Carpenter did understand what it was like to worry and yearn, and why take out my heartsickness on a friend who had never been anything but kind? But I couldn't say the *I'm sorry* that was called for. I just couldn't. Instead, I set the pot and cups down on the desk and left without speaking another word.

Bert Gruber hadn't been seen all night, the clerk at the Gooseneck Hotel told me, and no, he didn't know where Bert was and no, Bert hadn't left a message for me or anyone. "He goes away like that sometimes," young Miltie Barber explained. "Gone a day or two and then back with never a word of explanation. Not that I mind 'cause he pays me a little more to be in charge when he's not here."

I met Lonnie at the door of the telegraph office, earlier than his usual Sunday hours, and I appreciated that he had changed his routine because of the situation at the schoolhouse.

"Got some answers coming in already this morning," he told me and shoved a fist of paper messages into my hands.

"Anything?" I asked before I looked at the wires and knew by the shake of his head that I wasn't holding any good news.

"But I'll stay here and if anything comes through you need to see, I'll bring it right out to you."

Caroline Moore's was the first message I read. She was sorry to tell me that my sister had disappeared one night a while ago, and even Marty Chip didn't know where she went. She would ask more questions and let me know if there was news.

Not Martha but someone I didn't know from Potter sent a short wire saying the Alice Variety Theatre was long gone weeks ago, and no one knew anything more about them. There was a brief postscript: Do they owe you money, too?

Three law officers all sent the same message: Regret no knowledge of either Fannie Newell or Florence Delarose.

Each message a disappointment and a failure.

When I returned to the schoolhouse, Monty stayed behind while John stepped away for a while. The day promised late-October sun and a constant wind strong enough to make the tree branches bend.

"Likely see our first snow before the month's out," Monty said, but when I protested, he replied, "Just be glad this ain't Montana Territory. Now that's cold."

"Was that your home?"

"No, I wouldn't say that, but I spent some of my younger years there."

I wanted to ask more but felt that was too nosy and contented myself with asking, "What brought you to New Hope?"

"Cows. I come along with a Texas herd to pick up the railroad here and I just liked it. People were nice to me and it seemed like a place where I could settle down. Now that I been here a while, I don't plan to leave. I liked the name, too. New Hope. I liked that."

"Me, too," I said. Our conversation was interrupted when Archie Sloan opened the schoolhouse door with a flourish and stepped into the doorway.

"Sheba, you still there?" Sloan called, laughing a little. "Hell, if I'd known you were sitting out in the cold all night I'd have invited you in to keep me and the boy company. I know some ways to keep a woman warm." At Sloan's voice, both Monty and I stood.

"I'm going to make sure Jem's all right." I bunched my skirts and took a few steps with Monty hurrying right behind me.

"I don't think that's a good idea and Bliss ain't here."

I turned so I could get a look at the young man's face. He looked concerned and uncertain, for that moment as much a boy as Jem.

"He won't hurt me," I told Monty. "He wants to know if he'll get what he wants, and he knows I'm the only one who can tell him that. Watch but stay out of range, and we'll be safe enough for the time being."

Monty reached behind him for his rifle. "All right, but if you need me, you call and I'll come running."

I sent a smile to the serious young man, now standing with legs apart and the rifle cradled in his arms. "Thank you."

Sloan watched my approach without speaking.

"I want to see my nephew," I said when I was close enough to speak without shouting.

"Not 'til I get what I want."

"My sister's on the way, but she's no more a fool than you are. She'll want to be sure her son's alive and unharmed."

As I came closer, Sloan studied my face, not sure I told the truth. "So you knew where she was all the time."

"Not exactly, but close enough."

"Well, son of a bitch," he said, not without approval, "you nearly had me believing you didn't know any more than I did."

"I'm a good liar," I replied, "but what difference does it make now? You'll have to wait for the late train if you want the money. I want to see Jem."

He stepped to the side and I walked in past him, determined not to flinch or jerk away as my shoulder brushed against his chest. The man smelled of whiskey and cigarettes and sweat. Jem was still tied to the desk leg, but the length of rope was long enough to allow him to move and reposition himself under the chalkboard at the front of the classroom.

He looked awfully small, and the sight of him kindled such a fire of outrage and hatred inside me that I had to take a deep breath before I could crouch beside him and smile. He smiled in return, but I could tell his heart wasn't in it. Why would I expect anything different?

"He didn't hurt you, did he?" I asked, alarmed by the boy's expression, which I couldn't quite make out. Was he mournful? Embarrassed? Afraid?

"No, but—"

"What?"

Jem lowered his voice. "He said I couldn't go out back and I had to – you know – over in the corner. Right here in school. Three times." He looked and sounded mortified at the enormity of the offense. In school, of all places.

"Oh, honey," I said, relieved, "that's fine. We'll clean it up later." With Mr. Stenton's blood soaked into the floor, more than that corner would need a good scrubbing. "How did you sleep?"

"I missed Othello," a statement that placed me in the proper pecking order.

"He missed you, too."

"Archie says Mama's coming. Is she?"

"Yes, I believe so." Jem's eyes lit up and to keep him from pursuing the subject, I asked quickly, "Are you hungry?"

"A little. We ate something called hardtack with some bread and Archie offered me something from a bottle that he was drinking from, but I didn't like it and I had to spit it out.

When can I go home?" The question felt as sharp as a knife to the breast.

"Pretty soon."

"Can I come with you now?"

"No, not just yet. You need to be brave a little while longer." I saw his mouth droop slightly with disappointment, but he recovered his usual sensible attitude.

"All right. Wish you'd have brought my book."

"Next visit," I said, but Archie Sloan, standing behind me, had heard enough.

"Not gonna be a next visit. You need to get out and go wait by the train station. I'll be listening for the whistles. I figure you got less than twelve hours now. Better pray there ain't no delay on the tracks."

I said to Jem, "Remember, stay brave a little while longer. Everything will be fine. You'll be home in a twinkle," earning me a small smile in return. I stood and with Sloan too close knocked my shoulder into the man as I walked toward the door. "The boy's more of a man than you'll ever be." Scorn thickened my voice, but I was immediately sorry I said even that much because I feared he might take his anger out on Jem. To my surprise, Sloan nodded with admiration.

"Got Sloan blood in him, that's for sure, and more me than Cole." His words to me weren't nearly as cordial. "You bring her here as soon as she's off the train. Bring her straight here and tell her what I'll do if she don't have the money with her. Him having Sloan blood ain't gonna keep me from lopping off an ear."

I didn't respond to the provocation but lifted my skirts away from him, the way a woman would do if she were trying to keep them out of the muck, and stepped outside. Two men stood in the distance now, both still and giving the schoolhouse their full attention.

John walked forward to meet me. After a quick look at my face, he said, "The boy's all right then."

"Yes. He's never been a complainer, but John, I think I may have said the wrong thing. I told Sloan Dee was coming on the late train. He'll expect to see her here by suppertime."

"I think that gained us a couple extra hours, Sheba, so it's not a bad thing. Are you still planning to sit out here?"

"Yes. Lonnie Markman said he'd deliver any wires with hopeful news, and except for the telegraph office I don't have any place to be. You and Monty can take care of your own business if you want. Monty has his rounds to make around town, and I've learned enough about him to know he's a young man who takes his duty seriously. And maybe you could check on Arthur and see if anyone's seen Bert recently."

Both men followed through on my suggestion and walked off together, still deep in conversation as they disappeared over the nearby ridge. I wasn't alone for long, however, because Isaac Lincoln joined me too quickly for it to be an accident.

"I don't want to take you away from your family, Isaac," I protested.

"That Jem of yours almost seems like family by now, Sheba. I believe Frederick thinks as highly of him as he would a brother." He paused. "Frederick had a little brother, but we lost him in '79, the year before we came to New Hope. Lost another one late last year."

"I'm sorry. I didn't know." But I should have known, I thought sadly. Maybe I could have done something to ease their sorrow. They were my neighbors, after all. The woman I was before Jem seemed more and more a stranger to me.

"After losing Moses to fever, Harriet told me she was expecting again, and for a while I thought maybe what my mother always says about the Lord giving and taking was true. But Harriet lost the baby early on. For a while, I feared I'd lose her, too. It was a bad time. I credit Doctor Danford with saving her life. Harriet's not over it yet, but she's not one to complain." I could tell from the tone of his voice that it wasn't only Harriet who was still grieving and healing. "It's losing our Moses that made her take to Jem so quick."

"Jem's good medicine," I said.

Isaac caught the slight quaver in my voice and laid a hand over mine. "He'll be fine, Sheba. You'll see."

"How can you be so sure after what you've lost?"

"It's always better to dwell on hope. I was born a slave just like my mother, but I knew the time would come when we'd be free. I just knew it. It was a matter of waiting and hoping and waiting some more. Now I own my own business, my son goes to school same as all the children in New Hope, and I can buy my wife a new dress made just for her. I was born into slavery, Sheba! If that can happen to me, then you shouldn't be thinking the worst. There's no future in that."

I would remember that talk with Isaac and his kind advice at unexpected moments all that long afternoon. *Waiting and hoping and waiting some more.*

When I didn't return to the shop for any kind of luncheon, Ruth brought me a plate of ham and bread and pickles, everything about her exactly as it always was. Same smile. Same warm concern. Same encouragement. I might never have snapped at her or reminded her of the many, many nights she kept a despairing vigil at the bedside of a dearly loved and dying husband. I was sorry I had spoken so harshly to her in such a mocking, angry tone, but I could not tell her I was sorry. I don't know why the words stuck in my throat, but I simply could not say them aloud.

John came and went. Monty did the same. The wind picked up and blew in clouds that covered the sun. Sloan had left the schoolhouse door open after my departure and every once in a while, he came and stood very briefly in the doorway. Was he doing the same as I? *Waiting and hoping and waiting some more?*

By late in the afternoon, I was unable to sit for nervousness. I'll hear the train whistle in an hour or so, I thought, and what will I do then? When no Dee appears and greenbacks do not rain from the heavens? What will happen? What will I do then?

John had to put a gentle hand on my shoulder to put an end to my pacing. "Come and sit down, Sheba. We should talk."

I stared at him, hearing something ominous in the words, and then followed him to the bench. He wanted to take my hand in his, but I wouldn't allow it.

"Just tell me what you have to say," I said. "I'm not a child in need of comfort. Just tell me."

"All right." For the moment, John reminded me of Ruth this morning at the boarding house, patient with my bad temper and not inclined to take offense at anything I said or did.

"We can't count on your sister getting to New Hope in time. You know that as well as I do. I think you're right about Gruber knowing where she is and that he went to get her, but after he got off the train at Willow Island, nobody knows what happened to him. I've wired people I know there, but they can't tell me anything. If Gruber had to go farther north than Custer or farther south than Daviesville, there's no way he could get her back to New Hope in time. That's the truth of it, Sheba."

"I understand."

"And while I don't think there's a man in New Hope who wouldn't step up to help if asked, they're not men used to guns or being in a fight, not like Si or Luke, and Ruth says Si won't get back before nightfall no matter how hard he pushes. Except for the part you have to play – and God knows if there was a way around that, I'd lock you in the bank vault before I'd have you anywhere near Archie Sloan – Monty and I figure we're better off on our own."

"Don't delude yourself, John, that even you can make me go anywhere I don't want to go." He needed to get that straight in his mind for whatever the future held between us. "That's the only disagreement I have with anything you've said so far. Now tell me what you and Monty have in mind."

John took a deep breath and then released it in a long, soft exhale. "You understand there's no way Sloan is going to give Jem up. The boy's his only ticket out of here. As long as he has Jem, he knows we won't risk any harm coming to him so

Sloan needs to hold on to him."

"Oh." I hadn't thought that far ahead. Get the money and make the trade was as far as I had got, but with John's words, I realized how woefully bad I was at thinking the way a bad man would think.

"So we have to get Jem outside where we can see him and know where he is. I'm not telling you it's not dangerous, but it's better than having the boy hogtied to a desk and unable to run. Sloan'll keep Jem close, but we've – you've – got to convince him that there's no deal until your sister sees that her son's safe. You'll need to make him believe that she won't put herself or the money within his reach until she sees that Jem is alive and well. That's your part."

"But she's not even here." Maybe it was being tired that kept John's words from making sense.

"No, but you are, and from a distance, the two of you look a lot alike. With your hair down and in different clothes, you can distract Sloan, make him take a second look."

"But when he realizes I'm not Dee, he'll be furious. He'll hurt Jem for sure then."

"Listen to me, Sheba." What a patient man John Bliss was! A virtue I had never appreciated in him before but especially needed then, with my mind moving at the pace of molasses in January. "I told you why Sloan won't let Jem go. He knows he won't stand a chance of getting out of here without having the boy as ransom for safe passage, but it's worse if he gets away with Jem because having the boy along will draw attention Sloan won't want. The law will be looking for the two of them, and it will be a lot safer for him if he's a man traveling on his own. As soon as Sloan gets out of sight, having the boy along will mean nothing but trouble for him. Do you understand what I'm trying to tell you?" I did. Of course, I did. John couldn't bring himself to say the words out loud, but I heard them, nevertheless.

"Yes," I said in a small voice. "Yes, I see." What I saw was an unbearable picture, and I had needed John to paint it for me.

"There's no good plan here, Sheba. No guarantees. But Monty and I think if we can get Jem untied from that desk and in a place where he can run if given the chance, and if we can distract Sloan long enough for one of us to get close, we might be able to end this with nobody getting hurt."

"With Jem not getting hurt, you mean," I said.

"Jem or you, Sheba. I'm thinking about both of you." He was quiet then and sat back and away from me to give me the space I needed to think about everything he had told me. I tried to think of alternatives, something less tentative, something without the potential for violence or at least with a greater potential for success, but I couldn't. Because, I thought, with a vicious man and an innocent child hidden away inside a building with only one door and no windows, there wasn't an alternative, especially not with the time we had been given. Monty and John had done the best they could with the little they had to work with. It was up to me to do my part with equal resolve.

"All right," I said finally, "go over everything with me, what I need to say and where I should stand and where you'll be and where Monty will be – just everything."

"Good girl," John said and leaned toward me to explain in detail what was likely to happen in just over an hour.

17

I've found through the years that memory is seldom trustworthy. Words a person remembers slowly change over time into the words she wanted to hear. People are recalled as taller or shorter, wittier or prettier than they really were. Happy occasions become happier. Sad occasions slowly lose the sharp edge of grief that sent us collapsing to the ground from sorrow at the time. Memory adjusts itself to the longings of the person remembering.

But for me, every moment of that October Sunday afternoon outside the schoolhouse in New Hope, Nebraska, is like an etching done on fine crystal. Clear and unshaded, deep and permanent. If I choose to, if I let myself, I can relive every step and hear every word from the moment the whistle of the last train announced its arrival. I will – I can – never forget it.

Sloan heard the whistle the same as everyone else. Monty hiding in the shadows among the trees and John and I seated on the bench pretending that life and death weren't marching right toward us.

"Well, there it is." I meant the whistle, and John understood.

"Yes," a pause, then, "Maybe this isn't—" I could hear the sudden doubt in his voice, but I didn't let him finish.

"It's all we've got. I'll be careful, and you be sure you do the same." I gave him a quick smile and started walking toward the schoolhouse.

"Ain't you going the wrong way?" Sloan asked from the doorway. "Train station's on the other side of the hill."

I pulled one of my useless telegrams from a pocket. "Dee wired to say she needs to see Jem safe and in one piece before she'll go ahead with what you want."

"She's not the one giving orders."

"Maybe not, but she's the one with the money."

"You can tell her you saw the boy and he was fine."

"Why do you think my sister would believe a single word I said?" I sent him a scornful look. "I could tell from the way you talked that you and your brother were a lot like Dee and me. No love lost between us, that's for sure. Wouldn't we have tried to find each other over the years if it made a difference to either of us? You know how my sister is, how she always expects to get what she wants, and what she wants is to see with her own eyes that you haven't harmed her son."

"She can come in and have a little visit then, like you done."

"Do you really think she's fool enough to get within arm's length of you and give you the chance to hurt both her and Jem? I gave you credit for more brains than that."

Archie Sloan looked at me a long time, so long that I thought he must somehow be able to read on my face every detail John and Monty and I had planned, but at last he said, "Well, you go get her and I'll think about it."

"I'm telling you—" but those were three words too many.

He raised the hand that dangled half-hidden from my view and aimed the long-barreled revolver directly at me.

"You ain't telling me nothing," the words drawled and deliberate. "You just bring her here, and her and me'll work it out."

I shrugged. "Have it your way then, but don't think you and Dee are that different. Money's always been as important as people to her." I turned and walked away at a steady pace, unrushed, with all the time in the world.

Behind me, Sloan called to John, "You be sure to keep the hell out of the way, Bliss. I owe you for that little business in the alley the other day, and I'd just as soon kill you as look at you. Everybody told me how dangerous you were, but all I see is a man hiding behind his woman's skirts." John was too smart to reply just then; his response would come later.

Once down the ridge and out of sight of the schoolhouse, I hurried to the dress shop. Mort Lewis, town lawyer, tried to get my attention by calling to me from across the street, but I shouted, "Later!" in response and went inside to change clothes and stuff my old traveling valise with fabric grabbed from the front of the store. The bag was believable, looking like it could be filled with money and heavy enough to hold greenbacks yet not so heavy I couldn't lift it. I stopped and took a breath, trying to gauge how long it would take to collect a person from the train station on the far north end of town and get her to the schoolhouse. Don't rush, I told myself, but don't dawdle, either. For the briefest of moments, I realized how impossible this was, how ridiculous and doomed, but I also remembered Isaac Lincoln's words about waiting and hoping and waiting some more. The waiting was finally over, but not the hoping. Never the hoping.

I decided against the constraint of a hat and simply unwove my heavy braid, removed the hairpins, and ran my hands through my hair so it looked wild and full. Then, dressed in my old traveling suit, I lifted the bag and stepped outside. I knew people had to see me. This was New Hope, after all, but it was late Sunday afternoon and Sundays are the quietest day of the week. On a cool, windy afternoon they were likely to be reading the newspaper they hadn't been able to get to all week or writing letters to faraway family or enjoying an innocent game of jacks or marbles with their children. That's the kind of place New Hope was, a place that had learned to take in and absorb evil, as it had done three years earlier, and yet somehow hold on to its decency. Many of the people who saw me walking with unmistakable purpose back toward the schoolhouse would be praying, too.

Ruth would be one of them, a woman who believed praying possessed some kind of power, believed it even when doing so had failed her and left her a widow. I had wondered often enough if that made her a fool or a saint. Now I better understood how a person might consider desperate, even impossible measures, if it meant you could hold on to a person you loved. Wasn't that what I was doing? Neither fool nor saint. Just human.

I crested the hill and started down the other side, stopping as soon as I saw there were two figures in the schoolhouse doorway, one big and one small. I took a few steps closer so Sloan would be sure to see me and stopped again, dropping the bag at my feet. The wind, which had picked up, played its part and blew my hair up and across my face. There would be no way Sloan could know Dee had been black-haired the last time I saw her, and from a distance my hair would look the same color as my sister's.

"Well, well, well." Sloan had seen me. "Look who we got here. Where'd you leave your sister?"

I made an exaggerated shrugging motion, picked up the bag, took a few more steps forward, and halted again. I didn't look at John, who I knew would be standing by the bench inching his way forward while Sloan's attention was fixed on me.

"You got yourself quite a boy here, Fannie."

The man had a tight hold on Jem's upper arm and gave it such a hard jerk upward that Jem gave a subdued squawk. "Ow!"

With that one small exclamation, I felt such a spurt of rage that it was all I could do not to rush forward, screaming names at him as I went. I didn't do anything like that, of course, but I must have done something, jerked or stiffened, because he saw it. It was then, because the man had the instincts and the urges of an animal, that he suddenly seemed to question the scene, began to wonder what exactly was occurring in front of him. He gave Jem's arm another jerk.

"Time to talk to me, Fannie. I ain't got all day. You

wanted to be sure your boy was alive. Well, look at him. He is now. But there ain't no telling how long that'll last." He raised the same hand with the same pistol he had aimed at me earlier and held the barrel against Jem's temple. "Boy won't be so smart with his brains all over the ground."

I couldn't risk play acting any more. I knew the plan was for me to distract the man and keep him talking long enough for Monty to slip from his position among the trees and reach the north side of the building and for John to reach a range where he could use his Winchester to advantage, and I knew I hadn't given either man enough time to do what was called for, but I trusted my own judgement. Archie Sloan held the long barrel of a revolver pressed against Jem's head and I believed taking even one more slow, mute step forward would be a mistake I would regret all my life.

I picked up the bag once more and walked quickly forward, my gaze fixed on the man's face. His eyes made a sweep of the area and he shouted at John to stop where he was if he didn't want somebody to die. The words sounded half-hearted, however, because by then Sloan had turned his attention back to me, looking slightly hesitant and puzzled enough to let the gun droop slightly. I knew from his expression the exact moment when he realized I wasn't Dee.

"What the hell?!" he said. "You ain't Fannie!"

He raised the gun, once more briefly hesitating but this time I believe it was because he couldn't decide whether to kill me first or Jem, he was that furious at the deception.

"That's right," I cried, "I'm not." I was ready to say more, ready with words to make him so furious that he would choose me as target, not Jem, but it never came to that.

From my right, on the far side of the bench where I had spent most of the night, a woman's voice called, "Oh, Archie. Smart as ever. You're so right. She isn't Fannie. But I am."

I turned and stared at my sister. She was an actress, after all, and while I knew she must have raced here – Bert Gruber was far behind Dee, only just then appearing at the crest of the small hill with his chest heaving from the effort – there was no breathless tremble to my sister's voice. Despite the wind, it carried strong and firm. She was used to speaking over the noise of bar rooms and brawls.

Dee took a few steps forward, dropped her carpet bag to the ground, and bent to open it. "Somebody told me you wanted something I've got," she called when she stood upright again.

In one hand she held a wad of greenbacks that she waved at him as if gesturing a friendly greeting to an acquaintance. Her hair was no longer black but was back to the color we shared, and like my hair, the wind lifted hers and blew it all which ways. She was a glorious sight!

"Is this it, Archie?" With her other hand she pulled one of the bills free and released it. The wind took it up in the air and then away. "Is this what you want? Is it?" She opened her hand wide and all the bills whirled wildly toward the heavens.

"You crazy bitch!" Sloan was staring at her. "You crazy bitch!" he cried again, as if he didn't have the words for what he saw. "I'll kill this boy. You know I will."

As response, she picked up the bag, walked closer to the schoolhouse, halted, and once more set the bag on the ground.

"Here's the only deal I'll make with you," my sister said, her voice cool and unflustered. She could have been picking out a new hat. Reaching once more into the bag, she stood in front of him holding a fist full of money. "You're going to turn my son loose or I'll send these into the air just like I did the others." She gestured down at the bag. "I'm not bringing it any closer until my son is out of your hands." The big carpet bag sat at her feet, enough distance from Sloan that he would need to take several strides out from the protection of the doorway to reach it. If he shot Dee, the money would still lay out of reach. I could almost see him thinking through his next step, figuring out what would best suit his desire for the cash and his need for a hostage to keep pursuers at bay.

"But if you do what I say in the order I say it, I'll carry this bag right to you and drop it at your feet." Dee continued in the same cool voice. "You won't have to step out of that doorway to have everything you want and then some because you want me, too. You've always wanted me."

"What's your deal?" The words furious and surly but amazing, too. How had Dee gotten the upper hand?

"You send my son out and away. I won't move, and if I do, shoot me. The moment Jem's out of range, I'll bring the bag and drop it at your feet. You'll have me as hostage standing right in front of you."

"You used to carry that little pearl-handled pistol, Fannie. You think I'm fool enough to let go of the boy just so's his mother can get close enough to kill me?"

With her free hand, Fannie reached under her traveling jacket and pulled a small pistol from the waistband of her skirt. "Here you go. Fancy you remembering that, Archie." She let the elegant ivory-handled thing fall and at his order kicked it out of reach.

After another shout to John to stay where he was, I realized Sloan had no idea of Monty's presence among the trees, that he thought John was there on his own. Surely, that had to work to our advantage. Except for the wind, the world around me and everyone in it were suddenly still, waiting for Archie Sloan's decision.

At last, mind made up, he said, "All right, Fannie. Have it your way. You for the boy. You'll make a better target, anyway. Pick up the bag." She did but stood unmoving.

"Send him out first, Archie. You've almost got everything you want. Don't spoil it now." My sister's voice possessed a kind of mesmerizing confidence. In it was the promise of pleasure and satisfaction combined into the fulfillment of all of one's dreams. I had thought her talented when I saw her on stage, but here she was hypnotic. For that brief moment, I believed Archie Sloan would do anything Dee said.

Sloan let go of Jem's arm and with a rough push to his back, sent the boy stumbling out the doorway. Jem turned immediately toward his mother as if he would run to her, but without looking at him and with a dismissive slice of her hand, she said, "Not now. Run past your Aunt Sheba and past Mr. Bliss and go over by Mr. Gruber. Run as fast as you can." Jem balked for a moment, squinting at her, but the boy recognized the tone of his mother's voice as one with which he had better not argue, and with one last look over his shoulder at Dee, he raced away.

Dee moved forward with the nonchalance only an actress could manage considering the circumstances and dropped the bag almost on Archie Sloan's toes. I didn't know what to expect next and as unlikely as it sounds, I don't think Sloan did, either.

"Go ahead," Dee said. "Take a look inside if you want. It's all there. Well, except for what's floating in the wind around New Hope, Nebraska." If she had been tall enough, I believe she would have shoved her face into his. "You wanted a hostage and you got me in the bargain. Do whatever you want with me. I won't try to get away. But whatever you plan, whatever you do, I want you to know you'll never be the man your brother was. Never, no matter how hard you try. Poor Archie, Cole used to say, can't play a winning hand, can't satisfy a woman. Just a failure at every last thing he tries. I used to laugh about it, but Cole – he always pitied you. Poor slow Archie." The last three words, drawled and contemptuous, seemed to cut as sharp and deep as the knife in John's boot. Color rushed into Sloan's face and turned it blood red. It was so sudden and so startling that I had a quick and terrible image of blood exploding from his eyes and nose and mouth.

"I never needed his pity, did I, 'cause I'm the one standing here in front of you and he's the one that's dead." Sloan sounded like a man trying to convince himself of something that deep in his heart he knew was never true. "Guess you picked the wrong brother."

Dee said nothing but slowly, slowly raised her arm and finger by finger unfurled the hand that clenched the bills, scorn in every small movement as the wind caught the money and carried it up and away.

"You poor, pathetic fool," she said as the last bill disappeared. "Did you really think I'd go anywhere with you?"

Archie Sloan was so enraged at that moment that he would have killed my sister, hostage or no hostage. She had betrayed him again, had stolen more than money. How many betrayals did that make for the man? Around his feet lay the shreds of his pride. I saw his intention in every muscle of his face and hand and arm. Surely Dee saw it, too.

I shouted, "No!" and intended to rush forward, at Sloan or perhaps at Dee to push her aside; I couldn't have said what I intended to do. They stood facing each other. Was Dee now the Fenway sister with the dare in her eyes? A slight slump to her shoulders made her look more tired than afraid, as if she had finally wearied of running and hiding and pretending and simply wanted it all to end. Even as I took a step forward, I knew I would never reach either Sloan or Dee in time to make a difference.

That would be left to someone else.

I stopped abruptly as Monty stepped around the corner of the schoolhouse and walked purposefully toward Sloan. No weapon in his hands; perhaps with Dee standing so close he didn't want to risk it. There was nothing belligerent or threatening about him, just a fair young man who looked as menacing as a schoolboy. He came to a stop a little behind Dee.

"I'm the law, Mr. Sloan," Monty said in a voice both relaxed and stern, "and I'm telling you to let this woman be."

"Like hell I will," Archie Sloan responded and then several things happened in a blur of activity. Sloan raised his arm to shoot. Monty grabbed Dee by her right arm and flipped her back and to the side with such force that she stumbled and fell flat onto the ground. And exactly at the same moment Monty lunged at Sloan, Sloan fired.

That young deputy charging forward like an engine at full-steam into the barrel of a loaded, aimed gun held by a man fueled by fury and frustration was the bravest thing I have ever seen in all my life, before or since. He seemed unstoppable

But no matter how much I might wish it were different, no human is unstoppable, and Monty was human, flesh and blood and bone just like the rest of us. My writing of that crucial moment by the schoolhouse doorway makes it seem as if it went on forever because I cannot write it the way it happened, can't stack word on top of word on top of word. I have to write the words one after the other, but time isn't always like that.

Anyone would have realized that it would take Archie Sloan less time to pull a trigger than it would take Monty to reach Sloan. Monty must have realized it, too, but he was a young man intent on his duty. *I'm the law, Mr. Sloan.*

The bullet hit the deputy in the chest and while there was no doubt even to my untrained eye that it was a mortal wound, for a moment it looked as if somehow Monty had escaped the bullet altogether. He managed another fierce and forward step, but at Sloan's second shot, he fell, first dropping onto his knees and then face down to the ground with both arms outstretched as if attempting to fly. At his collapse, I was suddenly grounded, shocked into immobility, my legs and feet like lead.

"What have you done?" I breathed, horrified. Blood began to seep from Monty into the earth beneath him. I couldn't take my eyes away from the awful sight.

"Sheba, get down." John's call was so sharp and urgent that I immediately dropped to my knees and threw both arms over my head. From behind me John spoke again, just one loud word, "Sloan."

The man heard his name and whirled to see John standing with his rifle against his shoulder, in range now and close enough that he would not miss. Faster than a breath, I heard a shot and looked up quickly to see Archie Sloan fall, collapsing in loose-limbed death atop the carpet bag of money Dee had set at his feet just a few moments before. How fast death can come! One moment we're here and then not. Like a stone into the river and hardly a ripple left behind.

My sister didn't bother with a look at anyone else, whether dead or alive. She skirted Monty's body as she turned and began to run back toward the small hill behind us, the hill where she had sent Jem. The man in the doorway and the money in the carpet bag were gone from her memory. There was only one thing in her mind and on her heart.

"Jem!" she called. I turned slowly and followed her progress, watching as the two of them met by the bench.

The wind carried one small and wispy word in my direction: "Mama!" Something in the child's voice, the sound of a great and endless yearning at last satisfied brought tears to my eyes. Jem made a leap into his mother's arms as she fell to her knees, wrapped her arms around her son, and drew him to her to stroke his hair. Like a small creature, he burrowed against her. Jem was Dee's son, and the wall that surrounded them, the wall that for the time being kept the rest of us out, was one I could not begrudge, even if being temporarily invisible to the people I loved carried with it a slight but sharp prick to my heart.

Behind me, John knelt by Monty. I looked away from Dee and Jem and went to stand by John as he turned the body over. Together we looked down at the dead young man's face. Angelic still, I thought. Blood continued to spread under him, but his face was untouched by violence. I remembered how the deputy had looked with the moon behind him. For a long moment, I rested both my hands on John's shoulders as he knelt, ashamed that I could stand beside the body of this brave and decent man, gone before his time, and still feel a spurt of happiness that John's heart pumped and his chest moved with breath. Oh, I was so confused by everything I had seen and everything I felt! I couldn't seem to make sense of it. Finally, I knelt beside John and rested an arm across his back, hoping he felt the comfort I longed to give him. For the first time, I saw John Bliss as a man as vulnerable as the rest of us, with the same longings and fears as everyone else. His face held regret and sorrow, but when he turned to me, I saw love there, too.

"I'm sorry," I said, and it was true, but at the same time, Jem was alive and Dee was alive and John and I knelt here side-by-side with the future stretching out in front of us. How was it possible to feel truly and deeply grieved, yet at the same moment experience the stirrings of relief and gratitude and even hope? How was it possible that death and joy could live together in the same heart? John stood and reached down a hand to help me stand.

"I'm sorry," I said to him again. "He was a fine young man, and what he did was the bravest thing I ever saw." John put an arm around my shoulders, and we stood there even longer, both of us lost in our own thoughts. Finally, I turned into his arms, pulled him tight against me, and whispered, "Thank you for being alive, John."

His words were as soft as mine. "I don't think it's me you should be thanking." Even today, I couldn't say if he was talking about God or the young man who lay at our feet or someone else entirely.

18
Epilogue

Following that outburst of terror, violence, and ultimate salvation, I felt drained of all vitality, and if John hadn't sent me on several errands, I might have stood there by the schoolhouse for another night. I could have told John that the citizens of New Hope did not need me to report on what had happened. Someone somewhere would have been waiting and watching, the same as someone somewhere would have been waiting and praying. That was how New Nope, Nebraska, handled both life and death, but later, I came to understand that John wished to get me away from that scene of blood and death. The bench sat empty, Dee and Jem and Bert Gruber nowhere to be seen. Isaac Lincoln came down the hill as I trudged up, but neither of us spoke.

"I'll stay with him," John told me, looking down at Monty's body. "I won't leave him alone, so I need you to tell Harold to get two coffins up here and some men to help with the bodies."

I did that and then started back toward the boarding house to see Ruth. Suppers were left to cool as doors opened along the way and people spoke to me. I must have answered something that made sense, but I don't recall any of the conversations. Across the street, Pleasant Lincoln stepped outside with Harriet behind her. Neither woman spoke or even gestured. *A wicked man is loathsome, and cometh to shame,* the old woman had told me, which was the way it should be but not at such a dear cost. God should be able to figure out an easier way than the death of a good man to make His words come true. Can there never be love without sacrifice?

Despite the twilight sky and cool air, Ruth waited for me outside in the rocker on the porch of the boarding house. She wore a long barn coat over her dress and a heavy shawl of some kind wrapped over the coat. She rose when I pushed open the front gate. With a closer look at my face, she gave a little gasp and came down the walk to meet me.

"Oh, Sheba, not Jem!"

"No," I said quickly. "No, he's fine and Dee and John, too. It's Monty."

Ruth repeated his name as a question and came closer. "You don't mean—?"

"Yes. I'm so very sorry, Ruth. I know you and Si were fond of the young man."

Light from the front porch lantern made the tears in Ruth's eyes sparkle, the same way the sun sparkled on the Platte River in the painting on the wall of her foyer, the painting Monty so admired.

"I should be the one to tell Lizbeth," Ruth said.

"Lizbeth?" My face must have matched the blankness of my tone. "Why Lizbeth?" and then, "Oh, Ruth. Monty and Lizbeth? I didn't know."

"You had other things on your mind, Sheba," and although that was true, it was no excuse. I should have known. What else had I missed in all the years I lived in New Hope?

Ruth used her fingertips to wipe the tears that escaped down her cheeks. "I don't think her heart will be broken because I don't think it had got that far yet, at least not for Lizbeth, but Monty—oh, he just thought the sun rose and set in that girl! But her heart will still have a bad bruise, and it will hurt to the touch for quite a while." Ruth took a deep breath.

"I need to be the one to tell her. I don't want her to hear about it from someone else in passing, the way people comment about a fire or a flood. Can you watch Alexander? I'll have someone, Luther or even Mort, maybe, take me out to the farm. I know Lizbeth. She'll take the news and wait until I'm gone to grieve. She's a private girl."

"Ruth, I'd do anything to help, but watch a baby? I don't know the first thing about babies." Ruth was already hurrying back up onto the porch and spoke with her back to me.

"Alex was just fed and he's sound asleep. With any luck he'll stay that way for the next four hours. If he doesn't, just pick him up and rock him or read to him or talk to him. Paint him a picture, for goodness' sake. You'll figure it out, Sheba. I need to see Lizbeth now."

Alexander, an obliging baby from what I had seen of him, woke up the moment his mother walked down the front porch steps. His cry was so lusty that at first, I thought something had happened to him, been bitten by a spider or somehow bumped a part of his little body against the wood of the cradle. Or did he need a change? But no, nothing like that, only a baby crying. When I picked him up, the crying stopped immediately. It was arms he wanted, and the beat of another person's heart in his ear, and a soft voice talking about this and that, all things any human might long for and all things I had the power to give. When Ruth returned, Alex and I both slept in the rocking chair.

At the sound of my name, I woke, saw my friend backlit by the kitchen light, and stood, by that time so comfortable holding a baby that I almost forgot I had one in my arms. Without a word, Ruth took him from me and planted several kisses on his little head and face. I tried to catch a glimpse of Ruth's expression.

"How was she?" I asked at last. Ruth dropped one last kiss on the top of her son's head and gave a sigh.

"It was a sad thing, Sheba, and hard to see, but Lizbeth is made of strong stuff and after the first hurt has past, after it's had time to settle into her bones and become a part of who she is, she'll be stronger because of it."

I saw Lizbeth at Monty's funeral the following Tuesday. Everyone was there; not a single establishment in New Hope remained open. To honor the young deputy, the men had on their Sunday suits, even Si Carpenter, who as I recalled hadn't worn a suit even on his wedding day. Lizbeth's parents were there, but it was Ruth who stood with her arm around Lizbeth's shoulders as Reverend Shulte said the last words over the grave and it was Ruth who wept, not Lizbeth. The girl was pale and quiet and attentive to all the words the pastor said. Where did she think Monty was now, I wondered? And where would she find her comfort?

When everything was over, and people began their slow walk back to town from the cemetery located behind the church, I gave John's hand a squeeze and told him softly, "I'll see you later. I want to say something to Lizbeth." He tucked an errant hair under my hat – since Sunday afternoon, whenever we were together, he could not keep from touching me often and in small ways – and moved away to catch up with Si and Lucas Morgan, New Hope's one remaining deputy. When Ruth and Lizbeth reached where I stood, I put out a hand to Lizbeth's arm.

"I'm so sorry for your loss, Lizbeth. I don't have the words, but I want you to know that Monty—"

"His name was Ulysses Calvin Montgomery," Lizbeth said, her voice soft and firm and proud. "Ulysses. Calvin. Montgomery. He allowed Monty because he said his given name didn't fit, that it sounded too important for a man like him, but he had a true name, and it was Ulysses Calvin Montgomery."

It's my heart, not hers, that's going to break, I thought, and said aloud, "I didn't know but now that I do, I think it fits him perfectly. I want to tell you that I never saw anyone do anything as brave and noble as what I saw Ulysses Calvin Montgomery do. And I want to tell you that I believe with all my heart that he saved my sister's life, and probably my life, too. I don't know if you think it was a fair trade, but I want you to know that people are alive because of Deputy Montgomery's courage."

"Oh, Miss Sheba." For a moment, I caught a glimpse of the old Lizbeth in her voice and tone. "Lives aren't traded one for another. That's not how it happens or why, but thank you for those kind words. I will treasure them always." As if to comfort me for my lack of understanding, she gave me a light kiss on the cheek before walking away holding onto Ruth's arm.

The path to the cemetery is well-worn by the feet of the grieving, but somehow it isn't a sad place, at all. Once I surprised the Shulte children playing hide-and-seek among the headstones, and Lydia Shulte came over to say quickly, "I hope this doesn't bother you, Sheba. They don't mean any disrespect, but I can shoo them home."

"No," I said. "There's no need for that. I doubt that anyone resting here is bothered by the sounds of children playing."

There are always flowers by the marker with the name Ulysses Calvin Montgomery engraved in graceful script, often placed there by Jem and Dee, or Lizbeth or Ruth or me or even Harriet, by any number of others who had known the young man. Most of whom, I'm ashamed and saddened to admit, knew him much better than I did. Perhaps they had even known his full given name. I was there at his death, but how I regret not knowing him in life!

That Sunday night, after Ruth arrived back at the boarding house from breaking the awful news to Lizbeth, Silas came rushing into Ruth's kitchen as I prepared to say good night to her, gave her a quick kiss of greeting, heard the news from both of us about what had happened, and left for Bliss House. I followed him out and saw him hurry into the hotel in search of John Bliss, whom I hadn't seen since he had sent me off on errands several hours before. Maybe, I thought sadly, he's still standing guard over the body of his young friend.

Dee was seated at my kitchen table when I finally got

home that night. Once inside my front door, I saw a light shining from the kitchen and because I had lived in trepidation of Archie Sloan for such a long while felt an immediate, reflexive fear. Then I remembered Sloan's body lying limp across the carpet bag of cash in the doorway of the schoolhouse and walked with brisk purpose across the shop to push the bead curtain aside. Dee sat staring at her hands that were folded on top of the table. Praying or sleeping, but neither seemed like something she would be doing just then. She looked up at my entrance and gave a tired smile.

"Jem?" I asked, still standing.

"Oh, he's a hardy boy," Dee said, motherly satisfaction in her voice.

A steady diet of Shakespearean mayhem and murder, of Iago and Lear and Lady Macbeth will do that, I thought.

My sister continued, "He ate his weight in supper and then fell asleep at the table. It was easier finding a bed for him at Bert's than carrying him down here." She smiled at the memory. "Besides, I'm going to marry Bert Gruber so Jem might as well get used to living in his new home." I wasn't surprised by the news.

"Do you plan to stay in New Hope then?"

"Yes, unless your Sheriff Carpenter sends me to prison for possessing stolen property. New Hope is Bert's home, and Jem loves it here, too."

"I can't pretend to speak for Si Carpenter, but if you plan to return the money to its rightful owners, I'd guess he can pull enough strings to keep you out of jail. You're an actress. Make up some story about how you were forced to hold on to all that cash out of fear for your life."

"That wouldn't be far from the truth, Sheba."

I sat down across from her. "Are you sure you can stay in one place? Bert Gruber loves you. I'd hate to see him get hurt."

She offered a roundabout answer to my question. "I was in Stockville on Saturday doing a little play acting to keep myself fed, and Bert showed up. I usually let him know where

I was, but I told him to keep away because I was afraid Sloan would track him to me. Bert always did what I wanted, but that day everything changed. He waved Sloan's note in my face and told me in no uncertain terms that I needed to choose between the money and Jem because anyone with half a brain could see I couldn't keep both. Bert was fierce with me and he was right to be. Everything he said was true, just like everything you said in Ogallala was true. I was just so used to running and I had other plans—" Her voice trailed off. "I've made some very bad mistakes, Sheba. I don't deny it, how could I? I'm sorry about the young man. I wish I'd left that money behind."

For weeks, as we tried to settle back into our lives, I would remember Dee's sorrowful regret and Lizbeth's words at the cemetery – *Lives aren't traded one for another. That's not how it happens or why* – and try to make sense of everything that occurred. If Dee had acted differently, would Monty be alive and someone else dead in his place? What if I had acted differently? Over time, I've had to learn not to dwell on what I can't change, and I can't change the past. But it's still hard to leave it behind.

"I did it for Jem," my sister continued that Sunday night, "because I thought he deserved more than I could give him. It took Bert to show me that the only thing Jem needed to be happy was me, his mother, so that's what I'm going to give him. I believe the three of us, Bert and Jem and I, can make a home together. New Hope is the first place in all my life that feels like home. I never felt I belonged anywhere until now. I always felt different, and I thought running would change that, but then—" she made a sound somewhere between a laugh and a sigh, "after a while, I couldn't remember what I thought or why I thought it. Everybody's different in some way, aren't they?"

I nodded, content to listen in silence. In all our lives, Dee had never shared any of this before, and whether that was her fault or mine no longer mattered.

"Do you know what Bert told me? He said he'd take me

on any terms, and it would be enough for him. Any terms, Sheba, and no demands to be anything but the woman I am. Now. Here." She shook her head at the memory of his words, at the wonder of them, looked down again at her hands folded on top of the table, and stopped talking.

When we love someone, I thought, we either have to take them as they are or shut them out altogether. Bert had figured that out a long time ago, and while it took me longer, I had finally figured it out, too.

"I'm glad you're staying," I said and then stood. "Go find Bert, Dee. You look as exhausted as I feel. Talk to Si tomorrow and tell him the truth about the money. He's not a man easy to fool, and it will be easier all around if you just tell him everything. A lot of people, including the governor, are indebted to Si Carpenter for one reason or another. They trust him and hold him in respect. I have a feeling it will be all right."

It was very early Monday morning by then. I went into my little bedroom, experienced a small pang of loss but a greater pang of gratitude at the sight of Jem's mattress on the floor, stepped over it, collapsed into my own bed, and fell instantly and dreamlessly asleep.

With the funeral and Dee's marriage and arranging care for Mr. Stenton while he recuperated and then needing to make a trip with Silas and Dee to Lincoln to explain to the governor the unfortunate circumstances around my sister's previous actions, express sincere relief that the stolen money had been returned to its rightful owners, and promise only honorable behavior in the future, it was well into November before I was able to make good on my unspoken promise to John Bliss. Spooned against him, content, recalling the previous night's activities with an equal mix of surprise and pleasure, I opened my eyes and there was *Indian Summer* hanging on the wall in a patch of dim early-morning light! John's arms were warm around me and I thought he still slept, which gave me time to examine the painting with a critical eye.

"Hmph," I muttered, or something similar, and was startled and then almost instantly distracted by John's lips on the back of my neck and his warm hands against my skin.

"What?" he asked in a murmur, preoccupied but doing his best to show interest in maintaining a discussion.

"It's the painting," I tried to explain, but it was becoming difficult for me, too, to concentrate on my art.

"What about the painting?" John's actions indicated that what he had on his mind had nothing to do with paintings, but I persevered.

"There's altogether too much gold in it," I said. A small, surprised, and involuntary gasp escaped me, but I was determined to complete my observation. "I remember that morning, and the sky was more rose than gold."

"Sheba." John's voice was so thick that my name was only a growl.

"Yes?" I managed to get out the one word, by then scarcely more than an exhaled breath, and would have thought it too soft to be heard by a man ruthlessly intent on rearranging us to suit his own purpose.

"Paint me another one and make it as rosy as you want, but — not. right. now."

Considerably later, he lay on his side, propped onto one elbow, and looked at me with a grave expression. "I want to talk to you about something, Sheba," he said.

"Not the painting, I assume. Did we ever finish that discussion?"

"We brought it to a conclusion in a manner of speaking," he replied with a little grin but grew serious again. "I'm all in favor of Mrs. Woodhull, at least in theory. What man wouldn't think that free love had its attractions? And I know you find other people's opinions unimportant."

What he was going on about I had no idea, but he was clearly serious, slogging on with a subject that made him look and sound awfully uncomfortable for some reason. I turned fully onto my side and matched his posture so I could watch his face as he talked.

"I wouldn't say unimportant, exactly," I protested. "It's just that I'm not at the mercy of what other people think of me. I always pay attention to what's said, and I hope I give people's opinions fair consideration, but in the end, I'm going to do what suits me." I reached out a hand to play with his hair. "Why don't you just say whatever it is you need to say?"

"Do you plan to keep on living in New Hope?"

The abrupt question gave me an idea of what he might be trying to broach, and I asked, "Do you want to move away? Is that it? I thought you liked it here."

"I do like it here. That's the point."

I stared at him and then gave a hard tug to the strand of his hair in my hand. "What in the world are you talking about? Tell me right now and make it quick or—"

"Ow! I think we should get married." When I didn't respond, he rushed on, "This is New Hope, Nebraska, Sheba, not Paris or New York and they like things legal in New Hope. People get married here. It's what they do. You have a nephew who doesn't miss much, and what will you tell him about us cohabiting—"

"Is that what we've been doing?" I interrupted. "Cohabiting?"

"—when he notices?" John continued as if I hadn't spoken. "And you know Jem. You know he'll notice and ask all kinds of questions. What lesson will that teach a boy about life and being a responsible man, a decent man?"

"I was never very good at giving Jem speeches about life," I said thoughtfully. "I always walked away thinking he should be the one teaching me."

"I didn't care if people talked, Sheba. It never mattered before, but now it seems to me if we're going to live in New Hope and belong to the Merchants' Association and go to the Sunday School Christmas pageant—"

"Have you ever attended the Sunday School Christmas pageant?"

"No, but I might want to. You might want to if Jem's in it."

"Pastor Shulte is a good man, John. He'll let us attend the Christmas pageant whether we're cohabiting or not." I was trying very hard to keep any trace of laughter out of my voice. John Bliss was an easy man to love, even more so after I had seen him vulnerable and grieving next to Monty's body. He blamed himself for the young man's death – *wrongly* blamed, I tried to tell him – and would carry that burden a long time, maybe forever. I wouldn't hurt him again for all the world.

"Never mind," John said at last. "I'm sorry I brought it up. I hope you know I would never try to make you do anything you didn't want to do."

"I do know that," I said. "It's one of your finest qualities." I shifted closer to him. "I don't disagree with you. New Hope is my home and I don't want to live anywhere else, and you're right, it is an orderly community and we should try to fit in. Getting married will help with that. Besides, I'd like to spare poor Reverend Shulte the need to take us to task about our behavior. He has enough to do without that. So by all means, let's get married, and let's do it sooner rather than later, today or tomorrow or next week, whenever you want, but—John?"

I brushed the back of my fingers lightly and slowly down his cheek until my palm eventually came to rest on his chest. He felt like such a solid man under my fingertips, nothing but hard muscle and smooth skin. More of his finest qualities.

"What?" His voice had grown huskier as my hand descended.

"If you don't mind," I said, "not. right. now."

On our wedding day, my husband presented me with the gift of a house, and not just any house but the largest house in New Hope. Located behind the freight office on the opposite end of town from my dress shop, the elegant home had been abandoned twice by previous owners, one a family with two little girls and most recently, a woman whose husband was a rancher with thousands of acres in three counties but who nevertheless hated rural life. Clearly, it was not a marriage into which a great deal of thought had been put but then, who am I to talk? The first family's departure was a heartbreak; the woman's just the opposite. When she left New Hope for parts farther east, everyone – including her husband, I would imagine – breathed a sigh of relief. It is very difficult to make conversation with a woman intent on her own unhappiness.

What made John's gift so wondrous – apart from the indoor water closet – was the painting studio he created for me out of two rooms on the second floor. He removed a wall, put large windows on the east and north sides, and added a transom in the roof. We toured the house the evening of our nuptials, and I couldn't get over it.

'You did all this for me?" I asked, standing in the middle of the studio. It was night by then, but when I looked up, there were the stars sparkling against the night sky! "What a perfect gift! I wish I'd married you a lot sooner." Teasing him but not so very far from the truth.

"Me, too, but I'm not the one who needed convincing." He looked around the large and spacious room. "I guess it turned out all right." John and I are very much alike when it comes to revealing our true emotions, so he leaned against a side wall and pretended not to be proud of himself. I wasn't fooled.

"Yes," I said and went to put my arms around him. "It turned out wonderful! Thank you." I remembered not so very long ago holding John against me as a confusing blend of grief and joy washed through me and whispering a heartfelt thank you to him for being alive. If he would ever be able to recall that moment with the same gratitude I felt or if it would always be colored by the regret and guilt that mention of Monty inevitably brought remained to be seen. In my early years in New Hope, I had judged John Bliss to be an arrogant and unprincipled man, never imagining he had a sensitive bone in his body or that he might carry burdens on his heart.

In a way, he, like most of my neighbors at the time, had been invisible to me, because even then I had suspected the truth: if you let down your wall for one person, others will try to crowd in behind. How much could a person's heart hold, after all? And would there still be room for my art, for that rush toward light and the need to capture it? I guessed I would find out the answers soon enough.

I kept the dress shop as long as I could because I felt a debt to the enterprise and to the independence it first gave me, but when my paintings began to sell, I had to leave something behind and it was either the dress shop or John. My husband says he never doubted what I'd decide, but I always thought he seemed a trifle uneasy until the papers were signed and the new dressmaker took ownership.

"I want you to paint," John said out of the blue at breakfast one morning, as if there was ever any doubt to the matter. We were still newlyweds.

"You're giving me permission to paint now?"

He shook his head. "No. No, you know that's not what I meant. I might as well try to give you permission to have blue eyes. I just want you to know—" He hesitated, picking and discarding words until he found the right ones. "I want you to understand that I always knew I'd have to share you, that there was a part of you I'd never get access to. That's all. And I wouldn't have it any other way."

I raised an eyebrow as I reached for the marmalade. "You seemed more than satisfied with the parts you had access to last night."

A small twitch at one corner of his mouth acknowledged the hit, but he said, "You know what I'm trying to say – don't you?" The tentative tone, so unlike him, made me smile.

"Yes," I answered, "I do. It's why I worried about letting people into my life. I told you once that if I couldn't paint, I'd die, and that's still true. Painting for me is what breathing is for you, but when we talked then, I wasn't sure how much room my heart had or how much it could hold. I know now."

My husband didn't ask the question aloud but I heard it

anyway and said, "It has exactly enough room to hold everything and everyone I love. Isn't it amazing how that turned out?"

While I intended to paint regardless of my situation, I have tried very hard to balance that integral need with family and friends and community, with study and travel and even a little teaching at our school. Mr. Stenton decided it was time for the children of New Hope to appreciate some of the finer subjects and asked if I was willing to introduce them to some of the great masters of art as well as explain the proper application of color. The thought of facing an entire room full of children made me somewhat shaky, but it ended up being an enjoyable experience. Well, putting paint into the hands of children isn't always *enjoyable*, exactly, but I survived, and the children learned something – at least, I think they learned something – and in the end, even the demanding Mr. Stenton considered it time well spent.

I knew I would always paint, but I never expected to make money at it or have my name recognized by art fanciers, and if it hadn't been for Mr. Sidney Dillon, president of the Union Pacific Railway, I'm convinced my story would have ended precisely as I expected. But in a visit to New Hope on railroad business, Mr. Dillon saw my paintings hanging in Bliss House and bought two for his own home, which in turn were admired by several people distinguished by their independent means and their knowledge of art and suddenly, or so it seemed, the work of Sheba Fenway was in demand. In a way, you could say the railroad carried me to New Hope and then carried me away from New Hope and back out into the world.

To my astonishment, the Metropolitan Museum of Art in New York City offered me the opportunity to show one of my paintings in their new *modern* section, a temporary exhibition that if well received would become permanent. What could I submit that would be suitable for so eminent a setting? Miss Cassatt herself, one of the world's greatest living artists, male or female, submitted a painting for that same exhibition. I doubt I will ever recover from the glorious shock of my first view of her *Little Girl in a Blue Arm Chair* when John and I visited Paris for a delayed honeymoon, and the idea of sharing the same space as Mary Cassatt, the woman who created that splendid piece and so many other remarkable works, as well, made me breathless. I was prepared to refuse the honor.

"Refuse!" Ruth exclaimed when I shared my intention. "Have you lost complete control of your faculties? This is the opportunity of a lifetime! Any artist would love to receive such an invitation, but you were selected for the honor, and do you know why? Because the people in New York are experts and smart enough to realize that any painting of yours would be a wonderful addition to their museum." Then she frowned and added to be sure I didn't misunderstand her, "Well, not the painting of the Platte River that hangs in my lobby. That one's not going anywhere. Any *other* of your paintings, I should say. Take one more good look at everything before you say no."

So I roamed through Bliss House looking at what was on the walls there and then proceeded home where I examined every single painting propped or stacked in my studio. And still nothing seemed suitable for the grand Metropolitan Museum of Art.

Until one day when Lizbeth knocked on the front door carrying a painting in her hands, a dearly loved and treasured painting I had given to her from a full heart. I had worked on it furiously, not stopping until it was done and as soon as the paint dried, I took it to her. I feared she might balk at the title, but she didn't, only blinked away tears and with her usual self-possession spoke a quiet thank you. The painting has been hers ever since. I believed at the time, and still believe, that it was one of my finest works, but it was always for Lizbeth, in more ways than one.

"Ruth said you've been asked to send a painting to New York City to hang where a lot of people can see it, and I think it should be this one, the one you gave me. It's time to share it, Sheba. We both know what it means and how good it is. What do you think?" When she stepped into the front hallway, I took the canvas from her.

"Let's take it upstairs," I said. "where I have the best light."

Once there, we both stepped back and gazed at the painting where it basked in the sunlight streaming through the transom. Looking at it made my heart ache.

Not the sun but the moon illumined the picture, washed across the sky and set the clouds ablaze with white fire so that the trees and the small building in the distance looked deeper black by contrast. I had worked hard for that shade of black, adding more purple than usual and a touch of red, as well, to reflect the churning colors of fear and anger, lust and greed, deceit, jealousy, and resentment. The moon hung in the sky, small and undefined and so hazy around the edges that if it hadn't been for its clear and streaming light, a person might not even recognize it as the moon. Yet for all its lack of pretense, wherever the moon's rays touched the earth, they left an unfading splash of brilliant light behind in the darkness. If the artist kept on working, the painting hinted, it was only a matter of time before all the darkness would be transformed into moonlight.

"Oh, Lizbeth," I said, turning to her, "are you sure?"

"Yes. It has so much hope in it, and that's something everybody needs. I'll miss having it near, but I have to let it go. I want to let it go. It's time." We held each other, sniffing the way women do when they're trying not to cry, and then walked back downstairs.

After Lizbeth left and before John got home, I went back into the studio and pulled a chair closer to the easel so I could sit in front of the painting and study its details. How was it possible that a piece of canvas and some strokes of oil paint held the power to touch emotions so deeply?

In that picture I can almost see what it could be like if we took better care of each other. Peaceful like and bright.

No one else, from Paris, France, to New York City to

New Hope, Nebraska, could have explained with more eloquence what I looked at, what I hoped for, and what I tried to say through my art. I sat there a long time.

Later, as daylight slowly faded to twilight, the front door at the bottom of the staircase clicked open and shut, and then John called up the steps to let me know he was home. I stood, stretched, and went closer to the easel where Lizbeth's painting rested. From the start that's how I thought of it, as "Lizbeth's Painting," but I had called it something else, and when I accepted the Museum's invitation, I would use the proper title, the one I had scrawled next to my initials in the lower right-hand corner of the canvas. Not *Lizbeth's Painting* written there but just one word, one name.

A word bright as sunshine on the river. A name bright as the moon.

Monty

ABOUT THE AUTHOR

If you enjoyed *Surprised by Shadows*, don't stop here. Book one of the New Hope Series, titled *What We Carry With Us*, is available at Amazon.com, in the Kindle Store, and at BarnesandNoble.com. You'll have the chance to reacquaint yourself with many of the citizens of New Hope, especially Sheba's close friend Ruth, whose back story has its own share of heartbreak and danger, hope, risk, and love.

All of Karen's books present characters and places you won't soon forget. With her writing described as "satisfying" * and her research as "flawless," you can't go wrong. (*Akron Beacon Journal, 2010)

The Laramie Series by Karen J. Hasley

Lily's Sister

Waiting for Hope

Where Home Is

Circled Heart

Gold Mountain

Smiling at Heaven

The Penwarrens by Karen J. Hasley

Claire, After All

Listening to Abby

Jubilee Rose

Stand-alone novels by Karen J. Hasley

The Dangerous Thaw of Etta Capstone

Magnificent Farewell

The New Hope Series by Karen J. Hasley

What We Carry With Us

Surprised by Shadows

~ Remarkable Women. Unforgettable Stories. ~

All in Historical Settings.

www.karenhasley.com

Made in the USA
Coppell, TX
18 March 2023

14423366R00163